THE MOON'S
DEEP CIRCLE

THE MOON'S DEEP CIRCLE

by
David Holly

ISBN 13: 978-1-60282-870-4

This Trade Paperback Original Is Published By
Bold Strokes Books, Inc.
P.O. Box 249
Valley Falls, NY 12185

Printed in the U.S.A.

Credits
Editor: Cindy Cresap
Production Design: Susan Ramundo
Cover Design By Sheri (graphicartist2020@hotmail.com)

Acknowledgments

Taking a book from idea to print requires the delicate touch of many hands and the keen scrutiny of innumerable eyes. Writers merely fall into a fantasy and let it pour out their fingers as they pound away maniacally upon a keyboard, often far into the night. It is the publisher, editor, typesetter, designer, cover artist, distributor, and publicist who make the book a reality. Nor should we forget the humble bookseller, without whom authors would be writing to themselves. The list of appreciative thanks goes on and on, but I have to single out Kristina who proofread and whose thoughts improved this book immensely. Then, too, a special thanks to Cindy Cresap for her terrific job of editing. A heartfelt thanks to everyone at Bold Strokes Books, and a special thanks to Radclyffe for existing.

Dedication

For Kristina

Author's Note

While cities such as Portland, Baker City, Astoria, Pendleton, etc., exist, the names of high schools or community colleges and their swim teams used in this novel are wholly fictitious. Likewise, Cougar County and its towns are products of the author's imagination and bear no resemblance to any actual place. Anyone scanning a map in an attempt to place the locale of this novel would be hard-pressed. Cougar County seems to jump from the fertile agricultural land of the Willamette Valley to the sagebrush and junipers of the high desert depending upon the author's mood.

Part One:

The Journals

CHAPTER ONE

Tipper's Tale

The room where my brothers had grown up was the family shrine. At least, it was Mom's shrine. My pop never spoke of Thad and Tye, nor did he ever cross the threshold of their room. Once a week, Mom took the key that she wore on a black ribbon around her neck, opened the door, and cleaned the room. I had never been permitted inside.

Perhaps I had played there as a child when my brothers Thad and Tye were home and safe. Vague memories tickled the edges of recollection, but they were no more than tickles. My brothers were long gone, gone so long that I could not picture them, and as for why or where they had gone, I was clueless. Pop always said, "This family doesn't talk about that." And that settled the issue—at least in Pop's mind.

I had tried questioning Mom when Pop was at work, but a wary expression suffused her face when I asked, and she would draw her finger across her lips and turn away. Once, I tried following her into their room as she entered with the vacuum cleaner, but she ordered me out, her voice so strained I scarcely recognized it.

I had tried every Web search available, but I did not find my brothers. I found men with some version of their names, but they were never the right ages, and my e-mails had gone unanswered. The disappearance of my brothers remained the great mystery of my life, one I had always determined to solve. Then one day toward the end of my senior year at Muskrat Creek High School, when I was a grown man so to speak, with a voter's registration card and a selective service number, Mom goofed.

"Tip," she called, "I'm going to Albertsons. Do you need anything special?"

She knew my favorite foods, so she wasn't asking about those. She would buy those as a matter of course. She meant toiletries and such, but I had plenty of shampoo and toothpaste. I was running short of lube, but I could hardly ask Mom to buy personal lubricant so I could jerk off comfortably. Not in my family. Sex was never mentioned. I wasn't sure that my parents had ever *heard* of masturbation. I would buy my own lube at Rite Aid.

I heard the car crunching on the gravel as Mom pulled out of the driveway. Thinking about the lube had put me in mind to spank the monkey, which was best while Mom was shopping and Pop at work. In addition to the family farm, Pop owned a farm equipment dealership near town. I had a free day due to a teacher in-service day, when the teachers attend brainwashing sessions instead of imparting knowledge to their students.

My room was at the far end of the hallway, just past my brothers' locked room and the bathroom. My parents' bedroom with its private bath was on the other side of the house. Most of our house was wallpapered, but my walls were painted a clover green, and I had tacked up posters and cutout magazine pages of famous swimmers. One time Pop growled about all the swimmers being male, but I reminded him that I was male—and a swimmer. To the best of my knowledge, he had not entered my room since that night.

I started to reach for my secret stash where I keep my lubricant, but an urge to check the house compelled me to arise. My cock was already stiff in my jeans as I slipped out of my room. I padded toward the kitchen in my stocking feet and glanced out the window to make certain that Mom's car was gone. Turning back, I saw her mistake. She had cleaned my brothers' room earlier, and she had forgotten to take her key. I saw it sticking out of the lock with the black ribbon dangling.

My heart was in my throat as I glanced at the driveway to see if Mom was returning. She would rush back if she missed that key—

she guarded it as though it was the key to the U. S. nuclear arsenal. My pulse was racing as I turned the key and pushed the door open.

I don't know what I was expecting, but the room looked pretty much like every other boy's room. A few more books perhaps— really, a lot more books. However, the twin beds looked comfortably familiar, as did the twin dressers. The carpet was dark green, which matched the green-leaf pattern in the yellow wallpaper. I stepped to my brothers' window and surveyed the landscape. The fields of grain fell away to a thick wood, and I could see the mountain still heavy with snow away to the east.

That's when I noticed that the window was nailed shut. Not just nailed, but secured with big screws that bit deep into the wooden frame. The sight made me shiver, and I turned away from the window. Thad had been a bookworm, all right, so I scanned his shelves, lovingly constructed to accommodate the impressive collection. A hardback book titled *The White Goddess* caught my eye. Bearing a pagan dust wrapper, that book had been written by somebody named Robert Graves. I opened to the copyright page, discovered that it was a first edition, and decided to check its value on the Internet. Next, my eyes fell upon a twelve-volume set printed in the 1930s. It was the third edition of something called *The Golden Bough,* and it had old brown paper dust jackets.

I picked up one volume of *The Golden Bough* and found descriptions of dying gods and mourning goddesses and Osiris and Isis and Rites of Harvest. There were about five hundred books in all, and as I studied the titles, I realized that every book had something to do with paganism or witchcraft or other forms of occultism— including some disturbing titles. I replaced the volume and began opening the dresser drawers. The one held socks, bikini briefs, and some stuff with Tye's name on them. The other dresser was more interesting.

Thad's dresser also held socks and sexy bikini briefs and such, but in a bottom drawer, I discovered a pile of notebooks. I opened one at random and realized that I was reading the spidery hand of my long-lost brother.

❖

Thad's Journal: The Third of August

Last night, at the stroke of eleven, I slipped out my window into the warm August darkness. As I crept over the windowsill, I was careful not to awaken my brother Tye, who was sleeping in the other bed.

The ground beneath the window was soft, and I had raked away the leaves so my bare feet made no noise. No alarmed livestock gave me away, because our alpacas spent their nights in the barn where the predatory coyotes could not attack them. My path was well lit. The full moon glistened off the glaciers on the mountain that seemed to hang over me. The golden moonlight was so bright I could distinguish the green of the leaves. After I crept through my parents' yard, I pulled on my shoes before I crossed the cinder road and hurried through the cornfield. The scent and colors of summer hung in the air, the corn heavy, the pumpkins ripening, the breeze warm and dry. At the far end of the field, my best friend, Skip, stood waiting for me. Skip was a fellow initiate and my classmate in Greek mythology at Cougar Ridge Community College.

From far off came the faintest hint of piping. "Thad, that you?" Skip hissed. "You're early."

"So are you. Let's get farther from my house."

The wailing timbre of reed pipes grew as we ran over the long meadow toward the woods beyond. After a ways, we stopped to catch our breath. "Listen, Skip. Pan blows the pipes to summon the bacchantes."

The music stirred deep pagan feelings that reverberated through my cells as human lust. A throbbing excitement shook me, and my blood coursed hot in my veins. Skip suddenly pressed against me, and he brought his mouth close to mine. I met his lips with my own, slipping my hot tongue into his mouth. Skip sucked on my tongue. He teased it with his own. My cock grew hard in my shorts, and Skip fondled it as we kissed. His own dick was creating a stiff and striking distension in his shorts.

As we continued our impassioned kiss, I slid my hands down Skip's athletic back to his shapely rump. His ass was tight and his buttocks hard. The rounded shape awakened deep desires within me, desires I could scarcely name. The night promised total freedom, wild, willing, pagan, licentious abandon to the will of the old gods. While my hands explored his muscular buttocks through his shorts, Skip waggled suggestively as he pushed his tongue farther into my mouth.

After our mouths pulled apart, Skip moaned, and I said, "I love your ass, Skip."

He grinned at the bold implications in my words. "I've been working on my butt cheeks, Thad. Squats at the gym." He smiled promiscuously. "Wanna get your cock into it?"

"I imagine that I will now that we've been initiated. Just like you're gonna come in my ass."

Skip's hand traveled to my waist and slipped into the waistband of my shorts. His fingers explored my crack. "Hah, no underwear." He explored deeper, and as he did, the sound of the pipes reverberated louder across the fields.

"Were you watching Bromius last month?" Skip asked, his voice harsh with his growing need.

"Yeah, was he jacking off? I couldn't tell."

"The way you were sucking that priest's cock, you wouldn't have seen a gang of elves playing bareback leap frog," Skip said. Then he added, "I've been dreaming about riding Dr. Bromius's cock."

"Man, what boy hasn't? I'll bet every boy in our class dreams about taking the professor's thick cock up his butt."

❖

Tipper's Tale

As I leaned against Thad's dresser reading his words, I become conscious that I had a major boner. It was a shock beyond compare. I had never thought of myself as being G-A-Y (oh, yipes!), although I had never felt much interest in dating girls. That my brother Thad might have been gay, or even both of my brothers, was something I had never considered. Yet I was reading words that could hardly have been interpreted in any way but homoerotic.

My cock was not the only thing that was aroused. My curiosity was inflamed. I had to examine all of Thad's notebooks. But how? I closed Thad's dresser, keeping the notebook I had opened, and checked the room for signs of my invasion. When I was certain that I had left no evidence behind, I withdrew and locked the door behind me.

I rushed back to my room and slipped Thad's notebook under my mattress. Moving as fast as possible, I pushed my feet into my shoes without bothering to tie them and grabbed my wallet and car keys. Muskrat Creek Shopping Plaza was one mile from our house, and I broke speed laws reaching it. The Albertsons supermarket lay at the far end of the plaza next to the K-Mart.

Skip's Security Service was a hole-in-the wall at the breech where the shopping plaza turned into an L shape. I rushed inside and rapped on the counter. A guy somewhere between thirty and thirty-five emerged from the back scratching his stomach. "What can I do for you?" he demanded.

"I need a key cut—in a hurry." I handed him the key with the black ribbon.

The proprietor's eyes narrowed with suspicion. "I'm pretty busy just now. Do it for you in an hour."

"No, no, I need it right away." I pulled out my wallet. "I'll pay double."

"Must be an emergency," he said blandly.

Visions of my mother arriving home before me filled my thoughts. She was shopping at the other end of this fucking plaza. What if she saw my car? What if she came in and saw the black-ribboned key in my hand? I pressed the key into the proprietor's hand. "I'll give you five bucks," I offered, glancing at the sign that read $2.00 for key cutting.

He examined the key with agonizing slowness while visions of Mom loading the grocery bags into her car filled my mind. "Key to a simple inside lock," he said. "Bedroom door?"

"Bathroom," I screeched with a burst of inspiration. "My little brother's locked in, and I gotta get him out before Mom gets home and freaks."

The proprietor scratched his head. "That story doesn't hold up. If you've got this key in hand, you could let him out. Doesn't add up. You're up to something criminal."

"No way," I shouted. "Not me. It really is an emergency. And you're right. I'm not supposed to have this key. But I need it. I swear it's perfectly legal."

"I'll cut it for twenty," he said. "And you gotta show me ID."

I whipped out a twenty-dollar bill, which constituted rape with violence, and my driver's license. He studied my license painstakingly. "Terry Trencher?"

"They call me Tip."

"Any relation to Thad Trencher?"

My heart skipped two beats. "My brother."

"My best friend in high school," said the proprietor, suddenly becoming more cooperative. "We did a year of junior college. I'll have this for you in a jiffy."

I watched as he selected a key blank, eyeballed it against the key I'd given him, and stuck it into a machine. He punched a code onto a computer screen, and within a few seconds, I possessed a duplicate key to my brothers' room.

The proprietor was eyeballing me speculatively. "You're the captain of the Muskrats, aren't you?"

"That's right," I said.

"You going to shear those Corvallis sheep dippers?"

"Oh yeah, the Corvallis Shepherds will be swimming in our wake. But that's next week. This week we've got to out swim the Tillamook Big Cheeses."

"That shouldn't be too hard."

"No. We could beat the Big Cheeses floating on our backs."

He opened his cash drawer, handed me back my twenty and one more. "A little something for expenses," he said. "I believe in supporting the home team." I pocketed the cash, eager to get home.

"You know where Thad is?" he asked.

"No, sorry," I said, moving toward the door.

"If you hear from him, get him to call me," he said. "I'm Skip."

I was still so preoccupied with beating my mother home that the name didn't register with me then. Only as I was pulling out of the parking lot, just before I turned, I caught a glimpse of his sign again: Skip's Security Service. "Holy shit!" I said.

I tore up the road getting home. Luck was with me. I parked where my car had stood before and rushed into the house. I slipped Mom's key into the lock and hid the duplicate key in my room. I heard her pulling into the drive just as I emerged from my bedroom. I rushed into the kitchen, poured a glass of milk and took a swig, then smeared crunchy peanut butter and grape jelly onto a slice of bread and bit off a chunk, which I spit into the garbage. I dropped the sandwich onto a plate and pulled out a chair. Only then did I hurry out to help Mom with the groceries.

She was coming through the front door as I was going out the back. I grabbed four sacks from the rear seat and carried them around to the kitchen door. Mom was standing in the doorway. "Tip," she said, her voice oddly tentative, "did you…" She looked at the remains of my sandwich and the smear on my glass of milk. "Uh, never mind. Bring in the rest of the groceries, and I'll put them away while you finish your snack."

I went through the front that time. I kept walking, but my eyes slipped aside enough to see that the key with the black ribbon was no longer in the lock of my brothers' room. I brought in the groceries and watched my mother prepare our supper. She had just finished washing the beets when I decided that I had to ask about my brothers.

"Mom, I really need to know something," I began.

I saw her stiffen. "Please," I said. "You know what I'm going to ask. I have to know. Thad and Tye were my blood." *Were* sounded so deadly that I could not leave my supplication that way. "Are my blood," I corrected myself weakly.

Suddenly, Mom was sobbing over the sink. I rose to my feet, but she pulled away. "Don't you love me?" I wailed, but she was already out of hearing. She had shut herself in the bedroom. "Mom," I called, but she did not respond.

I sat back at the kitchen table and waited. Presently, she returned, gave me a stern look, and went back to the sink. "Don't you love me, too?" I asked.

I saw her shake again. "Yes, Tip. Your father and I love you. That's why we have to protect you."

"From what?" I demanded.

"From ancient night," she said, and despite my pleas, she refused to say more except to insist that I not bring up the subject when Pop arrived home. Pop's pickup truck barreled into the drive shortly thereafter, and after consulting with the buckaroos and inspecting our livestock, he washed up and sat at the table. Mom served our supper while Pop told about a difficult customer who could not make up his mind about a perfectly straightforward John Deere mower.

"I have swimming practice again tomorrow," I said, but my parents ate without responding.

Much later that night, when my parents were safely asleep in their bedroom, I pulled Thad's notebook from under my mattress. I scanned the pages I had already perused before I started reading in earnest.

❖

Thad's Journal: The Third of August, continued

With a hiss, Skip pulled his hand out of my shorts. "We gotta get moving, Thad, or we'll miss the casting."

The circle casting was the magical moment we never wanted to miss. After we broke our embrace, we jogged along despite being hampered by our cocks' hardened condition. Nonetheless, we made exemplary speed. The pipes summoning us to the monthly bacchanalia grew louder. As we trotted across the long meadow under the full moon, we saw far ahead other boys from Cougar Ridge Community College running toward the mystical circle on the edge of the forest. In that drawing circle, we would cast rational behavior aside and invoke the deities of intemperance. Naked in the mountain air under the golden moon, we would honor the eternal powers with our sexual frenzies.

"The lust of Dionysus is in me," Skip yelped as we broke into a gallop. The atmosphere we breathed skirled with the pipes, and the dirt beneath our feet throbbed with the drumming.

A great oak stood on a low hill, and Narcissus had already marked a ceremonial circle around it with cornmeal. Skip and I were late, and Apollo urged us to hurry. Skip and I stripped and stood gloriously naked in the cooling night air. Apollo, garbed only in a bull's head mask, produced the sacred amphora of anointing oil, which was not oil, but a water-based lubricant scented with aphrodisiacal herbs. Intoning a mystic chant, Apollo anointed Skip's forehead, his nipples, his navel, his erect cock, his tight asshole, his knees, and his feet with the sacred anointment. "Welcome, Osiris," Apollo said, invoking Skip's ritual name. He then kissed Skip's lips.

Apollo did the same for me, and I shivered with pleasure as he touched the warm liquid to the tip of my dick, and I moaned with delight as he sanctified my asshole. "Welcome, Adonis," Apollo said to me, and his kiss lingered sweetly upon my tongue. After Apollo had sanctified our bodies in honor of the hallowed Deities, Narcissus placed berry garlands around our brows, and Hermes handed us wands with ivy tendrils.

Behind Narcissus, like a guiding genius, a dazzling man stood in the center of the circle. Naked except for his ivy crown and his pinecone-tipped phallic staff, called a *thyrsus*, this awe-inspiring being embodied the path to the eternal. As he fingered his rigid cock and thrust out his rounded ass, he resembled a suntanned version of the ancient statue of the Divinity of the Starry Sky. Indeed, he taught us that the way to the everlasting serenity led through a sanctified ritual of unrepressed homosexual participation. He was my mythology professor Dr. Bromius. He was twenty-eight, a mere decade older than I was.

"Bacchantes," Hyacinthos announced, "This night we will invoke Chronos and Uranus. Enter naked and of your own free will into the vast circle."

One by one, we stepped into the sacred space where one of us would cast the circle. Our erect and pulsing dicks led us. The air felt warmer under the great sprawling oak, and the pipes sounded much louder. The drums began their sacred pounding, a rhythm that would become the rhythm of our heartbeats until we were all beating as one. Only the shafts of golden moonshine illuminated our naked skin. The air bore the scents with the holy oil, incense, and male lust.

Hyacinthos, a sophomore who had been Dr. Bromius's classroom assistant, commanded us to join hands while he selected

Attis to cast the circle. Stepping to the center while we joined hands, Attis turned three times, intoning the ritual words and pointing his thyrsus beyond the circle of boys.

"In the names of the gods of time and the starry sky, I cast a circle of protection around this brotherhood, a great glowing circle of protection closed around, above, and beneath. May Chronos and Uranus permit no evil to enter herein. I conjure the navel of the cosmos, the borderland among the worlds, the meeting of the real and the ideal, the fusion of the finite and the infinite, and the tryst of the being and the becoming. So mote it be."

"So mote it be," said we all.

Attis returned to his place, and Hyacinthos pointed his thyrsus toward me. "Adonis, you will sweep the circle." He held out a ritual broom, which I took humbly. I swept from the center outward, and the boys stood aside to let me sweep between their legs. My hand brushed hard cocks and protrusive buttocks as I swept and chanted.

"Let all fear and doubt be swept from this circle. Let our revels be pure and pleasing to the gods of lust of penis for hand, hand for penis, penis for mouth, mouth for penis, penis for ass, and ass for penis. Let our semen flow male to male in pure liberation as we seek the path to infinite bliss. Let all harm and cruelty, suppression and oppression, prudery and pretense, meddlers and busybodies be banished from this place. As I will, so mote it be."

"So mote it be."

"Merry meet," Apollo said.

Dr. Bromius, Hyacinthos, Narcissus, and Hermes echoed his words, and we boys replied, "Merry meet."

Fulfilling an elaborate ritual, Narcissus drew down the spirits of homosexual desire as he offered his ass to Apollo. As Hermes lit the four candles, I felt my need to fuck and suck growing. My left hand seized upon Skip's swollen cock. Orpheus gripped my cock with his left hand. Apollo's turn came next. He intoned the charms of the boy beautiful and offered his mouth to Hyacinthos. When Apollo finished his incantation, Narcissus bent and thrust his ass back. Apollo slipped his cock into Narcissus's rear. After he came, he dropped to his knees and sucked Narcissus's cock. Thus, our revels began.

Near the tree lay a wicker basket containing flavored condoms for blowing, extra-strength condoms for anal intercourse, and tubes of lubricant. I grabbed a tube and two rubbers.

Hermes, satisfying the function of a devotee of Uranus, placed his hands on his knees, stuck out his rump, and summoned us to form the unbroken train. Skip lubed Hermes's asshole, slipped a condom over his own cock, and wiggled his cock into Hermes's ass. Baal, a freshman like me, plugged into Skip, and Moloch fell into place behind him. I rushed forward, not wanting to be at the end of the line, but Ibreez jumped in front of me. Happily, Orpheus stood erect behind me, his cock hard, wrapped, and lubed. I lubricated Ibreez's little hole. Ibreez's ass was hot, and he waggled it as I fingered him. I drove my condom-covered cock into Ibreez's ass. While I positioned my dick, Orpheus was preparing my asshole. I pushed my ass back toward him, bringing my cock to the rim of the boy I was fucking, while Orpheus pushed his cock into my crack. I drew a deep breath and pushed my asshole open to admit him. Orpheus drove against me, his loins pushing against my bare buttocks. I was filled again with the incredible sensation of a hard dick entering my anal sphincter and driving steadily into my rectum.

"Uranus. Uranus. *Evoe*, Uranus," we chanted.

❖

Tipper's Tale

It was midnight and the house was silent. I could hear night sounds: the buzzing of insects, the coyotes calling down the moon, the owls hooting their hunting cries, and the wind whispering in the old Sitka spruce. Reading in bed, I felt a profound disquiet down deep in my soul. I was wearing nothing but my cotton underwear, a bikini style with wide green and yellow stripes. I was reclined on my left side, with my head propped on my left hand, so the gleams of my bedside lamp fell upon the perilous scrawl penned onto the blue-lined paper. Thad's words coming to me across more than fifteen lost years inflamed me beyond belief. My cock had hardened as I absorbed the dangerous images. My mind and body were stuck in a whirl of growing lust and social fear; yet even as Pastor Joe Kern's homophobic sermons flickered through my consciousness, my cock stiffened uncomfortably in my underwear. Despite the dangerous territory Thad was leading me into, I continued reading.

❖

Thad's Journal: The Third of August, continued

"*Evoe*, Uranus." The agreeable fullness in my rectum grew and ebbed as Orpheus rocked his hips against my ass. Over the past months, I had learned that I adored the sensation of a thick cock pushing into my ass. I thrust back to take all of his cock, and my own dick responded by growing heavier in Ibreez's ass. Ibreez had solid buns and a hot hole. As I thrust forward, his grainy rectum tickled my cock deep in spite of the protecting condom. Orpheus drew back until only the head of his cock was opening my asshole, then he plunged forward, wholly impaling my ass again.

Guys were thrusting, sweating, moaning, and calling upon the mystical powers. Hyacinthos let us come close to orgasm, but he knew our limits and ordered a halt before we could climax. The train of the fucked broke apart. Mad with desire to be filled and to spurt my own load, I cast my eyes upon Dr. Bromius. He had seated his divine butt upon a thick tree stump, his skin silvery in the moonlight and his eyes sparkling in the beams of the twinkling stars. Between his legs, his erect cock stood tall and thick, and even as I looked toward him, I could see a single glistening drop exude from the tip.

❖

Tipper's Tale

I had never read anything like this in my entire life. Gay sex, circle casting, magical spells, pagan rituals, arcane old gods whose names I could not even pronounce. Yet, these were my own brother's diaries, and as I read, almost agape with astonishment, the image of a chain of naked boys fucking in homage to unspeakable gods sent my soul twirling down a vortex of lust. My mouth was dry with my sexual heat.

I shifted my position, sitting up more so I could rub my cock through my underwear while I read. My dick was hard, as hard as it had ever gotten, which felt near to splitting open, and as I fondled it, a stream of thin fluid leaked from the tip. The front of my briefs was wet and growing wetter. I didn't mind coming in my underwear because semen washed out. However, I had learned that the lubricant left a dark stain in the cloth that did not wash away. I had to throw away several pairs before I learned my lesson.

I had never jerked off to such rampantly homosexual thoughts. Not until that night. Once the images were implanted in my head, I could not shake them out. I didn't even want to rid myself of them. I could picture the circle of naked college boys, my own brother prominent among them, and I resolved to read more about their wholehearted progress toward wanton homosexual orgies in honor of terrifying gods whom the world no longer knew.

❖

Thad's Journal: The Third of August, continued

Orpheus embraced me from behind and whispered into my ear. "May it please starry Uranus, I want to finish what I started. I want to honor the god by coming with my cock inside of you, Adonis. Will you receive me?"

How could I not accede to that holy appeal? Orpheus was paying me the supreme compliment by offering to plant in me the rod and seed symbolic of our gods. His cock was already lubed and ready with a new condom, so I dropped and let him take me doggy style.

"*Evoe!*" I roared as Dr. Bromius had taught us. "Praise be to the sublime deities." My cry was a wail that mingled with the wail of the reed pipes and the pounding of the drums. "Orpheus, that's so good."

My cock was hard still from our train fuck. Orpheus's cock drove deeper and deeper into me, stretching my asshole, opening me wide. Every thrust sent raptures up my cock shaft.

"*Evoe*, Chronos, increase my desire." My demands arose to the infinite; although I could not prevent my mouth from adding more. "You're really sticking it to me." Orpheus's cock head kept massaging my prostate, and it awakened a dark and delicious eroticism. "You're milking my ass, Orpheus. You're milking me. Keep it up. For the love of Uranus, do me like that."

"Your ass is hotter than Vulcan's forge, Adonis. Your ass is like the beauty of the callipygian moon." He pulled back and stroked my buttocks lovingly.

"Tell me more about my ass, Orpheus."

"You give good ass. *Evoe*." He drove his cock in to the hilt. "Great Chronos, Adonis, what a sweet fuck."

While Orpheus fucked me, I watched our professor throw himself upon his back amid a pile of freshly fallen leaves and draw up his shapely brown legs. In the full moonlight, I could see that his asshole was already dilated and ready to receive. I'd been hoping that I'd get my cock up my teacher's ass some night, but that night Skip got the prize. Apollo removed his Dionysian bull's head mask and slipped it over Skip's head. Thus attired, Skip looked primitive and bestial. Seeing him arrayed as the Bull God assured me that I was pleasing those forgotten Mystical Powers who demand the human acceptance of bliss. Fierce pride filled me. I rocked my ass back and forward on Orpheus's cock. I bore down with my anal sphincter, milking the rod in my ass with all my strength.

"I'm gonna fuck you, professor." The crow that came through the mouth hole of the bull mask on Skip's head sounded nothing like the voice of a bull; it was more like the raucous call of the crow. Nonetheless, Skip's cock was solid, and he was jerking it as he smeared it with lubricant. "Open your ass for the Bull God's cock." Skip kept shouting his demands as the student who had played Apollo slipped a condom onto Skip's dick. Thus prepared, Skip threw himself between our professor's legs and drove his hard cock up his ass. My dick stiffened harder at the sight, and my asshole gripped Orpheus's cock furiously.

"Dr. Bromius," Skip wailed. "Your ass is so tight. You're grinding my dick. You're gonna rip the fuckin' cum out of me."

Watching my best friend fuck my teacher was driving me wilder with excitement. I ground Orpheus's cock with my asshole, squeezing furiously.

Orpheus squealed with delight. "The friction in your ass is like fucking sandpaper, Adonis."

"*Evoe*, Dionysus, see how I take it for you." I was bragging, perhaps even gloating. "Orpheus is gonna give me all he's got. Orpheus, you're gonna blast big wads."

Orpheus humped me even harder, and I knew he was getting close. I wasn't ready to squirt yet; I wanted to save up. That was no reason not to bring Orpheus off, but Orpheus stopped humping and held his cock still in my ass.

"That's it, Orpheus," I said. "Hold off and go. Hold off and go."

"Yeah, it makes it more intense." That assurance from Orpheus sounded as a rasp in my ear. "Okay, I'm not as close now."

"All right. Get to humping."

Orpheus twisted his dick back and forth in my ass, and the sensation drove me wild. "I love that screwing." I moaned and humped my ass back, fucking his dick with my eager butt, while he banged my ass with his crotch.

I watched Skip, still wearing the bull head, bang Dr. Bromius. While Skip's cute ass was bouncing up and down, another bacchant fell upon him and thrust his cock into Skip's thrusting ass. Skip howled with joy and exploded his juices instantly.

He huffed through the mask, "Holy Dionysus, I'm coming. I'm coming a lot. *Evoe*, Uranus, my cock is spurting out the juice."

All around the circle, boys were fucking boys, moaning, groaning, wailing, and howling, some experiencing the intense thrill of thrusting and shooting cum into another boy's ass, and others were experiencing the great rapture of sucking cocks and receiving their loads of hot spunk. We were initiated bacchantes all, endowed by the gods and dedicated to pleasing the gods. Meanwhile, the pipers and the drummers continued their eerie rhythm, and our bodies attuned with the sacred music.

"Adonis, this is it," Orpheus said with a grunt. "I'm gonna come now. *Evoe*, Pan, I'm gonna come in your ass right now. Take it, Adonis; take the spunk of Orpheus."

Orpheus was thrusting hard up my ass, his hips slapping my butt cheeks as if he were spanking me. But it was a good kind of spanking, and I relished it.

Orpheus emitted the traditional bull roar as the first blast of semen spurted from his cock. "*Evoe*, ye goatherd gods. *Evoe!*"

His mindless howls drove me to milk him ever harder until his dick was spent and hurting in my grinding ass. I had not come while he fucked me, though I'd come close. Skip had climaxed in Dr. Bromius, and our fellow bacchant, a short boy named Scott, most characterized by his aggressive manner and outstanding dick, was climaxing in Skip's ass.

The boys were calling upon the gods, the ancient gods who asked only that we fully surrender our bodies to homosexual ecstasy. The piping and the drumming finally stopped as the musicians joined the sacred orgy.

Of course, in the eyes of the world, we were a gang of horny college boys indulging in mindless sex, but something else was happening. I felt the power of the old gods moving through us— we became bacchantes, half-satyr and half-nymph. I felt the mystic approval that my actions generated. With a cock in my ass, I revitalized the blazing exhilaration that our society tamed out of us. I rose above the sad social structure that at its best could merely present a dim, flat image of our rapture on a page or a computer screen for lonely masturbation. My parents attended a church with a lukewarm and insipid theology. Their religion did not defy government, thumb its nose at law and order, or bare its buttocks to social conventions. The followers of their faith did not sacrifice their bodies to the will of divine beings almost erased from human consciousness.

Five boys were linking into an oral daisy chain, and I considered jumping in on the action. However, each one had his mouth on a cock already, so the chain was closed. Then I saw another train forming. I hurried to the front of the choo-choo line and planted my ass on Ibreez's dick. He grunted as my rectum claimed his rod, and we all waved our ivy wands in honor of Dionysus as we rocked back and forth.

I slipped a fresh condom over my dick just before another boy took the lead from me. His round, grapefruit buns surrounded my dick, and I slid into his hot tube. He introduced himself as he pushed his buttocks back with reckless abandon.

"I'm Priapus. I was initiated last month, and I've been dreaming about your dork for the last thirty days, Adonis. I want you to come in me."

I broke apart from the choo-choo and took Priapus bending. Priapus had grabbed his knees and stuck out his butt, so I was happy to give it to him that way. "*Evoe*, Hail the great good Uranus, pump me," Priapus pleaded. "Pump it into me."

My cock was halfway up his ass. I pulled back to his sphincter and thrust home. "Do me like that. *Evoe*, in the name of the Uranian gods, do me like that."

His ass was good, and I wanted to give it to him just as good. I thrust my cock in his eager ass, thrusting and pounding, but I was already close to coming.

"I'm not gonna hold out long," I said and groaned as tingles raced through the head of my cock. "I'm gonna come fast."

"That's okay, let it fly. You're fucking me so good. I'm gonna go too. Adonis, you're making me come by fucking my ass. *Evoe*, gods of frenzy, I come when I'm fucked."

My dick head was tingling and rippling. The prickles of bliss were magnified as I thrust fast in Priapus's asshole. The tingles were growing into the eternal ruffles, the mad, shaking disturbances of the twitter and the pucker. My lips tingled and my nipples hardened. My eyelids fluttered so that I could but half see. I felt the explosions of the divine light in my brain and in my groin.

"Here I come. Here I come," I yelled.

My dick bucked, and the pleasure ran up my shaft. The muscles at the base of my penis contracted powerfully, and my first great spurt of semen shot forth. Spurt followed spurt as I rode the powerful waves of pleasure, shooting my spunk into Priapus's delightful ass.

Priapus was coming too. His cum flung free and fell upon the warm earth, glistening as it arched across the Sturgeon moon. "*Evoe*, praise be to Pan. I wanted this so bad. And it's even better than I expected. *Evoe*, all glory to Bacchus. Oh, Thad, I love your cock up my ass."

We remained locked together while our orgasms quieted. Then we rose and went to the altar where the refreshments awaited. Sitting together, Priapus and I drank the sacred ivy mead, ate sweet ritual seed cakes, and discussed every detail of our consecrated fuck. When we had replenished our tissues, we found our frank sexual talk had aroused us again, so we rejoined the Bacchanalia.

❖

Tipper's Tale

By the time I finished reading my brother's notebook, I was so close to shooting my load that I felt like I was already committed. I slipped off my briefs, which were soaked with my leakage, and tossed them onto the floor. My bottle of lube was sitting on my bedside table, evidence of my goal all along, and I grabbed a wad of Kleenex to catch my cum. I squeezed a dollop of lubricant into my palm. My cock felt great in my fist, as if it belonged there.

I lubricated the head of my cock, twisting around it before I slid my fist down my shaft. As I stroked, fantasies about the festival of Dionysus flickered across my eyelids. All my years of jerking off, I had tried to think about girls while I tugged my cock. I tried to picture myself fucking one of them, movie stars, girls at my high school, famous singers, a collection of motley whores granted celebrity status for nothing but their public shenanigans. Always, they had failed to satisfy, and always, before I rose to orgasm, my mind flickered across the other guys on my swim team and finally suppressed those desires and settled on vague, ambiguous images as I throbbed and tingled and blasted salvos of my wet spunk.

However, that night, my brother's journal freed me from the trap our parents and society had laid for me. I didn't get off thinking about females. I never had, and I never would. Guys were so much sexier, so much more desirable, so much more fun to be with. They were where my interest lay, and I suppressed my desires no longer. I fantasized that I was participating in the ritual that my brother had described.

I had never been fucked in the ass, nor had I sucked a cock. I had never even jacked off with a friend. I had never gotten off with a girl either, though I had dated some. Girls complained that I was a cold kisser, and I always backed out before I could become a lover.

Facing the truth of my disposition was liberating, even erotic, and as I beat my meat, I could hear the drums beating under the harvest moon and the pipes of Pan calling me to the celebration. Tingles coursed through my cock's head as I imagined participating in the train, plugged into a tight male ass even as some sexy guy plunged his slick cock into mine.

My orgasm peaked as if my brain had exploded. The pleasure came in rich, keen, red waves, so poignant that I could hardly suffer them. I had never felt a pleasure so acute that it hurt, but hurt so good that I never wanted it to end. The muscles under my scrotum pumped, the muscles at the base of my penis contracted, and a wet jet of cum shot out of my fist and across the room. I fumbled, trying to bring the wad of Kleenex to catch the blasts, but my spurts were beyond my control. I ejaculated freely and wildly, and when I finally finished, I sprawled on my back gasping for oxygen.

I rested and let my breathing return to normal before I climbed out of bed and wiped up the semen streaks on my carpet. My first shot had hit the wall seven feet distant. I could only hope that I had gotten all of the evidence. The stains on my briefs were obvious. I slipped down the hallway to the bathroom, hoping that neither of my parents would pick that moment to leave their bedroom for a late night snack. When I had cleaned myself and my belongings as well as I could, I pulled on a fresh pair of briefs and slipped between my sheets. Even still, sleep came with difficulty, for my mind could not release the terrific images Thad's words had evoked. I graced his notebook with a lasting look before I slipped it under my mattress. After a while, I slept and dreamed.

CHAPTER TWO

Tipper's Tale

A full day passed before I had a chance to try my key. On Saturday evening, my parents drove over to play cards at the neighbors. I waited for a few minutes before I tried the duplicate key in the lock of my brothers' door. It was sticky at first, but after a little jiggling, it turned the tumblers. No one had used the overhead light for fifteen years, so the bulb had died—Mom always cleaned in there during the daylight while Pop was at work. I illuminated my path to the dresser with a flashlight. The notebook I had taken earlier had been the third one down. I replaced it, and lifted the notebook on the top.

I opened the book to the first page and shined my light upon the text. As I scanned the first paragraph, I was certain that I was looking at Thad's first journal, the text that would give me the key to what had happened to him, to my brother Tye, and, I thought with a strange sensation deep down, might also happen to me.

Thad's Journal: The Twenty-Sixth of September

I'm going to start keeping this journal because of the tremendous awakening that occurred in my life. I certainly can't talk to Mom or Dad about what is happening, and my parents' church would think

I'd become the whore of the devil. Still, at some point Tye will read this, and maybe little Tipper too—someday.

❖

Tipper's Tale

I set aside the notebook until my heart stopped racing. Seeing my name, my childhood name, penned on the page stabbed me with a pain I could hardly express. I wanted to carry the notebook back to my bedroom, but I had to read just a few more words first.

❖

Thad's Journal: The Fifth of October

I know now that I'm gay; I think that I've suspected it all my life. I have no doubt that my brother Tye is gay, too. YES, I MEAN YOU, YOUNGER BROTHER, IF YOU'RE READING THIS. If anything, Tye is the gayest-acting boy I've ever seen. Even though he's still a high school student, Tye walks with an obvious sway that caused him to get bullied until he learned how to punch. Tye's effeminacy bothers our parents a lot, especially Dad. Dad calls Tye "Miss Panties" and is always trying to make a *man* out of him by dragging him off to church events, sports games, and a whole series of gospel retreats. Poor Tye has a bad time of it. He tells everybody he isn't gay. I've seen him practicing his walk in front of a mirror, trying to walk more like a boy, but as soon as he forgets himself, his butt wiggles like a cheerleader's.

Although our parents have strong suspicions about Tye's sexual outlook, nobody suspects me. I'm good at hiding the truth because I've been doing it so long. Even the few girls I've dated never suspected, or if they did, they kept their suspicions to themselves.

Perhaps the inclination toward homosexuality runs in families. It's too early to guess about my little brother Tipper, who is only three. Tye is only fifteen months younger than I am, whereas, my parents waited another fourteen years before they sprung little

Tipper on us. He is a cute little pest though, and I hope he turns out gay too.

❖

Tipper's Tale

I stopped reading, almost unable to believe the evidence of my own eyes. My brother Tye was a total swish? Thad hoped I'd turn out gay? I felt a weakness in my legs, but I picked up the notebook again.

❖

Thad's Journal: The Sixteenth of October

I feel so good about what I'm going through that I can't imagine what it would be like not to be this way. Perhaps homosexuality is a condition that our parents passed to us in their genes, though the condition/syndrome/what have you—maybe I'll refer to it as the good luck. Some would call it a curse, I guess, but after what I just experienced, curse is the wrong word indeed—anyway, the condition must have skipped Mom and Dad's generation.

Of course, my awakening is not only a discovery of how much I love gay sex. It also has to do with the old gods. It is rooted in paganism, which has freed me from the cruel bonds of Dad's religion.

This quarter I signed up for a course in Greek drama. Since I read *The Odyssey* and *Gilgamesh* in high school, I've felt an affinity for the ancient world, and I was looking forward to discussing *Agamemnon*, *Oedipus*, *The Bacchae*, and *The Frogs*. The boys at Cougar Ridge Community College have been saying that Dr. Bromius was the best teacher on campus. The girls disliked him, but most boys thought he was great. Inevitably, the campus was awash with rumors about Dr. Bromius: strange rites, orgiastic ceremonies, disturbing behavior, lawless performances, irrational titillating lectures, frenzies of sodomy under the full moon, and some unnamed reemergence of the ancient mystery rituals.

❖

Tipper's Tale

Bromius again, I thought as I perused Thad's text. The professor had been twenty-eight at the time. Dr. Bromius would be in his forties now. I wondered whether he was still teaching at Cougar Ridge Community College. How would he respond if I looked him up? Could he tell me anything about my brothers, things my parents were reluctant to reveal? Would he invite me to participate in pagan rituals of gay sex under the full moon?

More questions flooded my consciousness. Did homosexuality run in our family, as Thad suggested? "I am gay," I whispered to myself, as Thad had virtually prophesized. Saying the words, even whispering, felt liberating. I wanted to be gay because my being gay explained a lot. I felt no dismay over my homosexual inclinations. I was thrilled. "I am a homosexual," I said slightly louder. Hearing my own quivering voice, I rose from my bed and checked to make certain that Pop's pickup truck had not yet returned.

In three paragraphs I won't duplicate, Thad wrote about the necessity of coming out, revealing one's true nature to the world. Did he do that? Did Tye? Did I have the courage to follow their example? I tried to convince myself that I did, though I could picture how my parents would respond. I shivered cowardly at the thought. Pop would disown me. Mom would cry as she condemned me to hell. Was that what happened to Thad and Tye? Had they come out to Mom and Pop, and perhaps been banished from the family's book of record? Had Thad told our parents about his pagan orgies? Did they read his notebooks? They must have read them, or at least, Mom knew about them. She cleaned that room. She had access to the drawer where they were stored. Neither she nor my father had burned my brother's writings in a family bonfire, or even in a hotter fire down at the church.

I took the notebook, resisting the temptation to take two, and carefully closed the drawer. I inspected the carpet for telltale signs of my passing, but I had entered wearing clean socks, and the carpet bore no traces. I locked the door again and hurried back to my bedroom.

Mom and Pop had not yet returned. Doubtless, their church friends were entertaining with cakes and coffee, or my parents were imbibing intoxicants and Doris was getting mad whenever she picked up a "Draw Four" in their game of Uno. I had been dragged to enough of those games to know that Doris's Christian soul was drawn thin when she lost. I stripped to my T-shirt and briefs and reclined on my bed to read about gay sex orgies under the full moon. I was a bit surprised when Thad commenced with a history of the college.

❖

Thad's Journal: The Eighteenth of October

Cougar Ridge Community College was established in 1964, but the site has been a college of sorts for over a hundred years. Some buildings housed pre-World War II military barracks, and older buildings dated back to the Spanish American War. The jealous bunglers in administration had relegated Dr. Bromius's mythology class to a lecture hall in the oldest building on campus, a hoary brick structure overgrown with English ivy.

Skip was nervous as our feet made the ancient boards creak on our way to class. "You sure we should've signed up for this class, Thad? There's stories going around. Sounds like every boy who goes into this class comes out queer."

"You worried, Skip?"

"I'm just sayin'…" Skip started, glancing around nervously. "If my pop knew about you and me beating off together, he'd break out the fuckin' twelve gauge. Pop would shoot me and you too."

"Your pop is a total asshole, Skip. No offense, man, but you gotta wonder. Anybody who yells about faggots as much as he does must have something to hide."

"You suspect my pop?" Skip's voice trailed off in wonderment as we entered the classroom. "Pop blowin' the old skin flute?" I had given Skip a copy of *Tearoom Trade* a few months earlier, but I had never suggested that I suspected his father. Still, the glass slipper fit the princess's shoebox-sized foot.

Nearly a hundred students were seated in the lecture hall, only fifteen of them female. Because Skip and I were sitting in for our first day, we planted our butts on the back row. Two seats away, a boy with dark ringlets and an olive complexion swiveled in his seat as if he were turning on a cock. When he glanced at me with his sultry eyes, I could not help smiling back.

"First time taking one of Dr. Bromius's classes?" he asked, spotting a newcomer immediately.

"Yeah," I said. Strangely, the way this boy was appraising me gave me a hard-on. I felt a deep and primal sense of arousal; sensations and thoughts that were beyond my analysis washed over me. The boy was cute, no doubt of that, and somewhat out of the closet in his choice of dress, though he wasn't that odd. He was wearing a pinkish sweatshirt and eggshell jeans that fit him tighter than the current fashion.

"You're gonna love this class," he said. "Love every second Dr. Bromius is up there."

Our professor wasn't "up there" then, but after a few seconds, he entered through the back door and swept down the stairs. Dr. Bromius was dressed in tight green slacks, a creamy yellow shirt, and a green jacket. He flowed to the podium, which he gripped with his left hand, while his right traced a course through the air.

"There is a deep circle," Dr. Bromius said, "which no one can point toward. The center of this circle is everywhere, and its circumference is nowhere."

A world of meaning dangled from his words. The circle was eternity, it was the cosmos, but it was also something that spelled unspeakable eroticism. Images of boys fucking boys, vast circle jerks—just as Skip and I had teased the spunk out of our cocks—daisy chains of sucking boys, extensive trains of fucking boys, each plugged into the boy in front, and other actions too personal to describe flittered across the insides of my eyelids.

"A circle," Skip whispered, half to himself, half-mesmerized beside me. "I shoulda known that. The moon's deep circle." He slid his hand down to his crotch and touched his dick. He was not the only boy in the classroom who touched his dick at the sound of Dr. Bromius's voice.

By our third class meeting, I had utterly fallen under Dr. Bromius's spell—as had Skip and every other boy. I found myself staring dreamily at him during class. I was in love—or lust—with my professor. Meanwhile, seemingly oblivious to my homosexual desires, Dr. Bromius lectured about the rational and the irrational, and how we had to accept both sides, moderation and frenzy, and that Carl Jung wrote that repression creates an evil shadow that can destroy us. He lectured that we must periodically abandon ourselves to what Sheldon Cheney called "our ecstatic participation in the divine life."

Two weeks into the course, I visited Dr. Bromius in his office. My heart was thundering, and I felt a contraction in my throat that ran down into my crotch. Never before had I felt so edgy, so awkward, or so eager to please a teacher. Attired again in tight green and cream clothing, Dr. Bromius sat behind his desk, a wall of books behind him, a gigantic ivy wand hanging from the wall to his right, and a case of figurines on his left. In my sexually excited mental condition, the ivy wand seemed penis-shaped and the mythological figurines were distinctly homoerotic. I half hoped that Dr. Bromius would throw me over his desk and take me as he wished. The terrified other side wanted to run.

Dr. Bromius sensed that I wasn't there to talk about my grades; I was pulling straight A's. He sat behind his desk, reposed, unspeakably desirable, and looking for the entire world like one of the sky people of antiquity. As he waved a hand toward a maroon leather chair, his eyes took in my form from my hair to my shoes.

I dropped my ass into the seat and tried to speak, but the words stuck in my throat. I must have looked like a drooling loony. I tried twice to muster a sound, failing miserably until an embarrassing squeak emitted from my throat.

Dr. Bromius arose, walked around his desk, and placed a soothing/frightening hand on my shoulder. His touch was like a touch of flame, such a heat shot through my body. "It's all right, Thad," he said, surprising me. He knew my name. "I've seen you in class. I knew that you would come to me. Take a couple of deep breaths. Then ask for the thing you desire."

The question blurted almost unbidden to my lips. "How would I get initiated into the mystery religion?"

Dr. Bromius looked down at me, his hand still touching my shoulder, but lightly so that his fingers caressed my neck. I had the sense that he saw into my soul, though I knew that he was only human. He could not read my thoughts, I assured myself, though my deep superstitions spoke to the contrary. Still, he knew my desires.

He walked behind his desk again and removed a scroll from a drawer, handed it to me, and recited from memory:

Hear ye the words of the Uranian god, who has been Dionysus, Uranus, Apollo, Mithras, Anu, Osirus, Orpheus, Bran, Taliesin, Ganymede, Herne, Pan, Chronos, Lugh, and more names beyond counting, he whose feet stand upon eternity, and whose body enfolds creation:

"I am the splendor of the blue Earth, the change of the silver moon among the turning stars, and the mystery of the roiling water.

"I call unto thy soul, arise, and come unto me.

"My spilled seed gives life to the bending universe, and all seed returns to my body.

"Before my swollen phallus, beloved of gods and of men, let thy flesh and psyche be transported into the rapture of the infinite.

"Let my worship be the joyous heart, the masculine potency, the cosmic spasm, the spurt of semen, the receiving orifices, for behold, love and pleasure are my rituals.

"In our twelve-moon's morrice, thou diest not, but unto eternity thou risest.

"To thou who seekest me, know that yearning shall avail thee not unless thou tastest the mystery of the pleasure of men.

"If that which thou seekest, thou findest not within, thou shalt not find without.

"Behold, I have touched thee in the first unfolding of thy flesh; and I am won through thy offering to the desire of men."

So saying, my teacher smiled wryly and took the scroll from my trembling hand. "You must want, Thad, you must seek, you must ask."

"I want to be initiated, and I'm asking," I said, rising and embracing him. I missed his waist and grabbed my professor by his ass. Rocked by my own conduct, I still placed one hand behind his head, caressed his soft hair, drew his face to mine, and kissed his mouth. I knew I was violating any number of college regulations, but college administrators and state legislators are flying monkeys sent by the Blasted Bitch of the West and should be defied whenever possible. I slipped my tongue into my professor's mouth, and he was powerless to resist. He kissed me back, his tongue against mine, and his hand encircled my waist, slid lovingly down the small of my back, and caressed my buttocks.

With my professor's hand on my ass and his tongue in his mouth, I kissed hard, for he was the first man I had ever tasted. Somehow, kissing a man was so much more exciting than kissing any female, and I had tried a few of those while still a stumbling high school student, but this desire was better than any other. My cock was hard and tortured within my briefs, and I could feel that Dr. Bromius had also arisen to the occasion. His cock twisted to my left, forming a thick bulge in his tight slacks.

However, all things must end, and our kiss came to a conclusion. To my tremendous disappointment, he did not force me to bend over his desk, nor push me to my knees before him. He said, "Remember where we are."

I remembered. I was standing in his office, and other students waited in the hall outside. The time was not fortuitous. Still, he promised that he would send for me, that I had responded to the call of the god and to the pipes of Pan. With an affectionate pat upon my ass, he launched me on my way.

❖

Tipper's Tale

My brother's description of his first gay kiss drove me wild with jealousy. I told myself that it was only a kiss, a mere meeting of the lips, yet the intimacy of two boys kissing filled me with an envious longing to experience that sensation. That one of the participants was a college teacher and the other my blood relation—my brother—cast me into mystery. I was jealous of Thad, yet like he, I was also terrified of the feelings I was discovering within myself. Did I have the fortitude to confront the slights, insults, and derogatory terms imposed by school? The team? Mom and Pop's church? Mom? Pop? I couldn't imagine why the twisted repressors had bound my mind in the cold iron that had barred me from recognizing my own nature.

I set my teeth. My cock was hard, hardened by what I read, and I determined that I would act upon my lust. I resolved to find a partner to slake my sexual hunger, a lover, a boy lover who wanted me as I wanted him.

I was captain of the swim team; could it be so difficult to find a teammate of like mind? Guys who deliberately chose a sport that performed in skimpy swimwear—red Nike swimmer's briefs with the Muskrat Creek High muskrat mascot emblazoned on the side—could hardly be that straight. On reflection, I knew for a certainly that two were not. I pictured both teammates as I read and fondled my cock. Soon, the picture cleared like on an old-fashioned television with its rabbit ears tweaked.

❖

Thad's Journal: The Third of November, continued

On the next full moon after I kissed Dr. Bromius, I met, by arrangement, two boys who would lead me to my initiation. I recognized the obviously gay boy who had been sitting near me in mythology class. His name was Jim. He and I ate lunch together twice, and on our second lunch date, Jim suggested that Skip and I attend the next meeting of the college's Gay & Lesbian Alliance. However, before that meeting date arrived, Jim accosted me alone one day and told me to be waiting just beyond my dad's cornfield one hour before midnight during the next full moon. When the appointed night arrived, I slipped out my bedroom window, crept across the yard, and found Jim and another boy standing at the edge of the field.

"We have to blindfold you," Jim said.

"That's all right with me, Jim," I said, prepared to submit to the blindfold.

"Oh, Thad, my circle name is Attis," Jim said.

The other boy introduced himself as Orpheus. "We're your guides."

Orpheus and Attis tied a long sash around my eyes, circling my head three times. After checking my blindfold, they spun me, led me around in circles, and spun me some more until I lost all sense of direction.

Orpheus and Attis led me across the fields. I could feel the harrowed ground under my feet, and I had the sense we were gradually gaining altitude. After we had walked for forty-five minutes or so, they bade me halt.

"Don't touch your blindfold," Attis said. "Orpheus and I are going to take off our clothes. Then we'll strip you naked."

I heard rustling sounds, whispers of dropped fabric, and zippers slipping down. After a minute, Orpheus and Attis took my arms. "Don't try to help. Let us undress you. Don't touch your blindfold. Everything comes off but that."

As they stripped me, ordering me to raise my arms or stand on one leg as the occasion demanded, I could feel the brush of their bare skin against mine. Their touch was unbearably erotic. I wondered whether my cock was stiffening. With nothing binding it, I could not tell. I moved my hand surreptitiously toward my crotch, but one of the boys stopped me.

"No jacking off," Orpheus said.

"I wasn't." My protests exposed my vulnerability to ridicule as I stood naked and blindfolded.

"You were checking out your cock." My accuser spoke loud enough to be heard in Boise, Idaho.

An unfamiliar voice joined in my humiliation. "Why did you want to touch your cock?"

Another strange voice answered for me before I could defend myself. "Thad wanted to find out whether his dick gets hard when he's naked with the boys."

Someone's fingers squeezed the head of my cock. That touch was enough to tell me I was sporting a major boner.

"Thad was trying to play with his cock." That mendacious assertion came from Orpheus who laughed uproariously at his own fibs.

"Two boys get him naked, and wham-bam, he tries to spank his monkey."

"How often do you jerk off, Thad?"

"Come on, Thad. Tell us about it. Once a day? Twice a day?"

"He looks like a jacking artist. I'll bet he flogs that thing twenty times in a week."

Disembodied voices kept up a running stream of masturbation jokes at my expense while Orpheus and Attis led me up a steep rise. As we climbed, we passed through a gauntlet of scoffing, jeering, hissing, and taunting boys all intent on inflicting upon me every dirty dig and rude reproach they could invent. The boys' mockery became more homosexually explicit as we passed among them.

"Look at his lips."

"The boy does have a nice set, doesn't he?"

"Kind of puffy. Makes me want to slide my cock between them."

"How's your mouth, Thad?"

"Do you suck dicks?"

"With lips like he's got? You gotta believe Thad sucks dicks."

❖

Tipper's Tale

Sitting up in my bed reading those words, I felt Thad's embarrassment. I tried to imagine being naked and blindfolded while an unknown number of strange boys were jeering obscenely and jesting derisively and hooting catcalls. My face flushed, but even in my discomfort, I found that the situation aroused me. My cock was stiff and throbbing, as if I wanted to be led naked among the boys, sniggered at, bombarded with sexual slurs, and hear my sexual secrets burlesqued. Unable to reconcile my own mixed feelings, I read on.

❖

Thad's Journal: The Third of November, continued

"Wouldn't surprise me if Thad took cocks in both ends at the same time."

"Of course he does. Just look at his ass."

"Thad is a cupbearer."

"He's got a golden bowl."

"I'd stick my silver rod in his golden bowl."

"Thad would like that."

"He probably jacks off with a broom handle up his asshole."

I could feel my face burning, which made the boys snigger. "He's turning pink."

"He'll be pinker when we get done with him." The speaker or some other boy grabbed my cock then, and I knew that I was still erect. In fact, my dick was throbbing, as if the gibes excited me. On some level, I was enjoying the sexual attention, however ribald and humiliating. Somebody swatted my ass lightly. Then another hand patted my ass, lingering long enough to turn into a caress.

As I walked, unseen hands began touching me intimately as boys gripped my cock, patted my ass, tweaked my nipples, kissed my lips, and stroked my thighs. I remembered Dr. Bromius's lecture about the Eleusinian Mystery Rites. At Eleusis, the initiate would pass through a ribald crowd who would taunt him obscenely as he ascended to the sacred *omphalos*.

The raillery and the jests stopped as our ascent became precipitous. Attis and Orpheus guided me skillfully so that I never stumbled or stubbed a toe against a rock. I could hear other boys climbing ahead of us; I could hear their breaths and their bare footpads. I could hear the wind moaning in the trees, the owls hooting, and an eerie whisper as the ground flattened out.

"We're going to release you and step away," Orpheus whispered. "Keep walking straight ahead. Don't stop until you are told."

After the boys released me, I continued placing one foot before the other. Mere seconds passed until I met a new challenge. I felt the presence of boys in front of me. The boys rubbed their hard cocks against my cock and against my ass. As I pressed forward, bare and blindfolded, the boys told me that no one but an anal slut would continue forward. Each step brought new verbal slaps. They told me that a cocksucker might carry on, or a catamite, an asslicker, a habitual masturbator, a passive sodomite, an obsessive fellatiator. As I pushed forward against their bodies, they called me a sissy, a milksop, a pantywaist, a cream puff, a henhussy, a prissy Betty, a Miss Molly, a tame cat, a ladyfinger, a shirtlifter, and a mamma's boy.

When I reached the end of that challenge walk, I heard the thud of bare feet upon the packed earth as the boys reassembled. I continued walking until strong hands pressed against my chest.

"Seeker, you come to us trusting, though blind and humiliated, mocked and defiled. You have passed the test of will. Do you still seek to be made part of the Uranian brotherhood?"

"I do."

"Will you sacrifice your psyche to the homoerotic frenzies?"

"Yes."

"Will you sacrifice your body to give pleasure to boys?"

"Absolutely."

"Will you sacrifice a future of wife and progeny?"

"I do."

"Will you sacrifice all hope of approval from any society save ours?"

My heart was pounding hard. "Yes."

"Will you accept social ostracism, familial rejection, religious persecution, and sexual discrimination, so that you may serve the Uranian gods?"

That was a big one. I had to be in for all, or I would be turned aside forever. "Yes."

"Do you promise to commit your soul and body to unrestrained homosexual delights exclusively, for all of your days?"

I chose the path open to me. "Yes," I said. "I do."

"Do you promise to keep our rites secret, to tell no one what we do during our holy rituals?"

"Yes."

At my final agreement, sounds of jubilation arose from the assembled company. Pipes shrilled, drums boomed, and tambourines rattled. I heard hisses as many boys' sharp intakes of breath broke the tension. Gradually, the sounds stilled until only the beating of hearts and the whispers of the night remained.

"Now you will be anointed so you may enter into the sacred circle. I, Narcissus, shall anoint your body with the holy oil and with the sacred kisses."

I heard the speaker prostrate himself before me. "This kiss is for the feet that stand upon eternity," Narcissus said. His lips touched the tops of my feet, after which he dribbled warm, scented oil on them.

"This kiss is for the knees which stand between the step and the potency." Narcissus kissed my knees and anointed both.

"The third kiss touches the phallus that projects toward the heavens." Narcissus's voice was colored with an intonation of the ineffable. While his voice was still echoing over the distant mountain range, I thrilled as I felt his lips caress the head of my cock. I was rock hard and ready, pointing toward the heavens. Narcissus kissed my cock, flicking my cock head with his tongue. This kiss lasted longer than the previous two. When I was near to ecstasy, he anointed the head of my cock with oil.

Narcissus placed both hands upon my buttocks. "The fourth kiss worships the hole into which men shall pour their love," he whispered, pulling my butt cheeks apart and kissing my asshole. He lingered there even longer than he had at my cock. Finally, he touched an oily finger to my little hole.

Next, Narcissus kissed my nipples as marks of the duality of a man's gender, calling my buds "tits" before he touched them with the consecrated oil. I received a stronger scent of the oil when he rubbed it onto my nipples, and I was certain that I detected the scents of olive oil, perfume, and semen.

At the last, I felt his breath upon my face. "This kiss is for the lips that suck the pleasure of life," Narcissus said. His lips met mine, hot, wet, stirring; moreover, he electrified me with a kiss that made me nearly swoon. As his tongue slipped into my mouth, I sucked on it and played against it with my own tongue. My arousal knew no bounds, though I did not ejaculate. My body thrilled as though I passed through numerous orgasms and ejaculations, yet my cock remained in a state prior to spasm. I was utter potency, joining with the Uranian gods, preparing to enter into the eternal bliss of the moon's deep circle.

After my lips had been anointed with the sacred oil, I received a kiss upon my forehead. "The kiss that touches the psyche," Narcissus said, and he placed the anointing oil upon my forehead, tied a cord around my waist, and bade me step forward, blind to the world, into the circle of boys.

❖

Tipper's Tale

My vision had grown so bleary that I had to set Thad's notebook aside. I was hot with lust, hard as a fresh cucumber, and shaking like one condemned to the gallows. Tears were running down my cheeks. I took a handful of tissues to wipe my face and dry my eyes. I could not believe I was having such a strong reaction.

Thad's story was incredibly sexy, yet it bespoke feelings of sexuality that I could not grasp. His depiction of the ceremony evoked a yearning that pricked needs deep within my soul. His words were sexy, erotic, but more than sexual because they were charged with an appalling desire greater than eroticism. I felt strange all over, as if I were afraid, angry, horny, sad, ecstatic, and envious. Never had I imagined knowing my brother so closely, and never had I imagined the utter peculiarity of that acquaintance.

One thought I did distinguish out of the confusion: I was going to read all Thad's journals. Then I would read the books he read—if the reading killed me. Finally, I had to track down Dr. Bromius, wherever he might be.

Bright lights sweeping through the yard interrupted my thoughts. I heard tires crunching on the gravel and a cackle of unrest from the chicken coop. The alpacas and the sheep stirred in the barn, while in the pasture, the llamas lined up along the fence. Such activity could portend only one thing—Pop's pickup truck was pulling into the drive.

My hard-on deflated hastily. I slid the notebook under my mattress, dressed in cutoffs and T-shirt, and met my parents at the door. I could tell immediately that Mom had downed several glasses of wine, but Pop had stuck to a single glass.

"Tip," Mom said. "How was the cake?"

"What cake?" I asked.

"I left a cake in the cupboard. You didn't find it?"

"I didn't think to look."

The three of us sat at the kitchen table eating chocolate cake with big chunks of dark chocolate and raspberries in the frosting, and swilling down tumblers of cold milk. Pop discussed Doris's temper, and Mom nodded at appropriate intervals. Pop concluded that Doris needed an intervention. Mom agreed that Deacon Beacon should confront her with her indiscretions.

Sick of hearing my parents criticize their recent host, I ate my cake in silence. Fortunately, the family gathering ended soon, and we all headed for our bedrooms. I stripped out of my clothes again and reclined naked upon my bed. My cock arose before I could pull Thad's notebook from my mattress. I assured myself that I was a typical horny eighteen-year-old boy, except that my interest lay in other boys.

"What the fuck," I muttered. "I am what I am. I desire the form that appeals to me." And with a firm resolve to embrace homosexual paganism, I drew three deep breaths, released them slowly, and commenced reading.

Thad's Journal: The Third of November, continued

"Enter the sacred circle."

My guides clutched my arms and led me forward. To the sound of drums, pipes, bells, and tambourines, a boy with a melodious voice invoked a spell that closed the sacred space. A high magic ritual commenced, during which the priests invoked the watchtowers and banished baneful influences.

I stood between my guides while these rituals were enacted to the accompaniment of whispery voices. Following the banishing, I felt the breath of the priest upon my face again. A hand lifted the cord around my waist and pulled it taut.

"Seeker, a thin cord binds you to us now," said the melodious voice. "Do you seek bondage with a stronger cord, the pleasure link of boy with boy?"

"I do," I vowed, and the pipes and drumming, which had stilled while they awaited my response, commenced again, sending waves of erotic desire coursing through my body. Thus I stood, naked, blindfolded, surrounded by boys, some of whom must have been my classmates, and others whom I had never met, quivering upon the verge of salvation, paradise, hell, nirvana, ecstasy, submission, illumination, surrender, and fulfillment.

"Seeker, I am stag-horned Hyacinthos. I open the path of boys who live to give pleasure. Now you shall fulfill the great rites of our Uranian god. Seeker, if your vows have meaning, drop to your knees that you may kiss the holy phallus."

My guides assisted me to my knees. I knew from the priest's words that a boy's cock was about to touch my lips, and for an infinite second, the universe reeled. My mind whirled like the swirling stars. For the first time, I was going to taste a cock, and not in some private tryst, but surrounded by boys watching closely. I was naked. My cock was so hard I feared it would split, my knees pressed the warm earth, poising me to suck off any boy who wanted my wet mouth, and my mind was a confusion of fear and desire.

A soft night breeze rippled over my skin. I could see nothing except for a pale light that filtered around my blindfold. That light was the full moon, which was never to be denied. The thought that this experience might be a gag perpetuated against me, a horrific practical joke designed to expose my homosexuality in front of the whole college, flittered through my mind.

Just as that terrible doubt slipped unasked into my consciousness, the head of a dick touched my lips. In a panic, I pulled my head back, and doing so sent a pang of disappointment through me. I wanted to taste that cock, but I was afraid, and my fear filled me with shame.

"Seeker, let go of your trepidation." Hyacinthos's voice, directly above me, carried an offer of peace. "Free your soul from doubt. Feel the Uranian god as he courses through you. He is the throbbing excitement you feel. Now do as thou wilt."

The drumming grew louder, and the pipes whistled more shrilly. I pushed my head forward, and the dick again touched my lips. That time, I opened my mouth to receive it, and I heard an immense sigh emit from many mouths.

❖

Tipper's Tale

At that point, Thad ran out of pages. The notebook describing the remainder of his initiation ritual awaited me in his bottom drawer. I could hardly wait to snag it, but with Mom and Pop still stirring, I did not dare make the attempt. Thad's thoughts so closely corresponded with my own that I felt as if the notebook contained my own story. If only it did. Oh, to be the naked boy on the windswept heath with an unseen cock touching my lips.

My cock was swollen, my balls painful. I needed release so badly that I felt sick. I stood, switched off my bedside lamp, and slipped to my open window. My room faced south, so I could see only the whirling stars above the farm. A pasture with our herd of llamas stood not far from my window. A fresh spring breeze filtered through the window screen, carrying the pleasant scents of the pasture. I could see the corner of the barn, which housed the bunkhouse where Pop's buckaroos slept. Even craning my neck, I could not see toward the East, across the long cornfield, toward the mountains. Somewhere, in that direction, stood the heath where my brother's initiation had occurred.

I tried casting my mind back. I could not recall the sound of drums and piping from any night of my childhood. In the country where we lived, the sound should have carried for five miles. I resolved to take a hike toward the eastern hills soon. Perhaps I could find the place. I touched my cock as I stared at the night sky—the starry sky—Uranus—and uttered a sacred vow.

"I seek you, Uranus. I will do your will. I will accept your pleasure within my body. My soul shall arise unto you. I will take the emblems of your sacred phallus within my mouth. I will swallow your sacred seed. I will take you into my ass. I will receive the divine spurt of the eternal night."

My dick so throbbed that I gave the tip of it a squeeze. I was so close to coming already that the mere pinch inflamed me beyond reason. Standing naked before my window, I rubbed my dick and caressed my ass. Years of swimming and working out with weights had sculpted my buttocks until my muscles were hard and round. Examining my own butt in the mirror before swim meets, I had recognized that it was delectable. My teammate Lyle sometimes joked about my shapely buttocks, but I had not then caught the significance of his innuendo. Lyle was hot for my ass, which was all right with me; I was hot for Lyle's cock and his ass, too.

My hand slipped into my ass crack as I squeezed my cock. I don't know how far I would have gone up my ass, but I was too close to the edge to find out. I hadn't even lubricated my penis. A wet leakage dripped from my cock, and I used that as my lubricant. Jacking my dick and touching my butt crack, I gasped aloud as the overwhelming tingles rippled through my cock's head. My cock seemed to weigh a ton, as the ripples mounted into waves of orgasmic rapture. Without warning, a tidal wave of pleasure washed over me.

"Dionysus!" My voice warbled with a concoction of moans, wails, pleas, and sighs. "Pan. Satyrs of old. Fuck me. Take me for your pleasure. Use me for your lust."

The stars froze in their courses, yet, most paradoxically, they whirled hot and rhythmic, as my pelvic muscles contracted explosively, the powerful spurting muscles at the base of my penis jetting my spunk in an arc out the pisshole of my cock, through the night breeze, and splattering against the screen. I rocked my ass as I came, waggled it obscenely, and offered my body to the gods of homosexual lust. Squirt after wonderful squirt of my scented cum rose into the air and splattered.

At last, my contractions stilled, and I stood quavering, my heart racing as though it would burst, my lungs laboring to draw in the life-giving air, my legs quivering as though I had swum five miles, and my cock still seeping a fragrant drop of pure semen that oozed from my pisshole. I touched my finger to it, wiping the sticky drop from my cock. Then I touched my finger to my tongue and tasted my own cum for the first time in my life.

After I cleaned up my spilled semen, I slipped the notebook between my mattress and box spring, pulled up my cutoff jeans, and covered my chest with my white T-shirt. In the kitchen, I cut another generous slice of Mom's famous chocolate cake (whatever attributes or faults Mom possessed, she was a remarkably good baker), poured a glass of milk, and slaked my appetite with a midnight snack.

Afterward, I checked my e-mail, read three messages from our swim coach, and answered five from my teammates. Then I slipped into bed.

CHAPTER THREE

Tipper's Tale

Monday morning, I drove to Muskrat Creek High School, stopping along the way to pick up Rick Jecks, Israel "Jeep" Orbegoso, Martin Zambouski, and Lyle Fujimoto, four seniors on the boys' swim team. Since I had paddled my way into becoming captain of the team, Coach Reece considered it my "divinely ordained duty" to make sure my teammates arrived in time for their classes. After I objected to babysitting, the coach agreed to supervise the freshmen, sophomores, and juniors, if I would marshal my fellow seniors, whom he claimed caused "greater spiritual torment" than the other classes combined.

Though we seniors would graduate in June, we still had to win a number of important swim competitions. Coach Reece deemed it our "providential destiny" to uphold the reputation of the Muskrat Creek High Muskrats.

Our team uniform consisted of fire-engine red swimmer's briefs with the school logo emblazoned on the hip. Rick and Mart occasionally voiced objections to our uniforms, but I thought our swim briefs with the defining seam running up the butt crack made us look incredibly sexy, but I never said so.

Rick pretended that he was the school jock, even though, in the eyes of the community, he was just a swimmer. Though random strangers frequently gave us gifts and cash, the "real jocks" were members of the football team. Rick couldn't kick a pigskin any farther than he could a pig, which annoyed him because football players got to screw the cheerleaders. The basketball team also received regular servicing from the cheerleading squad, and the baseball players got in an occasional fling. Not even in a blue moon would a cheerleader approach a guy skilled in track and field, and they held an even lower opinion of boys who competed in slinky swimsuits. Though I had actually escorted a cheerleader to a couple of dances, I couldn't care less what cheerleaders thought, but the neglect worried Rick.

Laboring under the heartrending delusion that he was a cowpuncher, Mart wore Western shirts, square-toed cowboy boots, Levi's, and a black felt cowboy hat. Mart's family had been cattle ranchers since the days of the range wars. He claimed to be a descendent of Peter French, Henry Miller, or John Devine (the ancestor changed with each telling). He told anyone who would listen that he was a genuine buckaroo, though he was no more of a *vaquero* than Lyle.

Although Lyle was a fourth-generation Japanese American, he asserted that in 1942 his distant relatives bombed three Oregon towns. There was no historical record of a Japanese attack on any Oregon town except Brookings, so Lyle's claim sounded like nothing more than misplaced nationalistic fervor for a culture he had never known. In the case of Brookings, the Japanese pilot missed the population center entirely, dropping his ordinance on Mount Emily across the river from the town.

Jeep's parents emigrated from Bolivia. Jeep claimed as an ancestor a long-dead president of his country. In his case, at least, the name fit, although Jeep did not conform to the macho image of a Bolivian. Jeep walked with a slight sway, and he lisped when he got excited. Jeep, in particular, looked exceptionally effeminate in his competition swimsuit, perhaps because the seam cut deep between his prominent buttocks.

Coach Reece gave us *helpful advice* that was *certain* to make us win. "Boys," the coach would philosophize, "the Lord God created the whole universe with a few words. Words have power. So you've got to find power words that make you feel strong. While you're swimming, you've got to keep repeating positive affirmations. Say words like *smooth*, *strong*, *steady*, and *fast*, and keep on saying them." After delivering these homilies, he would meander back to his office and listen to Christian radio, while leaving me, a mere student, to coach the team.

"How about I repeat words like *electric cattle prod to your balls* when you sophomores keep paddling like dogs," I would suggest. "Quit paying attention to the antics of the boy next to you, freshman. Swim your own lane."

My first class of that late winter day was Middle Eastern history, which was enjoyable for a change because Mr. Lewis lectured on the ancient Hebrews writing laws against "men lying with men" in between running off to the temple of Baal every chance they got to bugger the boy prostitutes. We looked at some Bible verses that confirmed his opinion, though the true believers among us muttered imprecations about their vengeful God of wrath and the horrible pits of hell.

Physics followed, and once more, I did not blow up the lab. Trigonometry came hard upon physics, and the literature of England rounded out the day. In literature class, we hit upon the Uranian poets. Ms. Malcolm raked the room with her challenging eye as she discussed the Uranian philosophy. A few guys rolled their eyes, groaned in anguish, and made displays of puking as Ms. Malcolm talked about the Victorian British promoters of homosexual liberation, Edward Carpenter and John Addington Symonds. I looked around to see who was responding so theatrically, but my real interest lay in spotting those guys who perked with curiosity.

Ms. Malcolm read a poem by Fabian S. Woodley, whose words stuck me in a way no mere poem had before. I felt like the long lost son returning home as I made my way from class. Woodley's words echoing in my brain, I felt Thad's initiation throughout my being. I wondered about the new sensations that I was feeling and the Uranian life that should be mine. I was destined for my own initiation, I knew, though it might be quite unlike the one my brother had tasted.

Athletes were exempt from regular physical education classes, because our coaches, sadists to the core, Coach Reece being the most ruthless, demanded that we perform an even more intense workout.

Considering the facilities at the school gym to be inadequate, the taxpayers (against their will and without their knowledge) footed the bill for our memberships at a local fitness club. After our final class of the day, the swim team made its way, jointly and severally, to Beaver Dam Fitness Club. Naturally, Rick, Jeep, Mart, and Lyle piled into my car, so I chauffeured the seniors through our hamlet of Muskrat Creek and down the road to the larger town of Beaver Dam.

"How fast are you going?" Mart asked.

"Why?"

"Because you're about to get pulled over." No sooner were the words out of his mouth than I saw the lights of a Cougar County squad car in my mirror. I shifted to produce my license and lowered the window.

"Do you know how fast you were going?"

"No, sir. We were headed for the Beaver Dam Fitness Club. We're getting in shape to beat those ripe cheeses from Tillamook."

"You boys are the Muskrats? Of course you are. I recognize you." The deputy reached for his back pocket. I stiffened, but he removed only his wallet. There wasn't much in it, but he distributed five-dollar bills to Rick, Jeep, Mart, Lyle, and me. "Maybe this will help you boys buy lunch at the Tillamook Cheese Factory while you're over there."

"Thanks, sir."

"I'm Deputy Martin. Now you watch your speed, and we'll just forget about any legal infractions this time. You dive into the pool and win one for us."

As I pulled into the parking lot of the Beaver Dam Fitness Club, I thought wistfully that Cougar Ridge Community College lay only another dozen miles along this route.

As we changed into our workout clothes, I studied my teammates anew. I had always been aware that senior class swimmers looked good naked, and even stunning in their team swimsuits, but I had not been in touch with my feelings the way I was then. My brother Thad had awakened me to my long suppressed desires, and as we shed our clothes, my mouth went dry.

Rick had a thick cock, uncircumcised, but he also had a girlfriend whom he fucked regularly—or so he bragged (the louse)—and nothing about him suggested an openness to same-sex bonding. Mart had a cute butt that pushed out the rear of his swim briefs, and made me want to shoot a load into my pants watching him do squats. Still, nothing clicked. Jeep was more ambiguous. He had an effeminate quality about him, and I could well imagine him responding to an all male jack-off party. He often bragged about jerking off in public toilets and even once in a Macy's display window with a particularly erotic mannequin. However, he never made jokes about buttfucking or cock sucking, which could indicate that his mind was elsewhere—or he was covering. As I said, he was ambiguous.

Lyle just had to be gay. I had never been certain of it before that day, but a secret voice inside me spoke volumes. I knew. I was certain. If this was gaydar, then the stuff really worked. When I looked at Lyle, a little bell in my head tinkled *ding, ding, ding—Lyle is a gayboy.* I wondered what sexual adventures tickled Lyle's fantasy or whether he had ever been with a boy. I wondered whether he daydreamed about me. Was he attracted to me? Did he find me sexy?

Before that moment, I had never thought that much about Lyle. He was your standard American of Japanese descent. As that thought flickered through my consciousness, I pushed it aside in disgust. I despised my own stereotyping. Lyle was cute.

Lyle was pulling on a white shirt and red tennis shorts made by the same company. The clothes were tight on his form: his chest muscles defined his shirt, hard hours pumping iron had developed his arms, and squats had sculpted his butt. His ass was round and tight, and his anal crevice was deep. His cock made a natural pattern in the front of his thin shorts.

"I need to do squats today," Mart said.

"No way, Mart," I said. "Coach Reece told me we have to work on our upper bodies."

"Why don't you make a decision for yourself, Tip?" Rick's challenge drifted through the locker room like a football player's fart. "Quit doing everything the coach demands. He's not always right, and you know us better than he does."

"We're going to do what the coach said." I liked being captain, and I wanted to keep on being captain. "After all, he is the coach. Not me."

We worked with weights, spotting each other until our muscles were failing. After replacing the weights, we raced sprints on the stationary bicycles until we were pouring sweat. My heart was hitting 180 beats per minute when I glanced at the cycle beside me and saw that Lyle had taken his even higher.

"That's enough, guys," I said. "Let's hit the sauna."

We sweat harder in the sauna, though we sucked down bottle after bottle of sports drinks. We had changed into our swimsuits, of course, Rick and Mart into long board shorts while Lyle, Jeep, and I had pulled on our team swim briefs.

Rick shook his head as his eyes flicked over Lyle's bulge. "I'd think you guys would get tired of those pansy bikinis. I mean, that's what we gotta wear when we're competing, but they turn off the babes. They like their men looking like real men."

"Hey, Rick, you see this?" Jeep pointed at the bulge of his cock. "What the fuck do you think I've got there? You could be hiding a pussy in those shorts you wear. We're the real men." He threw his arms around Lyle's and my shoulders in a comradely gesture. I felt my cock stiffen in my swim briefs.

Rick came back with a wise-ass remark, which was a good thing because it kept everybody from noticing my crotch stretch. I was sweating heavily for more than one reason, but at the same time, I felt disappointed. I could have told Rick that I liked wearing swim briefs rather than jammers, and I particularly did not want to wobble around in board shorts. The briefs made me feel sexy. For all I knew, Rick bought his swimsuit at the tent and awning factory. How does a boy strut when he's wearing five yards of fabric? I strutted along the side of the pool in my red swimsuit.

For a wild second, I considered coming out to my friends. It could have happened in an instant; I had only to open my mouth. Yet I knew that it was the wrong time and the wrong place. You don't come out to guys in a small sauna when three of you are wearing next to nothing. It would be too threatening. I would be asking for a bad response, and would probably get just what I deserved. Feeling like a weasel, I sat quietly between Lyle and Jeep, drank a sports drink diluted with water, and let my pores flow. After a while, we showered, and then I drove the fellows to their homes.

Later that night, I was reading from my brother's third notebook, which I had secured while my parents were absorbed by some insipid television program. Thad was still describing his initiation ritual.

❖

Thad's Journal: The Third of November, continued

An unseen dick head caressed my lips as I knelt blindfolded within the circle. Pushing my head forward, I opened my mouth to receive the cock. *Ahhs* hissed from many masculine throats. The blissful sigh filled the night. I had never felt as naked as I did that night when I exposed my secret lusts to unseen eyes. Although it was night, I did not feel that night covered me. Even through my blindfold, I saw the moon's unnatural brilliance. Its illuminating beams shone like an arc light upon my first oral favor, and I shivered with excitement.

The breeze whispered through my hair and over my naked ass as I kissed the cock head. I had expected a bad taste. I feared that I would gag. I imagined the scent of urine and the nausea of a finger down the throat, but none of those horrors happened. The penis touching my lips had a pleasant, musky taste. There was the hint of something deliciously spicy—the forbidden spice? I wondered about that mystery as I touched my tongue to the smooth cock head. The tip of my tongue flickered over its peehole, but nothing disgusting ensued.

Without deciding to do so, I took the cock farther into my mouth. The cock head slid over my lips. I drew my teeth back, for I would not have nipped the delightful thing for worlds, and let it rest upon my tongue.

Slowly and carefully, I slid my head forward, taking the cock deeper into my mouth. When I felt it had gone far enough, I pulled my head back until my lips were again touching its smooth head. I tightened my lips around it and moved forward again, wrapping the underside of the head with my tongue. As I grew more practiced my tempo increased, and I started sucking harder on it.

The chanting started then. The drums commenced a slow boom that coincided with the chants. "*Evoe*, Pan; *Evoe*, Pan; *Evoe*, Pan; *Evoe*, Pan; *Evoe*, Pan."

The cock in my mouth produced sensations that traveled through my body. Every cell quivered with the excitement generated by the living organ I was blowing. Nothing about the act felt unnatural. Indeed, sucking that cock was a natural motion, no stranger than eating or elimination. My own cock was so hard that it throbbed, and the desire to jack off while I sucked was nearly overwhelming.

Of course, nothing was stopping me, except for my conscious awareness that I had an audience. (An audience was watching me suck a dick, I reminded myself.) My mind reeled at the enormity of my actions, and in that instant, my hand, unbidden, seized upon my cock. I massaged my dick head with my dry hand, wondering if I dare stop sucking so I could spit in it. However, another hand took my wrist, firmly, yet kindly, and pulled my hand away from my cock.

I recognized Hyacinthos's voice even when he was whispering into my ear. "You must save your seed for another, initiate. For the present, you may only receive."

At the words, I started sucking harder and faster. The tempo of the drumbeats increased. I heard, "*Evoe*, Pan; *Evoe*, Pan; *Evoe*, Pan," and I felt a throbbing sensation as the blood coursed heavier into the already swollen cock and the semen rose from the balls. Would he come in my mouth, I wondered? Should I pull my head away? Could I swallow? Spit it out?

I never got a chance to decide. The drumbeats reached a fever pitch. Tambourines and bells rang wildly, and the chant came wilder still. I felt a tremor as my classmate shot cum into the back of my throat, and my swallow reflex took over. The cum went down readily. I neither gagged nor choked. Drums pounded and pipes shrilled. The second shot painted my throat, and I found myself swallowing it. After that, I was committed. With a load of cum already heading toward my stomach, I could only keep swallowing until I had downed it all.

As I swallowed, the music collapsed into discord unrestrained by melody. The tinkling of bells and rattling of tambourines battled against the clamor of the pipes and the rough booming of drums, and the human chant degenerated into feral ululation. Then all music stopped. I heard a sharp collective gasp, followed by a single voice echoing, "*Evoe*, Pan."

The taste of semen was upon my tongue, a pleasant taste redolent of mushroom sauce, salt, and sweeteners. Reluctantly, I pulled my head back so that the shaft slid out of my mouth and the cock head reached my lips. As the cock passed over my lips, my heart skipped a beat because the head of another cock touched my anal cleft.

❖

Tipper's Tale

My heart also skipped a beat as I read Thad's narrative. My brother, my brave brother, had sucked his first cock blindfolded and trembling. He led the way to the cliff, blazing a path his younger brothers could follow, and leaped over the edge, plunging into freedom from our community's mores. He had overcome all fear and all doubt to suck and swallow before an audience. The image was nearly sufficient to make me shoot off into my briefs. I didn't even have to touch my cock. My mental pictures rather than my hands brought me to the verge of orgasm.

Yet exciting as the cocksucking story had been, I could clearly guess what was coming next. My brother was about to describe his first anal sex. He was going to tell me, through the medium of his spidery handwriting, about how he got fucked. For some reason, taking a cock in the ass seemed even more intimate than taking one in the mouth. It was the greater surrender, the ultimate submission, and the thought of it thrilled me beyond saying. I continued reading.

❖

Thad's Journal: The Third of November, continued

The cock touching my anal cleft was wonderful and terrifying. I'd always wondered what it would be like to receive a cock up my ass. What boy hasn't? In past times, I even tried pushing foreign objects up my butt while I was masturbating. I practiced with a couple of dangerous items like a banana and a candle. By good luck alone, I did not lose either of those up my rectum. I even used the well-slicked handle of a garden implement, which made my eventual orgasm vegetative, but flowery.

Skip and I discussed buttfucking one toadstool-tangled night after a quart of gin had mistakenly wandered our way. Ripping drunk, we sat on a rail fence on the west pasture, held hands, and owned up to our deepest secrets. Nothing came of that drunken confession though. We tried to jack each other off, but the experiment failed due to timidity, torpor, or intemperance.

I had learned that Skip wasn't any straighter than I was, which made me doubt whether any male was totally straight. Get guys wasted and they'll do *anything* sexually. They will lick ass, suck cock, and take cum in every orifice once booze or dope has blotted out the social conditioning. Although I'd been drunk when I made my admission to Skip, I knew that I didn't require booze or dope to respond to my innermost urges. I really wanted to get fucked like a butt slut. I was going to take it and like it.

❖

Tipper's Tale

My ears pricked for stray sounds, I became instantly alert when a door closed softly, and even softer footsteps approached my door. I shoved Thad's notebook under my pillow, pulled the covers over my prominent erection, and picked up my trigonometry text. Opening up without knocking first, as was her custom, Mom stuck her head in my doorway.

"Tip?" she whispered. "Tipper, did you fall asleep with your light on?" (My bedside lamp threw a telltale streak of light on the carpet beneath my door.)

"No, Mom," I said. "I'm doing homework."

Instead of going away, she entered and sat on the edge of my bed. She picked up my trig text, which I had laid aside. "I'm glad you take your studies seriously," she said, glancing at the problems I had penciled earlier that night. "But you need your rest. You're a growing boy."

Not so much now, I thought, as my cock deflated. "I'm thinking about college," I said disarmingly. I drew a deep breath. My mother was in a sentimental mood—perhaps I could surprise her during this momentary weakness. "Where did Thad and Tye go, Mom?" I asked. "They went to Cougar Ridge Community College. Did they graduate from there? Did they go on to the university?"

I had asked too many questions at once. Mom jumped up, dropping my textbook. "Tip, you know your father's rule."

"They were my brothers. They *are* my brothers. I have a right." My voice sounded desperate, pleading, even a bit whiney. I lacked the strength to make her tell me what had happened. She shook her head sadly, turned away, and hastily left my room. She didn't even pull my door tight. I had to climb out of bed and parade across the room. As I closed it, I wondered for the first time in my life why my room didn't lock. The room where my brothers had slept had always locked from the inside, but mine had never been equipped with a lock.

Stretching out again upon my bed, clad only in my briefs spotted with leaked bodily fluids, I opened Thad's notebook again. I could only hope that he would reveal a truth my parents were loath to disclose.

❖

Thad's Journal: The Third of November, continued

I felt warm lips close to my ear. Breath whispered, and I recognized Hyacinthos's voice. "Have you ever taken a dick up your ass?" he asked, as though he were asking whether I'd ever eaten strawberry ice cream.

"Never. I don't know how."

"Don't be afraid. I've taken hundreds. I love the sensation. There's nothing better than having a boy come in your ass. However, to enjoy it, you have to want it. You do want it, don't you?"

"Yes." I committed myself fully. I could feel hot bodies around me, flames, wind, and moonshine playing upon my bare ass. I smelled masculine sweat, incense, candle wax, semen, and wood smoke. I heard the whispers and the snickering, the bells, the tambourines, the drums, and the hornpipes.

"Good," Hyacinthos said. "Take deep breaths. Don't squeeze. Don't clamp down on it with your asshole. Push. Push as if you're taking a shit. Pushing opens your ass and lets it in. A squeeze means you're resisting. Trying to squeeze it out makes it hurt."

"Okay." I gasped as someone pulled my butt cheeks apart and pressed his cock head against my asshole. "Okay." I felt a tremendous pressure. I felt hands gripping the top rounds of my buttocks.

"Relax. Breathe. Push." Hyacinthos urged me to accept the penetration. "If it hurts, take deeper breaths and push harder. Soon it will start feeling good. Real good. Oh, Thad, you're gonna love riding a cock."

As instructed, I filled my lungs, blew my breath out slowly, and tried to relax. The pressure against my asshole increased. For a moment, I panicked and clamped down tight.

"Wait," I gasped. "I can do this." I drew several more deep breaths and pushed with my ass.

"That's the way," Hyacinthos said. The pressure against my asshole did not decrease. Instead, it grew more intense, and my rectum began to feel full and heavy.

"You've got Orpheus's dick inside of you now." The way he said it, Hyacinthos could have been our former high school principal making the morning announcements over the PA system. What's more, the crowd was listening, because a triumphant cacophony of bells and tambourines greeted his proclamation. "You have Orpheus's cock in your ass, Thad."

The pressure increased, but I continued taking deep breaths and kept on pushing. I felt no pain. Orpheus gripped my waist and gradually pulled me back. Deeper and deeper, his cock impaled my ass until his loins pressed hard against my butt.

"Thad, are you sure you've never done this before? You're taking Orpheus's cock all the way. You've got his thick cock in you to the hilt. How does it feel?"

"Nice," I murmured. "It feels good." I hunched forward an inch and pushed back again.

"Oh, you're ready to get fucked, aren't you? You like taking it up the ass?"

"Yes," I said, and the drums rolled, the pipes skirled, the bells rang, and the tambourines shook. Lusty male voices howled into the night, voicing encouragement, pagan abandonment, and the lust of man for man.

I pulled forward again and fucked my ass on Orpheus's thick cock. As it slid out, my asshole vibrated with intense pleasure, and before the head could pop out, I impaled my ass again. Orpheus met my strokes, and soon we were joining in a rhythmic buttfuck.

A low moan was issuing from my mouth, my cocksucking mouth, as the pleasure grew ever more intense. I could not feel the shape or the depth of Orpheus's cock; I only had a feel of its thickness and weight, but my asshole sang as each stroke rippled the vital nerves joining there. The air around me cooled as Hyacinthos slipped away, his function fulfilled.

My tight ass soon squeezed Orpheus to orgasm. His cock seemed to thicken, so that each stroke massaged my prostate, provoking a raging passion in my groin. My balls tightened, and my cock stiffened for eruption. Orpheus groaned with his own explosive orgasm, and I felt his cock twitch as he launched a salvo of spunk. More twitches followed as he moaned and begged me to take it all, as though I could refuse.

Orpheus's contractions stilled. I truly wanted to ejaculate with his cock still fucking me. I was close to rapture, but he stopped stroking. I ground his cock with my ass, working to bring myself off. To my dismay, before I could attain orgasm, he withdrew his cock. However, as helping hands assisted me to my feet, I surmised that there was more to come.

"Initiate, you have opened the way of the catamite. Are you prepared to see the circle?"

"Yes," I said, and two hands untied my blindfold.

For a moment, I stood blinking in the full moonlight. We were standing in a grassy clearing with a deep wall of dark woods beyond. To the east, I could see the moon illuminating Mt. Jefferson and Three Fingered Jack, and to the south, it shone off the glaciers of Mt. Washington. The group consisted of a dozen boys my own age, naked in the yellow moonlight. They stood evenly spaced in a circle around me. Everyone held a tambourine, hand bells, or a musical pipe, except for the two who pounded on drums. To one side of me, Orpheus stood, removing the used condom from his cock. He tossed me a salacious wink before he deposited the condom in a trash bag.

At the center of the circle, behind the fire pit, Dr. Bromius, also naked and incredibly gorgeous, sat on a wide stump, but his attitude seemed to be more of an observer than a participant. Incense burners, candles, and other ritual objects stood around the stump on which my teacher planted his bare ass. Flanking him were two boys, one masked as a bull, the other as a stag.

The air was warm in the circle, and every boy's penis jutted enticingly. The sexual tension was thick. As I tried to understand the meaning of this coven, my asshole began throbbing with a pleasant sensation, as though it remembered the pounding it had just received.

These assembled boys, my classmates, had witnessed me sucking my first cock and receiving my first buttfuck. In their eyes, cocksucking and dick riding were brave and noble actions. I did not feel humiliated in the least. My mind rejoiced with their contagious jubilation.

The boy wearing the bull mask approached me. "You have met my lover," he said, waving his hand toward the boy in the stag head, "the Priest of Hyacinthos. He has taught you the way of the catamite. I am the Priest of Apollo, and to me you must prove your worth by following the manner of Zeus. Behold the offerings."

With a gesture, Apollo waved his hand toward the circle of boys. Each turned, bent, and wiggled his bare ass with explicit suggestions. "Make your selection, initiate."

As he intoned the words of the command, the Priest of Apollo lubricated my hard cock and slipped an extra-strength condom over it. He lubricated the condom again. I turned, surveying the proffered butts. Every boy was begging for it. "Take me," one shouted. "No, me," offered another. "I'm the best fuck," another proclaimed.

One boy had tight curvy buttocks (as did they all), but his enticed me the most at that moment. I stepped forward and placed my hands on his hips. He dropped his tambourine and placed his hands on his knees. The other boys turned again, sweeping us closer to the fire pit before the stump altar where Dr. Bromius sat, and set up a wild clamor on their instruments. With their free hands, they stroked their cocks.

I slid my cock between the boy's buttocks, and his rosebud felt hot against my dick head, even with the thick condom's protection. The boy helped me by pushing back and positioning his asshole while I drove forward. He was no newcomer to this sport. My dick slid readily into his opening asshole. The chute was tight, hot, and rough, and I almost ejaculated right then.

His ass seemed to suck me in until I found myself buried all the way. I was smashing his hard little buns before I pulled back until my cock was barely inside. Before I could push forward, he drove backward, impaling himself once more upon my cock. I found myself thrusting to meet his rush.

We were on our feet, me thrusting, him bent at the knees and rocking back with his hips. Our meetings were wildly primal as I pounded his ass again and again. His hole was so tight on my cock that I could not hold out against the tremendous milking sensation. At the same time, the remembered sensations of the cock coming in my mouth and Orpheus's cock fucking my ass drove me mad with pleasure.

"*Evoe*, yeah, you're making me come." Tingles were rippling though the head of my cock. My cock was harder and tighter than it had ever been. I felt it throb. The tingles grew. They rippled through the head of my dick. They rippled up my shaft. My dick was heavy and growing heavier. "I'm gonna do it in your ass."

The music grew wilder as every boy sensed my approaching orgasm. I could see boys shaking bells or tambourines with one hand and jerking their stiff cocks with their other. The pipers and drummers were also doing their work one-handed so the rhythm of the music was lost in the pagan noise. I felt my cock gain tremendous weight as I thrust. My balls tightened, and my nipples crinkled. Twitches of pleasure vibrated through the head of my cock. Sparks of pleasure traveled up my cockshaft.

Then I could feel my lips grimacing and my eyelids fluttering. I knew that I was thrusting like a madman and an unbidden howl was escaping from my mouth. Somehow, I felt in tune with every boy in that circle, and part of a vaster circle of men stretching back to the dawn of humanity. I did not really believe in Apollo or Dionysus or any god; yet I was at one with all gods.

My soul exploded into the infinite void as fireworks burst in my brain, and rapturous waves of intense pleasure flooded my cock, and the powerful muscles at the base of my penis contracted, shooting a wild spurt of spunk up my cock and into the condom buried in my companion's ass. For his part, his blazing ass was milking me off, and he was growling with a deep anal pleasure as my cock massaged his prostate.

I seemed to orgasm and ejaculate for the longest time, and even as my ejaculations stilled, I felt a continuous ripple of pleasure in my cock head. After a time, I regretfully pulled my cock out of that wonderful ass. After I did so, he turned and smiled lovingly at me. He helped pull the condom from my cock and deposit it in the trash. Then he kissed me gently upon the lips before returning to his place in the circle.

Both priests detached themselves from the center where Dr. Bromius sat. "Thad, welcome to the circle of Dionysus," Apollo said. "You have embraced your nature and found it to be good." He kissed me upon the lips, and his kiss made my cock rise again, which I would have thought impossible after that tremendous and draining orgasm. "You have died to your old self. Thad is dead. Henceforth, in this sacred circle, your name shall be *Adonis*."

Hyacinthos kissed me next. "Adonis," he said, "you have enjoyed the sexual acts of initiation, but you will come to learn that gay sex is merely the path we use to the spiritual realm. Other witches have used drugs, pain, deprivation, and other means. Their ways are not our ways. We choose the path of giving and receiving, sexually, youth to youth, boy to boy, man to man, age to age. You have found pleasure in giving and receiving, and thereby, set your feet upon a path to a vast circle. For the rest of your life, you will walk the circumference of that circle, but while you live, you will never find its center. Welcome again to the circle of Dionysus and the cult of the Uranian gods."

After that lecture, I walked the circumference of the circle, kissing each boy upon the lips, lingering long with each. Finally, we sat together for cakes and ale, before the closing of the circle. And all the while, Dr. Bromius parked his professorial ass in the heart of our circle, eyeballed me as if I were his intrepid son, and offered not a taste of his own flesh.

❖

Tipper's Tale

Reading about Thad's initiation, I had been gently massaging my raging cock through the thin fabric of my briefs. Without warning, my orgasm reared up before I could properly grab hold of my cock. The tickles of pleasure in my dick head grew into a volcano of foaming eruptions. I rocked back against my pillow as my cock bucked against the tight cloth. Lightning flashes blasted my brain as my cells fired. Blending reality with fantasy, incoherent images flickered before my fluttering eyelids. My lips contorted in a grimace of agonized joy. I must have looked simultaneously stabbed, shot, garroted, poisoned, electrocuted, and drowned.

My bottle of lubricant sat unused as I spurted my own lubricant into my underwear, my tortured cock throbbing with long-denied release. I saw my underwear turning dark and wet with my semen. I gasped aloud and gripped the wooden frame of my bed. I panted and shivered throughout my frame as my palpitating cock continued to fume and seethe.

When my contractions stilled, I sprawled in a fluster on my back, and I stared bewildered at the whirling ceiling as I gasped for breath. I was bathed in sweat and heard my leaping heart thunder in my ears.

My heart rapidly recovered. As my sweat soaked into my bedclothes, I smelled the spicy scent of my ejaculated semen. My briefs were sopping with cum. Standing shakily, I examined myself in my mirror. My sodden briefs accented the shape of my cock. It was still standing, though not as firmly as before that fabulous eruption. For once, I was glad that I kept a bikini shave for swimming. Usually, I mourned the loss of my pubic hair, but then I was glad that I did not have hairs matted with drying spunk.

I tiptoed down the hall, jumped into the shower, briefs and all, and washed away the evidence of my boyish lust. When I finished scrubbing, I dried and listened at the bathroom door. Apparently, my parents had not stirred. I slipped into my room again, hung my wet briefs out the window, and pulled on fresh underwear. Satisfied, I scanned the story of Thad's initiation a second time. By the time I finished reading about the anal initiation, I was hard and toying with my cock again.

Thad had added a few words after his final description of the circle.

❖

Thad's Journal: The Third of November, continued

Our circle closed, and our gay coven went dark until the night of the next full moon. I dressed, kissed my friends good-bye, and hiked homeward, down the rugged, well-known butte, skirted a meandering creek, and ploughed my weary feet across the fields. After I had crossed the style and entered my father's farm, I slipped through the cornfield and crept past the bunkhouse where our buckaroos slept.

As I climbed back through my bedroom window, I saw Tye sleeping with his back to me. I quickly undressed, hoping that neither my clothing nor my body showed signs of my homosexual orgy. However, before I could slip into bed, Tye sat up. Despite his pretense, I knew that Tye had been awake and waiting for me.

"How was it, Thad?" Tye asked. Tye was almost seventeen, and usually, he was a cocky little Nancy boy, and nowhere near as endearing as our baby brother Tipper. However, he sounded sincere.

❖

Tipper's Tale

A strange feeling came over me every time I saw my name in Thad's journal. I shivered up my spine, as though a ghoul had just staked out my grave. My hard-on deflated, and I did not try to revive it. That night, there would be no second ejaculation, followed by a gruesome and risky clean up. I read on.

❖

Thad's Journal: The Third of November, continued

"How was what?" I asked. The smirk on Tye's face was something to see.

"Gay sex," he said. "How was it?"

I stood frozen. I was still naked, and the full moon illuminated my body. I had never felt so exposed. How did Tye know what I'd been doing? What had he blabbed? Dad was such a complete homophobe that if he suspected, he'd throw me out of the house. If he didn't kill me.

It was as though Tye was reading my mind. "It's okay, Thad. I know you're gay. And quit worrying—Dad and Mom don't have a clue—not about you."

"How do you know?" I asked, not too certain I wanted to hear the answer. From the moment I kissed Dr. Bromius, I knew the day would come when I would have to come out to the world. However, I intended to pick my time wisely. Some gay boys have supportive parents, but I knew that mine would not be.

"Same sex attraction runs in our family, Thad," Tye said. "Look at Uncle Beau. And someday you should ask Grandma Trencher about Gramp."

He didn't volunteer any more, and I didn't want to ask. *Gramp Trencher*? I wasn't sure that I wanted to know. Tye had always been closer to Grandma Trencher than I ever was. I loved her, but Tye was her confidante. Had she told him stories about our family that had been kept from me—because everyone assumed I was naturally heterosexual?

And what of Tye? I was certain that he was gay, but I had assumed that he was a gay virgin. However, his confidence in his sexuality suggested otherwise. Was my younger brother—my underage brother—more adventuresome than I was? Did he have male lovers? I suddenly felt like the stereotypical old maid, though I was certainly no longer a virgin—at least with boys—and I was only eighteen.

I pulled on my black silk boxer shorts with Marvin the Martian on them and climbed between my sheets. I was bushed, and the roosters would be crowing before long. Shortly thereafter, little Tipper would be bursting into our bedroom, doubtless jumping into my bed with a groping knee in my balls, as was the little fellow's custom.

"Thad?" Tye's question came as a coarse whisper. "Thad, did you get fucked in your ass?"

"Shut up and go to sleep, Tye." Perhaps he did. He didn't ask any more questions that night. Sleep eluded me, and I tossed on my bed, experiencing over and over the sensations of the ritual in my mind, still feeling the cocks throbbing in my mouth and ass, still feeling the solid mounds of the boy ass I'd plowed, still tasting the flavors of the night, still hearing the strange, discordant music, still mumbling the ritual words that bound me to the vast circle of men.

"Yes, Tye," I whispered. "I did get fucked. And I loved it."

❖

Tipper's Tale

I'd been a month shy of three years old on the night of Thad's initiation. That explained why my memories had not stuck. As I read about awakening my brothers in the mornings, another shadowy finger of memory tickled my brain. I remembered the summer sun streaming through their windows as they lazed beneath their covers. I remembered the musk and farty scent of their closed room in the winter months. I remembered the warmth of their bodies as I jumped into their beds, their howls, the way they would "rassle" me. I remembered that in spite of their loud protests, both Tye and Thad were always delighted to see me. They had loved me deeply. And I loved them so very, very much.

CHAPTER FOUR

Tipper's Tale

Inflexible high school administrators and hard-assed coaches expected us athletes to attend every class, five days per week. Daily swim practice fell hard upon the end of our last class. On weekends and weeknights when we did not have a swim meet, Coach Reece expected us to beef up our muscles at the Beaver Dam Fitness Club. And we had competitions every Friday, many requiring travel to another high school.

That rigorous schedule prevented me from driving to Cougar Ridge Community College, as I would have preferred. I made five telephone calls to the college, but I couldn't breech the wall of silence and institutional suspicion.

My first call through the college switchboard led to a dead end. "May I speak to Dr. Bromius, please?" I was standing beside my locker in my swim briefs. The rest of the team had already headed for the pool.

There was a pause followed by, "Can you spell that, please?"

After I spelled the name, she assured me that no one by that name worked at Cougar Ridge Community College. "He used to teach there," I said helpfully. "Who would know where I can reach him?"

Silence greeted that remark. "Hello?" I said finally.

"What extension would you like, sir?"

"I don't know. Who would know how to find Dr. Bromius?"

"What department does he work in?"

I was beginning to wonder if they had hired an idiot to work the switchboard. "He teaches mythology."

"We don't have a mythology department."

"How about religious studies?"

"Sir, we're a public community college."

"Humanities?" I asked desperately, glancing at the clock in the coach's office. Coach Reece would be pitching a conniption fit.

"Humanities is part of the English Department."

"Fine, give me the English Department." By then, I was hoping to talk to anybody but her.

"Tip," Rick yelled, turned the corner of the lockers, and saw me talking on my cell phone. "What are you doing? Reece is getting seriously pissed."

I disconnected and tossed my cell phone into my locker. I grabbed my swim goggles heedlessly, twirled the combination lock for security's sake, and ran for the pool. The coach started bellowing the instant he spied me.

"What were you doing, Trencher? Don't you know that these boys need practice?"

Rick loyally jumped to my defense. "Tip had the dribbling squirts, Coach Reece." Upon hearing that defense, the coach's jaw dropped like a fresh corpse's, and the freshmen giggled like thirteen-year-old girls. Unfazed, Rick continued inventing an excuse for my tardiness. "Had to get cleaned out before he jumped into the pool. Otherwise the custodians would've had to drain the whole shebang."

I caught Rick's arm and admonished him under my breath. "I'd have come up with a more dignified excuse than dribbling squirts."

"I could have said you were muffdiving a cheerleader," Rick whispered with a hint of sarcasm.

I elected not to stand on my dignity. I started organizing the boys, but Coach Reece decided that the team needed his personal touch. "Boys, in your body, God has created a magnificent sports machine. You can train your muscles to the pinnacle of endurance, but if you lack the spiritual tools, you can't creatively envision winning. The team with the most effective creative visualization is the team that's going to win. You've got to exercise your brain apparatus. You've got to visualize creatively. You've got to pre-experience the reaching of your object to be the victor."

Lyle noticed that I was preoccupied. "What's wrong, Tip?"

"Tell you later," I said out of the side of my mouth. Coach Reece was giving me his evil eye. The man needed some perspective in his life. We were only a high school swim team, but he seemed to think the fate of the universe hung upon our victories.

I decided to give the team my personal touch as well. I jumped into the pool behind a sophomore and tickled his toes mercilessly as he struggled to outdistance me. He floundered desperately down the lane, kicking like a demented newt. Swimming one-handed, I tortured him to the end of the pool.

By the time practice concluded, the college staff had gone home. The phone at the English office answered with a recorded message. I tried the next morning before my first class, but my high school schedule meshed too well with the college's hours. I didn't bother leaving a message.

I managed to reach the college during my lunch break. Naturally, the Cougar Ridge Community College English department secretary was enjoying a lunch break at the same time. I listened to half of the recorded message and disconnected. Lyle gave me a searching look across the table, but I shook my head. Lunchtime in Burgerpig with the other guys present was no time to talk about my problems.

"No charge for the Muskrats," the manager called. "The seniors on the home team eat for free." The manager was so thin that he belied the accepted beliefs about fast food. He whirled to the cash register, pulled out a wad of twenty-dollar bills, and handed us each five of them. We were used to people bestowing cash and gifts upon us, but a hundred each was surprisingly generous. After thanking the manager, we occupied a corner of the restaurant. I spent most of my lunch time fending off Mart who kept swiping my fries, even after eating his own supersized French fries, triple burger with cheddar, and large chocolate shake.

Late that afternoon, I reached the English Department secretary. I was standing by a locker in the men's changing room at Beaver Dam Fitness Club, watching the constant parade of naked male flesh pass, when I finally heard her voice. "I'm trying to find out the whereabouts of Dr. Bromius," I said quickly. "He used to teach there."

There followed a pause, which I interpreted as pregnant, but then her voice came back with another stall. "I've been here only two years. What years did he teach?"

"Probably around fifteen years ago. Is there anybody there who'd know him?"

"You say he taught composition courses?"

"Mythology."

"Ms. Opdycke teaches our mythology course. She's been here for years and years. She might know him."

"Is she available?"

"I'll transfer you to her office."

There followed a pause and a ring. Then another message in a brittle voice. Opdycke's voice mail didn't say when she would be available. I left a message, telling her I was trying to track down Dr. Bromius, and leaving my cell phone number.

I hurried upstairs to work out with the guys. Rick was doing a set of straight-legged dead lifts, while Mart, Jeep, and Lyle stood behind him. Rick was wearing new polyester gym shorts that clung to his ass as he thrust his rump into the "out the window" position. Mart snickered and pretended he was shooting rubber bands at Rick's butt. My cock tightened in my gym shorts. Those lifts were really paying off for Rick; I hadn't realized that his rear was looking so enticing. I wanted to shoot something at those developing curves with the enticing cleft in between, and it wasn't pretend rubber bands.

"You slackers quit making fun of Rick's ass and get to work. Mart, you need to be doing some lifts yourself. Meanwhile, Lyle and Jeep can spot each other on chest presses." After I made sure that my guys were hard at work, I proceeded to the hack squat stand and worked on my own rear end.

Rick had driven that day. He dropped me off first before driving the other guys home. I could tell that Lyle was burning to talk with me, but he would have to wait. The stars had not yet aligned in our favor.

By the next afternoon, Ms. Opdycke still had not returned my call. I asked the switchboard operator for her extension, and that time she picked up on the first ring.

"I called yesterday," I said urgently. "About Dr. Bromius."

Did I hear a sharp intake of breath on the other end of the line? I couldn't be certain. A pause followed.

"This is important," I said at length. "It's a long and complicated story, but I'm trying to find out something about my brothers, and maybe Dr. Bromius could tell me what happened to them. If I could find Dr. Bromius."

"I really can't help you."

"Did you know Dr. Bromius?"

"Oh, yes, I knew Buck Bromius. But I don't know where he is now."

Buck? Buck Bromius? Could that even be a real name? "What happened? Why isn't he there anymore?"

"I've said enough. Any information would have to come from human resources. Though I wish you luck getting *that* gaggle of paranoids to divulge information about a former employee."

"Wait, don't hang up. How about my brothers? Did you know Thad Trencher—or Tye Trencher?"

"They were students here at Cougar Ridge?"

"Yeah." That was only partially truthful. I knew that Thad had been a student. I wasn't certain about Tye.

"I don't remember them. Even if I did, I couldn't tell you anything. There are federal laws."

Old Opdycke knew more than she was saying, but I couldn't get any more out of her. I thanked her for her time, called the college again, and asked for human resources. I received a recording telling me that HR closed at 4:30.

Swim practice was particularly exhausting that day. We had clobbered the Big Cheeses at Tillamook and the Corvallis Shepherds in our home pool, and were preparing to swim against the Water Bucks in Pendleton, but I couldn't get my mind off Dr. Bromius or Thad's initiation. I wondered whether I should try talking to Skip again. He had asked me if I was in touch with Thad, proving he didn't know where Thad was. But maybe he knew something that would help. My wandering mind resulted in Coach Reece shouting at me, which rattled my nerves. Rarely did the coach get to me, but that day I made a hash out of swim practice. I was glad when it was over, and we seniors piled into Lyle's car.

Lyle dropped off Rick first, then Mart, and finally, Jeep. When it was just the two of us, he suggested I come back to his house. "You're acting all screwed up, Tipper," he said. "We gotta have a talk."

Carrying my bag, I followed Lyle up the stairs to his bedroom. His parents were watching television in their basement home theater. Lyle snagged some drinks, chips, and a platter of cheese and cold cuts from the kitchen. I was sitting on the side of his bed, and he sat beside me. I could feel the near heat of his body.

"What's going on, Tip? You're not acting like yourself."

"You know how I've always wondered about my brothers?"

"Yeah. They disappeared or something? It's a big mystery?"

"It's even weirder than that. My mother keeps their bedroom like a shrine. I'm not allowed to go in there."

"Creepy."

"Yeah, except I had a key made." I held it up as if he needed proof. "I found my brother Thad's notebooks, and I've been reading them."

"What do they say?"

"If I read a bit to you, do you promise not to get disturbed?"

Lyle snorted at that admonition. "Sure, Tip. I'll sure try not to get disturbed."

"My brother wrote about how his professor, Dr. Bromius, initiated him into the Uranian mysteries." I pulled one of Thad's notebooks from my bag.

"What are Uranian mysteries?" Lyle asked, losing interest rapidly.

"You'll hear in a minute. I want to know what you think."

"Oh, sure," Lyle said doubtfully. He settled back primed to be bored. My heart thundered as I geared up to read, fearful of Lyle's reaction. I thought he was gay. I sensed he was gay. But how could I be certain? The danger in coming out to him was real. How might he react? What if he denounced me to the team? My parents? The whole community? Uneasy in my body and mind, I selected a paragraph that sounded less graphic.

❖

Thad's Journal: The Thirtieth of October, continued

The air vibrated not only with the increasing tempo of the pipes and drums, but also with a raw sexual energy, the awesome power of the human male to generate lust and offer the power to Dionysus. We stood in a ring, and outside our circle stood four bonfires to hold back the cold. The wind blowing off the mountain snowfields was dry and icy, but the circle of trees blocked the gusts and the bonfires warmed our space.

Hyacinthos had passed deosil around the circle, dolloping lubricant into each boy's right palm. We chanted an invocation to the Uranian gods as we shuffled sideways around the circle, each grasping the erect cock of the boy on his right. At last, Apollo stood, flanked by Narcissus and Hermes, and he read the Great Charge to us, as Dr. Bromius read it to me that day in his office. After he finished reading the final words, "Behold, I have touched thee in the first unfolding of thy flesh; and I am won through thy offering to the desire of men," his eyes roamed around the circle. "Tonight, we shall initiate yet another who has sought and asked. I met him with the Holy Kiss, and he responded. Even now his guides lead him to this sacred place."

❖

Tipper's Tale

Lyle was staring at me, his eyes round and amazed as he squeezed out the words, "Holy shit."

"Yeah," I managed, trying to gauge his reaction.

"Is this about a gay sex orgy?"

"Yeah. Well, no, not exactly. It's a pagan ritual. The boys use sex to attune themselves to the eternal powers."

"Holy shit," he repeated, shifting to a more comfortable position.

"There's a lot more," I said with a quick glance at his crotch. I couldn't tell whether he was getting hard. "You want to hear it?"

"Yeah," he said. His face turned a tad pink. Then I knew. Lyle did want to hear all about it. He was interested in gay sex.

❖

Thad's Journal: The Ninth of March

Rumors circulated the college following my initiation, and soon everyone knew that I was a member of Dr. Bromius's circle. My instructors dropped verbal insinuations, and my fellow students asked explicit questions. I had joined the most secretive group on campus, and secrecy breeds suspicion—and jealousy. Of course, we initiates allowed few students and no faculty intimate knowledge regarding the significance of membership in the Bromius cult. Gossip and hints flew around the campus, but none of the rumors came close to the full reality of our revels. Skip began pestering me, but I had made a solemn vow. I told him nothing of the ritual.

"How do I join, Thad?" Skip demanded one day during wrestling practice. We had been stars of the Muskrat Creek High School team, so, naturally, we joined the Cougar Ridge Community College squad. I slid my eyes downward, down his delectable form in his wrestling uniform.

"Are you gay, Skip?"

"Huh?" he asked. I was looking for a little spring in his bulge as I planted the question, and I saw more spring than I'd expected. I pulled him behind the bleachers where no one could see.

"What're you doing, Thad?" Skip whispered as I placed my hand on his swelling cock.

"Just checking something," I assured him and planted my lips on his. For a second, he did nothing. My heart sank. Then he shocked me by kissing me back with a fervor I would never have dreamed he possessed. Our kiss was protracted, spun out, stretching toward infinity. It was a kiss without boundaries, beyond the pale, over the top, and out of this world.

We pulled apart, aware that we were taking too long. The rest of the squad would soon be wondering what we were up to. Not to mention that our coach was a kicked-in-the-head nutball who frequently shouted "damned fine morning" and "how the hell are they hanging" to the college president.

"Go see Dr. Bromius," I urged Skip. "Visit him in his office. Tell him what you want."

As the week progressed, I read *The White Goddess*, though I understood little of Robert Graves's dazzling "historical grammar of poetic myth." Dr. Bromius assured me that understanding would come in time. I also read two Dion Fortune novels, *The Winged Bull* and *Avalon of the Heart*. The college library had a copy of Frazer's *The Golden Bough*, but Dr. Bromius told me that it was a later edition with some of the more intriguing matter excised. The Christians had complained, just as they had historically persecuted, censored, and banned their competition. I began searching for a complete version, one that recognized the Christian savior as one among a long line of dying and reviving gods.

Skip's initiation fell during the full moon in March, several moonlit rituals after my own introduction into the ways of the moon's deep circle. By that night, I was seeing myth and ritual everywhere, and recognized almost everything we were learning in college as a metaphor for something that was so elusive that no mortal could capture it in words. My dreams were vivid. Yes, they were blatantly sexual. Explicitly homosexual, if you will, and I had several times awakened Tye with my nocturnal mutterings. Yet, I sensed that the sex was a path, a summoning of ecstasy in order to approach the unapproachable eternal reality.

❖

Tipper's Tale

"Holy crap, Tip," Lyle said, his voice hoarse. "Wow, your brother was a real...heathen." Lyle's words came out in a gasp, as if he was fearful of articulating the word he most wanted to express. His pretense might have convinced me if I could not see his raging boner. "Your brother really wrote that shit?"

"I can't think of his writing as *shit*."

"Sorry, don't take that wrong, Tipper. I didn't mean it the way I said it. Do you think it really happened?"

"Who would make up a story like that, Lyle? They're his private journals. Dr. Bromius's gay pagan coven initiated Thad and his friend Skip. Skip's initiation is in this notebook. Let me read it to you."

❖

Thad's Journal: The Ninth of March, continued

On the night of Skip's initiation, we Uranians raised energy to the eternal powers. I jerked the cock of the boy on my right as we danced among the bonfires, just as the boy on the left tugged mine. Only the pipers and the drummers held their position, but they also worked one-handed.

I did not know the name of the boy tugging my cock, but I hoped to know him better soon. He had a firm, decisive grip that bit deep as he stroked.

❖

Tipper's Tale

Lyle moaned loudly. That little piece of narrative had him sizzling. Lyle's face was flushed hot, and a telltale wet spot decorated his pants. He was trying to conceal his leakage and failing spectacularly. When he noticed me eyeing his leaked cum, he started babbling, "You're right. Thad couldn't have invented that stuff. It has to be true."

I was only half listening. My cock was rocky in my underwear. I had to free it, or I was going to die. Without thinking about what I was doing, I pulled down my zipper. A murmured gasp escaped from

Lyle's mouth. I looked at him and saw that his eyes were riveted upon my crotch. He did not seem to be aware that his hand was sliding toward his cock. He pulled down his zipper, just as I had, and his cock nudged through the opening. He was wearing chocolate-colored bikini underwear of a soft, stretch fabric that showed the imprint of his cock head.

Without asking for his say-so, I fingered Lyle's cock through his underwear. I traced the head with my forefinger, swollen with lascivious purpose and sticky with his leaking pre-ejaculate. "Hot shit," Lyle said, and his words rang like a church bell. He was praying that I would keep teasing his dick.

I pulled off my sneakers and socks and dragged my pants over my feet. Lyle sat spellbound while he watched me undress. We had seen each other naked hundreds of times, being pool jocks, but never had we been intimately bare while our thoughts were inflamed with gay lust. Never had we been intimately turgid while our cocks throbbed for dramatic participation.

I completely undressed until I stood before Lyle, flushed, hot, and erect. He reached for my cock, touching it lightly with his fingertips. Liking what he felt, he gripped the shaft. Another gasp slipped from his mouth.

"I never touched another guy's cock before," Lyle said. He squeezed my dick. He gripped my dick head and twisted it with his fingers as if he was trying to open a screw top bottle. The most intense sensation shot through me.

"Take off your clothes, Lyle. Let's jerk off."

"You want me to jerk you off while you're doing me?"

"Yeah."

"That's pretty gay," he said. His voice carried no doubt that he wanted to do it. He was trying to come to terms with what he was, and he still doubted my inclinations.

"Jacking each other off is gay, Lyle," I said. "That's what I want us to do. Gay sex. You and I masturbating each other. Let's do it."

Doubt and distrust disappeared from Lyle's face, leaving him with a smutty looking mug. "Yeah. What the fuck am I hesitating for?" he mumbled crudely. He nearly tripped over his pants trying to undress himself. I helped him untie his sneakers. He pulled off his shirt. He leaped to his feet, kicked his jeans onto a chair, and stood before me in his soft, brownish underwear with his cock jutting so trustingly.

"Allow me, Lyle." I slipped my thumbs into his waistband. I pulled his boxer briefs down ever so slowly, over the head of his thrusting penis, which popped free, tall and proud. I pulled the briefs down to his knees, pushed his bare ass down on his bed, and pulled his underwear over his feet. Then we were both naked, in addition to being young, sexually stirred, and eager.

"Do you have any lubricants?" I asked urgently.

"Lube," Lyle said, jumping for his stash and displaying a nearly full bottle. "Loads."

"That's what I use too," I said. Lyle pulled out three unopened bottles. "My, you sure do have a lot of it," I added, picking up the nearly full bottle. "This one bottle should be enough. How often do you spank your monkey?"

Lyle grinned roguishly and admitted nothing, but I knew a big time masturbator when I saw one. I wanted to bet that I had him beat. I'd been honing my skills for many years, and I was sure that I had perfected my talents.

Easy enough to brag. Spanking your own monkey is straightforward. Spanking another guy's monkey is more difficult. Trying to stroke each other simultaneously takes talent. When I got Lyle on my right so I could jack his cock, he had trouble pounding mine with his left. We tried it facing each other, fucking each other's fist, but the coordination was still complicated. Every time we got into a good rhythm, and my cock started feeling heavenly in his fist, one or both of us stumbled. We kept pulling apart, and every time we did, we ended up with a case of the giggles.

"We're a bit nervous. Let's try it lying down."

We faced each other. Still, we were shy about what we did. I wanted to slide a hand over his silky ass, but I wasn't ready for that step. Our groping was adolescent, but Lyle said, "I won't be able to see you come. I want to see you come."

That gave me an idea. "Do you mind getting it on you?"

"Your cum?" Lyle blushed. "No, I wouldn't mind. I'd like that."

"How about we try it this way? You lie on your back. I'll get on your stomach and jack off on your chest. You can reach around me and jack your cum onto my ass."

Lyle promptly got into position, his eyes glinting with excitement. "Let's try it."

I crouched atop his stomach with my legs bent beneath me. I straightened so that my cock was pointing toward his chin, lubed my hand again, and began jerking off. The old, much-practiced rhythm was my own, and though Lyle's hand had been fun, my own knew how to milk my dick. I squeezed it harder than Lyle had, and I wrung my cock head.

The fine downy hair on Lyle's well-muscled stomach tickled my butt cheeks. For a second, I closed my eyes so I could feel his heat all the better. When I opened my eyes again, I saw that Lyle was smiling at me. He hunched his hips, bumping his cockhead against my ass crack. A hot thrill shot through me.

"Excuse me," Lyle said, blushing because he'd touched his cock to my ass. Little did he know that his inadvertent bump nearly drove me to toss prudence aside and pierce my asshole upon his jutting cock. It would have been so simple. I would have only needed a small change in position. However, the moment passed.

"No excuses, Lyle." I jacked off even more furiously than before. "I like your cock, Lyle. You can rub it against me. You can shoot your cum all over me. Shoot your spunk into my butt crack, if you can."

My wanton invitation would have made Lyle whoop with joy had he not been mindful of his parents watching television two floors below. He did allow one loud panting hiss to escape, a wheeze rising from his thundering heart and gasping lungs. In spite of his physical distress, Lyle jacked his cock against my butt. I kept on jerking off, sliding my sweating ass along his taut stomach.

"I'm about to come." I found that I was emitting a low moan, a howl almost, low in my throat, like an animal trapped. I struggled to bring out more words. "Do you want me to hold off?"

"Fuck, no, Tipper, let me have it. I'm there, too. Oh, yeah. Ah, Tip, I'm gonna decorate your ass."

His fist was furious, as demonstrated by the quivering of his arm as it circled my butt. Ripples of pleasure were already teasing my cock, and I felt the heaviness that signaled I had passed the point of no return. The ripples were growing in intensity, and nothing I could do would stop them. Even if I stopped and waited, my cock was destined to squirt. Cum was rising from my balls. I was committed to ejaculation.

"Here I come, Lyle." My voice was hoarse.

Lyle's voice was raspy too. "You feel that? Did you feel that, Tip?"

I had felt a warm, wet splash strike my butt crack. Another followed, and another. Lyle moaned. His moaning shifted into a groaning sound that elevated into a keening overtone. Splats of his rich semen were hitting my ass, decorating me, lubricating the crack of my butt, and splattering down my legs and up my back. Lyle was trying to stifle a screech of pleasure. "You feel my hot semen, Tip? I'm giving you a sperm job. A spunk bath on your ass, teammate."

The thumping drums of orgasm were shaking my own cock, and mighty contractions sent my first shot of cum splattering over Lyle's chin. I tried to keep my cock down so that I creamed his chest, but my third squirt went high. I saw my cum splatter his lips and the side of his nose. I was losing all control. Big, wet splats were hitting my ass cheeks and even into my spread butt crack. Getting wet made my own orgasm even more exciting. I let fly with one last hard burst that spread over Lyle's chin, painted his lips, and splashed into his nostrils.

Only gradually did our contractions ease. Our muscles returned to their normal state—eventually. I still sat on Lyle's stomach. Lyle gasped. I wheezed. We both panted from our exertions. Our cocks grew flaccid, and after long minutes of protracted release and slow oozing, Lyle's cum dripped slowly down my crack. I could hardly go home with Lyle's semen decorating my skin. I was drenched.

"Do we have to sneak down the hall to the bathroom?" I asked, envisioning a setup like my own.

Lyle laughed and pointed toward a door. "That's one advantage of being an only child—I have my own bathroom."

A few minutes later, we scrubbed off the "evidence" under the showerhead. Before I let Lyle clean me, I washed his chest, neck, and face.

"I think I'm blowing your cum out of my nose, Tip." I held the washrag to his face. There was considerable support for those words. I was glad that he had shown no disgust at my giving him an unintentional facial. In fact, I caught him licking his lips when he thought I wasn't looking.

When I finished cleaning my cum off Lyle, I handed him the soap and washcloth. Then I turned around. "Man, I sure did unload on you, Tip." Lyle soaped my behind and ran a washrag between my ass cheeks. "Your whole ass is covered with cum."

Washing was a lot of fun, and we lingered in the shower. We were toweling each other off when we heard Lyle's mother's voice in his bedroom. "Lyle, I brought some milk and cookies for you and your little friend."

"Not so little," Lyle whispered, squeezing my cock with the towel. "We're in the shower, Mom," he yelled.

"You boys are showering together?"

"We shower together all the time, Mom," Lyle yelled. "It's no big deal. We're on the swim team."

"Oh, yes, of course," she said, buying that line of bullshit.

"Did you hide the Astroglide?" I whispered.

"Yeah."

"What about the smell? Think about how much spunk we shot. Your room has got to stink like a semen factory."

"My bedroom always smells like that. Don't worry. Mom can't get a whiff of the cat's litter box. Her nose hasn't worked right for years."

We poked our heads around the bathroom door and discovered that Lyle's mother had gone back downstairs. Still naked, we hurried toward the snacks she had left. I helped myself to one of the lemon bars and two of the pumpkin cookies.

"These are great, Lyle."

"Yeah, but that pumpkin will give you the worst gas you've ever had."

"That's okay. I'll be home by then."

"Don't forget that I have to drive you home. Don't take it as an insult if we go with the windows down."

Lyle was right about the pumpkin cookies, but that's another story. They were still delicious.

CHAPTER FIVE

Tipper's Tale

The next morning brought my turn to drive again. I picked up Lyle first. He met me with a happy grin, but we didn't say much after we picked up Jeep, Mart, and Rick. Rick had fought with his girlfriend, so he was in a surly mood. He made a few spiteful observations about our school and the Muskrats' chances against the Copperheads. Mart took offense and told Rick off for the pussy whipped case that he was. For a moment, it looked as if he and Mart might duke it out in my backseat. Fortunately, we got to school without fisticuffs, and Rick huffed off to his first class.

I reached Cougar Ridge Community College's human resources office just at the end of my lunch break. The woman I talked to was even less helpful than Opdycke had been. She refused to confirm that Dr. Bromius had once taught there.

"Give me a break," I said. "There's no law protecting college teachers. Their employment is a matter of public record." Lyle had suggested that argument after we'd spent an hour in the computer lab researching Dr. Bromius. Google listed about 20,000 hits for *Bromius* and none for *Buck Bromius*. Of course, Buck was probably a nickname, short for Buckminster or Buckley or Randybuck or some such. Anyway, we didn't have enough information for a search. Still, I did learn that though FERPA regulations protected students' rights of privacy, the federal government had no interest in safeguarding the privacy of college instructors. As far as the feds cared, it was always open season on teachers. Dr. Bromius was fair game.

Cougar Ridge Community College's Human Resources Office didn't see things my way, however, and the woman refused to disclose any information. More and more, I suspected that Dr. Bromius had departed under a cloud, and no one would talk for fear of admitting further damage to the institution's reputation. Either that, or the poltroons were terrified of getting sued. Finally, the HR lady gave me one piece of advice. "Try the public library. The librarians will help you."

I wasn't convinced that the county library could help, but I disconnected politely enough. My afternoon classes passed by in a fog, and nothing memorable happened until swim practice. I was standing beside the pool in my competition swimsuit with my swim goggles pushed atop my head.

"No, Baldwin," I shouted at a sophomore. "You have to touch the end of the pool while lying on your back. Quit rolling over, and keep your ass in the water."

Coach Reece came barreling from his office. He was dressed in his red team shirt, with his stomach protruding over the waistband of his black pants. His face was redder than his reddish hair, making him look like a methamphetamine-addicted pit bull.

"Trencher, why do you have them practicing the backstroke? The backstroke is the second slowest stroke."

I kept my attention on the boys in the pool. One scrawny freshman was barely struggling along. "Carlyle. Keep your palms toward your legs, thumb side up. Your recovery is sloppy." I made a mental note to assign a personal trainer to him. Carlyle needed to bulk up if he ever hoped to look sexy in his swim briefs, much less swim competitively. As it was, his swimsuit had traveled south, displaying half of his scrawny ass.

The coach grabbed my arm and bellowed like a buffalo. "Get these boys practicing the front crawl. They need speed to win races."

Usually, I submitted to the coach's demands, but that day I was already exasperated. I pulled my arm away. "They also need form."

Coach Reece actually snarled at me. "You think 'slow and steady' wins the race?" He looked like a rabid dog with a secret vice. "What kind of team captain are you?"

"I'm the one you appointed," I shouted. I lowered my voice a little. "Look, Coach, speed isn't going to get us anywhere if half these guys get disqualified. Friday, we're swimming a two hundred meter individual medley against the Pendleton Water Bucks, and we've got guys performing in violation of the National Federation of State High School Associations' rules."

Stunned, Coach Reece stepped back and stared at me. I had never really stood up to him before then, and he was so flummoxed that his customary platitudes failed him. The whole team had stopped swimming. Some boys were standing on the bottom, and others were treading water, but everyone was watching awestruck.

"I'm waiting for lightning to strike Trencher dead," Mike Baldwin said.

"Coach has gotta be summoning down the wrath of God," Ben Defoe said.

I figured that the coach was going to take away my captaincy on the spot. I expected him to rip off my swim briefs like a furious major relieving an insubordinate sergeant of his stripes. However, Coach Reece merely raised his eyes heavenward and nodded as if he'd received a response from on high. "Tell that boy to pull up his shorts," the coach said anticlimactically, swiveled neatly on his heel, and stalked to his office.

The swimmers started to applaud, but I stopped them immediately. "Don't humiliate the coach. Back to work. If we can't beat those antelope fuckers in Pendleton, we'd best hang up our towels."

I kept them practicing the backstroke for an hour. When we returned to the individual medley, the team looked a lot better. Even the sophomores were following the rules. Toward the end of practice, Coach Reece stepped out of his office and watched carefully. Finally, he nodded. "Good job, Trencher. I was praying that you'd turn this team around, and the Good Lord has chosen you as the right vessel to perform His task."

"Uh, sure, thanks, Coach." My anal sphincter puckered at the thought of being the "Good Lord's" vessel.

Later, as I was driving the seniors home, the guys were unusually subdued. I dropped Rick off first, but before he climbed out of the car, he looked me directly in the eyes. "You really acted like our captain today, Tip," he said. He stuck out his hand for me to shake.

"I told the coach the truth. That's all. I've done it before." That statement was only half true, at best. "You guys just never heard me."

"But today you stuck to your guns," Mart said. "You didn't switch strokes like he wanted. You did what you knew we really needed."

"You were assertive," Jeep said. He batted his eyes in jest. "You were so manly."

That comment started a tirade of jokes, which made me more comfortable than their praise. I wasn't sure how to take the praise, whereas I was used to their ribbing.

"Yeah, Tipper, how'd you get so manly all of a sudden?" Lyle asked, his eyes dancing with merriment. He pointed dramatically and demanded with great presence, "Have you been having manly sex?"

And at that moment, I knew that something had changed within me. All Lyle and I had done was jerk off on each other, but the act had given me confidence. Enough confidence to speak truth to the power of the community, and damn the consequences. And I wondered where the newfound assurance would lead—to more manly sex, I hoped.

By diabolical design, I dropped off the other seniors before Lyle, but not before I got pulled over again. Luck was with me. Once again, Deputy Martin approached my car window.

"Holy shit," Jeep said, but the deputy was amiable.

"This is a forty-five zone. You were hitting eighty-five."

"Swimmer's leg. I've got a terrible case of it. Makes the leg kick out. Causes me to press down too hard on the accelerator. Completely involuntary, of course. It's ironic that the same condition that helps me to win races against the other teams interferes with my driving."

Deputy Martin started laughing halfway through my explanation. "Trencher, that's the worst excuse I've ever heard." Looking at the carload of swimmers, he mused wistfully, "I ought to ticket you."

However, once again he let it pass. He even gave us a few dollars more, after extracting a promise that we'd go to the finals. I dropped off Mart and Jeep, saving Lyle for last. As we pulled into his driveway, Lyle twisted in the seat, laid both hands on my thigh, and grinned wickedly. "Wanna come up?"

"Damned right I wanna come, Lyle. That's why I dropped off the breeder boys first."

"I thought I detected a wily hand in your machinations, Tipper."

As we trooped up the stairs, Lyle called down to his parents. "I'm home. Tip is with me."

"All right, dear," his mother responded from the basement. "Your little friends are always welcome. Have a good time."

"Little friends?"

"Not so little." Lyle cupped my buttocks with both hands and pushed my ass up the stairs. "You have big, strong butt muscles."

I turned at the top landing and kissed Lyle. His lips were hot against mine. I felt his dick responding in his undershorts. As I wrapped my arms around him, hugging him tight, his heat warmed me. His lips pressed mine, and his tongue warred against me. My cock arose, twisted painfully in my underwear. Lyle's hands slid down my back and cupped my ass again. I wiggled my buttocks against his hands, which rubbed my cock against his. Our bodies burned as we dry humped. We kissed deep and long, so long that we ran out of air.

"I'll bring up a snack for you boys shortly," Lyle's mother shouted, just as Lyle and I released our hold and broke for oxygen.

"Isn't your mother going to start wondering what we're doing?"

Lyle shook his head. "She'd have to catch us in the act before she started getting suspicious." He laughed. "Even if she did catch us, it'd take me two minutes to convince her that she saw us doing homework or working out a new swimming technique."

Safely ensconced in Lyle's room, we made ourselves comfortable by removing our outer clothes. We left our T-shirts on and our undershorts. Lyle's underwear was black, of a stretchy cotton fabric, and mine were bikini style and seashell colored. Our cocks were distorting the shape of our undergarments.

Lyle touched the tip of my cock. "What about your mother?" I asked. I was afraid she would walk in on us. Yet, even as I shivered with dread, I felt a strange excitement as if I wanted to get caught.

"Don't worry about her. She'll take hours getting a plate of cookies and a pitcher of milk ready. We'll hear her coming up the stairs."

"We didn't hear her yesterday."

"We were in the shower."

"Okay. Does the idea of having your mother walk in while we're having sex excite you, Lyle?"

He rolled his eyes as if I were joking. "Read some more of your brother's journal. We didn't finish yesterday."

"Finish?" I couldn't resist ribbing him. "We hardly got started. I read only a couple of paragraphs before you started feeling me up."

Lyle feigned a dismayed expression. Then he pantomimed a look of illumination. "I seem to remember you grabbing my dick."

"Do you?"

"Couldn't keep your wicked hands off a sweet young thing like me. My innocent cock was prey to your homosexual lusts."

"You revel in those homosexual lusts." I touched his cock. "I was the 'sweet young thing' led astray by your evil impulses."

"How's that for an evil impulse?" Lyle said, sliding his hand over my ass. His groping fingers pushed my underwear into my butt crack. As he traced his forefinger up my cleft, a hot feeling invaded my crotch, suffusing me with warmth. My cock swelled harder, and an unfamiliar sensation ran up the underside my balls. The strange, pleasant tingling continued up my ass.

"Damn, Lyle. I've never felt anything like that. It's good."

"Is it good?" He listened for a second, and his eyes flickered toward his door. "No, she isn't coming yet." However, he pulled his hand out of my butt crack. "Read first. Then we'll play."

I was hot to play then, but I was no hotter than Lyle. Relying on his judgment, I opened Thad's journal to the place where we'd stopped the previous day.

❖

Thad's Journal: The Ninth of March, continued

Because the magical purpose of our cock-tugging dance was to raise power for ritual spell casting, the priests decreed that our circle jerk must proceed to orgasm. Dr. Bromius arrived while we pagans were cavorting, gamboling, leaping, capering, frolicking, and jacking. His eyes glinting with mirrored enchantments, our professor tossed off his clothing and danced toward the masturbating celebrants. As we flung cum in all directions, we greeted Dr. Bromius with blown kisses.

I was glad to see Dr. Bromius. I had been wondering what had detained him. The circle had not seemed quite the same without him. His personality infused us with a pagan intensity that we students could not yet emulate.

Hyacinthos and Apollo also seemed relieved—and inspired—at Dr. Bromius's arrival. Hurriedly, they erected the altar and passed out brooms to the participants. Wet with our tossed semen, we swept the circle of all baneful influences until it was pure and ready to provide a ground for our carnal power. Dr. Bromius took a broom and swept vigorously. While he whisked the dry earth, he chanted:

"Spirits of doubt,
We sweep you out.
Spirits of fear,
Be gone from here.
Fairy boys, make hay, go lay,
Let our fairy thoughts be gay."

Apollo handed Dr. Bromius his athamé, and our professor cast the circle, starting at the north and continuing around three times. I watched his thick cock swing as he worked, and his buttocks tighten as he drove the ceremonial dagger through cosmic thought. As he cut, he chanted:

"I cast a circle of protection around this sacred space and around these assembled fairy boys. Let the acts of homosexual lust enacted herein meet the favor of the Uranian gods: Pederast Zeus, Radiant Apollo, the Dog-Men of Edom, Partridge Baal, Hyacinthos, Bran the Crow, Amathaon the Fellatiator, Plutonian Orpheus, Argonaut Hercules, Dionysus of the Vine, Melkarth, Wood-Cock

Narcissus the Holy Masturbator, and Jabbette Ganymede.
Let this circle guard our orgies of Sodomy and the Holy
Secret."

Dr. Bromius's words moved me deeply. He made me feel how
terribly special was my sexual nature, and how cosmically significant
were my sexual acts. Even as my heart leaped, my cock grew harder,
my lips tightened, and my asshole twitched. Flaming desires filled
me. I wanted to fill a mouth or an ass, and even more, I wanted my
mouth and ass filled. I had delivered my psyche to the old gods of
Uranus, and they were working though me. The names Dr. Bromius
had summoned commanded me to submit my body to their will.
Their impulses would be my impulses. My submissions were their
submissions. My discharges were the discharges of the gods. My
penetrations were the penetrations of the everlasting powers.

The yellow moon shone through the breeze that our bonfires
warmed, and the heat and light seemed to melt my flesh while the
pipes and drums, the bells and the tambourines, and the measured
chant of my fellow Uranian pagans propelled me toward ecstasies
of lust.

Then Skip arrived, naked, blindfolded, led by his guides
Orpheus and Attis. Skip looked scared and eager, and a part of me
wanted to reassure him. Yet another part wanted to watch him suck
a cock in mystery, not certain where he was, not knowing who was
watching. The gods were working through me—mystery won over
reassurance. Skip must capitulate to fortune.

With two sweeping slices with his holy knife, Dr. Bromius
cut a door in the circle. I followed the other boys out of the sacred
space into the world of time and process. We formed a double line,
a come-if-you-dare challenge, which Skip must pass.

Last November, I had been the blindfolded college freshman
nakedly daring the baffling, vulgar, and touchingly personal boys.
This time, I saw all. I saw Skip stripped of his clothing and hauled
bound and nude to the challenge. Before that night, I had never
fully appreciated Skip's naked body. As wrestlers, we had showered
together numerous times, but boys are taught not to gawk at other
boys' cocks and asses. The lessons are subtle, socially mandated,

and cleverly insinuated. The heterosexual propaganda works. We forsake our natural homosexual impulses and believe that "the way of a man with a maid" is the *natural* order.

Skip and I had kissed. We had jerked each other off. But even with my best friend, I had resisted giving over to the fullness of homosexual desire. I had not yet learned to love the naked masculine form.

Even in our nakedness, we had been private. However, our privacy was nothing more than ignorance. Nothing private existed in the eternal realm; the gods of Uranus saw all, knew all, tempted all, dared all, and completed all. Skip was gloriously naked for all to see, naked to the gods, and naked to his classmates. His cock was hard, and its hardness hexed into reality an existence that all must acknowledge.

Skip entered our gauntlet, naked, blindfolded, hard, horny, and confused. Boys goaded him, jabbed him, mocked him, pressed him, and grasped him. As he drew abreast, Skip had his back to me. The boy across was caressing Skip between his thighs, hands massaging the underside of Skip's balls. Moved, I cuddled against Skip's rounded buttocks, even pushing my hand into the deep cleft between. I had always known that Skip had a nice ass, but his muscular development and sculpted flesh was even firmer and hotter than I had imagined. I felt his ass up briefly before he was swept down the line. I watched as other boys caressed him, assaulted him, mocked him, patted him, and prodded him. After we had molested Skip in the way of the mystery cults, we moved back through the invisible doorway and assumed our places in the circle.

I listened while Apollo submitted Skip to the ritual questions, the ritual anointing, and the ritual kisses of the body. My boyhood companion Skip answered quickly, vowing himself to a lifetime of sex with men. When Skip pledged his mouth for bowl and rod, Apollo cut the sacred circumference with his athamé, permitted Skip entrance, and closed the circle behind him.

We pagans had swept our circle, but it had been opened and closed several times. Taking no chances against the slippery spirits of homophobia, Apollo invoked the watchtowers and banished all baneful influences. No spirit of fear, no spirit of impotence, no spirit of homophobia could enter our ritual place. We were free to conduct our gay orgiastic celebration.

Dancing among us, Dr. Bromius drifted his gaze over the assembled circle of boys, each one his student, each one his devoted acolyte, each one his potential sex slave. Our beloved professor smiled at my eager stare, but he did not appoint me to the ritual task. Skip had to be attuned to the homosexual rapture, so my turn was not yet. I was too new to the circle.

Dr. Bromius picked a different boy, a well-hung, horsy, extroverted lad whose name I did not yet know. The boy had shaggy blond hair that hung over his ears, skin tanned all over, and buttocks that looked as though he could drive a spike.

The boy placed his cock before Skip's lips. I wished that I had been chosen, but I could merely watch. Had Dr. Bromius selected me, I might have missed the significance of my own ritual suck. Enraptured, I watched as my best friend accepted the reality of the cocksucker. Blindfolded, Skip prepared to receive the cock that would symbolize the penetration of the almighty powers. When Skip was ready to receive the divine fluid, Hyacinthos invited Skip to drop to his knees and kiss the Phallus of the God.

I watched, entranced, as Skip received the boy's cock into his mouth and began blowing it with lusty eagerness. "Suck it, Skip." My voice was lost beneath the wild musical accompaniment. "Suck that boy's cock, Skip. Let him come in your mouth."

❖

Tipper's Tale

"Hot shorts!" Lyle said. His shorts were bulging provocatively. "Where do I go to join?"

"I wish I knew." Lyle didn't have the only hard-on. Mine was stiff as a Sitka spruce. Adjusting my tumescence in my bikini briefs, I continued reading.

❖

Thad's Journal: The Ninth of March, continued

Blindfolded, enraptured by the ritual, Skip mouthed the big cock with feral passion. He sucked the boy's dick head as if he were a young goat sucking its mother's teat. I watched with rapt attention as Skip took the thick cock deeper into his mouth. The boy he was sucking glowed with pleasure. However, by degrees, his glow faded and perplexity fogged his visage. He flung his arms out in desperate supplication. Skip only sucked harder. The priests grabbed the boy's hands to give him strength for the ordeal and to restrain him from cupping his hands behind Skip's bobbing head and feeding Skip his cock.

Even the musicians watched in awe. The music lost volume as the players were thunderstruck in the face of such powerful cocksucking. A low moan rose from the assembled witnesses. Even Dr. Bromius stood flabbergasted, his thick cock flaring up and northeast as he watched.

Skip was a sucking creature, drawing the boy's dick deeper, teasing its fluids, robbing its essence. His lips would wrap tightly around the dick head and then ooze down the shaft until the entire cock disappeared into his mouth. He was swallowing the boy's dick head into his throat with every thrust. The boy getting sucked grew pale at the ferocity of Skip's cocksucking. He cast a desperate look toward Hyacinthos, but the priest merely gripped the boy's left hand and smiled benignly as though he were blessing the hallowed juncture.

"*Evoe*, Dion, Dion, Dion-Bacchus," the boy screeched. He flung his face toward the yellow moon and rocked his hips in time with Skip's mouthy motions. My hard cock tightened in sympathy, but a green jealousy shot through me. My asshole tightened, and my legs shook. I had engulfed a cock, sucked as well as I could, but I had failed to make my boy howl. I did not overwhelm him, not the way Skip was doing. Everyone recognized that Skip possessed a cocksucking talent born in the bone.

Skip was enjoying that cock in his mouth, enjoying it to a degree that I could never approach. He was relishing the shape and texture, relishing the semen that had to erupt, and relishing his power to bring a boy to explosive and mind-altering orgasm with his lips, tongue, and throat.

"Oh, Uranus, Dionysus, Bran, and Orpheus." The boy's screech echoed off the distant mountains, but his cry to the Uranian powers did not move Skip to mercy. Skip was inspired to suck harder. I saw how his lips bruised the boy's cock head and squeezed his shaft. Skip's tongue worked too. He lapped at the cock head, and nibbled around the edge. The boy emitted a keening wail that drowned out the other sounds of the night.

"*Evoe*, Dion-Bacchus." His praise of pleasure died as language failed him altogether, and his throat allowed no more than animal cries. His squeals joined with the voices of the coyotes in the hills, yipping at the full moon.

The two priests released the boy's hands. He flailed briefly before gripping his own buttocks with both hands. Wild gasps, pants, and wheezes interjected into his frenzied cries. We watched in near orgasmic awe as he shuddered up the pinnacle of orgasm. His balls were emptying, his pelvic muscles were twitching, and his ejaculatory spasms poured spunk into Skip's throat. Skip swallowed triumphantly, and when the boy was finished, drained, and depleted, supported on his feet by both priests, we still stared in awe at our blindfolded initiate, my best friend Skip, who had out-sucked everyone, who had proved his worth as the mightiest cocksucker of our pagan clan.

❖

Tipper's Tale

Thad's description mesmerized Lyle and me to such a extent that we bowed before the pervasive omnipresence of the glorious deities of homosexuality. Surrendering our souls to the gods, we sat staring into each other's eyes. My cock was nearly bursting with a need to ejaculate. I let my eyes drift down Lyle's stomach to his soft briefs. As my eyes travelled down, my homolust grew—as did Lyle's. His erection dangerously distended the cloth. As I looked, I half expected to see his piercing prick rip through the stretched fabric. In addition to being stretched severely, Lyle's briefs were wet with his leakage.

Lyle was looking at my dick as he muttered, "That was a thrilling narrative." Ms. Malcolm's literature class was having a deleterious effect on Lyle's psyche; he was beginning to talk like a nineteenth century professor.

I used more contemporary diction. "I'm about to shoot off in my pants."

"I'd like to meet this Skip guy, Tip." Lyle's underwear was throbbing. "A world champion cocksucker. I wonder what he looks like."

I was watching Lyle's cock, which seemed to be imitating plate tectonics. It was moving under the cloth, sliding with glacial speed and power toward a roomier position. His cock's relentless slide under the landscape of his briefs created erotic patterns in the strained cloth.

"I wonder whether you can tell just from looking at him."

Lyle was still thinking about Skip. "I've met him." I was still fascinated by Lyle's cock. "He works not far from here. I'd bet that he doesn't know about the journals. He sure doesn't know that I've been reading them."

Lyle said, "I've got to get a look at him." He tried to shift his cock with his hand, but his briefs were stretched too tight.

"You'd never guess Skip's talent by looking at him." Lyle's cock made a sudden sideslip that carried it somewhat to his right. It was more fascinating than any serpent. "I'll take you by and introduce you. I wanna ask old Skip a couple of questions anyway."

"Old?"

"We're reading about stuff that happened fifteen years ago. Skip has to be thirty-three."

"That's not old. I've seen lots of hot-looking guys that age. The gym is packed with them. Like you haven't noticed. I've seen your wandering eye in the locker room."

That was a revelation. I had not realized that I'd been revealing so much of myself. Especially parts of myself that I didn't even know about before I started reading my brother's stuff.

"I've been checking out other guys?"

"All the time, Tip. You've got a roving eye."

"Holy crap! I didn't know I was doing it."

"Relax, Tip. You know the old cliché—it takes one to know one."

"You've known all the time that I was gay?" I asked, rubbing Lyle's cock.

"I was damned sure of it," Lyle said. "The other guys don't have a clue."

"Jeep does."

"Well, yeah, Jeep. Jeep has a terrific ass. From behind, he looks like a girl wandered into our locker room."

"Just because he has a nice ass…"

"You don't think so?"

"That's not what I mean, Lyle. Jeep has a bountiful ass. But that isn't what I mean."

"Gaydar, Tip."

"Huh?"

"Don't play coy. You have gaydar, too."

"Yeah, but Jeep gives off mixed signals. I'm pretty sure he's interested, but he tries to hide it."

"So did you, Tip. So did I. Then the truth came out." His mouth was close to mine then. I was looking into his eyes, but I could feel the close proximity of our lips.

"Is your mom coming up with those cookies?" I whispered, no longer sure what we were talking about. Lyle didn't answer—our mouths met. We kissed hard and long; his tongue slipped into my mouth. I found my tongue playing against his. Then I was sucking his tongue, and I wondered how much different sucking his dick could be. I pushed my tongue into his mouth. My hand was on his dick. He slipped his hand into the waistband of my bikini briefs, where my cock was stiff but twisted in the fabric.

I pushed Lyle's semen-scented underwear down, over his ass, below his knees. He raised his feet so I could pull his damp briefs over them. I withdrew my lips from his so I could concentrate on his lower parts. His dick was hard, sticky on the uncircumcised tip, and seemed even thicker than it had been the previous day. My seashell-spotted bikini briefs bulged ferociously, as though my stiff cock would tear through the sweat damp fabric.

Before I could push down my briefs, Lyle kissed my cock though the cloth. Instantly, I was wetter with his hot mouth and a sudden leakage.

"You're leaking, too, Tipper. I smell your spunk."

"Taste it, Lyle." Lyle raised his eyes to my face. He looked apologetic, even fearful. "Go ahead." I stroked his black hair, cut short for the pool. "It's all right. I've tasted my own cum."

Lyle touched his tongue to the wet spot on my briefs. He shuddered, and the enormity of what was happening sent a shudder down my spine. Nevertheless, that shudder was a quiver of surrender, not a tremble of dismay. I gave in to my impulses, submitted to my nature, and surrendered to my desire.

Embracing his own homosexual nature, Lyle gripped the waistband of my briefs with both hands. I stood to make it easy for him, and pulled them off my ass. My cock bobbed blessedly free. Lyle pushed me back onto his bed and pulled my briefs over my feet. He stripped off his T-shirt before he lifted mine. I raised my arms so he could strip me naked.

"Suck me, Lyle. Suck my cock, and I'll suck yours."

Without undue ceremony, his mouth traveled to my cock. His tongue tortured my cock head, his lips caressed my shaft, and his teeth nibbled my skin. Slowly, painstakingly, Lyle allowed my cock to pass through his lips and glide along his tongue.

"Oh, Lyle. I want to suck you too. I want to suck your cock while you suck mine."

"Yes, that's what I want too. I've wanted to suck you off since I first laid eyes on you." His hands glided over my chest and stomach while he talked. His fingers probed my navel, and explored down to my groin. My cock was standing tall, thick, tight, and slick with his spittle. "When I first saw your bulging cock and curvy ass in your red swim briefs, I wanted you." He gripped my cock and jacked it; I fell back with a gasp. "Whenever we're together in the pool, or when you're walking along the edge barking orders at the freshmen, I've thought about how your dick would feel inside me."

No doubt feeling that he had talked too much, Lyle kissed my cock again, and after that, he couldn't utter another word. He could only make low moans and quiet smacking sounds. For a few minutes,

I sprawled, enraptured, savoring the movement of his mouth on the head of my dick, and completely unable to keep my vow to suck his dick as he sucked me. Lyle was, after all, giving me my first blow job, and I'd never felt anything so good. His mouth working at my dick was more electrifying than the innumerable hand jobs I'd practiced on myself.

Lyle's mouth stimulated me better than a thousand hand jobs; his lips pumped my cock shaft like a Saudi oil prince going for the liquid gold; and his tongue licked deep like a tiger's mouth. Staring at his ceiling, I was all cock in a universe of sucking mouths. A vast ring of mouth had enclosed my cock, and I was lost within it. Yet even as I yielded my flesh, my eager flesh, to Lyle's oral power, my heart wanted to give as I got. My mouth yearned to suck a cock. I wanted to taste the flesh, to savor the smooth skin, to feel the thick shaft gliding farther and farther back into my mouth, and to taste the delicious cum that must inevitably erupt.

Of course, Lyle's cock was the cock of the moment. The harder he sucked me, the more I yearned to suck him. I imagined the semen rising from his musk-scented balls, rising up his cock tube like lava, and erupting as a thick, sticky pudding onto my tongue.

Lyle was gripping my buttocks with both hands as he worked my dick. His hands felt good on my ass. I liked having him touch me in that way. So familiar, I sighed. Like my ass was his to fondle at will. Then I knew that I couldn't wait for him to finish on me before I started on him. I had to get my hands on his tight ass. I had to get my lips around his thick cock.

"Lyle, let's suck each other off. At the same time. Let's do the old sixty-nine."

Almost reluctantly, Lyle pulled his mouth off my dick. "Sure," he said. I adjusted my position until my face was near to his crotch.

"Is that better?" he asked, but without waiting for an answer, his left hand gripped my ass and his mouth found my cock again.

I pressed the tip of my tongue against Lyle's cock. Tonguing another boy's dick was an extraordinary thing, an activity foreign to me, yet paradoxically natural. My mouth knew what to do without any advice from my imagination. My right hand slid across his upper buttock, so that the tips of my fingers brushed his ass crack. From somewhere below, I heard the doorbell bong. I heard Lyle's mother say something, whether greeting her guest or calling up, I could not guess. I didn't give the arrival a second thought. I pressed my lips to Lyle's cock, kissing his cock head. I kissed it and licked it, then I slowly licked down the shaft. His balls were tight with silky black hair growing on them. I licked Lyle's balls, savoring the exotic taste. The doorbell bonged a second time as I licked his shaft.

Lyle's mother shouted again; that time she *was* shouting *up* from the foot of the stairs. I could not remember whether we had locked the door. We had intended to, but with one thing or another, we might have skipped it. A delicious premonition of peril crept up my spine, which made Lyle's dick-suck-smacking more provocative.

I pressed my lips to Lyle's dick head again, letting his cock pass over my lips and enter into my mouth. Lyle was already leaking a thin fluid, which had a sweet taste as though it were composed entirely of sugar. Nothing about it was objectionable. It certainly wasn't like having someone "go to the bathroom in your mouth," as one deluded detractor from the notorious Oregon Citizens' Alliance had described it (the homophobic spawn must have sucked thousands before they concocted that qualifier). I took Lyle's cock deeper, letting it ride along my tongue, while I pulled it toward my throat by gripping his tight ass.

Having Lyle's cock in my mouth was the most stirring sensation I had ever experienced. My mouth was full, and the great weight slid along my tongue. I was about to come in Lyle's mouth, so intense was our sexual tension, and he was just as close to ejaculation. I felt an introductory tingle, not quite a commitment to orgasm, but a discrete demonstration of feelings to come, when I heard the scraping of Lyle's bedroom door. A fresh breeze swept across my bare ass as the door pushed opened fully.

"Guys, I was calling and..." The voice trailed off with a dead sound, followed by a sharp inhalation.

Lyle and I rolled over as one. I saw Jeep staring at our tryst, his eyes wide with astonishment, and his mouth agape. Jeep tried to say something else. I tried to speak too, but words completely failed me.

Before Lyle or I could unfreeze, Jeep whirled, thundered down the stairs, and burst out the front door. Cries and exclamations followed this abrupt departure. During the hubbub, Lyle and I dragged our pants over our wet cocks and bare asses. As we struggled hastily into our T-shirts, we could hear Lyle's mother rushing up the steps, fearful that we had met with some catastrophe.

She stopped in the doorway, gripping the frame. Her eyes slowly swept the cluttered bedroom. "What was the matter with that boy?"

"We surprised him," Lyle managed, scarlet-faced, standing to conceal his semen-stained briefs that were still lying on the rumpled bedspread. I glanced around for my own underwear, but I couldn't spot them. I hunched frozen beside Lyle, saying nothing.

"Surprised him? Is he crazy?"

"No, Ma, it was just a stupid joke. I'm sorry."

No sooner had Lyle's mother left his room, shaking her head in puzzlement, than Lyle darted to his window. "Jeep's still there," he said. "He's sitting in his car. Maybe we should go down and explain it to him."

"And say what?" I asked. "What possible explanation would work? He saw everything. He's not gonna believe we got snake bit and were sucking out the venom. He knows we were sucking cock."

"Yeah." Lyle sounded as if he were strangling on the word. "Do you think we should try to deny it? It'll be all over school tomorrow. You think we should stonewall?"

I drew a deep breath and squared my shoulders. "Hell, no. Did you like sucking my dick?"

"You know I did."

"Well, so did I—I liked it a whole lot. I want to finish sucking your dick, Lyle." I thought about how my father would take the news that I was a cocksucker. He would not react well. Still, truth had to win out in the end. "I don't want trouble at school, especially with the homophobes, including Coach Reece, but if the word gets out, we should walk proudly and say that we're gay."

"Yeah, Tip. I'll come out if you will. But we're gonna get a lot of flak. Hey. Jeep just opened his car door. He's getting out."

I rushed to the window. I saw Jeep's vehicle, but I didn't see Jeep.

"He's come back in," Lyle said, turning toward his door. We heard Jeep's feet on the stairs, and a second later, he stepped cautiously into the doorway to find both Lyle and me standing dressed and ready to confront him.

"Uh, hey, guys…" Jeep said before his voice trailed off.

"Hey, Jeep," I said.

"Uh, yeah," Lyle managed.

"What's happening?" Jeep said.

Lyle and I turned and looked at each other as though we could not believe our ears. "What's happening, Jeep? What's happening with you?"

"Uh, I don't know what to say, Tip."

"What did you just see, Jeep?"

Jeep flushed dark red. He tried to speak, but he only managed a stutter. However, I noticed a curious bulge in the front of his jeans. Were they sticking out just a bit farther than was natural for a flaccid penis? Did Jeep have an incipient erection?

When Lyle caught the direction of my gaze, a mysterious half-smile twitched over his lips. "Come on, Jeep. Tell us what you saw."

"I saw you two guys naked on Lyle's bed."

"Not just naked, Jeep." Suddenly, I was having fun.

"Yeah, Jeep." Lyle was coaxing to come out with it. He was enjoying the moment too. "You know what you saw. You witnessed us sucking each other's dick."

"Yeah, what's up with that?" The bulge was increasing. His dick must have been half-hard.

"So why did you run?" I asked as if cocksucking were an everyday event.

"Why did you come back?" Lyle asked simultaneously. I guessed that the same answer could reply to both questions.

Wretched with embarrassment and fear, Jeep wheeled as if he would scurry again, but I snatched his arm. "Don't be afraid." I pulled him closer. He did not resist. I touched my fingers to his bulging erection. He pulled away, reconsidered his reaction, and pushed closer to me. I brought my lips to his and kissed him passionately. Keeping my eyes open, I witnessed the wild panic in his eyes. Jeep made a token gesture of drawing his head back before relinquishing entirely. His lips pressed against mine. His eyelids fluttered with yearning before closing dreamily. His arms encircled me as his tongue met mine.

I felt Lyle join the embrace, his arms including us both, as his lips brushed Jeep's ear. "I'm glad you decided to join us," Lyle said, but Jeep said nothing, for his mouth was occupied. He was sucking my tongue.

Without warning, Lyle pulled away. "Watch out, guys. My mom is coming up the stairs."

"Oh, shit," Jeep said, his panic returning.

"No sweat," Lyle said. He glanced at Jeep's raging boner. "Sit down. Whatever she asks, say it was a joke." Lyle pushed Jeep down on the bed. I hurriedly adjusted my pants, and began coolly investigating a model spaceship dangling from Lyle's ceiling.

Lyle's mother bumped his door with her foot. "I have a snack for you boys," she called. Lyle opened the door. She entered bearing a large tray with sandwiches, a cold pitcher of cider, and a pile of frosted cupcakes. Lyle took the tray and set it on his desk.

"Thanks, Mom."

"Are you all right?" she asked Jeep. "Would you like me to call your mother?"

Jeep turned deep red. "No, sorry, Mrs. Fujimoto. The boys played a joke on me. I didn't mean to give you a fright."

"Lyle, that was not polite," Mrs. Fujimoto said, shaking her head. "You boys play nice now. And eat some sandwiches before you eat the cupcakes."

At her invitation, I poured a glass of cider and grabbed a sandwich, which turned out to be roast beef with a dash of horseradish. Mrs. Fujimoto kept jabbering while we ate sandwiches, though her conversation centered around the latest doings on a television game show. Lyle rolled his eyes behind her back, but Jeep and I could only fix grins at her while we ate. She didn't leave until we started in on the cupcakes.

As she was tramping down the stairs, I insisted that Lyle lock the door. Jeep looked into my eyes for the longest time before he turned to Lyle. "Yeah, Lyle. I'd feel better if you locked your door."

A few minutes later, we were naked and sprawled upon Lyle's bed. Jeep had a thick cock with a bouncy circumcised head. Of course, Lyle and I had seen it countless times, but we had never seen it in rigid glory. I gripped Jeep's cock shaft and rubbed the head with my thumb.

"Oh, shit," Jeep said. "This is gay."

I stopped his mouth with a kiss. Again, he responded. His tongue pushed into my mouth while I fondled his cock. Jeep kissed hard and let me masturbate him, but he still had not summoned the nerve to grab my cock or Lyle's.

"Tip." Lyle was feeling left out. "Quit hogging the goodies." He gripped the head of Jeep's cock with two fingers, forcing my hand down the shaft.

"Are you okay, Jeep?" I asked. Lyle and I were still hot from our unfinished blow jobs, and we had already made our peace with our sexual desires. Jeep was still in the virgin stage, uncertain whether he dared follow his inclinations.

"Yeah," he said. "It feels good."

"I need to come." Lyle had become rather insistent. "I was right on the edge when we got interrupted."

"So was I." I tossed Jeep a significant look. He responded by reaching for my dick. He emitted a loud gasp as his hand made contact. He huffed his breath out as he squeezed my shaft and felt the head of my dick.

"That's a hell of a thrill, isn't it?" Lyle asked rhetorically. "The first time you grab a cock—it's like nothing else."

"Yeah," Jeep muttered, half dazed. "Blew the heterosexual shit right out my ass." He grinned at us. "Not literally. I didn't poop." His eyes glinted. "How about we get back to what you guys were doing when I interrupted?"

I turned my head to Lyle and spoke softly. "How about you suck off Jeep, while I blow you?"

"Really?"

I grinned at him. "Yeah, you said I was hogging Jeep's dick."

"You haven't stopped hogging it."

"That's a contemptible lie," I said, shocked at the perfidy of it. Lyle and I both had our hands on Jeep's cock. I was pounding the shaft relentlessly, while Lyle was twisting his fist around the head.

"Hey, guys, quit talking about me. I'm here," Jeep said.

"How about your cock, Tip?" Lyle said. "Maybe Jeep doesn't want to suck you off." I stopped stroking Jeep's cock. Lyle kept his fingers on the tip of it, but he also ceased stimulating it.

"Then he doesn't have to do it," I said, watching Jeep's reaction. "I only said that you would suck his dick. I didn't say that Jeep had to do any sucking."

A baffled expression suffused Jeep's face. He opened his mouth as though he wanted to say something. He shut it again without uttering a word.

"It's okay, Jeep," I said hurriedly. "Nobody has to do anything he doesn't want. I'm going to suck Lyle's dick because I want to. I want him to come in my mouth."

Jeep nodded at Lyle, who had already fastened his lips on Jeep's swollen penis. Jeep's bafflement turned into wonder as Lyle's eager mouth performed its duty. I turned toward Lyle's cock, but I kept my own erection pointed so Jeep would have easy access when he broke down. I knew that he would give in to his natural impulses; it was only a matter of time.

Lyle's cock was just as wonderful as before. His dick head slid between my lips, my no-longer virgin lips, my lips that had touched his cock before, and passed along my tongue. It was in me, in my mouth, and it was wonderful. I pulled my head back and tortured his cock's head with my lips and the tip of my tongue. I licked down his smooth shaft and tickled his balls with my tongue. The hair on his balls had been clipped close, because he, like the rest of the team, wore a bikini clip. High school coaches did not want stray public hairs bushing out the sides of our swim briefs. The close trim made his balls feel fuzzier. I licked them for a while before I returned to his dick head. I had allowed him a respite, so he would not spurt too soon. Nevertheless, his dick grew thicker as I resumed sucking. The head of it became rock solid. When Lyle came, it was going to be a blast.

As I blew Lyle, Lyle continued sucking off Jeep. Lyle's mouth was making wet, smacking sounds, similar to the smacks my mouth made on his cock as it smoothly slid toward the back of my mouth. I wondered how deep I could take it. I've always had a powerful gag reflex, but I was no more gagging on Lyle's dick than I would eating a bowl of banana ice cream with chocolate chips and cherries. Except that Lyle's dick was better than ice cream.

As I sucked, I felt a curious sensation. A wet mouth touched the head of my dick, still erect and ready to blast. Jeep had broken through his inhibitions, made his peace with the gods (the if-it-swells-ride-it divinities, not the thou-shalt-not-enjoy-thy-neighbor's-cock authorities), and joined our three-way blowjob. Surprisingly quickly, he passed through the apprehensively tasting and exploring phase, and was soon blowing me like a seasoned cocksucker.

I was close to coming before Jeep started on me; within two minutes, I could hardly hold out. Jeep began to squirm as he sucked, writhing so flamboyantly that I knew he was hitting the peak of orgasm.

"Umm, umm." Lyle was moaning as Jeep's cum poured into his mouth. I worked Lyle's cock harder, feeling it arch tautly as it filled with the semen pumping up from his balls. I tasted that sweet, spunky fluid, and I let it paint my tongue before I swallowed it down. Somehow, the cum entering my mouth inflamed me more, or I was just ready, because I felt the ripples of approaching orgasm again. But that time there was no interruption. No one burst through Lyle's door as my virgin throat took Lyle's cum, and my own semen spurted with untamed discard into Jeep's mouth.

Jeep was swallowing, just as I was swallowing, and Lyle was swallowing. We consumed one another's spunk, and the vast circle of our desire was unbroken, as we lay twisted and still wriggling with hot gay pleasure as the last holy drops oozed from our cocks into one another's mouths.

We lay connected for a time in satiated bliss. Finally, we broke apart and stared at each other with amazement. "Holy, fuck!" Jeep gasped at length. "Do you guys realize what we've just done?" He was commenting on the enormity of the change in our relationship, but the way he said it sounded ridiculous. I was about to make a sarcastic remark about "realizing" I had just come in his mouth, but Lyle chipped in.

"We took the gay path," Lyle said. "Tip and I were talking about it earlier."

"Yeah, Jeep. I'm gay. Homosexual. All the way."

Jeep's face went ashen, and his eyes widened. "Are you planning to announce this? I'm just asking. My poppa will probably pull out his nine millimeter and shoot me deader than a run-down possum." He looked scared.

I shook my head. "That's a decision we're gonna have to make together. It affects all of us. If I come out, or Lyle does, then we're all affected. Even Rick and Mart; not to mention, the younger guys on the team will get harassed if everyone knows that we like gay sex."

"It's not like that anymore, Tip," Lyle said. "It's okay to have gay friends."

"In rural Oregon?"

Lyle looked crestfallen. "Yeah. That's true. We're a farming community. There's lots of bigotry—especially from the churches. Especially if they discovered the pagan connection."

"Guilt by association," Jeep said. Lyle's last comment struck him belatedly. "What pagan connection?"

"I don't feel guilty," I said. "I'm feeling euphoric."

"Yeah, I feel that too," Jeep said. "What did you mean about being pagan?"

"Let's not decide tonight." Lyle's eyes lit up with mischief. "Read some more from your brother's journal. Not about Skip's initiation. Find a different passage. Let Jeep feel what we've been feeling. Let him feel your voice."

"My voice?"

"Yeah, Tip. It's the way you read Thad's journal aloud. Wait until you hear him, Jeep. Tip gets into that pagan ritual and the hot sex, and I get into his voice. Tip, your voice goes through my whole body."

"Hot shorts! Pagan ritual? I want to hear about that."

"Yeah, wait until Tip starts reading. You'll feel it. It's like his voice licks your dick and pushes up your ass."

I had lifted one of Thad's later notebooks, way out of sequence, because I wanted to scan it for any mention of what happened to my brothers. I opened at random and started reading.

❖

Thad's Journal: The Fourth of April, continued

Hyacinthos held his ivy *thyrsus* in his left hand and his cock in his right. He rocked his hips to the rhythm of the throbbing music as he jacked his cock toward the circle of celebrants. The Uranian power was emanating from his jutting penis, and the power passed through us like radiation.

"Bacchantes of Dionysus, the moon is full, the crops are ripening, and the wheel of the year has passed its center. Once again, we taste the rod of potency and consume the seed of the spasm. Once again, we abandon ourselves in consummation of the anal mysteries."

He raised his wand, pounding his pecker wildly, while the drummers pounded with ever-increasing tempo. We tossed our used condoms into a receptacle, and placed new ones on our cocks. Apollo seized Orpheus and began humping his ass riotously.

❖

Tipper's Tale

"Holy shit, that's hot." Jeep was panting with lust. "Where did you get that, Tip?" His hand having slid into his groin, he was rubbing his bare cock.

"It's his brother's journal," Lyle said again. "His brother was initiated into a gay pagan cult, and we've been reading about it."

"And sucking dicks," Jeep added, grinning mischievously.

"No, we just started sucking today," Lyle said with refreshing honesty. "Are you ready to come again?"

Jeep removed his hand from his dick. "After the way you sucked me off? I won't come again for a week." We laughed at that ridiculous exaggeration, and Jeep looked a little shamefaced as he corrected himself. "At least for another hour."

"Lyle," came a voice from down below. "Dinner is ready. Will your little playfellows be joining us?"

Lyle shot us a helpless look, which provoked giggles. I glanced around Lyle's room, with his laptop depicting competition swimmers on its screensaver, his brightly painted model spacecraft, and pictures of guys in bright colored swimsuits pasted on his walls.

"Does your mother think you're still eight years old?" Jeep asked.

"Yes."

"Then she's just like mine."

"Holy shit," I said, remembering that my mom had promised corned beef and cabbage for supper. "I have to be getting home. I'm late."

"Me, too," Jeep said. "I better go, Lyle."

"Nuts," Lyle said. "Call your parents and tell them you're eating here."

I tried to imagine sitting at the table with Lyle's parents, while I had their son's semen in my stomach. "It wouldn't be fair to your mother," I said, pulling on my briefs. I dressed quickly, as did Jeep.

Lyle watched us, grinning as we covered our goodies. "How about tomorrow?"

"Yeah. After we work out."

"Me, too?" Jeep asked.

"Of course, Jeep," I replied. "We're a team."

Jeep grinned. "A swim team? Or a cocksucking team?"

Lyle's answer was enigmatic. "Both of those."

"And much, much more," I said.

CHAPTER SIX

Tipper's Tale

When I rushed through the door with my book bag and gym bag, my parents were sitting at the table. Mom looked miffed, and Pop was downright pissed. "Where have you been?" he demanded. "Your mother promised your favorite supper."

"Give me a break, Pop." My eyes lingered on the platter covered with a steaming corned beef brisket surrounded by cooked cabbage. "We had swim practice right after class, and we had to work out. Then Jeep, Lyle, and I got together for a research project." I left that one vague, omitting the details of that research project. I didn't exactly lie, but I did create the impression that our research was school related.

"Okay, wash up," my father said. Did I detect a note of relief in his voice? What did he fear?

"If I'd thought I would have been five minutes longer, Pop, I would have telephoned."

"Your mother and I will wait for two minutes."

Such an authoritarian. My natural rebellion bubbled up, but I suppressed my urge to retort. Maybe I was maturing. I realized that my father's abrupt manner and general bossiness came from fear— fear mingled with love and loss, though his loss was probably self-inflicted.

"I'll just be a second," I called over my shoulder as I thundered down the hall.

I shut the bathroom door and examined my face in the mirror. Was this the face that sucked Lyle's cock? No sign of my recent activities could be detected. I did not look a whit different, save for a secret smile that I could not utterly erase. I rinsed my mouth—just in case my parents could smell dick on my breath. I checked my clothes for stains, but found none. I looked presentable. I looked completely normal. But I felt far from normal. And I wanted to shout to the rafters that I had relished *everything* I had done with my friends.

When I was seated at the table, Pop asked me to say grace. Praying before meals wasn't always the custom in our house. On holidays, or when the three of us gathered for dinner, Pop sometimes asked. Often he skipped the ritual. That night, based upon some mysterious *raison d'être* or *raison d'état*, he selected me to mumble the words.

I bowed my head, pressed my palms together, and entreated, "I pray that all humanity find peace and harmony." Feeling that was the prayer that would do my parents the most good, I picked up my silverware and speared a piece of corned beef.

My father's eyes were bugging out. "What was that?" He pointed into the air above my head to refer to the ascending supplication.

"A prayer. You asked me to pray. I prayed. I thought it was rather good." He should have been grateful that I didn't pray to Dionysus for greater pleasure during gay sex, but I didn't mention it.

My explanation caused Pop even more outrage. "You didn't even mention God. You could have been praying to Buddha, for all I know." Thankfully, he didn't ask me to try again, but picked up his knife and fork. The garlicky scent of the corned beef was enough to overcome a true believer's religious duties, much less my father's. Pop was a big time churchgoer, and Christianity ran in his blood, but I secretly suspected that in Pop's mind God more resembled a John Deere harvester than an old man in a white robe.

I forked a piece of corned beef into my mouth along with a chunk of cabbage that Mom had cooked to the perfect texture. It was ambrosia, and as I swallowed, I pictured it sliding down to mingle with Lyle's semen. The image was surpassingly pleasant.

My parents were drinking authentic English-style bitters, but I was given an off-brand cola. Not even Coke or Pepsi. I would have preferred the bitters too, but I knew better than to suggest it. My father would pitch seven kinds of conniptions if I requested an alcoholic beverage. I concentrated on my glazed carrots and chewed my corned beef. Dessert turned out to be a tall chocolate cake. We all enjoyed gigantic mugs of milky coffee with our cake.

"Tipper," Mom said tentatively. "Tomorrow night is the election for officers of the Muskrat Creek Christian Association. You know that your father is vying to be elected president of the association."

During the election two years previously, Dieter Hardrein had clobbered Pop. Since losing by a landslide, my father had sharpened his political skills, while Dieter Hardrein had been photographed leaving a white power meeting at the grange. Though people in our neighborhood were hardly open-minded, even they drew the line at overt racism. Pop was running against Dieter Hardrein again, and I hoped that my father trounced the despicable Hardrein. If Pop won, he would be too busy to pry into my affairs.

"Yeah, good luck with the election, Pop," I said. "I've been pulling for you." *Pulling* was the literal truth. To enhance Pop's chances of getting elected, I had jacked off six times while reciting a chant for success, which I discovered in one of Thad's books. I hoped the spell would work because I didn't want that much ritual masturbation to go to waste. I timed my orgasms to coincide with prescribed ritual words, which was more difficult than I had imagined. Up until then, I had masturbated without any deep thought and let my semen fly when it would. I ruined three pairs of briefs getting the timing right. There was no way I could toss stains like I'd produced into Mom's laundry basket, and as for undressing in front of Rick or Mart—forget it. Those wretched breeders still thought of masturbation as self-abuse, rather than a sacrosanct commemoration of a boy's concord with timeless night.

"Anyway, the point is, Tip," my father added, "you'll be on your own tomorrow evening. Your mother and I will be gone from six o'clock until late. You shouldn't expect us home before eleven. So if anything should happen, call down to the bunkhouse."

"I'll fix a meat loaf," Mom added. "Some potatoes you can heat in the microwave, and some green peas."

"That will be fine," I said. "Do you mind if I invite a couple of friends over?"

"For a party?" Pop asked, his face darkening and his eyebrows pulling together. His face was a darker shade of red than his carroty hair.

"Not a party, Pop. I know better than to do something so stupid."

"How many friends?" Mom said. "Not the whole swimming team?"

"No, no. Just Jeep and Lyle. Like I said, we're involved in a research project. For school. It's taking a lot of time. I guess that's what life is like for high school seniors."

Pop's eyes met Mom's, and some bizarre breeder communication passed between them. Their communion was enough to send a cold chill up my spine and drop a blue sink down my gullet. However, the result was different than I expected.

"I imagine that will be all right," Pop said. "Jeep and Lyle seem like responsible boys. Just make sure that you clean up after you eat. Wash your dishes, and don't leave a mess for your mother."

Then I knew. Pop and Mom were planning to host a party for their fellow Christians following the election. They wouldn't be home until two. Jeep, Lyle, and I could make gay whoopee—just so long as we cleaned up afterward.

After supper, Pop helped Mom load the dishwasher. I had just sat in front of the television, when Pop cleared his throat. "Tip, your mother and I have to go out for a bit." That was all he said.

"Are you going to indulge in some last-minute campaigning, arm-twisting, and calling in old favors?" I asked. My father actually grinned at me. I was astounded. "Pop, if I can help in any way? You want me to come with you?"

"No, you're not part of the adult group yet," he said, looking pleased. "You relax this evening."

I watched television while Pop made two telephone calls and Mom changed into a dress. When they were ready, I walked them to their car.

"Show them that you know where the bodies are buried, Pop."
My father actually laughed. I tossed a shovel into the backseat.
"Hold this up as a prop."

When Mom and Pop were safely distant, I took my secret key
and opened the door to Thad and Tye's room. I replaced several
notebooks that I had already studied and extracted a couple of others.

Confident that I was safe from detection, I searched deeper. I
pawed through Thad's socks and briefs and found nothing. Under
Tye's underwear, I discovered a silver neck pendant with a satyr
design. The satyr's erect penis was shiny, as though well rubbed.

Before locking the door, I checked for evidence of my presence.
As I scanned the room, I lingered upon the bookshelves. It occurred
to me that the books might hide letters or instructions. Suppose
either Thad or Tye had foreseen his fate and left secret clues for me
to stumble on later?

Thus far, I had not paid enough attention to Thad's books. I had
read a few random tomes, and I was using spells from one book.
But I had hardly begun to look through them all. I began to remove
books from the collection, leaf through them, and replace them as
they had been.

Thad had collected books on a variety of subjects, some of
them unnerving. More carefully this time, I examined titles of
subjects like witchcraft or Wicca, pagan rituals, occultism, folklore,
anthropology, primitive races and customs, mythology, ancient
magical practices, and ritual and initiation. None of those appeared
to be particularly threatening, but somewhat more ominous were
those that featured secret societies, the Rosicrucians, Egyptology,
the Temple of Set, the Church of Satan, the O.T.O., the Golden
Dawn, and Freemasonry. Other books dealt with people like
Aleister Crowley, Andrew Chumbley, Anton LaVey, Austin Osman
Spare, and Michael Aquino. Finally, there were sinister looking
tomes discussing ceremonial and black magic, grimoire, alchemy,
hermetics, the Kabalah, chaos magick, demonology, and Satanism.

Thad's fascination had carried him pretty fucking far into the
twilight world, if this collection was any evidence. The thought of
black magic and devil worshipping gave me a sick feeling in the
pit of my stomach. I couldn't imagine my brother getting involved

in something like that. However, I consoled myself that reading about Satanism was a far cry from practicing the dark side of the Christian religion, and nothing in Thad's journals suggested that he was a Satanist. As far as I could tell, he had joined this neo-pagan brotherhood so he could enjoy their flamboyant sex orgies.

I slipped one book titled *Homosexuality in Wicca* from the shelf. The chapters described groups like the Minoan Gathering, the Fellowship of the Phoenix, the Radical Faeries, the Brothers of *Cannophori*, the Cult of Cybele, the Apollo Brotherhood, the Hectite Tradition, the Feri Faith, and the Green Man folklore. These sounded somewhat like the group my brothers had joined, and I hoped the book's descriptions would give me inspiration. I packed the bookshelf loosely, so my mother would not notice the disappearance of a single volume. I sincerely doubted that she read them ever.

Back in my room, I selected appropriate passages for the next evening's reading. I decided that I would read the rest of Skip's initiation to Jeep and Lyle. After they had been immersed in the vivid details of Skip's anal initiation, perhaps they'd be open for an anal ritual of our own devising. I checked my supply of lube and two boxes of extra-strength condoms I had bought on the way home.

"Whatcha need extra-strength for, Tipper?" Mr. Tubbs, the crapulous druggist had asked. "Them rubbers are for the back-door crowd."

"They sound safer," I said, delighted that Tubbs had confirmed my assumptions. I wanted the best condoms for anal sex, but I wasn't sure how to ask for them. I couldn't fucking well say, "Gee, Mr. Tubbs, I'm expecting my friends to buttfuck me tomorrow night." Such barefaced honesty wouldn't fly in the rural community where I lived.

"Well, they're the toughest buggers," Mr. Tubbs said, his chins jiggling obscenely as he nodded. "But mainly the fudge packers use 'em. You're not into buggery, are you, Tip? Just because you're an athlete don't mean any pop's gonna like you stretching his daughter's butthole."

"I can't imagine any father would be overjoyed about any teenage boy buying condoms. But here you are selling them to us."

Mr. Tubbs chortled merrily. "I'm not *selling* them to you, Tipper. I'm giving them to you." He extracted a fifty-dollar bill from his cash till. "Here, take this. It will help pay for gas and food when you drive to Klamath Falls on Friday."

Still chuckling, he handed me the condoms and the cash before waddling back to his prescriptions.

❖

The next day was misery on wheels. Middle Eastern history started the day with an in-class essay about T. E. Lawrence's contribution to Anglo-Arabic diplomacy. In physics, I discovered a way to transport matter into another dimension—or so I claimed when I lost my lab notes—but my teacher didn't buy my explanation. In English literature, Ms. Malcolm slammed us with a multiple-guess quiz on *Wuthering Heights* that made me want to barf upside down and backward.

Later, the team spent an hour in the pool, but none of us could do anything right. The water was much colder than usual, and one of the sophomores got a muscle cramp and had to be rescued. As I was swimming my laps, the fierce cold shriveled my cock until it withdrew into my pelvis. Losing my dick would throw a damper on the sizzling gay sex I had planned with Jeep and Lyle.

At Beaver Dam Fitness Club, we worked our lower bodies in preparation for our next swim meet, two nights away. We had trounced the Pendleton Water Bucks the previous Friday, so we would be swimming against the Klamath Falls Dippers. The Dippers were only noteworthy for their choice of swimsuits so we were favored to win. Thrashing the Dippers would pit us against the invincible Silverton Copperheads two weeks later. We pedaled on the exercise bikes, ran the gluteal programs on the step climbers, squatted with barbells, stepped up risers with weights, and worked our quads, our calves, our hamstrings, and our asses off. In near agony, we changed into our team swimsuits in the locker room, even Mart and Rick dressing as team members, and headed for the sauna.

Picking our way past the senior citizens thronging the edge of the pool, we encountered five guys in brilliant yellow swim briefs prancing toward us. "It's those fuckin' yellowtails," Rick hissed confidentially, loud enough to be heard two miles away. *Yellowtails* was a belittling term we'd pinned on the Silverton swim team. They attended Copper Valley High, so they called their team the Copperheads. The school's teams wore trademark golden yellow uniforms to reflect the various ores mined in the town during the nineteenth century.

When he saw us, the captain of the Copperheads minced and faked a girlish pose. "Oh, it's the Rats from Muskrat High."

"Why don't you transsexuals call yourselves the *Tumbleweed Pussies* and be done with it," another Copperhead said. "No sense in you ladyboys beating around your sage bushes."

"Ignore these crow shit yellowtails, guys," I said.

"What are you doing this far from Silverton, yellow britches?"

"We drove down to teach you llama pokers how to trample water."

"You've got too much chlorine up your poop tube," Mart said.

"Don't argue with them, Mart. A few weeks from now, they'll be watching our asses while we swim away to the state finals." We had to beat the Copperheads to match up against the Fur Traders in Astoria. If we won there, we would face off against one final team.

The temperature gauge in the sauna was reading one-twenty degrees. A rotund woman was occupying one side. We climbed to the top racks of the other two sides. I would have preferred to stretch out, but there wasn't room. I drank my water and felt it flow out my pores as fast as it went down my throat.

As usual, Rick had an objection. "That was a weak comeback, Tip. Who wants the yellowtails watching our asses?"

The heavyset woman raised her head. Due to the steam, I couldn't see her clearly, but I sensed her outrage.

I poked Rick's bicep and explained patiently, as if to a brain-damaged infant. "If our competitors are watching our asses, then it means we're ahead of them. Us winning—them losing, which is the way I prefer it."

"Me, too." Jeep gave Rick a straight look, certain that our teammate still did not get it. "If we're watching their asses, then we're the losers."

"Can't you boys choose a more elevating topic?" the woman asked without anyone inviting her to join the debate. "All this talk of human derrières is so demeaning."

"We're speaking metaphorically, ma'am," Lyle explained, using language only he would understand. He probably aced the *Wuthering Heights* quiz. I was glad that he spoke up, because Rick would probably have advised the woman to "get stuffed," which could get us in trouble with the club management. An incident would draw Coach Reece into the picture.

"Metaphorically?" the woman sniffed.

"Yes, ma'am," Lyle continued. "We are the Muskrats. We'll be swimming competitively against those rude boys in the yellow swimwear, and they were making obnoxious comments to us. We only responded in kind."

"So you're our home team," she said. "Forget what I said. I hope you boys whip those Yellowtails."

Jeep drove that day. His father had bought him a 2008 burgundy Honda Element with four-wheel drive. Lyle sat in the front passenger seat, Rick and I sat on the fold down rear seats, and Mart sat on the floor. I had offered my lap, but Mart froze me with a direct look and dropped his butt onto the rubber mat. Jeep dropped off Mart first, and then Rick. He drove a mile down the road from Rick's place before pulling onto the shoulder. Then he leaned across the console and kissed Lyle. The sight of my friends kissing sent a thrill through me. The beauty of two boys kissing awakened feelings I could never describe. I felt an ache, a deep ache, a good ache, an ache of longing and satisfaction combined.

They kissed for a long time. When they broke apart, both boys heaved a sigh.

Jeep turned in his seat and studied the logistics. "Don't feel left out, Tip. I'm gonna give you the same treatment, as soon as I can reach you."

"Back to my place," I said. "My parents should have left by now." I pointed at the sky, which had turned dark green. "Better hurry. A storm is coming."

CHAPTER SEVEN

Tipper's Tale

As we pulled into our drive, I saw that Pop's car was gone. Mom's car was parked beside mine, which was to be expected. Our alpacas were safely tucked away in the barn, and the buckaroos were crowded into the chuck wagon next to the bunkhouse, where they were enjoying Ol' Cookie's fabulous pork roast.

Just as we stepped out of Jeep's Element, the sky opened. The hailstones rained down vengefully, and we raced for shelter. The house was dark, but the porch light beamed with welcome glow. Mom had left a note beside the microwave, telling me how to heat up our dinner.

Mom had prepared a meat loaf, as she had promised. It was already sliced so I added a little extra spice and dumped a substantial amount of barbecue sauce over it. I set it in the microwave and turned it to high heat. "Shouldn't you cook that on medium heat?" Lyle asked, swatting my ass.

I swatted him back. "Yeah, but I only know how to punch in the number of minutes and hit start."

"Tip, that meatloaf is gonna dry out if you cook it on high."

"I loaded it up with barbecue sauce to keep it moist, Lyle."

"Gourmet cooking at its finest."

"Sarcasm is low humor Lyle."

While Lyle was messing with the microwave, I turned to get the plates. Without warning, I discovered that Jeep was right in front of me, his face pushing toward mine. "Your turn," he said just before our lips met.

My heartbeat increased as my lips pressed against Jeep's mouth. His lips were hot, slightly moist, and alive with need. Every cell in his lips worked against my cells, yet still they cooperated in making tiny movements, retractions, contractions, shifts, and tingles. I had never thought about the mechanics of a kiss, and I didn't then either, but I felt the hot motion against my own lips. Then came Jeep's tongue, pressing first against my lips, then pushing between them, parting them as our kiss became more open-mouthed.

Jeep purred like a kitten as his tongue probed deeper into my mouth. My arms were around him; I let my hands slide down his back until I was gripping the cheeks of his firm ass. As I sucked his tongue, I rubbed my hard cock against his own erection. I gripped his butt tighter, pulling him against me.

"Come on, boys, knock it off," Lyle said. "We will have ample opportunities to play after we eat. Meanwhile, dinner's ready, and I'm starved."

I glanced out the window before sitting at the table. The hail had stopped, but the rain was coming down hard. Distant flashes of lightning lit up the peaks of the surrounding mountains.

The meat loaf was not dried out, and everything looked steamy delicious. A natural cook, Lyle had heated the dinner to perfection. My own efforts, however well intentioned, would not have been so well performed. Before we sat at the table, Jeep produced a bottle from his bag.

"How about a bottle of nineteen ninety-four Cabernet Sauvignon?" he asked.

Lyle grinned ebulliently. "Wine. Now we're pissing with the full-sized dogs."

Jeep used an attachment on his pocketknife to open the bottle. My parents never drank wine, so we didn't have any wine glasses. I provided the best I could, and we dashed generous slugs into orange juice glasses.

"Have you been carrying this bottle around school all day?" I asked, examining the label.

"I was careful with it."

"Can you imagine what would have happened if Coach Reece had found out you had it?"

"Whatever you say about Coach Reece, he's not a snoop," I said. "But Principal Relish is another story. He'd look up our asses in a heartbeat."

"Principal Relish wouldn't have found the wine bottle in my rectum. It wouldn't fit."

"Did you try sticking it up your ass?" I asked. "You know that from experience?"

Ignoring my witticisms, Lyle asked, "Where did you get it?"

"It's a Bolivian wine. Costs a fortune in the United States, if you can find it. My parents have two thousand bottles stacked in the basement. They'll never miss one."

After we had eaten everything, I buried the empty wine bottle in the bottom of the trash and carried the sack out to the garbage can. I shuddered to think what would happen if my parents found that bottle. A vicious inquisition would be the least of my problems. Pop would probably order me to quit the swim team.

Mom's note directed me to the refrigerator, where I discovered our dessert. My eyes widened at the sight. I lifted out the banana cream pie quivering in multiple levels and topped high with meringue. I sliced thick wedges, leaving two slices for Mom and Pop when they returned from their night of celebration—or pity party if Pop got trounced.

Disdaining the dishwasher, Lyle began hand-washing our dishes, Jeep dried, bouncing his butt against Lyle's every time he grabbed a plate, a fork, or a glass. I received the towel-dried items from Jeep, along with a buttock bounce, and carefully put them in their proper place. A gay camaraderie had arisen among us, a sexual understanding both covert and intense. For some time over three years, we had showered together, swum together, competed and cooperated together; we had been a part of the same team. But now we shared something deeper, a secret passion and knowledge that linked us tighter than anything we had known before.

When the dishes were finished, I took Jeep's and Lyle's hands and led them to my brothers' room. Both boys fell silent as we entered, as though they were walking upon sacred ground. Walking barefoot across the carpet, I showed them Thad's books, the view from the nailed windows, and the drawer full of notebooks.

"Are you going to read to us before we…uh…have sex?" Lyle asked. He was taking the sex for granted, and I liked his assumption that gay sex lay in the offing. His stutter excited me. The hesitation in his voice suggested that he was prepared to go further than we already had.

"Yeah," I said, my voice going suddenly nectarous. "I planned to read more of Skip's initiation."

"What happens next?" Jeep said. "Skip already sucked a cock." He stopped talking, his eyes widening with inspiration and his face reddening with some emotion that was not embarrassment. "Oh. Did he…I mean, did Skip…oh, man."

"Yeah, oh, man," I said. "It's a description of his anal initiation. Skip gets buttfucked—just like Thad." I placed sticky emphasis on what I said next. "He gets buttfucked—and *likes* it. After one of them fucks Skip, the boys remove Skip's blindfold. Then Skip has to choose a boy from the circle and fuck his ass."

We inspected my brothers' room, after I impressed upon my friends the importance of keeping it just as my mother left it. I locked the door, and we slipped into my own room. Lyle and Jeep promptly stripped to their underwear and flounced down upon my bed. I pulled off my outer clothing and sat beside them.

"Let's hear about Skip's anal initiation."

I drew a deep breath, released it slowly, and began to read. My cock was stiffening in my briefs before I uttered the first word. My voice grew raspy with wanton lust as I mouthed Thad's words.

❖

Thad's Journal: The Ninth of March, continued

"*Evoe*, Bacchus. *Evoe*, Pan," I whispered sibilantly as my blood throbbed in my veins. The untamed piping and drumming beat upon my ears. "Here it comes. Skip is going to get fucked."

Hyacinthos asked Skip the essential questions, the same life-changing questions I had been asked.

"Don't be anxious. You gotta want it."

"I want it." Skip's face was flushed, whether from pleasure, or embarrassment, or lust, or some other emotion, no one could say. His face flush spread across his shoulders and down his body until the cheeks of his proffered ass reddened.

"Good. Take deep breaths. Don't squeeze. Don't clamp down on the cock with your asshole. Push. Push as though you were taking a shit. When you push, you're letting it in. If you squeeze, you're resisting. When you squeeze, anal penetration hurts. Getting fucked should feel good. It should feel good the first time and every time. If taking a cock starts to hurt, draw deeper breaths and push harder. You gotta relax and let it happen."

I was so close to Skip that I could hear every word, words so like those Hyacinthos had used to help me take my first cock.

I watched Skip suck in a deep breath and blow it out. His body loosened with unconditional acceptance. Sandes, an anally skilled sophomore, was chosen to stick his dork into Skip. Sandes was wearing a sanctified smirk as he pressed his thick cock against Skip's asshole. I could see Sandes moving closer to Skip, gradually worming his cock into my friend's callipygian ass. Due to Skip's blindfold, I could not see his eyes, but I witnessed the curl of his mouth. A feral lust twisted Skip's lips as Sandes's phenomenal cock invaded his asshole.

❖

Tipper's Tale

"That's hot shit," Jeep said. "What the fuck was that word?"

I snickered because I knew what word he meant. When I first read that passage, I had to look it up too. "Callipygian," I said. "It means having shapely buttocks."

Jeep giggled and checked out his ass in the mirror.

"You're callipygian too, Tipper," Lyle said, brushing his hand across my butt. The sensation of being touched so intimately hit me like a bolt from Zeus. I felt like the divine catamite. The room swam until I feared I'd pass out. I set the notebook on the floor, prepared to offer my ass on the spot.

However, Jeep yelped, "Hey, keep reading. This is making me hot."

❖

Thad's Journal: The Ninth of March, continued

Skip's cock was hardening again, swelling between his legs even as he hunched on all fours, taking Sandes's cock up his ass.

"That's the way," Hyacinthos said. "You're taking it like a horny catamite. You're a natural, Initiate."

Skip moaned as Sandes thrust forward. Sandes was pressing his hips against Skip's buttocks, and a grin split Skip's lips as he pushed back against the cock within him. Just as he sucked dick, Skip took Sandes's erection up his ass with a hint of braggadocio. Skip's cock gave a distinct lurch; it bucked with a squirt of pre-cum that spurted thinly from his pee hole.

"You've got it inside you, Skip," Hyacinthos said, as a triumphant cacophony of bells and tambourines sounded. "All the way. You have a cock in your ass."

❖

Tipper's Tale

My hand had been rubbing my dick as I read the last two paragraphs, but I was unaware of it until Lyle grabbed my wrist. "Don't jerk off, Tip. Save it for us."

"Yeah." Jeep's voice was raspy with lust.

❖

Thad's Journal: The Ninth of March, continued

"I like it," Skip said and moaned. "I like having a cock in me. It feels good." He hunched forward and pushed back. "I'd take every one of you. Gang bang my ass to orgasm."

The drums rolled, the pipes skirled, the bells rang, and the tambourines shook. I rattled the tambourine someone had placed in my hand, and I heard my own voice, husky with lust, howling words of gay abandonment at my friend while the silvery moon illuminated my swollen cock.

❖

Tipper's Tale

"Oh, yes." Jeep's cock was swollen in his briefs. He rubbed his protuberance against Lyle's ass. Lyle did not try to pull away, but let Jeep dry hump him. Lyle wiggled his ass cheeks to give Jeep more friction.

I felt left out. "Guys, you gotta wait for me. Don't start fucking without me."

"Finish reading this shit first." Jeep was insistent that I continue reading while he continued rubbing Lyle's dick. "I wanna hear what happened. It's hotter than fuckin' hell."

Lyle whispered something into Jeep's ear, and Jeep gave another wiggle with his ass. "Hotter than our red swim briefs," Jeep repeated for my benefit. I was tempted to stop reading and pile in beside them, but they stopped acting out our ineluctable wishes, so I went back to the story.

❖

Thad's Journal: The Ninth of March, continued

Sandes thrust against Skip's ass, pushing deep inside. Skip grinned with pleasure as Sandes's dick opened him; he demonstrated his lust as he waggled his ass upon the impaling flesh; he proved his worth as he drew forward. Sandes pulled back, an expression of amazement coloring his face. Then Sandes pushed forward again as Skip thrust his ass back to meet him. Sandes grunted as Skip's hot wrestler's ass ground his cock, squeezing it within the tube that would not hold still.

I despaired of ever using my ass the way Skip could wiggle his callipygian buttocks. Sandes was moaning with impending orgasm after a few thrusts, but Skip showed no mercy. Even blindfolded, my friend ground his ass upon Skip's protuberant pecker, just enough to bite deep into Sandes's cock. Sandes' face paled as his blood flooded his pelvis, hardening his cock to near-impossible stiffness.

"*Evoe*, Pan, *Evoe*, Pan, *Paniskoi*, *Aegipan*," Sandes shouted, his head thrown back, his throat naked to the white moon. "*Evoe*, Pan, *Evoe*, Pan."

Skip was bouncing his ass violently against Sandes's cock. Sandes was thrusting, but Skip looked more like the aggressor. He was fucking Sandes's cock with his asshole. My own cock was near to squirting as I watched the ritual. Sandes's orgasm lasted longer than I would have believed possible, and Skip continued to milk the cock in his ass long after its last drops were spent. At last, almost in relief, Sandes pulled back from Skip, and his cock popped free.

Stunned by the exuberant passion there unleashed, Hyacinthos approached Skip with some awe. "Initiate, you have most sublimely followed the path of Hyacinthos and opened the way of the catamite. Are you prepared to see the circle?"

"Yes." Skip's shouted agreement was still echoing off the mountain crags as Orpheus removed the blindfold.

Apollo, his head concealed in the bull mask, spoke to Skip. "You have met my lover Hyacinthos," he said, just as he had spoken to me. "Hyacinthos has taught you the way of the catamite. I am the Priest of Apollo, and to me you shall prove your worth by following the course of Uranus. Behold the offerings."

We who had been initiated turned and presented our eager rumps. I bent, placed my hands on my knees, thrust my ass back, and wriggled in open invitation. I sincerely hoped that my friend would fuck me.

"Make your selection, Initiate." While Skip made his decision, Apollo lubricated Skip's hard cock and slipped an extra-strength condom over it. He lubricated the condom again.

"Take me," I shouted, glancing over my shoulder. "Fuck my ass, Skip."

"No, take me."

"I give the best ass."

"My fuck-hole is hot for you."

Other guys were making their offers, each vying to receive Skip's cock. Competition was fierce. Later, I was never sure whether Skip even recognized me from my rear. Whether he chose me out of loyalty, or whether my butt cheeks offered the most enticing package, it was my ass he selected.

I yelped with joy when Skip placed his hands on my hips. Grumbling with disappointment, the rest of the circle re-formed around us. We were pushed close to where Dr. Bromius sat. Every boy, along with our professor, began masturbating freely with one hand, while with the other they played upon their musical instruments.

"Hi, Thad," Skip breathed in my ear.

"Call me Adonis," I responded with a gasp as I felt his thick cock slipping between my buttocks.

❖

Tipper's Tale

Lyle was moaning like a horny cow. "Ohmigod! That's so fuckin' hot."

Jeep added his sharp gasps to Lyle's moans. "Are we gonna do that?" Shyness and eagerness combined in Jeep's expression. "Holy shit, Tip. Boys fucking boys—that's the big one. Are we gonna do that?"

"I hope," Lyle said in a barely audible mutter.

"Do you want me to stop reading?" I was so hot with lust that my vision was blurring, and my cock was stretching my briefs so dramatically that I wondered whether the fabric would ever resume its natural shape.

"Don't stop," Lyle and Jeep responded in unison.

"We gotta hear all the details."

"Specially if we're gonna fuck each other," Jeep added. He flushed slightly. "I mean, if that's what you guys have in mind."

"That's what I have in mind." Lyle slid his hand over Jeep's ass.

"*Evoe,* Pan." Jeep's moan filled the room.

"You boys *really* want to hear more? I don't think I can hold out much longer. We could try buttfucking now and read later."

"No, read some more." Jeep was adamant.

"We've got all night," Lyle said.

I glanced at the clock and sighed. "Not all night. But there's plenty of time."

❖

Thad's Journal: The Ninth of March, continued

The drummers beat riotously and the pipers piped with sheer frenzy as Skip pushed his cock into my asshole. As I opened for him, the wild discord of tinkling bells, jangling tambourines, and bawdy shouts rang upon my ears. I fancied that I could hear the piping of Pan while Skip pushed his cock into my ass, inch by breach, second by minute, depth by width—as though my coeval was, indeed, a goat-shaped demon.

Oddity and rapture intermingled in my mind. I felt my pagan soul moving beyond the realm of the comfortable into the terrifying beyond. The irrational beckoned me, and I had no will to resist. My cock was hard, dripping with my own leakage, as my best friend pushed his cock deeper into me. Somehow, taking Skip's cock committed me more than the buttfuck of the previous month. Yet, however absolute and fear-provoking the commitment, it was a commitment that I relished.

I was falling out of time, being pushed out of space, as Skip drove deeper into me, his hot breath rasping endearments in my ear. "*Evoe*, Adonis. I love your ass. It feels so good, Adonis."

Skip kept filling me. The weight of his cock grew greater as he ever-so-slowly drilled deeper, opened me wider, and fucked me gayer than I could have imagined. My asshole was alive with delicious sensations. As he slipped his cock inward, my anal sphincter throbbed pleasantly as it dilated. As he pulled his cock back, I experienced a gratifying impression of irrepressible slippage. "Yeah, take me, Skip. Fill me with your dick."

My cock was throbbing. I couldn't keep my hands off so I started jacking off, which drew riotous cheers and jeers from our audience. Skip finally filled my ass to the extent of his cock, held steady for a minute while I accepted the full length, and then pulled back until he was on the verge of pulling out of my dilated asshole.

I gasped as he pushed forward again, filling me with his whole shaft. Faster then he pulled back and fucked forward, screwing my ass with greater vigor. The thick meat of his swollen cock combined with the growing sexual frenzy of his motion to trigger profound vibrations in my rectum. I felt a powerful, milking sensation as he hit one special spot up my ass.

Skip gasped. "I can't hold out. Your ass is so hot, so tight, so grinding. You're milking my cock. I'm gonna come hard. I'm gonna come right now."

I felt Skip's cock growing heavier as I jerked my dick. The idea that my most intimate friend was going off in my ass excited me beyond comprehension. I gripped his bucking dick with my asshole, clamping down as best I could, while the tingles of approaching orgasm filled my dick. I squeezed my dick head between my fingers and pounded my shaft.

"I'm coming in you, Adonis. I'm giving it all to you right now."

That was it for me. Skip's words finished me off. My cock squirted out a shot that must have blasted over the low-hanging moon. I was pumping it out hard and heavy while Skip was pumping his own load into the condom in my ass. My fingers were sticky and wet with my blasted cum as I continued to massage my cock and urge out the last drop.

My legs buckled with a sudden weakness, and I would have fallen had Skip and I not been linked. Skip's strong arms encircled my midsection, embracing me from behind. "Watch yourself, Adonis," Skip said, holding me up.

I drew a deep gasp and wondered how long I had been holding my breath. I felt like my world had exploded.

"That was fuckin' terrific, Skip," I said as we pulled apart. His dick exited my ass with a popping sound that made some boys giggle.

"You gave our new initiate a tight fuck, Adonis," Baal said, compliments and envy combining in his tone.

"Well performed, Adonis," echoed another voice, an achingly familiar voice that I heard three mornings per week in the classroom.

Thrilling from the ends of my hairs to my toenails, I returned to my place in the circle while the two priests welcomed Skip to the Circle of Dionysus. They kissed Skip and explained to him the holy nature of our homosexual ecstasies. At last, they bestowed the name Osiris upon him. Thus blessed, Skip/Osiris kissed each boy in the circle. Though we had already fucked magnificently, his lips were hot on mine and his tongue played with significant invitation within my mouth. My flesh could not forget the feel of his lips on mine or the fullness of his cock in my ass, even as we sat together for cakes and ale, before the closing of the circle.

❖

Tipper's Tale

"Holy fuck," Jeep gasped, numbed with wonder.

Lyle appeared equally stunned. "I'll echo that oxymoron." Both boys had raging hard-ons that threatened the integrity of their briefs. My own were positively ruined. Another pair I'd have to replace secretly lest my mother discover the extent (not to mention, the nature) of my lust.

"Where do I go to join up?" Lyle finally asked.

"You want to get initiated?" I asked. "So do I, Lyle. But I don't know where we go. I don't know where my brothers are, or whether they are alive. I don't know where Dr. Bromius is."

"Maybe Skip knows," Lyle said.

"He asked me if I knew where Thad is. I think he's clueless. Though he might know some things we don't."

"We can go pump him," Jeep suggested. Both Lyle and I widened our eyes, but Jeep hadn't caught his own double meaning. Puzzled by our hard stares, Jeep added, "Not right now, guys."

"What do you want to do *right now*, Jeep?" Lyle purred, sliding his hand over Jeep's round ass.

"You know," Jeep said after only a short hesitation. "We can initiate each other."

Without another word, I opened my drawer and pulled out the condoms and lubricant. I met Jeep's eyes, and saw a resounding "Yea." Of course, I was not surprised to see the same look reflected from Lyle's dark eyes. I pulled off my briefs, so my hard cock popped free and my swimming-pool-and-gym-shaped ass protruded so invitingly that they both stroked it. Their frisky hands felt so familiar upon my butt cheeks that—for the first time in my life—I fainted.

I didn't know what had happened. "Oh, uh," I said as Jeep slapped my face lightly. "What the fuck?"

"You fainted, Tip."

"Oh, hell, no!"

"When we patted your ass, you went out like a light."

"Must have been that Bolivian Cabernet Sauvignon shit."

"No fuckin' way. My folks can down four or five bottles in an evening."

"Your parents' alcoholic propensities do not reflect upon me."

"Are you okay?"

"Yeah. Let's do it."

"We were about to do it. That's when you fainted."

"Fuck my gay ass."

"Don't lose consciousness."

Lyle slipped an extra-strength condom over his dick. I helped Jeep lubricate Lyle's sheathed member. A funny feeling came over me when I asked Jeep to help lube my asshole. However, his finger rubbed around my rim without any disasters ensuing. "Oh, that's nice," I moaned. I felt the pressure of Jeep's finger. He pushed the tip of his forefinger slightly inside, opening me just a little. I moaned with pleasure, so he entered a little deeper.

"Slip it into me."

His finger was slim, so it slid in with little effort on my part. I didn't fight against it, but I didn't push to receive it either. I just let it happen. I was vaguely aware that he was going a little deeper, and a little deeper still, and then he was slipping it in deep so that I felt the knuckle dilate my anal sphincter.

"Oh, Jeep."

"You're taking it, Tip. Want me to try it with my dick?"

"Yeah."

Jeep pulled out his finger and changed his position. I was on all fours on my bed. I pushed back my butt to entice him. Abruptly, I felt something thick against my asshole.

"Is that your cock?"

"Yeah. I'm gonna push it in just a little bit. Tell me if it hurts, Tip. Try to relax."

"Yeah, slide it into me.

"Tip! Tip! Tipper, man! Are you okay?"

"Wha...?"

"You fainted again. That's twice."

"I never."

"Why are you lying on your side? Why is my cock pulled half out by its root?"

"Huh?"

"Man, you passed out. You were gone for thirty seconds, at least."

"Maybe we better not do this," Jeep said.

"Bullshit, Jeep," Lyle said. "You want to do it too."

"Yeah, but..."

"But, nothing. It's just a reaction to fear. That's why Tip passed out. Something deep down in his subconscious is knocking him out. After we do it the first time, he'll be all right."

"Okay, how about you slip your cock up my ass first?" Jeep said. "Tipper can watch us. That'll show his subconscious there's nothing to fear." Suiting his actions to his words, Jeep assumed the position on all fours on my bed and stuck out his ass. "Go ahead, Lyle. Stick it to me."

Jeep's ass did look enticing. Lyle tipped me a wink, so I nodded back. I had lost my erection when I fainted, but it returned like a faithful friend. I rubbed my hand over Jeep's buttocks, while Lyle's hand glided into Jeep's butt crack. Lyle's fingers were slick with lube. "Oh," Jeep said, his voice ripe with surprise.

"Does that hurt?"

"It feels good. I didn't know it would feel so good."

"I haven't done much yet, Jeep. That's just my finger."

Lyle twisted his finger in Jeep's asshole, twisted, probed, and turned until Jeep was moaning. I thought that Jeep might shoot his load right then. However, Lyle removed his finger, wiped it on a napkin, though it had nothing on it but a little lubricant, and slipped a fresh condom onto his dick. I squirted a bit of lubricant into my palm and stroked Lyle's wrapped dick.

"Tell me you want this, Jeep," Lyle said, placing his hands on Jeep's butt mounds.

"Yeah, I want it. Push your cock into me."

Lyle mounted Jeep. I could see the head of Lyle's cock in Jeep's butt crack and I knew that it was pushing into Jeep's asshole. Why did I have to faint? Why couldn't I have been the first? I was jealous, and I felt a mild regret, but my emotions were slippery. I was also glad that Jeep was going to get it first. I didn't have to be the first among my friends to take the pansy route. As the thought slipped across my cerebral cortex, I wondered where I had heard the words *pansy route*. Some time in my past, I heard something terrible, something that I had blocked from my memories. I knew then that whatever had happened, it concerned my brothers, and it involved my parents. And I was a witness to something so terrible that I could not recall it, no matter how hard I tried.

"Oh, yes, that's good," Jeep gushed. "Oh, that feels so fuckin' good, Lyle. Oh, yeah. I like it. Push your cock into me. Let me have it all the way."

I felt a sharp pang because I could have been the one receiving the first dick, and I despised the buried psychological condition that had prevented me. Jeep was moaning louder, and an expression of pure bliss suffused his features. Lyle was pounding harder against Jeep's butt. Jeep was pushing his ass back to meet Lyle's thrusts, and I saw that he was wiggling it.

"Ah, Jeep, I never felt anything like this," Lyle grunted. He gripped Lyle's hips and thrust harder. As his ass sped up, I saw his facial expression change. I was looking at the face of orgasm, and I was close to shooting my own load just from the sight. Lyle's tight round buttocks thrust, and his lap slammed repeatedly against Jeep's outthrust ass.

"I'm giving it to you, Jeep. I'm giving it to you."

"Come in me, Lyle. Let it go, man."

Lyle thrust several more times. Then his face relaxed beatifically, and his thrusts slowed. He pulled his cock out of Jeep's ass, gasped in a deep breath, and pulled off the condom with a paper napkin.

"Let me catch my breath." Lyle's face was pinkish and perspiring. "Then you can fuck my ass, Tip."

"No, Lyle," Jeep said gently. "I'm gonna fuck Tip. I'm hot and ready to go, and we gotta help Tip past his phobia." He smeared a little lubricant onto his cock, pulled on an extra-strength condom, and lubricated the outside. "Stretch out on your face, Tip."

I did as he commanded. I lay face down and pulled up my right knee as the best illustrated books on anal intercourse recommended. The position made my hard cock more comfortable. "Do I look like an anally receptive homosexual?" I whispered.

"Yes," Lyle said.

"It's a beautiful sight, Tip," Jeep said. I felt his weight on top of me. "That's my cock you feel pressing against your asshole."

"Push it in."

"Don't faint."

"If I faint, slide it in anyway."

Lyle suddenly laughed loudly. I was afraid the buckaroos could hear him in the bunkhouse. "That's the spirit, Tip. You're going to take Jeep's cock, conscious or unconscious."

I didn't pass out. My heart was beating fast, but I remembered to push with my asshole as the pressure increased. "You've got it in you, Tip," Jeep said. "I'm going deeper."

"Yeah, drill me, Jeep," I said.

Lyle pressed his face close. "Man, that looks hot. Tip, I can see his cock sliding into you. It's disappearing into your crack. I can't see it going into your asshole, but I know that it is. It looks so fucking sexy. I wish I had my camera."

"How does that feel, Tip?" Jeep asked.

"It feels wonderful. It's filling me up, and it's triggering good feelings in my asshole."

"I know what you mean. It's about to get even better." He rose up, and the sensation of his cock pulling out of my ass was astonishing. Then he pushed down again, filling me until his front pressed hard against my butt. "I'm in you all the way, Tip. As deep as I can get in this position."

Then I knew that I was not going to faint again. A delirious sensation of complete surrender came over me, a dreamy, cock-filled sense of being penetrated and relishing it. "Yes," I said. "Yes, fuck me. Give it to me. Come in me."

After receiving his own first buttfuck, Jeep was already teetering on the edge of orgasm. His dick rose and fell, burrowing deep and then pulling back to the rim. As his tempo increased, I felt a deep down heat, almost a burning that vibrated up my ass, and also reverberated through my anal walls and up my cock. I felt tingles in my cockhead. The tingles were similar to the tingles that precede orgasm, but they were not quite the same. It was a pleasurable sensation, but I knew that Jeep would have to fuck me for a while before he triggered an orgasm. And I knew that Jeep did not have that much time. He was so close to coming that any request that he extend the fuck would be futile.

"I can't hold out," Jeep gasped. "I'm going off, Tip. Oh, yeah. I'm gonna come in your ass. Oh, fuck, I'm coming now."

I was grinning. I couldn't wipe the satisfied smirk from my face. Jeep was coming in my ass. A guy was getting his rocks off in my ass. In some unexplainable way, his getting off inside of me was better than my own orgasms. Even though I wasn't coming, I felt a fabulous euphoria. And there was another emotion that I could not identify at first. Then I knew what it was. I felt proud. I was proud that I had taken his dick. I was proud that I was getting fucked. My whole body flushed with pleasure as Jeep moaned and thrust. I wiggled my ass to give him more friction and strove to tighten my anal sphincter around his cock.

Jeep stopped humping me. He lay atop me, his dick still in my ass, his full weight pressing me down. His breath came hot and heavy in my ear. "That was fuckin' great, Tip."

"My turn," Lyle said.

"You already got your nuts off." I was teasing him. I knew what he meant.

Lyle looked frustrated. "I mean that you've got to fuck me, Tip. Then the circle will be complete. I fuck Jeep, Jeep fucks you, and you fuck me. The moon's deep circle."

Jeep pulled his cock out of my ass. My asshole made a popping sound as he pulled the head out, which made us giggle.

"How do you want to take me?" Lyle demanded. "Doggy style like I screwed Jeep? Or on my face the way you got it? Wait. How about I lay on my side? Let's try it that way."

Jeep and I lubricated Lyle's ass while he lay on his side. Of course, being the reader he was, Lyle had researched all the positions, and we were using the three best starting positions for anal beginners. The one he had chosen is called the *spoons position*. It is a less submissive posture than the doggy style anal sex position Jeep had taken and classic rear entry position I had elected. The spoons position gives the receiver control over the depth of penetration and prevents the penetrating partner from going frighteningly quick.

Both Jeep and I had taken a pounding—and liked it. Lyle, for all his big talk, was the biggest wuss. However, neither Jeep nor I called attention to his wussiness. Lyle wanted to take it, so I was going to stick my cock into his ass and keep fucking him until I cured him of this tiny reluctance. Just as Jeep had cured me of my fainting spells.

I snuggled against Lyle's back. His asshole was lubed and fingered open, and my cock was lubed for action. My own asshole throbbed in a pleasant way as I touched my cock against Lyle's hole. I grabbed my cock with one hand and directed the head against Lyle's rectal opening. "Push, Lyle."

Lyle drew a deep breath, and my cock found easier entrance. I promptly slipped it past his anal sphincter. "Oh, wait, stop a second."

I stopped with my dick head slightly inserted. Lyle drew another deep breath, and I felt his asshole open. Without his inviting me, I pushed my lap toward his buttocks. His hole was tight around my wrapped cock. The friction going in was spectacular. "Oh, that feels good, Lyle. So good."

Jeep took hold of Lyle's cock and pumped it while I slipped my cock deeper into his ass. Lyle was moaning and biting his pillow. He let go long enough to say, "Oh, guys. I'm taking it. I'm taking a cock. It's true—I'm really gay."

Jeep's eyes met mine briefly and his eyebrows rose sardonically. Lyle hadn't already figured out that he was gay? I winked at Jeep, pulled my cock back, and thrust forward. I penetrated Lyle a bit deeper with that thrust. My cock was halfway into him.

"How does that feel?"

"It's starting to feel better. I'm trying to wiggle my ass for you, but I can't in this position."

"Don't worry about that, Lyle. You're giving great friction. Your asshole is massaging my cock like a sucking calf."

Lyle sighed and appeared to relax somewhat. Jeep winked at me as he kept masturbating Lyle's cock. I kept rocking my hips, sinking my cock deeper into Lyle with each stroke. After a minute, I was pushing all the way into him. "You're taking my whole cock, Lyle. That's as deep as I can go."

"It's feeling good," Lyle said. "Oh, yeah. *Now* I like it."

I grinned at Jeep. Contained in that shared smirk was an entire commentary on human complexity. Jeep had been the most reluctant of the three of us to accept his homosexual nature, yet he had been the first to receive a cock in his ass. Lyle had been the most willing, and yet he had the hardest time taking his first anal prodding. And I, who had initiated the whole business, had fainted—not once, but twice.

"Oh, Jeep, you're jerking me off so good. Tip, you're fucking me nice. Now, let's change positions."

I stopped humping his ass. "What do you want to do?"

"Let's try the cowgirl."

I pulled my cock out of his ass and rolled onto my back. Facing me, Lyle straddled me and positioned his anus on my dick head. He pushed down slowly and carefully, using his strong swimmer's legs to lower his weight. This time his anus muscles relaxed promptly around my cock. Grinning and erect, he accepted my cock until he was resting all his weight upon my middle.

He raised himself, grabbing his own cock and jacking it. Then he began riding up and down on my cock. He varied his rhythm and speed to suit himself, which was fine with me. What was good for him had to be good for me. My cock was already tingling.

"I'm going to come, Lyle."

"That's what I want," he said, jacking his cock harder. He had already ejaculated once that night, but he had recovered nicely. He was ready to shoot again.

So was Jeep. He lay beside us, jerking himself off. Sprawled helplessly on my back, I could not help but notice that the holes in both cocks were pointed directly at me.

"You don't mind getting a facial, do you, Tip?" Jeep asked.

"Not at all." The tingles in my cock were rippling down my shaft. My fresh-fucked asshole was contracting already. Something warm hit my face, and I saw that Jeep was ejaculating on me.

"Oh!" The full force of orgasm hit me. Lyle was practically bounding on my cock. He was flogging his dick as he milked mine. An explosive rush flamed through my groin. I knew I had to be coming, but my orgasm was so intense that I could not count my individual contractions. Cum splattered onto my chest. My chin was slippery, and I tasted spunk. The semen hitting my lips had that sweetish Asian savor, not the spicier Latino tang that I associated with Jeep. Lyle was painting my lips with his cum. Still, he rode my dick, riding like a cowgirl, and never once did my swollen cock slip out of his tight ass.

So that night Lyle, Jeep, and I carried our activities to the highest and purest level of homosexual intercourse—the buttfuck. I watched as Jeep drove Lyle home, waving to them as they sped away in Jeep's Element. The rain had stopped earlier, the sky was clear and spangled with stars, and the quarter moon appeared to be sitting on the peak of Mt. Jefferson. I felt a gargantuan sense of liberation. With good will toward all, I penned a note and left it on the kitchen table.

Mom, the guys and I really enjoyed the supper. We saved two slices of pie for you and Pop. I hope that you got elected, Pop. Tell me all about it in the morning. Important swim meet tomorrow evening, so I'm heading for dreamland.

Tip

I didn't lock the front door. In the country, one doesn't often. I pulled the door of my room shut, slipped between my sheets, and remembered the exciting events of the evening. My last conscious thoughts were of my friends' cocks and asses as I drifted into a homoerotic dream state.

I never heard Pop and Mom arrive home. The roosters began crowing with lusty vim, the sun painted the sky with rosy streaks, and morning bolted in gloriously. I jumped from my bed invigorated to experience a new day. The daffodils were blooming with morning abundance, and new tulips were preparing to blow.

I pulled on khaki shorts and a fresh T-shirt and headed for the delicious aroma wafting from the kitchen. Mom was using the big griddle, and the circles of buckwheat pancakes were browning nicely. A gigantic slab of hot ham was already sitting on the table. Looking especially pleased with himself, Pop was sipping coffee and glancing at the sports section. The newspaper carried a photograph of me diving into the pool. The writer of the article was speculating about our chances of beating the Copperheads. No one expressed any doubt that we would trounce the Dippers that night.

"Congratulations," I said.

Pop's head jerked up from his paper. "How did you know I won?"

"From your expression." Pop's face clouded, so I added, "You look like a winner."

That brightened him up. Mom gave me a smile as she set a stack of pancakes in front of me. I cut a thick wedge of butter and placed it on top. Then I poured honey over it and took a forkful. Mom poured me a tall glass of milk and I helped myself to some ham.

"How many ballots?" I asked around the food in my mouth.

Pop's eyes were alight with braggadocio. "I won on the first."

"Way to go, Pop." I glanced at the clock and ate faster. "We're at the Muskrat Creek Aquatic Center tonight. Seven o'clock."

"I'll be there," Mom said.

"I'll try," Pop said. "You understand I can't promise."

"Yeah, I know." I never believed that the farm equipment business was that heavy in the evenings. I mean, if somebody's going to shell out for a tractor, isn't the buyer going to try it out in the daylight? The truth was that seeing me in a competition swimsuit shriveled Pop's nuts. All that young masculine flesh in red swimmer's briefs awakened his most homophobic impulses, and that night promised even worse because we were racing against the

Klamath Falls Dippers, who wore white swim bikinis cut narrow in the rear. By the conclusion of every race, the Dippers looked like they were wearing invisible thongs.

We Muskrats changed in the familiar locker room at the Muskrat Creek Aquatic Center, our home turf. The Dippers changed in the same accommodations, but our coaches kept the two teams apart. That was disappointing, because I wanted to see the Dippers naked before I raced against them. However, with Coach Reece's fat ass in the way, I didn't see dick.

As our team strode out together, strutting in our red swim briefs, I saw my mother watching from the viewing stand. Lyle's parents were there, as were the families of most of our team. However, my father had not shown up to watch us whip the Dippers.

The competition was hardly even close. Coach Reece was even swimming two of our sophomores against two Klamath Falls seniors. The only thing the Klamath Falls swim team did well was to look incredibly homoerotic in their swimsuits. At one point, we let them get a little ahead. We gave them a moment of optimism before Lyle, Mart, Rick, Jeep, and I crushed their hopes forever. The Muskrats would meet the Copperheads in Silverton for the next meet.

When the meet was over, we hit the showers together. I tried to talk to the captain of the Dippers about their swimsuits, but he wasn't receptive. He was feeling the stigma of being captain of the losing team, but I had only wanted to ask about their choice of a competition suit. They were definitely skimpier than ours, and the material took a direct glide path toward the swimmer's asshole. Rebuffed twice, I finished showering with my friends.

So one eventful day followed another. Lyle, Jeep and I got together daily. We varied our sexual activities: some days we fucked, some days we sucked, and other days we beat one another's meat. Finally, we were two days away from our competition against the Copperheads.

CHAPTER EIGHT

Tipper's Tale

Jeep and I were shaved smooth. I shaved Lyle's front while Jeep shaved his back. "Tip, I'd like to see you in one of those briefs the Klamath Falls Dippers wear," Lyle said.

"I'd like to see what *I* would look like in them," Jeep said as he finished the final stroke on Lyle's butt. We covered Lyle with lotion, showered him, and treated him again.

I pointed out that the Copperheads wore brilliant yellow swimmer's briefs. "They look pretty sexy too." I was thinking about Tizzy's ass.

"That Tizzy is kind of cute," Lyle said, his hand roving toward my dick. "I wonder whether any of the Copperheads are like we are."

He didn't wait for my answer. His lips touched my cock, which had stiffened at his touch. Jeep was hard already, so I touched my tongue to his cock. Lyle was pulling my dick into his mouth as I closed my lips over Jeep's.

"We're gonna make a daisy chain?" Jeep asked, jockeying into position. His cock pulled away from my mouth, so I had to shift too. Soon, we were closer, and each of us had a cock in his mouth. We squirmed closer, and our cocks penetrated deeper, past lips, gliding along tongues, going fearsomely deep.

Lyle's hand was on my ass as he sucked me. His forefinger touched my asshole, a forefinger slick with his spit. He probed me as he took my cock even deeper into his mouth.

I made my mouth a tube for Jeep's cock. His hips were rocking as he made fucking motions in my mouth. I had to swallow hard to keep from gagging. Swallowing did the trick because I didn't gag; I let his cock slip into my throat. After I took a couple of stokes in my throat, I pulled back and drew a breath. It was such a funny, delightful sensation that I tried it again. I swallowed Jeep's dick head into my throat. He fucked my throat, or rather, I fucked his cock with my throat, drawing back to gulp another deep swimmer's breath before going all the way down again.

Lyle's finger was probing deeper into my asshole. He was rimming my hole with his forefinger, and then opening me and slipping it inside. He slicked his finger with a little more saliva. Some drool was running out the side of his mouth and he was using that to slick his finger for penetration.

I tried the same trick with Jeep. I let the drool slip along his dick and caught it upon my finger. I slid my hand over Jeep's ass and slipped into his crack. Carefully exploring, I slicked my finger three more times before I penetrated his asshole.

The effect was electric. Jeep's cock bucked. His semen jetted down my throat. My cock throbbed as I took Jeep's cum. Flashes of sensation vibrated down my dick as I pushed my head forward and drove my finger deeper into Jeep's ass. I swallowed the head of his cock again, taking it all the way. The freshly shaved skin around the base of his cock touched my lips. I kept making swallowing gestures, keeping Jeep's cock in my throat while it ejaculated.

The roar of full orgasm claimed my dick. Swells of pleasure rose within me. My asshole contracted tightly around Lyle's finger. The pulse of muscular contraction shot my semen into Lyle's mouth. As I came, I drew my head back and took a breath, though Jeep's cock was still halfway toward the back of my mouth. I tasted the final seeping of his spunk on my tongue. More contractions shook me as the pleasure of orgasm swelled to its peak and then subsided.

With a moan, we broke our daisy chain. While our spit-and-semen-slick cocks stained my sheets, we could only stare at one another in wonder. "I know how Balboa felt," Jeep said.

"Huh?"

"Vasco Núñez de Balboa. When he saw the Pacific Ocean. I feel like a great explorer."

"We're explorers all right," Lyle agreed. "We're conquistadors."

"Get real, boys. We're the senior class swim team, and fuckin' Balboa was one of history's worst homophobes." No one in their right mind would have called me an expert on Spanish-American history, but I had looked up homophobia online and found Balboa listed.

The stains on my sheets were copious and telltale, evidence no boy should ever present to his mother. While we were loading them into the washing machine, Lyle broached another subject. "Tip, there's no swim practice tomorrow night."

"Of course not. We're supposed to rest up on Thursday so we'll be fresh to out swim the Copperheads on Friday."

"That's what I mean. So tomorrow, after school, you can introduce us to Skip."

For some reason, I had avoided confronting Skip until then. I realized I was afraid of the truth. Maybe I would learn something too horrible to know. I bit my lip. "Yeah. Let's talk to Skip."

"What about Mart and Rick?" Jeep asked. "They'll expect us to ride with them."

"I'll tell them that we have to do something else."

"I think they're getting suspicious," Jeep added.

"So what? Let them get suspicious."

"They're going to find out sometime," Lyle said. He looked a little scared after he said it. A clammy feeling came over me, but I put a brave face on it. Jeep was positively pale. None of us were really worrying about Mart or Rick. We were thinking about our families.

Once more, I followed Jeep and Lyle to their cars. That night they had arrived separately. I kissed them both, confident that none of the buckaroos could see me. I stood in the driveway, watching as they sped into the wet spring night. The rain had started earlier in the evening and continued to fall. Even through my clothes, the rain chilled my freshly shaven skin, so I hurried back into the house. Then I walked alertly, eyed the house critically, and sniffed suspiciously, but I could not detect a lingering scent of our activities. I loaded my sheets into the clothes dryer and waited so I could remake my bed.

❖

Lyle was driving, and Jeep had claimed shotgun, so I had the Sentra's backseat to myself. We drove slowly, not by choice, but because we were hampered by the tourists viewing the tulip farms. On both sides of the highway, fields of tulips, blowing in every hue, stretched toward the vanishing point. The horizon of tulips was only broken by the snowy mountains.

We had ducked out immediately after school, so we arrived at the Muskrat Creek Shopping Plaza at the busiest hour. Nonetheless, the largest crowds were converging on the Albertsons supermarket. Lyle parked near the covered walkway that passed between the sections where the L design met. Skip's Security Service was open. Skip was waiting on a customer who could not decide between two car alarms. When Skip saw me, his eyes widened with recognition. "Be with you in a second," he said, casting his eyes over Lyle and Jeep. Did I detect a hint of pederast lust in Skip's eye? I hoped so.

We dawdled around, examining alarms, dummy cameras, handcuffs, stun guns, key hiders, child leashes, pepper spray, and spy sunglasses. Finally, the customer left without making a decision. Skip cast a disgusted frown at his departing back. Then he twisted his face into a more inviting expression.

"You're Thad's brother. I forget your name."

"I'm Tip. Did you ever meet my brother Tye?"

"Thad's kid brother? Yeah. I guess I knew him."

"Did you ever see him wearing this?" I dangled Tye's silver satyr neck pendant before Skip's face.

Skip recoiled when his eyes lit upon the satyr with the silvery erection. "What do you boys want? I've got work here."

"Bullshit, Skip," I said. "I want to find my brothers."

Skip blanched, but he tried to bull through. "You boys are interrupting my work. You better leave. Right now."

I leaned across the counter, pressing my face close to Skip's. "Remember kissing Thad?" I whispered seductively. "Remember Dr. Bromius? Remember the night of your initiation?" My lips were close to Skip's then, but he did not pull away. He could have pepper sprayed or Tasered me, but he pushed his face closer until his lips met mine. I kissed his lips, lips only a decade or so older than mine, not so much in the stream of time, not a wide gap in the moon's deep circle, and as we kissed, Skip's tongue slipped into my mouth. I reached my hand behind his head and locked us together. Our kiss went on and on, until my cock was a fiery rocket. I heard Jeep and Lyle gasping behind me, but I also heard the patter of spring rain upon the roof of the shopping plaza. I could have sworn I heard the daffodils blooming.

"That was a fuckin' fantastic kiss," Jeep gasped when Skip and I finally came up for air.

"Do you remember Thad? His mouth? His cock? His ass? You have been better acquainted with my family in the past, my brothers both, but now I am here. I and my friends, and we know about your past. We know about Thad. We know the lust you felt then, and the lust you still feel." My language sounded strange to me. Jeep was giving me a quizzical look. Lyle alone appeared pleased—getting an A on that *Wuthering Heights* quiz had swelled his head, whereas I had barely scored a C-plus.

"How do you know that?" Skip demanded. "What do you know?"

"We read about the night of Thad's initiation—in splendid detail. And the night you got initiated—Thad wrote down everything. Wow, Skip, you're hot. You were hot then, and you're still hot. Any one of us would take you any way you wanted, oral or anal, top or bottom. Right here. Right now. Are you interested?"

I couldn't gauge the level of Skip's interest. The counter concealed his lower body, so I couldn't see if he was sporting a boner. Perhaps, however, he was not erect. He looked stricken. For a moment, I considered calling nine one one; Skip looked like he was about to have a stroke or something. After all, he had reached the advanced age of thirty-two.

"Where'd you boys read about this shit?" Skip asked.

"It's not *shit*, Skip," I said. "Thad left journals. Explicit journals."

Skip was gray and shaking, though spots of color burst out on his cheeks and his eyes glinted with hidden fires.

"Where is Thad now, then? After that night, why'd he leave me behind? Doesn't he know I loved him?"

I froze. I had thought this interview would be difficult, but I had not realized how difficult. Skip's questions floored me. Without preparation, I experienced the full pathos of his abandonment. Had my brother betrayed his best friend, his lover?

"What night do you mean, Skip? What happened?"

Skip merely shook his head, stuck in memories he would not reveal.

"Wow!" Jeep muttered. "This sucks."

"Yeah, it sucks. Skip, I'm sorry to bring up painful memories. I just want to find my brothers. Thad and Tye. I need your help."

Skip was half-stuck in the past. "You boys know about our revels under the moon?"

"Yeah," Lyle said. "You haven't done anything that the three of us haven't. We've taken cocks every way you have, Skip. We initiated ourselves."

Skip shook his head slowly. "You can't initiate yourselves. You have to be accepted by the circle. Otherwise, it's just sex. Besides, I can't talk to you about it. For two reasons. I swore an oath, and you boys are jail bait."

Lyle jumped on that whopper. "No more jail bait than you, Skip. We're high school seniors. We're all three past the age of eighteen. You can't get into legal trouble with us."

"You had to wait here, Skip. You had to stay for me—and for my friends. Thad should have told you that. He should have warned you."

"He trusted me," Skip said, a look of wonder suffusing his visage. "He went through hell, but so did I."

The guy who had been trying to decide between the two alarms returned then, dragging his wife in tow. "Tell me the difference again."

Skip gave a helpless shrug, but he tipped me a wink before Lyle, Jeep, and I departed. It had been one hell of a kiss.

❖

After eating breakfast, I hurried to my room, completed my bathroom routine, and read my e-mail messages. I had just finished dressing and loading my gym and book bags when I heard Rick's 2002 Ford Expedition. He had Mart with him, riding shotgun, so I jumped into the backseat. We picked up Lyle and Jeep and barely made it to homeroom before the first bell.

The day sped by. No teacher pressured us. Not a single quiz to torment us. The school held its collective breath. We were the first Muskrat swim team to come close to the finals.

Even Principal Relish sounded enthused as his voice warbled through the loudspeaker. "We are going to beat the Copperheads tonight. Next week, we're going to out swim the Astorian Fur Traders. It's a great time for Muskrat Creek High, and I hope everybody appreciates our finest team."

"*We*? Where does he get off with *we*?" Mart whispered hoarsely. "I'd like to see Principal Relish compress his ass into the Muskrat swim briefs."

If we won in Astoria, then we would compete against one final team to claim the state championship. The principal would probably take credit for that too.

After classes, we bounced into Rick's SUV. We grabbed dinner at a fast food joint on the drive north to the Silverton Swim Club. Rick and Mart ate cheeseburgers with loads of onions—gloating that the ensuing gas gave them buoyancy—while Lyle and Jeep ate the fish filet, and I made do with a chicken sandwich. Of course, we consumed a super-sized mountain of fries based on the latest medical supposition that we should "carb up" before the big event. We washed down this banquet with colas and milkshakes.

The Copperheads arrived at the Silverton Swim Club ahead of us. We ran into them in the men's locker room. Tizzy Gates, captain of the Copperheads, the same yellowtail who had harassed us at Beaver Dam Fitness Club, was standing naked before his locker. I don't think I had ever noticed what a cute ass Tizzy had. He acted as if he knew it too, because he waggled it with a distinctly gay panache as he bragged about how he was going to leave us lapping his dickwater.

"Tizzy, you're a perv," Mart said.

Rick had to add his own homophobic bullshit. "Dickwater? That's super gay. Isn't it, dude?"

"Go sit on a floatation device, Jecks," the Copperhead captain said.

I added my own jibe. "Y-E-L-L-O-W-tail. I'll be swimming the two hundred meter butterfly against you, Tizzy. You can't overcome technique with brute strength." Though he was not particularly tall, Tizzy was notorious for his upper body might. His chest and biceps bulged. "You know what's going to happen. Your recovery sucks, you can't catch the water, and you miss your window for breathing. You'll probably inhale the pool, and we'll have to go to the trouble of pulling you out and giving you mouth-to-mouth."

"Fuck you, Trencher," the Copperhead said, unable to come up with anything better. He pulled up his yellow swimmer's briefs and adjusted his package. The sight of his cock and balls disappearing into his swimsuit, then forming a juicy bulge, made me want to drop to my knees. I didn't mention my lusts to Tizzy though. I led my team to our lockers and stripped. Even as I pulled up my red swimmer's briefs, I knew that I was going to leave Tizzy's ass behind.

❖

An hour later, we were heading back for the locker room. "Did it look to you like Tizzy was crying?" Jeep asked.

"Had to be the pool water running down his face," I said. "He'd hardly be weeping just because I swam faster than he, just because we're going to face the Fur Traders, and the Copperheads are going to have to win another match if they want to face us at the finals, and just because they're going into that competition having lost once this season."

"Fuck, yes, the little pansy was crying," Rick said. "Tip whipped his yellow ass."

Mart and Rick leaped up and gave each other the high five at the thought of Tizzy crying. I put a smile on my face, because I was happy that we had won. That the other team had to lose so we could win did not thrill me. I was thinking that Tizzy might make a fine addition to our little gay sex society. Something in his demeanor shrieked out, "Take me. I'm gay." I wondered whether I was developing gaydar.

Still, Rick had called Tizzy a pansy. Did Rick have gaydar, too? Rick sure wasn't gay; he was so heterosexual I couldn't figure out how he kicked his legs to swim. Suddenly, I wasn't sure about anything. It seemed as if the whole world had shifted around me, and I didn't know anything. All I knew was that I wanted to find my brothers, if they were above ground, and I wanted lots of hot sex with other boys.

I felt my lust rising. I glanced at Lyle, who was changing beside me. "Can you get away tonight?"

He gritted his teeth. "I can't. My parents are having a party for me. Family crap. I can't duck out, damn it."

Earlier, I had heard Jeep telling about his Tió Augusto arriving from his *hacienda* in the *pampas*. Tió Augusto was taking the whole family to celebrate after the swim meet.

The Copperheads drifted into the locker room. Rick started taunting them, calling them "yellowtails," and making other remarks. The guys in the yellow swimmer's briefs ignored Rick until Tizzy arrived. He didn't look like a guy who'd been sobbing. "We'll get you red butts next time," he said. "We have another meet too, and after we win that one, we'll claim the championship by whipping your girly butts."

"They do have girly butts," another Copperhead chipped in. He suddenly grabbed Lyle and whirled him around. Lyle was still wearing his swim briefs. "Look at the way that seam pulls up his crack. They all have that butt seam."

The taunts were juvenile, as usual, so I pretended to ignore the yellowtails. They would not be swimming against us again. In spite of Tizzy's boasts, the Copperheads were no match for the Portland Professionals. The Professionals would surely defeat the Copperheads, and if we won in Astoria, we would swim against the Professionals.

Tizzy stepped into the shower in his swimmer's briefs and stood under the spray. I took the stall beside him, where I washed out my swimsuit.

"How're you doing, Tizzy?" I asked.

"What the fuck do you want to know for?"

"Quit being a sore loser. I'm just asking. It doesn't have to be dog-munch-dog-ass all the time, does it?"

He looked at me as if he were seeing me for the first time. "No," he said hesitantly. "I don't like losing, Trencher."

"It was a fuckin' high school swim meet. On any given day, one team is bound to lose. It doesn't mean shit."

Tizzy let the spray wash the pool chemicals out of his chestnut hair, the golden streaks looking reddish under the weird neon bulbs. He stepped out of his yellow swimsuit, rinsed it, and wrung it with both hands. At last, he hung his swimsuit over the shower rod and looked into my eyes.

"You're all right, Trencher," he said, extending his hand. We were both stark naked then. I took his hand and gave it a squeeze. If he returned my gesture, then he was interested. Sure enough, he squeezed my hand before letting go.

"My name is Tip, Tizzy. Short for Terry. Some of my friends even call me Tipper."

"Sounds kind of gay." At that, I turned my back on him and began soaping my cock. It had been just a little bit swollen, not noticeably, I thought, but it deflated completely at Tizzy's remark.

I heard his breath draw deep, with the faintest rasp in his throat. I wondered whether he was looking at my ass. I could only hope. I heard a soft sound issue from his mouth and I felt his hand on my arm. I faced him again.

"You're a nice boy, Tip. I'm sorry I sounded like an asshole."

Nice boy. What high school senior tells another that he is a nice boy? A girl might say that. Never a boy. Unless? Unless Tizzy was toying with me.

"How many boys on *your* swim team are gay?" I asked nonchalantly. I might have been talking about the pool's salinity.

Tizzy hesitated, but he did not hesitate long. "What do you have in mind, Tip?" Tizzy responded, tossing back the come-on.

"I wasn't suggesting that we settle the competition with a jerk-off contest," I said. Did Tizzy's cock stiffen at my response? I thought so.

"Why not?" he said. "You might win that one too. All that practicing, you know."

"Yeah, Tizzy, like you don't spank your own monkey about fifteen times a week."

Tizzy suddenly laughed, a barking snort if I ever heard one, and grabbed his cock suggestively. "Twenty. You must've lost count while you were looking at my asshole."

"Is your asshole something to be admired?" We were openly flirting by then.

"A rosebud."

"I'd like to get my cock into it some time," I whispered. Tizzy's cock sprang upward. "Tizzy, at least three members of my team are gay—including me."

"That makes us brothers, Tip," Tizzy said. "Five of my boys are on the side of the angels—five that I know about. And that doesn't include me, though I like a cock as well as anybody."

It was an ambiguous statement, so I asked, "You like pussy too?"

"No fuckin' way. Twats are trouble, no matter what you do. Besides, dicks are more interesting. I just love to see those bastards spit."

My cock was flying high by then. Tizzy was hard too. I reached for his cock and tweaked its tip. "Do you have plans for tonight?"

Tizzy's face fell. "I can't tonight, Tipper. Family crap, you know. My folks would kill me if they knew I liked playing skin flutes. Silverton is cosmopolitan compared to my home. I live near Silver Falls, which is about as redneck as Oregon gets."

I could have disagreed with that comment. Silverton advertises itself as the gateway to Silver Falls State Park, and Silverton was the first town in the United States to elect an openly transgender mayor. Despite the homophobia rampant in Oregon's evangelical community and among dwellers of the high desert and Eastern Oregon, the old buckaroos were cornholers and cocksuckers to a man. Shrugging Tizzy's innocence aside, I said, "I understand. My folks don't know about my tastes either."

We toweled off side by side. For some reason, our teammates left us alone in the shower. However, once Tizzy and I hit the drying area, the rest trooped into the showers. Tizzy and I walked to the benches. When we were out of sight of the teams in the shower, I reached for his cock and rubbed it. Suddenly, he had hold of mine too. Deciding to find out how Tizzy measured up to Skip, I pushed my lips toward his. We met, and I pushed my tongue into his mouth. We kissed for about thirty seconds. I gave his bare ass an affectionate pat before I hurried to my own locker.

Our kiss must have lasted longer than I thought. Rick and Mart had finished drying and were heading for Rick's Expedition. Jeep and Lyle joined me at my locker. Tizzy glanced at them.

"It's all okay, Tizzy," I said. "I've done just about everything with Lyle and Jeep."

Jeep and Lyle exchanged a look, but I shook my head at them. "Tizzy is as gay as we are, guys."

Tizzy tore a page from his notebook and jotted down his cell phone number and e-mail address. I gave him mine too. Then three Copperheads joined us, thinking that we were ganging up on their leader.

"Josh, Bobby, and Lee are cocksuckers from way back," Tizzy whispered. Josh, Bobby, and Lee looked rather awkward until Tizzy said, "These Muskrat boys are queer too."

"We gotta get together on this," Lee said.

"We will. Maybe we can start checking out all the other swim teams too."

"Did you guys check out the asses on those Klamath Falls Dippers?" Jeep said.

"Especially the way their bikinis creep up after they've been kicking their legs a bit," Bobby said. "Oo-la-la! I like to stick my dick between those buns."

"Let's not get too energized. I'm going home, where I'm going to jerk off and devastate my briefs. So are the rest of you boys, because we're all stuck with families and teammates. We can't do much about our homophobic parents, but we can get our teams to come out."

"That's what I think too," Tizzy said. "What kind of guy chooses to join a team where he gets to wear swimmer's briefs? You know the answer."

"So let's get them all out, and then we'll form our own band of brothers."

Nobody was watching, so we hugged and kissed a little bit, just a get-acquainted kiss, not a gonna-jump-your-butt-here-in-the-locker-room kiss.

Outside the locker room, Principal Relish and Coach Reece were congratulating each other on a job well done. They watched

Jeep, Lyle, and me walk past, but neither of them thought to congratulate us, though it was our swimming skill, hours of practice, strategy, and eons spent at the gym that had won the evening for Muskrat Creek High.

Earlier in the evening, before the match, Coach Reece had practically excoriated me for not riding on the school bus.

"You should have been with the freshman and sophomores." Why was our coach yelping at me minutes before I had to swim against the Copperheads? The man was wholly lacking in tact. "You boys had no business driving yourselves down here. After this, any away meet, you seniors have to ride the bus with the rest of the team. Build morale. Terry, if Jesus were here, what would he do?"

"Was Jesus the captain of his high school swim team?"

The coach howled loud enough to be heard in downtown Bumfuck. "You know what I mean. Our Lord would lead the group by example. Not ride down in a private car and scarf up fast food on the way."

Perhaps the image of Jesus Christ swimming while wearing red competition briefs inspired me to swim so strongly that night. For whatever reason, we Muskrats were on our way toward the state finals—providing we won against the Fur Traders.

After listening to the principal and the coach congratulate each other, Lyle, Jeep, and I exchanged sardonic leers and headed for Rick's SUV. Rick and Mart were waiting impatiently in the parking lot. "What kept you pansies?" Mart asked.

"Don't be an asshole, Mart," I said, making it an order. "We were talking with the other team. It's called being gracious. Didn't you notice that we won?"

"It's called being wussy," Mart said.

I felt my blood pressure rising. I wasn't going to let Mart challenge me that way. "Who is captain of this team?"

"You are," Jeep said.

Lyle was also on my side. "You are captain, Tip. So don't get defensive."

"I'm not defensive. I don't like being challenged. If I want to talk to the other team, then that's my right."

Even Rick turned against his sycophant then. "Yeah, who is our captain, Mart?"

Mart's face had gone deep red. "Tip, you are. Sorry. You're not a wuss."

"We gotta stick together as a team," I said. "Next week we'll be swimming against the Fur Traders. Nobody has beaten those boys for three years."

"We're gonna whip their asses," Rick said.

"That's right, Rick."

The drive home to the parking lot of Muskrat Creek High School from Silverton took more than an hour. Had we been riding on the school bus with the rest of the team, the time would have been far longer. I broached the subject as delicately as possible.

"We're gonna have to ride the bus to Astoria."

Rick howled in dismay. "Fuck, no. Not the bus." The other seniors looked stricken.

"I hate to break it to you, but Coach Reece lowered the boom. We gotta ride the bus."

"Shit on the fuckin' school bus," Mart said. He spoke for us all, but we all knew in our hearts that come the next Friday, we would be riding the bus to Astoria.

❖

Rick dropped off Lyle and Jeep first, due to their pressing family business. A few minutes after nine, he and Mart left me off at my front door. The days had been growing longer, so the buckaroos were just herding our alpacas into the barn for the night. I stopped and visited with a couple of the little fellows (the alpacas, not the buckaroos). One little dark brown fellow with an extremely long neck, who looked like something out of a Dr. Seuss illustration, was reluctant to leave me. Finally, I had to go to the barn with him.

"Did you win?" asked Lopez, one of our buckaroos.

"We won." I scratched between the alpaca's ears. At least the buckaroos were rooting for me.

Tearing myself from the alpaca herd, I thought about Lopez all the way to our front door. He was a wiry little buckaroo, and I bet that he swung a mean dick.

Brother Deke's car was parked in front of the house, between my black Prius and Pop's blue Ford F150. Brother Deke's wife Doris was proclaiming *UNO* at the instant I sauntered through the door. Mom, Pop, Brother Deke, Sister Doris, Deacon Beacon, and Mrs. Beacon were seated around our dining room table. Packs of Uno cards lay in abundance, testament to the orgy of card dealing that had taken place while I was swimming my heart out.

"We won," I said, hefting my gym bag.

"Good lad," said Deacon Beacon. "God was on the side of the home team."

"Sure." I didn't believe that a personal deity would devote an iota of consideration to the home team. Deacon Beacon's theology was warped, not to mention that his own daughter, Mary, was an ardent gay rights activist in California.

I grabbed a cold supper from the refrigerator. Mom had left a standing roast and vegetables I heaped a generous portion onto a plate and stuck it in the microwave. Beers that I had never seen sat in the refrigerator as well. My parents well occupied, I sipped from a bottle of stout, ate at the kitchen table, and topped off my meal with blueberry pie.

I checked on the card players again, but they were oblivious to me. I slipped into my room and pulled off my clothes. Standing naked before my mirror, I watched my cock swell. I wished Lyle and Jeep were with me. Or Tizzy. I wondered what sex would be like with Tizzy. I had a suspicion that it would be pretty fucking good. I imagined Tizzy sliding his cock into my ass and riding me. The more I thought about it, the more I wanted action. I had said I was going to jerk off, but masturbation is lonely. I wanted a partner.

Suddenly, I thought of Skip. There was no way Skip's Security Service would be open this late, but what if he was working on some project? I called information for the number, and then called his shop. All I got was a recording: "Skip's Security Service. We're closed now. Our hours are eight to six, Mondays through Saturdays. If this is an emergency, call your local police department."

Skip's message left considerable to be desired. I was having an emergency, but I wasn't about to call the cops. I was stymied. I didn't know where Skip lived. I didn't even know his last name. That was frustrating because I was certain that Skip and I would have had a great time together. Even considering he was an older man.

Feeling almost dizzy, I raised my screen and stuck my head out the open window. The scent of the alpacas carried by the wind off the mountain snowfields cleared my head. I could smell the new corn sprouting in Pop's fields. Thad had trod those same fields on his way to his gay pagan orgies under the moon. Thinking of Thad reminded me that I still had an unread notebook hidden under my mattress.

For security purposes, I pulled on my briefs before I removed the notebook, switched on my reading lamp, and stretched out on my bed. Opening the notebook, I saw that it started with an undated section that seemed to be a continuation of some missing part.

Thad's Journal

We had cast a Circle of Set upon the withered heath. The spirit of sexual abandonment touched me, infused me with its presence, excited my mind, and inflamed my body. My mouth puckered, my cock swelled, and my asshole dilated. The electrically charged atmosphere raised the hairs upon my naked skin. Rare lightning bolts cracked across the purplish night as the mountain peaks shattered the lowering clouds. A light cold mist fell upon me, but it did not chill my flesh. My cock vibrated with urgency. I swelled with the desire to penetrate and to be penetrated.

"Adonis. Oh, Adonis." Ibreez brushed his erection across my taut buttocks and growled lustily. "A storm is coming." Whether Ibreez meant the storm of the sky or the storm raging through his cells, he gripped his cock and brushed it back across my ass. He did that twice, and then he hugged me from behind so that his stiff cock nestled between my butt cheeks. He did not try to penetrate me; he merely rubbed his cock up and down my crack. My mouth was dry with lust, and I felt my hair standing.

In the center of our circle, Bromius turned his face to the sky. Our professor's eyes glinted with lust, and a lewd grin split his face. Written upon his features was the same debauchery that I felt; that night I would do anything. All acts of sexual gratification were my rituals. I was a citizen of Sodom. I made my home in Gomorrah, of whom nothing is spoken. I was a Dog Priest of Sirius, prepared to indulge in frenzies of anal sex at the rising of the Dog Star. I was a catamite of Baal, and the cocksucker of Moloch. We all embraced our destiny as butt-sluts and come-mouths in the Circle of Set.

As Bromius invoked the Magpies of Sexual Bondage, Ladon the hundred-headed dragon, Typhon the spewing volcano, Orthrus the two-headed wolf, and Apep the pitch of chaos, I pricked with greater lust. My body felt dry, and I longed for men to restore me with their juices. Just as Set devoured the penis of Osirus, I craved semen in my mouth and semen in my bowels. I needed that flood of manseed, that flow of the divine fluids, the influx of the cosmic cum that would restore me, annihilate me, resurrect me, destroy me, reincarnate me, endanger me, and protect me from the vicissitudes of time.

"Shoot into me the timeless rapture of the infinite flow," I shouted, my plea lost in the universal cry. "Bind me to the Chthonic powers. Let me serve in sexual bondage."

"Fuck my gay ass," Skip shouted. "Come in my mouth. I live to receive the bounty of men's balls."

"Let me be Apep's Fuck Toy," Sandes screamed. "Mighty Apep, bind my ass and use me for your pleasure."

As we made our declarations, Apollo and Hyacinthos tied long red ribbons to our arms and legs. The ribbons fluttered in the wind, symbols of our bondage to the deities. As the drums and pipes tossed their vibrations against the approaching thunder, we formed a sinuous line, each boy holding the bare hips of the boy ahead, and danced around the circle. Other than our ribbons, we were naked in our rite and our cocks were erect. The ribbons flowed as we danced, emblems of our thrall to pederast masters.

❖

Tipper's Tale

If my cock had not been about to rip through my briefs, I would have supposed that Thad had lost his marbles. However, I could see that this rite involved some bondage ritual required by the deities invoked during that full moon. I wished that I possessed the notebook that placed the ritual into context. I rubbed my throbbing cock through my briefs, and decided that I would ask Skip about this ritual when he and I finally got together.

I had never considered bondage; by homosexual standards, the oral and anal sex Jeep, Lyle, and I had engaged in was vanilla oral sex and anal sex. I wondered whether we might introduce a game of some sort. The idea of being tied up and pretending to be fucked against my will appealed to me. The fantasy of submitting sexually to a master intrigued me. I could imagine being ordered to suck the master's cock.

I guessed that the Circle of Set appeared as a part of Thad's ritual cycle. I had the distinct impression that it did not occur often, and that I was reading about a special occasion. Enthralled, I read on.

❖

Thad's Journal: The Fourth of February, continued

Dr. Bromius approached me as I stood watching the bondage ceremony. "Why have you stopped participating, Adonis?"

My ploy to seduce my professor was working. My sudden and feigned disinterest interested him. I rubbed my right buttock against my professor's cock. "Master, I would willingly be your slave." His cock had been half-hard. As I pushed back against him, I felt it swell to its full glory. I was surprised at how thick it was. I turned, dropped to my knees, and kissed it.

"I want *you* to dominate me," I said. I slowly rose, kissing his cock, kissing up his stomach to his nipples. I sucked his left nipple. I licked and worried it with my tongue until Bromius stood moaning. The skin on his cock was stretched tight. A tiny drop of pearly fluid dripped from the tip, but it fell to the ground before I could lick it off.

"It is *you* who are dominating me," he said, shivering with passion. "So it has always been. The master submits to the desires of the slave, the lord to the serfs, the deity of the clouds to the hinds of the field."

I raised my head so I could kiss his lips. It was the first time we had kissed since that morning in his office, all those long months past. Bromius's tongue slid sweetly into my mouth with the fervor I well remembered. As his insatiable ardor grew, his hands explored down my back, tracing every muscle and bone. His caress wandered down my ribs and reached the jutting tops of my ass mounds. On down his exploring hands went, over the rise of my buttocks, my hard, brawny wrestler's butt, until Bromius was kneading my buttock muscles with his strong hands. He threw his whole soul into his caress. Yet even as his attention centered upon my ass, I sucked his tongue long and kissed him deeply. My tongue played in his mouth until he was moaning with irresistible yearning.

Suddenly, he pulled his mouth away and looked into my eyes. Awed at my passion, he looked pleased as well. Then a sense of place and purpose flooded back. We had cast a Circle of Set. One must be the slave of the other.

"Fuck me, master," I said. "Dominate me. Use me for your pleasure."

My chest throbbed as I waited for his response. I felt the wind upon my skin, mingled with the charged heavens. The lightning was moving toward the Three Sisters and Brokentop, yet danger still hung in the air. Around the circle, boys were submitting to one another. Skip/Osiris had been bound ass up over a tree stump while Apollo buttfucked him. Orpheus and Narcissus were holding Moloch's head and forcing him to suck Hermes's cock while two other boys forced Hermes to submit to the oral domination.

"Yes, my young slave," he said. "I will fuck you, Adonis. Turn again and rub your ass against my cock."

I pushed back my ass and rubbed my buns against his dick. I stroked his solid erection between my cheeks, up and down my crack. "Your cock feels good against my ass." I rubbed his dick harder.

"Don't speak unless I order you," he said. "The Ritual of Set demands your absolute obedience. You may say *Yes, master*."

"Yes, master."

"Now fall on your knees, place your face in the rotting leaves, and thrust back your buttocks."

Bromius slipped a fresh condom onto his erection. On my knees, I placed my face in the brown discards of withered heath. I pushed back my ass, wiggling with anticipation. My heart was thundering with excitement.

"Now beg for it, slave."

"Take me, master. Fuck my ass. Give me your sweet cock."

Dr. Bromius dropped behind me, and his hands caressed my ass mounds again. I loved the feel of his hands on my ass. I suddenly felt slutty, but slutty in a good way. The spirits of the gods of submission were moving through me as Bromius mounted me. I felt his weight upon my back and his thick cock pressing against my asshole.

"Are you my dog, slave?"

"Yes, I'm your dog," I said. "Use me, master; use me as your dog."

Bromius inserted his massive member into my anal canal. My asshole dilated around his dick. I felt an enormous pleasure as my sphincter stretched to its limit. He slowly pushed deeper, never ceasing the pressure that penetrated me. I felt full, and fuller still as the tremendous fullness invaded deep into my rectum.

Bromius's voice came with a hot sexual rasp. "I give you permission to praise me, slave."

"My master," I shrieked over the pipes and drums. "I'm so full. Your cock is so good. So good."

Bromius reared his hips back and thrust as if to rend me into two halves. Yet my asshole remained intact. I took him; I took all he could give me, though I could not have taken even a tiny bit more.

"Master." The word was rendered almost intelligible by my uncontrollable moan. He did not comment on my disobedience in speaking without permission. In answer, he thrust again—savagely; he was really putting it to me. He rose and thrust again and again while moans, grunts, and groans escaped unbidden from my lips. It was as if he was drilling me, and ripping me apart at the same time, but I prayed to Set that it would never stop. My cock was hard and leaking pre-cum onto the winter ground, and I knew this fuck would take me over the edge. I was going to have the fabled anal orgasm.

"Servant of the Demiurge, you give good ass," Bromius wailed. "Your ass is so fucking good. Oh, I'm going to shoot. Your ass is too tight, Adonis. I can't hold out against your insatiable sphincter—you're squeezing the spunk out of my dick. Thus the slave forces the master; thus the slave milks the master of his bounty."

I wanted him to have it as good as it gets. I squeezed his dick as he pulled back, and the sensation of him emptying and filling me while his cock head milked my prostate with each lunge drove me wild with joy. My dick started vibrating in a way it never had before; it bucked and lurched in the rotting leaves, and a pleasing sensation filled me that I'd never experienced. I knew that something spectacular was about to happen.

"Master, I'm about to come too. Master, fuck, yeah, go in my ass, man. Let it go in my ass."

"Adonis, oh, oh," he gasped. "It's getting so good. So good."

A ravishing sensation of almost unendurable delight grew in my ass, a savory weight. Blissful tingles replaced the disturbing vibration in my dick; the torturous undulations of bliss regaled my cock head and grew in intensity. Throbbing detonations echoed up my shaft until my pelvic muscles blasted a spurt of cum into the leaves. As my cock throbbed joyfully, Dr. Bromius's dick bucked in my ass, and I shot load after load of wet cum into my herbaceous bed.

Slowly, the sensations subsided, until I was left with only a dull ache that was not unpleasant. Dr. Bromius gasped, shuddered, and pulled his tortured dick out of my ass. "In the name of Bacchus, lad, you give great ass," he wheezed as he rolled off my ass and fell beside me on the ground. I lowered my tender ass and collapsed beside him. "Help me with this, slave," he demanded, indicating his cock.

"Yes, master." I unrolled the bloated condom from his dick and threw it into the receptacle. He patted the ground beside him, so I lay back down on the leaf meal.

"It's been a long time since I came that much. You milked me."

Thunder rolled far down over the South Sister. I looked around the circle. One boy was tied with his back to a sapling, hands over his head. Other boys were taking turns nursing upon the captive's swollen cock. I thought of joining the fun, but my asshole was pulsating delectably, and Bromius allowed me to rest my head upon his heaving chest. "Thank you, master."

By the time the priests called for the conclusion to the orgy, we were a drained, spent crew of young men. The storm had moved off, so no dark clouds drew across our bright moon. We sat naked together eating plum cakes and drinking pear juice. Skip joined me, lowering his bare ass so it pressed against mine.

"That bondage stuff was fun," Skip said.

"As long as nobody takes it seriously," I added.

"These boys know it's only a game. Nobody is really a slave or a master."

"We're all slaves of something, Skip," I said wistfully, "and despite our pretensions, none of us are masters of our fate."

"What's wrong with you, Thad?" Skip whispered. "That's fuckin' depressing."

"I just have a feeling," I said. "Call it a premonition."

Shortly thereafter, Dr. Bromius banished the four Magpie-watchtowers: Ladon, Typhon, Orthrus, and Apep. Attis and Orpheus closed the Circle of Set until the next year. We dressed and departed toward our individual homes. Skip and I walked together. He kept questioning me, but I couldn't tell him more than I had. I only felt sad, because I knew that family and community were pitted against us. Already my heart longed for the passing of the uncertain month until our next bacchanalia under the silver moon.

CHAPTER NINE

Tipper's Tale

Forgetting that my parents had guests in the house, I had been rubbing my dick vigorously through my briefs until I reached the final paragraphs of Thad's description. Thad's premonition spoke of events to come. Unfortunately, Thad was not writing down the things I most wanted to know; for instance, what was happening at home? Had our parents begun to suspect my brother's secret? I couldn't guess, and only two notebooks remained to be read. Would they solve the mystery? Would they tell me where my Thad and Tye were now?

I heard footsteps in the hallway, and a hand on my doorknob. I tossed a pillow over the notebook, leaped to my feet, and grabbed my baggy blue shorts. Luckily, my erection had subsided.

"Tip," my mother said, opening the door. Had the woman no sense of my privacy? "We'd like to talk to you." That sounded ominous. I was trying to pull my shorts over my ass as Mom entered my room.

"I was changing," I said accusingly.

Oblivious to my discomfiture, she continued, "Your father wants you to come to the living room right now."

"Let me get my shirt on, Mom. Is your company still here?"

"Yes, Tip. Make yourself decent." She left without bothering to close my door again.

Make yourself decent—too late for that. I shut my door and changed into my jeans and a T-shirt. I pulled carpet slippers over my bare feet, checked my appearance in the mirror, and padded toward the living room.

Brother Deke was sitting in one armchair and my mother in another. Sister Doris, Deacon Beacon, and Mrs. Beacon occupied the couch. My father was standing near the window. Thoughts of the Holy Inquisition flooded my mind, and I looked for the coming of rack and rope. What followed was less terrible than I feared, and more ghastly than anything my imagination could conceive.

"Terry," Deacon Beacon began with a faint *ahem* in his address, "what do you know about the sin of homosexuality?"

It was enough to cause me to dash from the room, shrieking at the top of my lungs. Having some presence of thought, I adopted a puzzled demeanor. "Huh?"

"A young person wishes to join our congregation," the deacon said. "It goes without saying that this individual hails from the godless city of Portland. This supplicant has confessed to me and to Pastor Kern the trials of being long beset with that ghastly desire."

I could have released a terrific sigh. Whatever was going on, it had nothing to do with my activities.

Brother Deke piped up with one of the more pathetic church clichés. "As we say, love the homosexual, hate the homosexuality."

"Love the sinner, hate the sin," Sister Doris said by way of correcting Deke.

My father made a low, disgusted noise down in his throat. "I don't love them," he muttered barely loud enough to be heard. Something horrible and hollow rang dully in his voice, as if he was lying to himself.

Love the bigot, hate the bigotry. "I'm confused, Deacon," I said. "Are you talking about your daughter?"

Mrs. Beacon gasped and turned bright red.

"Tip!" Mom's rebuke was as sudden as the wrath of God, and Pop shot me a furious look.

Deacon Beacon blushed crimson, but he had the gumption to stick up for me. "I guess that would be a natural question, considering the circumstances," the deacon said. "Although I'm taken aback to learn that Terry knows about the case of my wayward offspring."

Know about Mary Beacon? Everybody in Muskrat Creek knew about Mary Beacon. Everybody in the United States knew about

Mary Beacon. I didn't apologize for bringing up a painful subject. Love the homophobe, hate the homophobia. At least, Deacon Beacon's words had partially mollified my parents.

"We're talking about a young fellow," Brother Deke said, "not a thirty-year-old diesel dyke."

"Deke!" Doris's shout was so vehement that everything stopped. She was favoring Deke with a killer look far worse than the one I'd received from Mom and Dad.

"Oh, yeah, sorry, Deacon." Brother Deke did appear to be sincerely abashed. (If I looked abashed, it was because I faked it well.)

"Anyway, to get to the point," the deacon pressed along, "we're holding a deliverance for this young man on Sunday."

"We're going to pray the gay out," Mrs. Beacon said. "Just the way they did for Jesus." What the hell was she referring to? "It's important that all the young men in our church attend."

Finally, I saw how I fit into this scenario. "Tip will be there" Pop's promise was delivered in a tone that barred any argument.

"I wouldn't be comfortable seeing something like that." Would I never! How could any self-respecting homosexual allow himself to be so abused and abased? The idea revolted me. If I had possessed the courage, I would have told them the truth about myself then and there. But I didn't. I was afraid.

"I share your discomfort, Terry," Deacon Beacon said. "The idea of men deliberately perverting themselves with other men is repugnant to all of us. But it's important that you be there. You will need to suppress your revulsion for the deviants long enough to help us cleanse the devil out of this degraded youth."

Pop looked stern. "Tip will be there."

A horrible thought occurred to me. "Do I know this guy?"

"Oh, I'm sure you don't."

"What's his name?"

Deacon Beacon looked uncertain. He looked at my father and Brother Deke and the three women for spiritual guidance. "What's wrong with telling him the pansy's name, Bob?" Sister Doris asked.

"Perhaps we should keep the name private for the moment," the deacon said.

"I want to make sure I don't know him—like from school or something." However, by then I was convinced that this guy was nobody I knew. Then another thought occurred to me. "What does he look like?"

"Oh, for heaven's sake, Tip," my father said. "What do you care what he looks like? You can't always identify a faggot by the way he looks. Besides, you'll see him on Sunday—for certain—because you're going to be there."

Shortly thereafter, I escaped from the nest of homophobes, my father foremost among them. I stopped in the bathroom and brushed my teeth. By the time I returned to my room, I was no longer in the mood to masturbate. The session in the living room had sickened me. My mind was a whirl of thoughts. I had the distinct sense that if my parents ever found out that I was gay, they would throw me out of the house. The prospect of wandering desperate and homeless was horrible to me, but even more horrible was the loss of my parents' love. In spite of their prejudices and faults, I did love them. Nevertheless, even as I thought about the way they had cared for me, I knew that they bore some guilt for Thad's and Tye's disappearance.

I listened to the sounds of the night. I heard the guests' cars pull away, and I heard Mom and Pop retire to their bedroom. Sleepless even after my hard night swimming, I pulled out a book I had sneaked from Thad's shelf and started reading at random. It was a volume of *The Golden Bough* titled *Taboo and the Perils of the Soul*. Finally, I drifted off to sleep disturbed by the vague feeling that the local taboos would imperil my own soul.

I awoke after a cascade of wild erotic dreams. During the final seconds of sleep, my unconscious had transformed taboos that imperiled the soul into a joyful orgy involving Tizzy, Lyle, Jeep, Rick, Mart, Skip, and several other guys, including the unnamed, unseen guy from the church. I dreamed of sucking Tizzy's cock while Mart fucked my ass. I kissed down the side of Tizzy's cock until my mouth met his balls. I tea-bagged his ball sack, sucking on it while Tizzy moaned. Mart pushed his red swim briefs down to his knees and was humping my ass ferociously. I felt his cock sliding deep into me. My anal sphincter sent ripples of pleasure up my back and down toward my cock with each stroke.

I kissed Tizzy's cock from stem to tip, slipped my lips over his cock head, and took the whole erection down my throat. Tizzy was moaning with approaching orgasm as I fucked his dick with my throat. Pulling up for air, I wrapped my tongue around the head and top part of his shaft. When I knew that he was committed to come, I pulled my mouth back, grabbed his dick, and jacked it into my mouth. I stuck out my tongue so that his fresh cum erupted onto my taste buds. Mart was coming in my ass then, thrusting so hard that he shook me. I couldn't hold Tizzy's dick still and ended up jacking it onto my lips. His hot cum splattered against my lips and ran down my chin.

My body was shuddering as I felt his warm semen on my face and tasted it on my tongue, even while Mart humped my butt furiously and called me his "boy toy," his "butt slut," and his "anal angel." A hot throbbing filled me, but the sensory vibration shifted into a familiar jingle. I heard a chorus of bells, and awoke aware that my phone was sounding. At the same time, my mother's voice echoed through the house. "Tipper, breakfast is ready." Outside, Ole' Cookie was banging the gong to summon the buckaroos to the chuck wagon for their morning vittles.

"Okay," I shouted for Mom's benefit and grabbed up my phone. I hit the answer key and mumbled a greeting. "Hey, Tip, did I wake you up?" Lyle's voice came chirpily through the airwaves.

"Right out of a wet dream."

"Really?"

"Yeah, really."

"Did you come in your pants?"

I was, in fact, attired only in my briefs. They were slightly swampy, damp with sweat mingled with a few drops of pre-ejaculate. "I was just about to unload, but you woke me before I went over the edge."

"Oh, sorry, I guess," Lyle said. "Oh, fuck it, I'll make it up to you."

"Tipper!" Mom screamed. Outside, the breakfast gong rattled so loud that the llamas in Sisters could have heard it.

"Lyle, I'll call you back."

"Wait, how about a trip to Cougar Ridge Community College this morning? Jeep and I are going."

"Yes. I have to eat breakfast with my family. I'll call you back as soon as I can, Lyle."

I stripped off my briefs, wiped my asshole and dick on yesterday's towel, pulled up my tan shorts, sans underwear, slipped a Muskrats T-shirt over my torso, and paraded down the hallway. Mom had fried sausage patties, scrambled eggs, and cooked hotcakes filled with raspberries. She had also whipped up a pan full of grits and made gravy from the sausage grease. I figured the fat and cholesterol would kill the entire family before we had a chance to cast the demon of homosexuality from a brain-rinsed Portland boy.

"I have to get down to the shop," Pop exclaimed, checking the clock as if I had delayed him. "Japheth Farms is in the market for a fleet of tractors with all the accessories."

"Is old man Japheth coming himself?" I asked, hoping to keep Pop off less comfortable subjects.

"He'll be at the shop at ten," my father said solemnly. "At the least, his sons, Shem and Shawn, will be coming to see us. Would you like to help me make the sale, Tip?" His voice contained a strange hope I had never heard before that morning.

"Oh, I wish I could, Pop," I said, sincerely meaning every word. "I promised I would go with Lyle and Jeep. We're heading over to the community college. We want to check out a few things."

My mother shot my father a significant look, which was not lost on me. "Of course," Pop said swiftly, "your education comes first. I can always sell tractors, plows, and disks. I really don't need you to help me do that." He stopped, as if uncertain what to say next. "But I'd love to have you selling them beside me. I'd love to see you take over the family business."

I choked up then. Pop's dream would come to nothing. The so-called family business was doomed. The equipment my father sold was suited for the family farm, but the family farm would not exist in another twenty years. Computerized tractors would replace those human operated John Deere models, and gigantic greenhouses on orbiting space platforms would eventually replace the farm.

I poured raspberry syrup over my pancakes, before I scooped scrambled eggs and sausage patties onto my plate. My mom filled my mug with cocoa.

Pop left before I was finished. Mom was washing the dishes as I deposited my plate and utensils into the soapy water. "Can I help?" I asked.

"No, go see what the college has to offer, Tipper." Without any warning, she burst into tears. She stood sobbing at the sink, and nothing I could offer would console her.

"Mom!"

"Go, Tipper."

"Is this about Thad? Or Tye? Tell me. I have to know."

"Shut your damned mouth, Tipper. Leave me to my own hell."

I retreated down the hall, stricken, confused, and determined. I knew that she was vulnerable, but she was also volatile. What was the key to the secret, besides the one she wore constantly around her neck—which I so furtively possessed?

I shaved my face, brushed my teeth, showered my stinky body, and dressed appropriately to the day. When Lyle's yellow Sentra appeared in our driveway, I jumped into the backseat. Lyle gassed us through Muskrat Creek, through Beaver Dam, and on toward Cougar Ridge.

The campus was attractively located on a precipitous ridge overlooking Cougar Creek. Near the edge stood a long border of Scotch Broom, brilliant with yellow blossoms. The campus was dotted with Noble Firs, Western Hemlock, Douglas Firs, and Sitka Spruce with winding walkways running between wisteria shrouded halls hewed from native stone. The college boasted of a thriving horticulture program, so the trees and bushes were labeled. We passed an island of attractive greenhouses surrounded by a pond filled with colorful fish.

"We gotta check out the library," Lyle said as we passed Clock Tower Hall. "I'll show you guys what I found."

Unlike the administration building, the library was open on Saturday. The library was five stories tall, and the first flight of steps led down to a shocking collection of old magazines and journals, most bound like hardcover books. I opened a couple of news magazines and read about the opinions regarding a military draft. The issue was dated 1939.

Jeep urged me on. "Come on, Tip." He swatted my ass to get me moving. "Let's see what Lyle is talking about."

"We gotta find the occult section," Lyle said.

"Don't you know?"

"I haven't been here. I got into the library's catalog online."

The assistant librarian who had been following us since our arrival spoke up when we reached the section on paganism and the occult. "Can I help you boys find something?"

I looked at him for the first time. He had soft brown hair with highlights, a creamy complexion, smooth features, full lips, and a nice build. He was wearing a pastel blue shirt and brown slacks that fit him nicely.

"Yeah, we're looking for a book called…" Lyle stopped as he caught a good look at our librarian. "Wow!"

"Yeah, wow!" I echoed. I wanted to grab this assistant librarian's ears and plant a big wet kiss on his lips.

Jeep looked around for eavesdroppers. "Come on, guys. Try to be a little discreet."

I didn't care who was listening. I wanted that man. "I can't be discreet. I'm in love."

"Me, too," Lyle said.

The librarian blushed prettily. He tried to talk, but he ended up stuttering. Finally, he managed a question. "Are you boys college students?"

"Seniors in high school," Jeep said, dropping the deadly H.S. bomb. What man would be willing to fuck high school boys, whether they were of fuckable age or not? Exposure would result in the worst possible publicity. Newspapers and television news stations would speculate about criminal charges, even though nothing illegal had occurred. The least terrible thing that would happen would be the certain loss of his job.

All those thoughts and more must have flashed through that librarian's mind, because he turned pale and backed off three paces.

Lyle waved his hand at the bookshelf where popular books on Wicca by Margot Adler, Hans Holzer, Scott Cunningham, Starhawk, and Raven Grimassi rested. "We're looking for a book titled *Gay Paganism*."

The librarian recovered sufficiently to help us. "That one is right over here. He lifted a trade paperback off the shelf. Lyle took it from him and displayed it proudly.

"So what?" Jeep said.

Lyle moved his thumb, which had been obscuring the author's name. He was holding *Gay Paganism* by Adonis.

The librarian started jabbering nervously. "We have an extensive section on the occult, particularly Wicca, witchcraft, and neo-paganism," he said. "Fifteen years ago, some professor, no longer with the institution, pushed the head of the library to stock up on those. Even after that professor left—under a cloud of scandal, I heard—the head librarian kept adding to the collection. The current head of the library would like to weed out this section."

"It can't be," I said.

"No, that's the real reason why we have such an extensive section on paganism," the librarian said, misunderstanding me completely.

"When was this book written?"

Lyle opened to the copyright page. "Ten years ago," he said. He handed it to me, so I opened it at random and began reading aloud:

Gay Paganism
by Adonis Tempter

In heterosexual covens, initiations are rites of passage to incorporate the initiate into the coven. The initiate fears the unknown, which leads to belongingness. Our rites are different. Our initiations provoke both release and rebellion. The initiate does not lose himself in the group. The initiate is freed to damn his authorities and to spit in the eye of his censor. The initiate opens to the mystery, but that opening inspires personal creativity. Our group has no ruler, no control. We conquer the conqueror. Once the initiate has passed through our boundaries, he has entered the vast circle. It is a dangerous place. The initiate is no longer safe, but he does not seek safety. He seeks freedom.

"It sounds somewhat like Thad's writing." I looked in vain for information about the author. "The name Adonis Tempter doesn't tell us much." I turned to the librarian. "Can we find out anything about this writer? Like where he lives?"

"Who's Thad?" the librarian asked, *apropos* of nothing we wanted to discuss.

"An old friend of the family," Lyle said. "Does the library have a book of writers' biographies?"

"Well, some writers." The librarian hesitated. "Adonis Tempter is clearly a pseudonym, and our book about pseudonyms covers only famous or popular authors. I can tell you that Erle Stanley Garder wrote as A. A. Fair and that Stephen King wrote under the name Richard Bachman."

"Who the fuck cares?" Jeep whispered, and Lyle shushed him. The librarian consulted a dozen reference books, but met with no success. The author Adonis Tempter was as baffling as everything else that involved my brothers.

The librarian gave us the address and phone number of the publisher. I called immediately on my cell, but the publisher had been bought out by another company five years earlier. "Surely, you maintained the former publisher's records. What if that writer submitted another manuscript to you? Wouldn't you want to know that you published him before? Wouldn't you even care to see the sales numbers on the earlier book?"

The woman with the thick New England accent couldn't answer any of my questions. She wasted ten of my cell minutes checking her files, but she didn't find out anything about Adonis Tempter.

"You don't even know where the other publisher sent the checks?" I asked.

"No," she said. "Maybe there weren't any."

"Fucking wonderful," I said and disconnected.

"Today has been unproductive," Jeep said.

"No shit. Even my wet dream got interrupted."

The librarian's eyes widened. Fortunately, we were the only students in the library, though we weren't students of the college. I wondered why no one else was using the library. It seemed like a perfect time to write research papers or catch up on studies.

Suddenly, I felt slightly superior to these college students. I might not have been a straight-A student like Lyle, but at least I did my homework. And since I had discovered Thad's collection of books, I had read more than I ever had in my life.

❖

After we left the college, we drove to Burgerpig, where we downed burgers, fries, and milkshakes.

"I'm surprised that he let you check out this book, Tip," Lyle said flipping through the pages. "Maybe he had the hots for your butt. You aren't even a student of that college."

"I suppose the college is desperate for anybody to check something out. There didn't seem to be a lot of students studying in the library."

"Let me see that book," Jeep said, grabbing for the book and splattering a dot of ketchup on a page. "Does it have pictures?"

"Hey, be careful, Jeep. I'm responsible for that."

"Just a tiny spot." Lyle wiped the ketchup with a napkin. The thought that my brother may have written this rare tome flickered through my brain, but I didn't bring up that objection. I didn't want Jeep to know that I resented him getting ketchup on words Thad may have written. I understood something of the complex emotions my mother must feel when she dusted my brothers' room. At some time in the past, she had made their room a household shrine, a *sanctum sanctorum*, a holy of holies—probably against my father's express orders.

Jeep wiped his hands carefully, so Lyle handed over the book. I dumped more ketchup on my fries and savored them one at a time.

"This guy makes gay sex sound like something holy," Jeep said, which drew stares from the family of eight at the next table. Lyle flashed them a cheery smile and pointed toward the book Jeep was holding. The father of the family sounded as if he was growling deep down in his throat.

"That man is snarling like a rabid dog," Jeep said.

"An actual *paterfamilias*," Lyle said.

"Breeders," Jeep said as if the thought sickened him. "Look at them. They've popped out six kids. It's enough to turn your stomach."

"Fuckin' disgusting."

"Will you guys quit it? It's just your typical rural Oregon family having a Saturday lunch. Do you want to get thrown out of Burgerpig?" I spoke too late. The looming form already bearing down on us was the restaurant manager. Needless to say, nobody stopped to fork over cash to the home team there. We even had to pay for our half-eaten lunch.

Leaving Burgerpig to the breeders, we drove to the Beaver Dam Fitness Club. At the far end of the men's locker room, we selected three empty lockers and changed into our gym shorts and T-shirts. Two men were headed toward the swimming pool. One was wearing a slinky pair of green jammers and the other was wearing half-pink and half hibiscus-flowered Asian swim briefs. The Asian man looked so incredibly gay that I wanted to follow him to the hot tub. However, my self-discipline restrained me.

"Did you see that guy?" Lyle gasped, demonstrating an embryonic erection through his spider-web-patterned blue exercise shorts.

Another man turned to look at Lyle, and I saw that the stranger's thoughts were anything but platonic. For a moment, I wondered whether every human male was, in essence, desirous of sex with other males, but I pushed the conjecture from my thoughts and concentrated upon my task.

"We need to do cardio today," I said. "Forget about whatever hot butts might be sitting in the hot tub. Think about sprinting your heart rate."

We did not keep a steady pace on the cardiovascular machines. Whether riding elliptical trainers, stationary bicycles, treadmills, stair climbers, or whatever, we started at resting heart rate, increased to a hundred by six minutes, drove up to 130 for two minutes, dropped to 110 for three minutes, increased to 140 for three minutes, and so on. Our goal was ever-growing endurance and ever decreasing fat deposits. Within forty-five minutes, we burned off all the calories we had consumed at Burgerpig. After that, the rest of our burn was gravy.

I had soaked through my gym clothes, Lyle was sweating hard, and Jeep was creating a puddle under his machine when I called a halt. Then we accomplished three repetitions each on the butterfly machine, the rowing machine, the biceps machine, and the triceps machine. We were in fair agony by the time we hit the showers.

Lyle's naked ass, an ass I had fucked, preceded me into the shower. Jeep followed my behind, which he had also fucked. In spite of our history, our main thoughts did not center around sex, but around our next competition. We discussed the next meet as we showered in adjoining stalls. "Do we have a chance against the Fur Traders, Tip?" Lyle asked seriously. "They're supposed to be invincible."

"No team is invincible," I said. "That's a big lie put out by the entire city of Astoria."

"Yeah, but can we win?" Jeep asked.

"Yes, if we really want to win," I said. "What is it worth to us?"

"Huh?"

"Do we have to win? Do our lives depend upon winning? Does winning or losing determine our very future?"

"I guess not."

"Wrong fuckin' answer, Jeep. We have to swim our hearts out. We have to swim our guts out. We have to swim our asses off. We've got to leave those Fur Traders wondering what the *hell* happened."

"That would be fun," Lyle said.

"Yeah, that's the secret. That's what it's all about, Lyle. Winning is fun."

Sudden applause erupted throughout the shower room, and the clapping echoed into the locker room. To the residents of Beaver Dam and the residents of Muskrat Creek, we were heroes. We might have been gay boys swimming in slinky bikini swimsuits, but to the community, we meant something. Men were applauding us. Naked, soapy, dripping, Lyle, Jeep, and I stepped out of our shower stalls and took a deep bow.

"You guys want to go back to my house?" Jeep asked as Lyle accelerated his yellow Sentra out of the fitness club's parking lot. "My parents are protesting for Latin American issues in Washington this weekend. Tió Augusto is there too because he has a meeting with two senators, and perhaps the president."

"Of course we'll come to your house," Lyle said, handing me the envelope full of dollar bills we'd collected from the men in the locker room.

"Yeah." I was feeling rather horny by then, and I counted on some hot sex with Lyle and Jeep to put me right.

Jeep was sitting in the backseat and I was riding shotgun. Jeep pushed his head between the Nissan's bucket seats and licked my ear. "I've been wanting to get you two boys into my bed," he whispered seductively.

Jeep's family lived in a sprawling three-story farmhouse, situated in the center of three thousand acres covered with junipers and sagebrush. The sage scented the air and gave off a purple glow in the late afternoon sunlight. We bounced over a cattle guard and rolled along the dusty road through a verdant pasture where Jersey cows watched us with speculative eyes.

Shortly, we passed a man seated on a black mare. Two border collies stood beside the horse, and the rider was wearing a costume I had only imagined. He was decked out in voluminous brown *bombachas* with a *chiripá*, a garish yellow shirt mostly covered by his poncho, a flamboyant red neckerchief, and a wide-brimmed hat with little balls hanging from its brim. He was carrying a *boleadoras*, a *facón*, and a *rebenque*.

"Is that man a gaucho?"

Jeep turned his head and waved out the window. The gaucho tipped his *boleadoras* to his hat in response. "Sure, he's a real gaucho. That's Paco. He taught me how to ride a horse. He's been with my family forever."

"Go, cowgirl," Lyle muttered. Jeep didn't hear him, and I didn't repeat it.

Jeep had not mentioned that the servants would be present while his parents were away. To Jeep's way of thinking, the humans who served his family didn't actually count as people. We passed a cook and two maids on our way upstairs.

Lyle regarded the servants nervously. "They won't tell your parents?"

"Of course not. Besides, we're not going to invite them to watch us."

"You could invite that gaucho," I said.

"Oh, you naughty boy." Jeep followed those words with gay sounding squeal that must have confirmed whatever suspicions the servants entertained. Then he swatted my ass, providing additional evidence. After he led us into his bedroom and locked the door, I breathed a sigh of relief and fell back into our game and swatted his ass.

"How naughty am I?"

Jeep grabbed my butt with both hands and pulled me close. "Really naughty."

Lyle pressed close behind. He reached around and unfastened my belt. "I agree. You're a bad boy, and now you're going to get it."

Jeep licked the side of my face, barely brushed my lips, and moved to my ear. Lyle unfastened the waistband of my pants and pulled down my zipper. Jeep was nibbling at my earlobe as Lyle pushed my pants down. My cock was so hard that my bikini briefs were ridgepoled. Jeep's tongue slipped into my ear. He probed and licked. Then he whispered, "You're gonna get it, bad boy. I'm gonna suck you hard. I'm gonna suck your dick until you beg me to stop."

Lyle pulled off my sneakers and socks before dragging my pants off my feet. Jeep continued frenching my ear, in between describing how he was going to suck me until I cried for mercy. He stepped back for a second while Lyle pulled my T-shirt over my head. Then I was standing only in my cock-stretched briefs while my friends, both still fully dressed, ravished me with their mouths. Jeep kissed my lips, long and lingering the touch of his hot lips, and then he slowly descended. His tongue touched my throat and ran down my jugular. He reached my nipples. Then he was sucking my left nipple.

Lyle started with the insides of my knees. Have you ever been kissed in the bend of the knee? Kissed by a true friend—I mean a lover of the same sex? Explosive raptures traveled up my nerves. The kiss upon the back of my knee was like a kiss on my asshole. I puckered with the vibrating sensation.

Jeep pulled my nipple with his lips; he puckered my skin and sent quivering vibrations down my stomach. He worked my left nipple, and then he worked my right. As Jeep switched to the right nipple, Lyle inserted his fingers into the waistband of my briefs.

Previously, Lyle had touched my ass with every one of his body parts, but for some reason, that afternoon, the insertion of his fingers into my waistband nearly tipped me. I thought that my dick would erupt right then.

"Guys, get naked. I want to see your bare asses and jutting cocks."

Ignoring me, Lyle worked my briefs over my ripping hard-on, while Jeep worked at my right nipple. By then both nipples were swollen and felt bruised—but in a pleasant way. After Lyle managed to worry my underwear down to my feet, he indicated that I should raise a foot, which I did, and he pulled them over my heel and off my toes. He did the same with my other foot. I did not think too much of his messing with my feet until he kissed my toes.

My lungs drew hard, producing an audible gasp in my throat. The sharp blast of air filling my lungs cut like a stiletto. Lyle licked across my toes and touched his tongue to my other foot. Slowly, he licked upward until he reached my ankle. Jeep, on the other hand, finished with my nipple, and he kissed my skin leaving a path of rosy blemishes down to my navel. Lyle sat up and pressed his lips to the back of my knees again.

I literally wobbled. Jeep grabbed my buttocks to steady me. Still holding my ass cheeks, he pressed his tongue into my navel. He swished his tongue around, not in a clinical way, but in a manner that conveyed deep desire. Everything in the touch of his tongue communicated a deep desire to tongue my navel, and—as if I were receiving paranormal signals—I felt his lust, his desire to please me, his determination to enrapture me, and my mind and body responded to it. I quivered as though every nerve was broadcasting vibrations of pure pleasure.

Lyle was kissing the back of my thighs. As his lips rose to my butt cheeks, Jeep's strong grip separated my mounds. I felt Lyle's face against my butt crack. At the same instant, Jeep dropped to his knees and took my cock in his mouth. Lyle's tongue slipped between my butt cheeks until I felt the soft, wet, probing tip circling my asshole.

"Oh, I can't stand it," I said between my clenched teeth, while Lyle rimmed my ass and Jeep slid his tongue along the underside of my cock, took my dick head deep, pulled back until his swollen lips worked the head of my dick, and then rode forward again.

Lyle pushed his tongue into my hole, dilating my anal sphincter and going inside. Rolling raptures electrified my dick head. Palpitations, shivers, quivers, and twitters flared in my cock's shaft. Titillating sensations ruffled from the invasion of Lyle's tongue and sent a glowing heat through my bowels. The blood in my pelvis seemed in a boil, lashed to a fury by the two invasive mouths. Jeep still gripped my butt cheeks and his hands kneaded my gluteus muscles while he provoked my dick head with his lips. Ruffling tremors claimed me. My legs shook, but Jeep held me erect as his hard tongue, working lips, soft mouth, and wet throat exacerbated my twitches.

My heart was going pitter-patter-pit-a-pat as a turbulence greater than any hurricane, a sucking more powerful than a tornado, an eruption no volcano could match, and a tremor beyond the madcap shakes of an earthquake rippled, fired, palpitated, infused, jolted, and thrilled me. The muscles at the base of my cock contracted furiously and flipped a gargantuan squirt of my hot cum into Jeep's throat.

Lyle rimmed my asshole as my contracting sphincter pushed his tongue out. Jeep took me with all his might. He drank me down. I couldn't think, or utter a coherent word. "Oh, ah, let me, ah, good, fuck, yeah, let it," rushed from my lips and burst upon the infinite. I felt the moon, the fullness of the moon, the deep glowing circle, raptures of the infinite enfold me. I was all and nothing, one with eternity and non-existent, a resident of infinite bliss and the partaker of the happy nothingness.

As my contractions stilled into oblivion, I nearly collapsed. I had never experienced such a mind-blasting orgasm. Jeep held me up, his firm hands still gripping my butt. Jeep pulled his tongue away from me, rose, and steadied my shoulders. Only then did I realize how hard I was shaking or that heavy tears were running down my face. I laughed loudly, loud enough to bring a servant knocking softly at Jeep's door.

"Bring some food," Jeep yelled. "A platter of cold cuts, chips, some fruit, and soda pop."

The servant departed, determined to carry out Jeep's complex order. I was still weak on my pins (as the old cliché goes), so my friends helped me to the bed. "You guys haven't gotten off yet."

"We will, Tip. Lyle and I are going to do the old sixty-nine on each other—while you watch. By the time we get our rocks off, the servants will arrive with our snack."

I stretched upon the bed and watched closely as my two most intimate friends sucked each other's cock. I saw their swollen cocks disappear into their mouths. I watched their lips and tongues work. I saw the way their hands caressed each other's ass cheeks as they pulled deeper. I pushed my face close to the lipped dick heads, and I pulled back to watch their butts thrust as they shot their hot semen down each other's gullet. No description in mere words can convey the emotions that swept over me as my friends rippled through intense orgasm and shuddering ejaculation and socially disapproved swallowing. Yet each illicit gulp was a revolution, and I was captain of the revolutionaries.

Jeep and Lyle rushed into Jeep's connecting bathroom when the first knock sounded on the door. I pulled up my briefs and strode unflappably toward the door. The servant surveyed my underwear with hot Latino eyes but his demeanor spoke of acceptance, if not nonchalance. I took the platter of sliced fruit and carried it into the room. The next knock was more feminine. Still clad only in my underwear, I opened the door to a sultry Peruvian servant. Her charms were lost on me. I explained that her master Jeep Orbegoso was taking a shower after our exertions at the gymnasium, and I didn't mention Lyle. Her black eyes knowingly wicked, the servant answered with a gesture that proved she guessed what was going on. I took the plate of cold cuts and set it upon the table beside the window.

Jeep and Lyle were showering together. I stripped off my briefs and jumped under the spray with them. For a while, we had fun soaping each other's cocks and butt cracks, but we discovered that we were hungrier than we were horny. After we toweled each other off, we raided the goodies.

CHAPTER TEN

Tipper's Tale

Pop's pickup truck was gone, and I found a note on the kitchen counter. Mom had left a plate for me in the microwave, while my parents departed on some unnamed mission. I had been feeling chipper after the mind-boggling sex with Jeep and Lyle, plus I had received a sexy, teasing phone call from Tizzy while Jeep was driving Lyle and me back to our homes, but a finger of discomfort tickled the edge of my consciousness. Somehow, I just knew that my parents' unexplained absence had something to do with a thus-far unnamed gay guy at church.

I wasn't hungry after the huge snack at Jeep's, so I left my dinner until later. I took my key and entered Thad and Tye's room. The days were getting longer, and the evening sun glowed yellow upon Thad's bed. I rummaged through Thad's notebooks, replacing the one I had borrowed previously, and taking the next to last in the stack. I felt a strange sense of disappointment to think that I was reaching the bottom of the drawer, and still I had not received any clue regarding my brothers' fate.

I checked the room for telltale signs of my passing and carefully locked the door again. In my own room, I shoved the library book under my mattress, stripped naked, and reclined to read. Another of Thad's sexual escapades with the gay pagan cult was just the thing I needed to dispel the dark cloud of homophobia that was pushing against my sunshine. I opened the notebook and touched the head of my dick as I began to read.

❖

Thad's Journal: The Eighth of March

I've tried to keep my personal life out of this journal and to concentrate on the purely spiritual. Though not everybody would consider gay sex orgies a spiritual path, they were for me and for the other boys. I experienced a spiritual awakening in Dr. Bromius's circle, so that the sucking and the fucking became avenues to eternal bliss. However, this evening something happened that left me feeling creepy about myself.

The family sat down to dinner. Dad prayed over it, as usual, and everything was normal until my brother Tye reached for the gravy. His fingernails were bright green.

"What's wrong with your hand, Tye?" Mom demanded.

Innocently, Tye displayed his fingernails. All ten fingers were bright with green fingernail polish. "After school, Mary Beacon invited me over to her house. Some of her friends were there, and they got the idea about painting my fingernails."

"So you just let them?" Dad demanded, his brow furrowed. His voice took on an Old Testament resonance. "You let them paint you like a faggot?"

"It was just for fun," Tye said, pouting. "It was only a dress up game."

"Dress up?" Dad raised his voice. Mom looked utterly stricken, and little Tipper started crying. Dad pushed his plate away and laid his hands on the table. "Dress up? Did they dress you in woman's clothes?"

"It was just for fun."

"No son of mine is going to be a Nancy boy," Dad shouted. Mom was crying too by then. I sat frozen in my chair, unable to speak, but Tipper was bawling at the top of his lungs. "I won't have a homo in this family."

"It was innocent," Tye said, his face ghostly. He told me later, after the family had calmed down, that the girls had dressed him like a teenage girl, complete with panties, padded bra, and short skirt. They'd made up his face and painted his nails. However, Tye told me that the girls were laughing and saying that there was no need to teach him how to walk like a girl. He already did.

"I won't have it," Dad said. "Our church won't have it. God won't sanction it, and I won't either. From now on, you stop mincing around like a sissy, Tye." He pointed toward me, making me cringe. "Be more like your brother."

"Dad," Tye yelped, and my heart skipped two beats while I waited to hear what he was going to say. Would my brother reveal my secret? I sat glued, terrified of what would happen, and too afraid to speak up. I knew that I should spring to Tye's defense. I knew that I should take his side, which was also my side, against Dad's prejudice. But I couldn't. I was too scared.

"Deacon Beacon asked me about you just the other day," Dad said, his lip curling with his disgust. "He asked whether you were a homosexual. I assured him that no son of mine would become an abomination. Then you do that—that—in Bobby Beacon's own house. Under his roof. You let his strumpet daughter paint and dress you like a catamite."

Tye gasped. Mom grabbed Tipper and carried him out of the room, and I did what I do best. I sat doing nothing. Just as if I agreed with Dad. For his part, Dad stormed out of the dining room leaving Tye and me alone.

"Thanks for sticking up for me," Tye muttered sarcastically.

I felt so sick that I could say nothing. I went into the family room where I found Dad sitting in his chair reading from the family Bible.

"The woman shall not wear that which pertaineth unto a man, neither shall a man put on a woman's garment: for all that do so are abominations unto the Lord thy God," Dad quoted. "Deuteronomy, twenty-two, five."

I felt so sick that I wanted to die right then.

❖

Tipper's Tale

I lowered the notebook, my stomach churning. I felt just as sick as Thad must have felt. Yet I understood why Thad failed to speak up. I had never stood up to Pop either. He dominated us all, and his religion was the official religion of our family. Pop's values were all of our values, by God, or else. More and more, I found myself speculating what "or else" might portend.

❖

I saw a young fellow, perhaps years my senior, slouched in the front pew. He had his ass planted firmly as if he feared his next steps would carry him to the lethal injection chamber. The sight of him caused my necktie to tighten. Haltingly, I began to approach him, but Pop nudged me and steered me into our pew—left side of the altar, third row from the front.

Most of the people attending that church had known me all my life. But they didn't really know me, and I felt like the scriptural stranger in a strange land—or as Jeep would declare, "the bastard at a family reunion." When I was little, the church was an important part of my world. Now I had grown and changed, while it stayed the same.

I saw two members of my swim team sitting in pews behind us. They were both sophomores. They waved, and I gave them the victory sign. "We're gonna drown those Fur Traders," I stage whispered across a sea of gossiping Christians.

"Tip. Shut up. We're in church."

"But, Pop, it hasn't started yet. Everybody's talking."

"Well, you sit quietly. I won't have you carousing. This is a particularly solemn day."

Especially solemn for the poor cocksucker in the front row, I thought.

The ushers called for quiet then, and the congregation whispered while the choir filed in. Little Alma, who stood about four seven but whose sizable ass would have made her taller if she had been sitting down, cranked up the festivities with a rousing hymn about getting free from bondage. When that horror finally ended, Pastor Kern made his grand entrance, flanked by his deacons. He laid a shuddering benediction upon us before he called upon the Holy Trinity to kick out all the evil spirits. I felt like leaving with the evil spirits, but Pop's eye was on me.

Then we had to stand for a prayer, distinctly homophobic in its tone, with hints of racism, anti-Semitism, provincialism, chauvinism, and xenophobia. When Pastor Kern had finished spewing his intolerant rubbish, he called upon Little Alma to do her "Duty to the Lord" again. Two more hymns followed. Then they dragged some stage-struck eighth grader forward to read a Bible verse.

"I'm gonna read Romans, chapter one, verses twenty-six and twenty-seven," the kid said, eyeballing his audience warily. "For this cause God gave them up unto vile affections: for even their women did change the natural use into that which is against nature: And likewise also the men, leaving the natural use of the woman, burned in their lust one toward another; men with men working that which is unseemly, and receiving in themselves that recompense of their error which was meet."

Deacon Beacon beamed down on the poor deluded upstart. "And now, tell us, lad, what is to become of these miscreants?"

"Huh?" the kid said.

"Read the next verse I gave you."

"Oh, yeah, that's First Corinthians, chapter six, verses nine and ten."

"Well, read it, you little jerkoff," the deacon hissed.

The kid scanned his page and found his place—guided by divine inspiration, doubtless. "Know ye not that the unrighteous shall not inherit the kingdom of God? Be not deceived: neither fornicators, nor idolaters, nor adulterers, nor effeminate, nor abusers of themselves with mankind, nor thieves, nor covetous, nor drunkards, nor revilers, nor extortioners, shall inherit the kingdom of God."

The verse was totally depressing, but it no longer had power over me. My father's church dealt in bondage. Christianity, Judaism, and Islam are slave religions, not only because they promise the slaves a better life after death if they obey their owners in this one, but because they bind their believers to a consciousness of sin.

Thad's religion was freedom. Thad celebrated what he was. He accepted his nature, and he reveled in it—like all of Dr. Bromius's fortunate students. The great sex I'd been enjoying with Lyle and

Jeep was no sin. I was going to do it again, and I was going to do it with other boys too. I knew that I would be putting out for Tizzy before the sun set that day, and I was looking forward to it. He had called me that morning, before we left for church, and I had arranged to meet him in the afternoon. I was going to milk the cum out of him.

I would have liked the courage to stand before the congregation and proclaim, "Yes, I am gloriously homosexual. I don't want to change. I am not bound by your *sin*."

Of course, I didn't have the courage—or desire for self-destruction—to say anything. I watched the kid slip back to his pew considerably less stage-struck than when he had arrived. Even at his tender age, he was already realizing that he had been manipulated and used for the ends of men who sought power over their fellows.

Deacon Beacon and his fellow deacons took their seats flanking their reverend pastor. Pastor Kern rose behind the pulpit as if he were some Old Testament hotshot and fixed us with a steely eye. The words that came out of his mouth were pure scripture, "But before they lay down, the men of the city, even the men of Sodom, compassed the house round, both old and young, all the people from every quarter. And they called unto Lot, and said unto him, Where are the men which came in to thee this night? Bring them out unto us, that we may know them."

Know them? What did that imply? *Know them* could suggest that the men only wanted to get acquainted with these strangers staying in their town. Maybe the men were Homeland Security and they wanted to ascertain that the strangers weren't terrorists—which in light of what happened to the Cities of the Plain wasn't such a weird thought.

Pop touched my arm. "You listen carefully, Tipper." His command sent a shiver down my spine. What did my parents suspect?

The reverend was warming to his task. "I am, of course, referring to those degraded spirits whom Timothy referred to as "them that defile themselves with mankind." He cast a significant glance at the poor soul still seated alone on the front pew.

You old bastard, I thought. I'll bet you say that to all the boys.

Heating up his rhetoric, Pastor Kern trotted out Leviticus, "Thou shalt not lie with mankind, as with womankind: it is abomination." He followed that one up with, "If a man also lie with mankind, as he lieth with a woman, both of them have committed an abomination: they shall surely be put to death; their blood shall be upon them."

Nice, I thought sarcastically. We'll kill them and it will be their fault. They made us do it. The wife beater's lament: See what you *made* me do.

Following the sermon came the deliverance. The young fellow in the front pew was hauled forward and introduced as Roger Thomas. With an unheard of burst of affection, my father wrapped his arm around my shoulders. "I know this is painful, Tip," he whispered. "You have to watch."

"Why, Pop? What does this have to do with me?"

"The family curse," Mom said.

"No, Barb."

"We need to tell him, Frank."

"No," my father shouted. Everything stopped. The entire congregation stared slack-jawed at our family unit. The pastor, the deacons, and Roger Thomas stood stricken in their tracks.

"What's the matter, Frank?" Deacon Beacon asked following a pregnant pause. The deacons appeared dismayed by Pop's outburst, while Pastor Kern just looked damned mean.

The words "family curse" were not lost on me. I damned the fact that we were seated in a pew because I was missing my best chance to get the truth from my parents. I gripped my father's hand. "Let's go home, Pop. Let's just get up and go."

My father was realizing the enormity of his offense. He had shouted just at the commencement of one of Pastor Kern's famous deliverances, when he would cast the demon of alcoholism, gluttony, gambling, or some other sin out of a publically humiliated specimen. Getting his hands on an actual homosexual had been the pastor's lifelong ambition, and Pop had just spoiled the dramatic moment.

My father's face was beet purple. "I apologize, Reverend," he said hoarsely. "I forgot myself. My family is experiencing a moment of domestic disharmony."

I sat impressed, though slightly discouraged. I had never known my father to utter bullshit in such ponderous terms.

The congregation was growing restless, and Roger Thomas was eyeing the exit door nervously. I hoped that he would bolt and end this nightmare. Then Deacon Usher spoke up. "Perhaps, we should take a short break."

"Break?" thundered the pastor. "Do you think this is one of those godforsaken college classes? There are no breaks from the Lord's work."

"Still," Deacon Beacon said, "Deacon Usher has made a point. Perhaps we should give everyone a few minutes for prayer or contemplation, or a chance to head out for a cigarette."

I had never smoked a cigarette in my life, but I was desperately hoping for a cigarette break. I would have willingly lit up a stinky stogie with the foulest of tobacco fiends. With a strange turn of mind, I realized that I did not want to smoke—I wanted to take a leak. I needed to pee in the worst possible way. "I've got to go to the bathroom," I whispered to my parents while Pastor Kern was trying to make up his mind. Without waiting for a response, I pushed past Pop and hurried down the aisle.

The men's room was located on the south side of the vestibule. I was almost running by the time I reached the door. I dashed to the closest urinal, pulled down my zipper, pulled my cock out of my underwear, and let fly. For a second, I felt a deep pain as my bladder unloaded. I whizzed with a great fury, so that I was grateful for the splashguard. Otherwise, I would have soaked the floor, my pants, and anything else handy.

Another male joined me at the next urinal. Turning my head, I witnessed Roger Thomas pulling down his zipper, pushing down his thong underwear, and pulling out a sizable penis.

"That's a thick one," I said, fixated upon his exposed member. A yellowish stream flowed from the head.

"Yours is no slouch," he said. "Nice cock."

"So you still like dick?"

"Of course. This wasn't my idea." He glanced suddenly over his shoulder. "Shouldn't I say that?"

"You can say anything you like to me. I like cocks too. What the fuck are you doing in this church? Why are you letting our asshole pastor debase you?"

"It's not my idea. It's my family. They're rural Oregonians, you see. I was dancing in a thong in a gay bar in Portland when my father and his brothers showed up one night, got into a terrible row, and pulled me out. That's how I ended up here."

"Then you don't expect to be turned into a breeder?"

"Hardly. I tried it a couple of times. Part of the 'cure,' you see. I had to fuck a couple of hookers."

"Did you do it?" I was fascinated.

"Yeah, but I didn't like it. Sex with a guy is pure ecstasy. Sex with a female is mundane. I got my rocks off, but I didn't feel much pleasure—not like the charge when a real man gets you off."

"Roger, you gotta get your ass out of here. Hit the door and keep running."

"Yeah, I know." He zipped his thick cock back into his pants. "But there's my family."

"Screw your family," I said, but even as I said it, I pictured my own pop and my mother. "Oh, fuck, Roger. Don't listen to me. I'm a hypocrite."

"So am I. I gotta go back in there."

"You're sure?"

"Yeah, I wanna get this exorcism over with. I've got a date this afternoon."

"A date? With a guy?"

"Sure. You should see him. What a muffin! I could just lick him to death."

I snickered. I was feeling better about Roger already. "So you don't think this deliverance is gonna change you?"

Roger laughed quietly. "Shit, no. Soon as I have the demons of homosexual lust cast out of me and am cured of my perversions, I'm gonna duck out, shoot up to Portland, and tongue bathe my guy."

"That's the spirit!"

As we were washing our hands, my cell phone warbled. I pulled it from my coat pocket. Tizzy was calling. I arranged to meet him after I finished lunch with my parents. I called Lyle and Jeep, asking whether they'd like to go for a four-way with Tizzy. They were willing. I disconnected and observed that Roger was ogling me with awe.

"Four boys in a bed?"

"Yeah. Usually it's only the three of us. Today is something new."

"And Pastor Kern calls me the sleazy pervert," Roger said with a sardonic leer.

Knowing that Roger was faking helped me get through the deliverance. When Roger was "cured" and stood beaming angelically over the congregation, the pastor led with a final prayer that no one in the church would allow the loosened demon to take possession of his soul. Did I feel an imp of the perverse rushing up my ass to claim me for the devil's own? Not a bit. I followed the procession down the aisle, which moved slowly because Pop had to shake hands with everybody. Finally, we were outside and shaking hands with Pastor Kern. Roger was standing beside him, and I wondered how the pastor would react if he knew Roger was wearing his stripper's thong under his suit pants. When I shook Roger's hand, he gave mine a squeeze and embellished the suggestion by twirling his forefinger in my palm.

❖

Mom had left a pot roast simmering on the stove. We ate around the kitchen table. Pop cut the meat, giving me the rarest piece as usual. Pop liked his meat "cooked dead," as he called it. He thought my tastes barbaric. I dished up potatoes, squash, turnips, and carrots and added a side spoonful of Brussels sprouts. Mom only cooked Brussels sprouts for Pop and me—she refused to touch them.

I waited until Mom was serving the dessert. "Can we talk about it now?" I asked.

My father stiffened but said nothing. "Mom called it the 'family curse.'"

"We're not going to discuss it," Pop said. "It doesn't affect you. Finish your dessert."

"It does affect me, Pop. Thad and Tye are my brothers. I'm eighteen years old, and my brothers have been gone for most of my life. Not to mention that locked room. Only Mom goes in there. Think about how weird that is. I live in this house, and I've never seen inside one room."

"You're not going to see it either. Don't you have homework?"

"Pop, for all I know there's an altar to Satan or something in Thad and Tye's room. Put yourself in my place for once. Think what I must imagine."

"Terry Trencher, this is intolerable," Pop shouted, throwing down his fork so hard that it chipped his plate. Mom's face was ashen. Pop walked to the sink, drew a glass of water, and drank slowly. Indecision was written on his features. At last, his facial lines softened, and he faced me.

"Go about your business with your teammates today, Tip. This family is going to take some time to simmer down. Your mother and I will discuss the matter of your brothers. Next Sunday afternoon, one week from today, either we will sit down and tell you everything or I will inform you that the issue is never to be brought up again."

The offer was the best I could hope for, so I agreed and headed for my room. Implicit in my father's words was the shade of ejection which would visit me should I broach the matter if he decided against telling me. I was hanging up my church suit and slipping into brown shorts and a T-shirt when I heard my father's voice through my door.

"Tipper," he said. "There is no satanic altar under this roof." I got the distinct impression that he was trying to put my mind at ease.

"Uh, thanks, Pop. I didn't really believe that. It was just an example."

❖

I had arranged to rendezvous with Tizzy at Burgerpig. I rushed through the door, fifteen minutes late, and sighed when I saw him twiddling his thumbs in a booth. "I had a family problem," I said softly, explaining my lack of punctuality. "Come on. We're going to Jeep's house. His parents are out of town until tomorrow night. Lyle is there already."

As we headed for the door, Tizzy swatted my ass. The swat was not hard, but it had a lingering feel, evoking an eroticism that the ordinary jock-to-jock butt slap did not produce. I flashed Tizzy a suggestive grin, but my face froze when I heard a bone gnawing reverberation behind me. Turning, I saw the same family Lyle and Jeep had offended the previous day. The father of the family was already into his growling like a rabid dog act when I bent toward him and whispered confidentially, "It's okay. We're athletes."

The *paterfamilias* was further enraged when a local auto shop mechanic grabbed my arm before I could get out the door, handed me a ten-dollar bill, and urged me to kick the Fur Traders in their nuts.

"I love it when they give us money," Tizzy said. "You could be the best scholar in the school, and the community wouldn't give you shit. Put on a team uniform, and the supporters throw cash like it's confetti."

Tizzy was driving a small Mazda pickup truck painted a brilliant yellow. "It's gorgeous. I didn't know they came in that color."

"I had it repainted so it matched the Copperhead team color," Tizzy said. "This isn't exactly factory issue."

Tizzy followed my black Prius to Jeep's parents' ranchero. Deviating from my natural driving habits, I held to the speed limit all the way. Of course, Deputy Martin would let me off, but if he found out Tizzy was a Copperhead, he would toss the entire motor vehicle code at him.

After we drove over the cattle guard, I kept an eagle eye out for Paco the gaucho, but I saw no sign of him. A servant admitted us through the door, and I led Tizzy up to Jeep's room. The door was unlocked, and I didn't bother knocking.

Lyle and Jeep were already naked. They were lying about five inches apart on Jeep's bed, their hard cocks pointing toward the ceiling.

"Fuckin'-A!" Tizzy exclaimed with approval and bent to untie his shoes.

I had thought that we would burn up some time getting to know Tizzy. I had been close to Lyle and Jeep for years before we discovered the joys of gay sex. I had only met Tizzy a few times, usually as rivals at swim meets. I never expected that our first date would start with *Hi*, and move next into *wham-bam*. The casual sex struck me as sleazy.

Then I thought of Thad, initiated into a pagan cult, blindfolded, risking all to become part of a ritual circle, a brotherhood lit by the round sphere of the moon's glow. Lyle and Jeep were sitting up to watch Tizzy undress. Tizzy removed everything except for his briefs, which were pleasingly pouched in the front and scrumptiously seamed in the rear. Like his vehicle and his team's swim briefs, his stretch microfiber briefs were brilliant yellow. The rear panels made for a sleek fit while the front paneled pouch lifted his package enticingly.

Tizzy did not pull off his briefs immediately. He groped his own ass, smiling dreamily as he performed this act of autoeroticism. Moving around his body, he masturbated his swelling cock through the stretching fabric, and while he played with himself he bestowed an expectant gaze upon me. Somehow, my mental image had not retained just how cute he could look. A smile twisted my lips as I kicked off my sneakers and dropped my shorts. I wasn't wearing socks, so I pulled off my red Muskrats team T-shirt. Then I was standing in my contrasting black and white animal print pattern briefs. I paid thirty dollars for them, but my mother laughed uproariously the first time she found them in the laundry. However, my mother was no gay boy. Jeep and Lyle hissed with pleasure at the sight, and Tizzy's erect cock throbbed in his briefs.

I flattered myself that it was not my underwear that made such a hit. It was the package the underwear contained, my cock and ass. Still, clever packaging always enhances the consumer's interest. Tizzy was ready to buy. He placed both hands on my buttocks. His grip tightened, pulling me closer. He massaged my ass as he drew my hardening cock toward his own trembling package.

I was forced to reach into my briefs to adjust my dick. Tizzy's eyes glowed as I did so. "Let me do that for you," he said, but his hands never left my derrière. My cock fully expanded and rubbed against his. I was slightly taller than Tizzy, and my height was in my legs so my dick head did not meet his. The head of his cock rubbed against my cock shaft.

"This is a great way to get to know you better."

"Huh?" he asked.

I answered with my lips. I met his mouth and forced my tongue into it. His lips were puffy, cocksucker's lips just like the ones my toothbrush passed between several times each day. I pressed my lips against his forcefully, kissed him passionately, and probed his tongue with my own. Tizzy's hands never left my ass; he caressed my buttocks gleefully. I knew then that Tizzy was an ass man. He liked ass, and I guessed that he liked it both ways.

As if to confirm my belief, Tizzy pulled his mouth away— briefly. "I want to fuck your ass, Tip," he said. "I want your cock up my ass. Oh, man, I love to fuck."

So Tizzy could perform the enchanting tasks of both top and bottom, just like Lyle, Jeep, and I. Our lips met again, wringing an eternal moment out of the cosmic sponge before we settled the conflict of our tongues. Tizzy probed my mouth, and I sucked his tongue for time beyond breath. When we broke to suck air, I murmured softly into his ear. "I pitch and catch too. Top or bottom, I do it both ways. So do Jeep and Lyle. Boys like us can ride and drive at the same time."

"How about we make Jeep and Lyle fuck us side by side? They will be the horny studs, while you and I play the sissies. How about that?"

I was unquestionably getting to know Tizzy better. "I'd love to play the sissy with you, Tizzy."

We pulled off our briefs and jumped into bed with Lyle and Jeep. Tizzy made for the headboard, gripped it, and stuck out his rump. I had never seen a sight so enticing. A sound bubbled up from my windpipe, but it could not match the lusty gasp that emanated from Jeep. Lyle's eyes were transfixed on Tizzy's curvy buttocks. I followed suit, gripping the headboard, and sticking out my rump beside his. Our shoulders were touching, and we bumped our hips together. I had never felt so sexy, so erotic, so available, so promiscuous, or so ready. "Fuck us butt sluts," Tizzy said, bumping my spread ass with his own as he wiggled with anticipation.

Lyle and Jeep could not agree about who got to screw Tizzy. Both wanted to stick their cocks into him, and considering that I was operating on my native turf, my gay ass was second choice. A coin toss solved the issue. Lyle lost, if getting off in my ass could be a loss. Jeep laid hands on Tizzy's swelling hips and pressed his cock against Tizzy's asshole. "I'm wearing a condom, and I've got it well-lubricated."

His prey was willing. "Slide it in, Jeep. I've taken five different guys' cocks about twenty times each. My ass is open and ready for yours."

"Tipper," Lyle whispered in my ear. "I'm glad I lost the coin toss. I'd rather stick my cock into your ass than anybody else's on Earth."

He could have just been saying that, but somehow his words rang true. I remembered that Lyle was my first Earthly love, my first boy love, my first sexual encounter with another human being, and whatever our society might think, we were lovers. I loved Lyle. He loved me. We both loved Jeep. Love and sex are not the same thing, and those who think otherwise are doomed to hideous consequences. In our care and compassion for one another, Lyle, Jeep, and I had found that love and sex can fit together like hand and glove.

Turning my head, I saw the reflection in the huge mirror mounted atop Jeep's lacquered mahogany dresser. I saw Jeep's butt muscles squeeze as he pushed his cock into Tizzy's ass. Tizzy thrust back with his *derrière* to meet Jeep's thrust, eagerly inviting the penetration. I witnessed the terrible beauty of a boy entering another boy's ass, terrible only because of the world's disdain, and beautiful in the way of Solomon's proverb that Pastor Kern had mouthed on Sunday, "There be three things which are too wonderful for me, yea, four which I know not: The way of an eagle in the air; the way of a serpent upon a rock; the way of a ship in the midst of the sea; and the way of a man with a maid." Seeing Jeep pull back so that his thick cock pulled most of the way out of Tizzy's ass, seeing Tizzy hunch forward and hump back again to meet the next thrust, and seeing Jeep drive his dick home until he slammed hard against Tizzy's rounded swimmer's buttocks, I concluded that no man needed a maid—not while guys had asses like Tizzy's.

I pushed hard with my asshole as I felt Lyle's thick cock pressing against it. "Enter me," I said. He pressed harder, and I felt a fullness that signaled that my rectum was being so superbly violated. I gasped, hardly able to control the wonderful sensations rushing through my body. Every time I received a cock, the pleasure grew. Each time was better than the time before. Stunned by the epiphany, I wondered why I should attempt to control sensation. Rather, I should celebrate sensation. Without meaning to, I let go. I just let go, hideous as that thought may sound, and as I released my cognizant self, my calculating I, and freed from control, I vanished like a candle flame snuffed by a huff as I dropped into the delight of the eternal blazing darkness.

Tizzy was grasping my shoulder as he shot his cum against the old South American headboard and onto Jeep's bedclothes. "Oh, God, Jeep, I'm coming on your pillow," Tizzy yelped, unable to control his spasm.

"Let it fly," Jeep gasped, coming hard in Tizzy's ass. Tizzy had no choice. His dick was erupting, and splatters of his hot spunk went everywhere. He even decorated my thigh as he twisted his ass upon Jeep's cock.

I could hardly respond. My entire body was an orgasm of bliss. The head of my dick was afire with ripples, but my most powerful tingles were exuding from my ass. For a sudden moment of consciousness, I feared I was going to clamp down too hard on Lyle's cock, but he kept it pounding into me. Lyle was groaning as my ass milked him of his fluids. Tiny orgasms rippled through my anal sphincter, up my rectum, and into my intestines. I felt a strange frenzy, an anal joy that defied description, as my cock tingled through my dick head. The tingles increased in intensity, their fervor rising to a pitch that blasted my conscious thought. I was all orgasm.

Lyle hammered my ass harder and faster, banging me with the intensity of his own approaching release. I, on the other hand, continued to release in ways that defied description. I blasted through portals never meant to be breached. I was the rock thrown through the plate glass window, the whistle in the dark, the dynamite at the anarchist's convention, and the fart at the public dinner. I fell into the absolute disruption of the cosmos, the proof, however terrifying and wonderful, that chaos has no limit.

"I'm coming so heavy," Tizzy said with a long moan. I echoed his words, but my experience was nothing that I could relate. I was the event of the moon's deep circle, and my feelings were truly the goal that any being possessed of a cock must inescapably attain at the end of pure yearning.

The cum was shooting from my dick. Cum hit the headboard, Jeep's pillows, Tizzy, and everything else. My contractions went on and on, and my orgasm deepened into the moment. Yet deliciously wonderful as my orgasmic tingles and ripping contractions might have been, they paled in comparison to the sensation of Lyle's cock sliding up and down my anal chute. I relished the sensations from my dilated asshole, and at the extremity of my ecstasy, I moaned, wailed, and howled. "Fuck my ass. Yes. I live to get fucked. Oh, yeah, fuck me." My invitation did not sound crude to my own ears. My words were music, a prayer even, a chant cast into the eternal night, lit only with the rounded radiance of the gorgeous spring moon.

CHAPTER ELEVEN

Tipper's Tale

Clothed in their team swim briefs, the sophomores stood in a row along the edge of the pool, their butts to the water. Some stood with their hands to their sides, while others less confident cupped their hands over their crotches. One boy stood with one hand on his flung hip while he gripped the shoulder of the abashed boy next to him with the other. I stalked down the row like an army drill sergeant, supremely confident in my own swim briefs, as I carefully enunciated my words, "These are the official *FINA* rules for the butterfly stroke, which apply to swimmers during official swimming competitions."

I made each sophomore recite the rules that I had taped to the window behind me. When they finished, I pointed toward the lanes. "Line up. Dive in. I don't want to see anything but your asses while you dolphin kick across the pool.

Swim practice was going badly. It was Wednesday evening already, and we were scheduled to swim against the Fur Traders on Friday. I found myself drilling a group of sophomores whose swimming skills made them look like a flock of drowning turkeys. Coach Reece hung around for a while, but his blood pressure elevated so dangerously that he merely quoted a few lines from *Exodus* or *Moby Dick* or something unrecognizable and fled, leaving me to whip the slackers into shape.

"You there, McMillan, suck it in every other stroke," I shouted. "Breathing on every stroke will slow you down."

"I need more oxygen," the sophomore cried.

"If it's easier on your little chicken lungs, you can breathe for two strokes in a row and keep your head in the water for the third stroke."

Lyle and Jeep were flanking me as I chewed out the sophomores, but Rick and Mart were leaning against the green tiled wall, their towels wrapped around their waists. Jeep and Lyle were showing off their team swim briefs, but Rick and Mart acted as though they were hiding theirs. That was my first intimation that a conflict was brewing. However, at that instant, I didn't have time to deal with Rick and Mart's issues, whatever they might be. I was determined that we should defeat the Fur Traders in Astoria on Friday.

"Canter, it's okay to dolphin kick after you glide." Brian Canter made a brave attempt to follow my directions, but his kick pushed him against the rope.

Groaning inwardly as Canter blew water out his nose onto another swimmer, I turned my attention to a sophomore who kept tossing his rump with every stroke. "Collins, the rules allow you to swim for fifteen meters underwater. Do it. It will reduce the drag on your ass."

As I yelled directions, Lyle abruptly swatted my ass. Jeep laughed as I turned upon my friends with a questioning expression. Rick and Mart passed a significant look between their disapproving faces. Neither Lyle nor Jeep noticed our fellow seniors' reaction, but a chill crept up my spine. I sensed that the time of our outing was drawing near, and I could not foretell what that might portend. Nothing good, I feared.

After practice, Lyle drove us home. He and Jeep were talking, but I rode in glum silence in the back. "Damn, I wish we could get together tonight," Jeep said. "After what we've been doing, I don't wanna go back to jerking off by myself."

Lyle laughed and rubbed Jeep's cock through his jeans. "Sorry, but my parents insist on my going to that cultural thing at the Japan Club tonight."

Between his moans of pleasure, Jeep laughed ruefully. "Yeah, I know. We've all got families."

"Maybe we should ask our parents if we could get together for a gay sex party," Lyle said playfully. "Invite the neighbors too."

"Oh, fuck me! I can hear my papa loading his forty-five caliber pistol."

❖

Mom's car was sitting in the driveway, but Pop's truck was gone. Jeep shot me a hopeful look, but I shook my head. "They could come home any second, Jeep. It's not safe. Best you jerk off on your own. Think of my ass while you spank your monkey."

"Think of mine too," Lyle added. Jeep swatted my ass again as I passed the passenger window. I hoped that no one was watching, but butt swatting is so common among athletes that the buckaroos might think nothing of it. After all, they crowded around the bunkhouse television for every football game, and football players are notorious bootie grabbers.

The house echoed eerily, as though haunted by ghosts of my childhood. I found Mom's note on the kitchen table, telling me that she and Pop had gone to play Uno and she had left a plate in the microwave and a dessert under the cake cover. I sneaked a peek at the white cake bejeweled with strawberries. The plate inside the microwave was garlanded with two slabs of ketchup-covered meatloaf, sliced potatoes au gratin, and green beans.

The plate was still slightly warm. I set the microwave for one minute and sauntered down the hall to my room. After placing my shoes in my closet, I removed my outer clothing. My socks were clean, so wearing only those and my aquamarine biker briefs, I took my secret key from its concealed hook high above the door on the inside of my closet. Checking the house again, I opened the door to Thad and Tye's room, replaced the previous notebook I had borrowed, and removed the final notebook containing my brother's musings. I concealed it in my room, removed my socks, and picked up my faded blue shorts.

As I moved, I caught my reflection in the full-length mirror attached to my closet door and stared at the way my push up underwear lifted my package. Feeling sexy as no one but a totally gay eighteen-year-old swimmer might, I sashayed down the hall clad only in my biker briefs.

Twenty minutes later, I was licking cake frosting and strawberry jam off my lips as I stacked my plates in the dishwasher. I rinsed each utensil as Mom would have done herself, but my mind was already focused upon masturbation. I could hardly wait to beat my meat while studying Thad's journal. I gave the table a last wipe with the dishcloth and scurried back to my bedroom. I was almost running by the time I reached my door.

I didn't want to ruin my expensive and somewhat flimsy biker briefs, so I placed them in my laundry hamper and laid a used gym towel upon my bed. Stretching out naked upon the towel, I took out my bottle of lubricant and opened Thad's notebook.

❖

Thad's Journal: The Tenth of May

Tye's eighteenth birthday party came as a complete surprise to him. I lured him to the barn with the promise of sharing a deep, dark secret. Tye was a sucker for deep, dark secrets. As he minced along beside me, he broached the subject uppermost in his mind.

"I want to get initiated."

I sighed. I had known the request was coming, and I was only surprised that he had waited until his eighteenth birthday to ask.

"I'll talk to Dr. Bromius. Now shut up about it." We were approaching the barn door.

"Why?"

"Somebody will hear you."

"You said that none of the buckaroos were in the barn. What's going on?"

"Tye! Tye!" Little Tipper's shrieks sent shivers through the night as he burst out the barn's side door. "There's cake. Ice cream."

Mom's face appeared at the door, aggravation written all over her. I could only laugh.

"You're pulling a surprise birthday party for me," Tye said, grabbing up Tipper and rushing through the barn door. I followed at a more sedate pace. Mom, Dad, and the buckaroos were standing beside the table. Everyone had been prepared to shout "Happy Birthday," but Tipper had stolen their thunder.

The buckaroos had decorated the barn with crepe paper streamers, multi-colored balloons, and other party decorations. They had brought in three of the cutest alpacas, and the animals were wearing brilliant crepe paper garlands on their long necks. The table was covered with hamburger buns, potato chips, nachos, tortillas, cheese puffs, guacamole, salsa, and a five layer chocolate cake with eighteen candles. A tub of ice held the jugs of lemonade and the containers of ice cream. Hamburgers and sausages were sizzling on the gas grill.

After we ate the burgers and chips, the buckaroos lined up and each one gave Tye a swat on the ass. Tye enjoyed every smack, but Pop watched with obvious discomfort. I gave Tye the final swat while Mom lit the candles on the cake.

"Cake!" Tipper shrieked. The little fellow loved sweets more than anything.

Tye made his secret wish, gave me a significant look, and blew out the candles. I didn't have to ask what he had wished for—I knew already. I resolved to talk to Dr. Bromius on Monday.

❖

Tipper's Tale

Thad didn't describe any more about the party. Nor did he describe his meeting with Dr. Bromius. His next entry jumped to a detailed account of Tye's initiation. I sighed with anticipation. Reading about my young self was not sexually stimulating, though I read the first passage twice. Finding no clue to the breaking up of our family, I touched my dick as I turned to the night when Tye entered into the moon's deep circle.

❖

Thad's Journal: The First of June

I was of two minds regarding Tye's initiation, but Dr. Bromius assured me that brothers by blood would never be put into an incestuous arrangement—in spite of our having jerked off in the same bedroom for years. Thus we met under the full moon in June, which the Native American tribes called the Strawberry Moon, the European pagans called the Rose Moon, and others called the Honey Moon. Strawberries, roses, and honey are symbols for love, particularly erotic love.

Far from city lights, and no electricity within sight, the stars spangled the sky much as they had done for our ancestors. They were not points of light, but brilliant sapphires, diamonds, emeralds, beryls, and rubies holding back the eternal night.

In honor of the night, we pagan boys wore rose-colored scarves around our necks and nothing else. The pipers were piping and the drummers were drumming and my blood trilled in my veins as I anticipated what was to come. Boys mingled, kissed, groped, and excited one another, raising energy to the Uranian gods before the arrival of the initiate and the casting of the circle.

Skip stroked my ass and tongued my ear. "Your brother is gonna love it, Adonis," he assured me.

At last, Orpheus and Attis led Tye up the slope bright with new grass and dark with dotted sagebrush toward our natural circle. Tye was blindfolded with a rose-hued scarf. As his guides harassed him with sexual banter, Tye laughed with lusty humor and strode bravely. His cock was erect already. We formed a line through which Tye must pass, and prepared to pelt him with jests, precisely as our ancestors had done to the initiate led up the path to the sanctuary of Bacchus.

Including my initiation and Skip's, Tye's was the fourth I had participated in, so I was used to the ritual questions. I listened while Tye made his vows, more eagerly than most, I thought, but perhaps we had all been just as eager as he. However, when Hyacinthos, wearing the horns of the stag, told Tye to drop to his knees and kiss the holy phallus, I felt the pagan spirit surge through me.

Tye fell eagerly as the priests selected Moloch and his thick rod. I knew Moloch as Arthur, a college student near graduation, just as I. Arthur had been Dr. Bromius's devoted student for two years, and he had confessed to me that the idea of moving on to a university was depressing.

"Art, they'll have a gay club. Gay straight alliance. Queers and Allies. Something like that. You'll meet a guy."

"There won't be anything like what we've got," Arthur said. "I live for our meetings under the full moon. I love the sex, but I love the magic more."

I understood what Arthur meant. I could not imagine life without our monthly gatherings. How could I live without the mystical participation in the deep circle cast by the shadow of the moon?

As I watched my younger brother touch his tongue to Moloch's cock, I did not feel the anticipated squeamishness. My heart swelled with deep emotions, but they were happy feelings. Pride, joy, revelation, exaltation, and mysticism combined to create a feeling that could not be described. Tye was fulfilling his destiny. As Tye kissed Moloch's dick, our mystery rites brightened into the most wonderful participation with divine love possible.

Blindfolded and naked, my younger brother licked Moloch's cock. He touched the tip of his tongue to the other boy's pee hole before he licked around the head. Then he kissed down the side of Moloch's dick until he was skirmishing with pubic hair. I grinned as Tye removed a loose hair from his tongue before he licked back up to the head.

"Those hairs do get in the way," Skip whispered.

"That's why I trim mine," I answered.

"Yeah, makes it more pleasant to suck your dick" Skip's hand brushed the head of my swollen cock as he said it, a gesture fraught with promise. A surge of hircine sensations coursed through my cells as Skip fingered my dick head. Meanwhile, Tye was taking Moloch's dick over his lips and into his mouth. My younger brother loved cock, as anyone could see. I felt immensely proud of him.

"That's my brother. Tye will suck Moloch's dick until Moloch is dry as dirt."

"Anyone hearing you would think you were deprecating your brother," Priapus said.

"Hardly. Tye moves like a sissy, but he's no Milquetoast. He has the courage of ten. He's stronger than he looks too."

"His mouth is sure strong," Priapus said. "His cock too. I'd dearly love to suck that thing."

"I'm sure you'll get your chance." I hoped that I would get to see Priapus suck Tye's dick. I'd watched my brother jerk off hundreds of times, so I knew the gusher of cum that he produced.

Tye was sucking harder on Moloch. Everyone could see that Tye was growing more and more excited as he sucked, as though the cock in his mouth stirred every cell in his body and fired every nerve with sexual elation. He lapped at the head of Moloch's cock, curling his tongue around it and then flicking the tip of his tongue against Moloch's dickhole. Tye rounded the rim of Moloch's dick head, around and around widdershins until Moloch was wild eyed with torment.

Tye laughed aloud before taking the cock into his mouth again. He bruised it with his lips; he popped his lips over the head, time and again. Then he let it slowly ride along his tongue as he took it deeper into his mouth. He took it halfway before he pulled back to the head. Then he plunged forward and began fucking Moloch's cock with his mouth. Each thrust or bob of his head drove the cock deeper into his mouth. At last, the entire shaft disappeared, so all knew that Tye was caressing Moloch's dick head with his throat.

Tye pulled back for a quick breath, and then he took Moloch deep again. He moved his head slightly, barely a nod, but such a nod that must have ravished Moloch's dick head.

"Oh," Moloch gasped. "Oh." He managed a weak *evoe*, but his mind was not focused on praising the sublime deities. Rather, he celebrated the gods in his body as he rode the rushes of his approaching orgasm.

As Tye drove Moloch toward greater heights of sexual transport, I fully understood—perhaps for the first time—that our rites were not merely enacting the raptures of the eternal powers. Even more, we were making our bodies the vehicles whereby the powers joined with us, rode us, as it were, and reveled in the sensations we felt. Our sexual sacrifice opened the gates between the real and the unreal and between the sacred and the profane. Our corrupt mortal flesh entertained Eternity, and Eternity found us pleasing vessels.

Tye was receiving Moloch's semen directly into his throat. Moloch was howling with feral mindlessness, like a wild beast in extremis. Yet, Tye bobbed his head, maintaining a slow, steady caress of his tissues that sent Moloch into spasms of delicious agony.

Finally, Moloch could come no more. "Stop. Oh, please stop. Oh, ye goatherd gods, I'm drained. I can't stand another tingle."

We laughed as Apollo helped pull Tye's mouth off Moloch's dick, but our delight was also a relief. I had been close to shooting my load spontaneously, and I was glad for the reprieve. When I came that night, I wanted to come inside another.

As we listened to the sacred words, my eyes flickered toward Dr. Bromius, who sat upon the stump, his cock flying, his demeanor reminding me of drawings of satyrs of ancient times. Our professor flashed me an approving grin, and I smiled back. My brother had distinguished himself with the quality of his blowjob. Next, would come the more important test—how would Tye perform anally?

"Orpheus," Hyacinthos said. "You shall open our new brother to the way of the catamite."

A minute later, Tye was on his knees with his elbows digging through the June grass into the warm earth. "Callipygian," Skip whispered, using our new word for shapely buttocks. "Your brother has got a callipygian set." Skip's voice was raspy with lust proving that he wished that he were about to mount Tye's ass.

Hyacinthos slipped a condom onto Orpheus's dick, while the priest of Apollo fingered more lubricant into Tye's rectal orifice. Orpheus eagerly mounted my brother, while Hyacinthos whispered hurried instructions into Tye's ear. I distinctly heard Tye admit that he had never yet been fucked—to his disappointment. However, for the past year, he had been practicing with an extensive collection of butt plugs and dildos. Tye assured the priest that he was ready to take a cock.

The information about Tye using various sex toys was new to me. I wondered where he hid them—then I realized that he could not have kept them at home. Tye had been sticking butt plugs up his rear at some friend's house. Some friend!

Orpheus's ass was blocking my view. I could not see his cock enter Tye's asshole, but I knew the moment it happened because a collective "Ahhh" arose from the assembled naked pagans. A louder gasp of sheer pleasure arose from my brother as Orpheus's cock pushed into his rectum. "Oh, yes," Tye shrieked. "Yes. Oh, I love it so."

I watched Orpheus's ass pull back and push forward again, impaling Tye all the way. Tye moaned joyfully as the thrusting cock went deep into him. He pushed his ass back to meet Orpheus's plunges. Driving his muscular buttocks, Orpheus slammed harder against Tye's ass. So forceful was Orpheus's thrusting that the priests ordered two boys to help hold Tye in place so Orpheus did not pound him face-first into the ground.

Everyone could see that Orpheus was banging Tye harder than we ordinarily fucked, but my brother was built to take it. His asshole was wide open, and the hardest thrusts did not tear him, but passed smoothly in and out. Tye's cock was dripping onto the fresh green meadow. I feared that he would spontaneously ejaculate, that the hard fucking would drive him to orgasm, and thus he would miss completing the ritual. My concern was multiplied when I witnessed that Baal, one of the two boys steadying Tye, abruptly spilled his seed. The cum spurted from Baal's dick and splattered onto the nape of Tye's neck.

Around the circle, boys gasped in awe and laughed nervously as they saw one of their own brought to ejaculation from merely witnessing this intense buttfuck. Sandes was holding Tye from the other side, and some of Baal's semen struck him as well. A heavy spurt from Baal's cock wet Tye's ear, but most of the flow hit Sandes's lower abdomen and ran wetly down to his swollen cock.

The hit was too much for Sandes, and he shuddered with orgasm. His own spunk blasted from his cock, a gusher that wet both Tye and Baal. His second spurt hit Orpheus full in the face as he hunched forward on Tye's ass.

"Oh, that did it," Orpheus howled. "I'm going. Oh, yeah, I'm going now." He thrust even harder, banging Tye's ass with all his might as the crashing orgasm blasted all thought from his brain. He humped hard, and everyone knew that he was shooting his spunk. Gradually, he slowed. He gave Tye three slow final plunges before he collapsed on my brother's back, threw his arms around Tye's chest, and buried his face in Tye's semen wet neck.

After a while, the boys helped Tye climb shakily to his feet. I could not tell whether Tye had ejaculated while he was getting fucked. His hard cock was silvery in the moonlight. Orpheus caressed Tye's ass cheeks, the golden cup that had given him such intense pleasure. When the priests removed the blindfold from Tye's eyes, he looked into the face of the boy who had fucked him and smiled at the wet stream of semen decorating Orpheus's face. Unasked, Tye kissed Orpheus on the lips, lips that were wet with Sandes's thrown sperm.

When the time came for Tye to complete his initiation by choosing one of us to fuck, Dr. Bromius drew me aside. He patted the tree stump beside him, so I placed my naked ass tight against my teacher's. The warmth of Dr. Bromius's closeness was intoxicating.

Then I heard the priests proclaiming Tye's choice. "He has chosen Osiris." Osiris? That was Skip. I watched Skip submit to anal lubrication, a leer of triumph smearing his face. He distinctly winked at me, gloating that my younger brother was about to fuck his ass.

"Does that bother you?" Dr. Bromius asked solicitously.

"No, I think it's sexy as hell." At my words, Dr. Bromius turned and latched onto my cock. Apollo rushed over with the lubricant, which he squirted into our professor's hand. I held out my palm, and so he filled mine too.

As Dr. Bromius and I slowly stroked each other's cock, Skip sprawled face downward on the ground. The priests placed a condom on Tye's cock and pointed toward the significant curve of Skip's ass. I wasn't listening to the ritual words. The words were already a part of me, and I was utterly at one with the moment. Dr. Bromius's cock filled my hand as I stroked up, and then down, pausing at the head to wring it, twist it with my fingers, and rub my thumb over the head.

Delighted at my manual skill, Dr. Bromius followed suit, duplicating my hand movements with his own upon my cock. Meanwhile, Tye had climbed onto Skip and was pressing his cock against Skip's asshole. I knew that this had to be a first for Tye. He was such a sissy that I was certain he had never imagined being the top before that night. However, in the moon's deep circle, we celebrants fulfill all roles. We are both the container and the thing it contains; our cocks are the silver rods, and our asses and mouths are the golden bowls.

I stroked faster on Dr. Bromius's dick as Tye pressed against Skip's buttocks. My brother's cock was driving deeper and deeper into my best friend's asshole, and both were finding joy. As I jacked my teacher harder, so did he jack me.

Tye was intoxicated by the rhythm of the instrument, the smell of sex, the brilliant full moon, the summer night, the distant mountains, and the taste of June. He hardly knew what he was doing as he plowed his hard cock in my best friend's asshole. Or so I imagined—in truth, how did I know what was passing through Skip's mind, still less my brother's homo-sex-maddened brain?

As I jerked Dr. Bromius's dick, I saw Skip push his ass up to meet Tye's cock, but I also witnessed my brother thrust his gay ass up and down so that his dick pushed into my friend's asshole.

"Oh, fuckin' yeah," Tye shouted.

"Yes, fuck his ass," the assembled pagan gayboys called. "Fuck his gay ass, and then fuck mine."

Dr. Bromius jerked my dick harder. I felt the tingles of approaching orgasm. My professor was going to make me come. I jerked his dick as I watched my brother penetrate Skip.

"Fuck Osiris." As that plea rose into the treetops, I wished that I was receiving a cock. However, I made the most of what I had. Dr. Bromius's cock was in my hand, and I was being given the thrill of jacking off my teacher. Dr. Bromius's hand pumped my shaft and twisted the head of my dick. As he manhandled my cock, he turned more toward me, and his hot sweet breath caressed my face.

I jerked him harder, squeezing the head of his dick and tapping his piss hole with my index finger. He puffed hotly at my ministrations, but his lips moved closer to mine. Then they touched my cheek. He kissed me chastely as I flogged his cock. I turned my head so that the edge of my lips meshed with his. His tongue slipped to the corner of his mouth and met my own.

Dr. Bromius's dick was velvet in my hand, and his hand was iron upon my cock. His lips were sweet, warm, and wet, and his tongue was a probing instrument.

Skip moaned loudly and he sustained it for a long time. "Ah, ah. You're fucking me so good. You're making me come."

Tye was just as noisy as Skip was. "I'm gonna come too. Fuck, yeah, your ass is grinding the spunk out of my balls."

Dr. Bromius and I turned our heads so that our lips no longer met, but we kept our hands busy. Tye was banging Skip maniacally, humping him hard and fast so that all could see that my brother was hitting the height of orgasm. Skip squirmed beneath him, showing that he too was shooting his cum into the new grass and the summer wildflowers.

"Oh, Adonis," Dr. Bromius said, his voice hushed and holy as I took him to the pinnacle of masturbatory ecstasy.

"That's right, professor. I'm gonna make you come. I'm gonna milk your cock until you shoot streamers."

Dr. Bromius joined his voice with the howls Tye and Skip made as they raised their voices to the moon. "Oh, Adonis. Oh, Adonis, Thad, Thad." My professor forgot himself and his place in the ritual as I drove him into a state of sexual extremity. He was pounding my cock just as hard, and my loss of control followed closely upon his.

Riotous tingles erupted in my cock head just as a hot burst shot from Dr. Bromius's cock. His semen arced high and created a silvery parabola of sperm seed in the moonlit night. My hand was wet with his spunk. I hardly noticed the semen on my skin, even though the touch of his sacred fluids heightened my joy.

As Tye gasped and pounded Skip's ass, slowing as both ejaculated their final drops, I was hitting the rush of full orgasm. Dr. Bromius was still coming, but his hand never slowed. He twisted the head of my cock, biting deep into my quivering flesh. My asshole tingled, and I felt a thrill of pleasure rush up my rectum as though I were getting dicked hard up the ass. But I wasn't. My brain gave me all the remembered sensations of pleasure, ass fucking, cocksucking, jerk offing, and any other sensation I had ever experienced. The muscles at the base of my cock contracted hard, sending a spurt over Dr. Bromius's head.

Raptures claimed me as I shot my next wad and the next after that. I emptied my balls, and still Dr. Bromius milked my dick. And as long as he subjected me to the delectable torture, I gave as good as I got until we both stopped. "No more, Adonis," Dr. Bromius said. "More is agony."

"No shit." I watched Tye and Skip climb unsteadily to their feet with the help of the assembled boys. Skip returned to his place in the circle, walking rather stiffly as though Tye might have fucked him into a paralytic state.

Wet and drained, Dr. Bromius hunched against me as he observed the conclusion of my brother's initiation. Erect but serene, the priests spoke softly to him, and Dr. Bromius nodded in agreement. Pleased with our teacher's approval, Apollo and Hyacinthos approached Tye.

"Tye Trencher, welcome to the circle of Dionysus," Apollo said. "You have embraced your nature and found it to be good." He kissed Tye upon his lips, so Tye's cock elongated again. "You have died to your old self. Tye is dead. Henceforth in this sacred circle, your name shall be *Ganymede.*"

❖

Tipper's Tale

Thad ended that entry there, but one more entry followed. I was in no condition to hold out until I finished reading. I had been lubricating my right hand and stroking my cock while I read Thad's description of Tye's initiation (clumsily turning the pages with my left). Some of the dick hot lubricant had dripped onto the unused gym towel, but most had gone to soak my shaven groin, and finding no hair to stop the rivulets, had leaked into my ass crack.

I placed the notebook on my bedside table, and fingered the head of my cock. It felt hot and dry, so I poured more lube into my hand and lubricated it. I circled my slick palm over the tip of my cock, going slowly at first, and then increasing my speed. Pleasurable sensations filled my dick, but I slowed again to prevent my coming too soon.

I rolled onto my back with my pounding erection pointing straight toward the ceiling fixture. I seized the foundation of my cock with one hand and stroked upward with quick, rounded motions. I kept the strokes short, so I did not quite reach the tip. My other hand slid into the crack of my ass. As I fingered my asshole, I kept varying the tempo of my circular strokes until the head of my cock was turning in the opposite direction of my hand stroke.

I squeezed lubricant onto my forefinger and inserted it into my ass. I pushed with my asshole, opening for my finger as I had opened for my friends' cocks. Finger fucking my ass was fun, but I was beginning to need both hands on my cock. My heart was hammering in my ears, and my body was tingling.

I gripped my cock with my left thumb and forefinger, which formed a ring around the shaft. I created another ring with my right hand, a little below the head of my dick. I turned both hands, spiraling my grip upward. I gripped harder as my fingers popped over the head of my dick, and each time my uppermost hand popped off, I started at the base again.

Rolling onto my side, I began to masturbate normally. I was getting close to coming, and I wanted my semen to hit the dirty towel. However, at the last minute, my good intentions took flight. I rolled onto my back again and traced light circles around my piss hole with my right forefinger. With my left, I gently pinched the movable skin on the underside of my dick head. Rubbing my fingers with my skin between them did not make much of an impression at first. Then the first tingles of orgasm hit, signaling that I had passed the point where stopping was possible. I was committed to ejaculation.

I continued rubbing my skin and circling my dick hole. My orgasm grew in intensity, mounting from tiny gusts into a tornado of sensation. The final funnel cloud sucked the sensation out of every cell to focus all pleasure in my cock. I erupted wildly. The terrific arc of cum shot from my cock and blasted toward my ceiling fixtures like a chemical rocket. The next spurt rose nearly as high, and my eyes crossed watching it. A warm splat hit directly upon my cheek. I squeezed my buttocks together to help pump the hot cum out of my dick.

My body seemed in a spasm. My eyelids were flickering so that the swim posters on my walls seemed to be caught in the light of a strobe, and my other tissues crinkled. The powerful muscles at the base of my cock kept contracting, sending out more streamers. I could scarcely believe how much I was ejaculating. At last, the final spasm hit me, a blast of pure pleasure that drained the last squirt of semen out of my balls. Then I sprawled, sweating and wheezing, hardly able to believe the intensity of the orgasm I had experienced.

After a while, I rolled onto my side again. I drew a deep breath and opened my eyes, surveying my room. Cum was not hanging from quite everything, but I had created a sticky mess to clean up. As I rose shakily, aware of the lubricant dripping from my cock and slicking my ass cheeks, I decided that whatever the time I must spend in cleaning my spilled seed, the pleasure had been worth the effort.

I wiped up the wet spots and made certain that my dick wasn't still oozing. After I had found the last squirt and wiped it from my headboard, I slipped down to the shower. When I was clean, I pulled on fresh black cotton briefs and a black T-shirt. I was feeling rather elated. My brother's initiation had stimulated me, and I felt a special kinship with all men.

I had to write an essay for the next day's English class, so I thought of something I had read in Thad's copy of *The Golden Bough*. I wrote about the *Battle of Summer and Winter*.

On May Day, in times and places when and where the folk were caught up in celebrating the natural forces and the changes of the seasons, different kinds of festivities occurred around the world. I settled upon one in which young men engaged in mock combat. The youths representing *Summer* dressed in ivy and mounted ivy draped horses. They engaged in a playful battle with their friends who represented *Winter*. The boys representing *Winter* wore costumes made of straw. I went to great lengths, inventing at will when I described the battle in homoerotic terminology. I knew that Ms. Malcolm would love it. A month earlier, Lyle had whispered that Ms. Malcolm was a confirmed lesbian who wrote girl-girl erotica under a pen name. She drove up to Portland once a month to participate in the Dirty Queers readings.

According to Frazer, after *Summer* vanquished *Winter*, the defeated combatants were set upon by their ivy-clad competitors and stripped of their straw. Using my imagination, and a dollop of inspiration from Thad's journal, I described a ritual in which the boys representing *Summer* buttfucked the *Winter* team after baring them before the assembled spectators. I went into vivid detail, even supplying discourse that Lyle, Jeep, Tizzy, and I had uttered in the extremis of our orgasms, and ended up writing a paper nearly twice the length Ms. Malcolm had demanded. Used to hand-spun essays of less than a page, the poor woman had failed to set a maximum. In my inspired, though thoroughly masturbated, condition, I conjured up five pages of holographic brilliance.

Only after I finished my homework did I take up Thad's notebook to read his final entry.

❖

Thad's Journal: The First of July

By the time the full moon of July arrived, Tye was bouncing with anticipation. However, he was the only one in a bouncy mood. The atmosphere in our home had grown downright hostile. Pop had not spoken one word to either of us for a week, and Mom went around as if she had Poe's raven perched on her shoulder. Little Tipper caught our parents' mood. He was fussy and cried over everything, which enraged Pop further.

Mom and Pop went to several counseling sessions with the church deacons and the reverend. I wondered what was happening with their marriage.

"Do you think Mom and Dad are thinking about divorce?" I asked Tye.

"Of course not, Thad. They haven't been fighting."

"They sure aren't happy. Why are they talking to the reverend again tonight?"

"It's not about their marriage," Tye assured me, bouncing his ass as he looked out the window.

"What else can it be, Tye?"

"I think there must have been some fraud at the church. Maybe one of the deacons robbed the collection plate."

"Why would you think that?"

"Because Mom and Pop are meeting the pastor and the deacons and Sheriff Douglas. I heard Mom talking on the phone with Sister Doris today."

I shook my head. Maybe in some ways I am more sensitive than Tye. I felt an ominous portent of evils imminent.

Things were not going well at the college either. I was taking my last course during the summer session, which meant that I would receive my diploma in August. Tye was taking Dr. Bromius's mythology course. Bromius seemed distracted. He had been summoned to meet with the dean due to some unexplained student complaint. Then Tye told me that right in the middle of Dr. Bromius's lecture on Midsummer Fires, the college president, his vice presidents, the dean, and the president of the faculty union had invaded the classroom and sat stony-faced on the back row.

Tye stood looking out the window into the moonstruck yard and across toward the hill where our rite would commence. "Shouldn't we go now?" Tye stuck out his ass as he talked, as though he were anticipating the cocks that would fill his tail. He was wearing thin running shorts that made his ass look naked.

"Soon. We'll meet Skip at the edge of the cornfield. Yes, Alan and Lane will meet us there too." I knew that Tye had a huge crush on Lane, called Baal in the circle.

"Dr. Bromius said that the July full moon is called the Buck Moon because that's when the buck deer grow their new antlers. And he said that it's also called the Thunder Moon or the Lightning Moon because of the summer thunderstorms."

"That's right. Looks like you're learning something."

"The important stuff. Now if the college would offer a gay sex curriculum, then I could declare a major."

I laughed. "How would you choose between anal class and oral class?"

"I'd go for a dual major." Tye smirked, still staring at the moon.

In various cultures, the full moon of July is the Mead Moon, the Hay Moon, or the Blessing Moon. The energies around the seventh moon evoked our gratitude for prosperity, the first harvests of vegetation, the buck deer's new antlers, and the thunderstorms of summer.

The alpacas were stirring under the rising moon. We watched as the buckaroos herded the pack into the barn. Tye and I climbed out our window. "Let's help them count," Tye said.

"Good idea," I agreed. "If anyone questions our sneaking out, the buckaroos can vouch for us." We slipped into the barn and helped count the herd. One spotted short-necked alpaca was missing, so we helped search for the lost soul.

"Over here," shouted a new employee when he found the lost alpaca devouring a clump of summer rye. Tye grinned at me as we slipped surreptitiously into the cornfield. The tall stalks of corn, five feet at the most, helped hide us as we crouched and pushed toward the lane at the end of the field.

"It's too low yet, Thad."

"Knee high by the Fourth of July."

"Lottery in June, corn be heavy soon."

I caught the reference to the Shirley Jackson story. "Hilarious, little brother," I said, poking his ribs. "In our rites, nobody gets stoned."

"Except when they get the stones put to them, Thad."

"The thought makes my asshole tingle."

We passed through the whispering corn stalks, far enough from the house then for us to stand. The full moon stood high, illuminating our path. Skip was waiting with Alan.

"Where's Lane?" Tye asked while I kissed Skip hello.

"That's fuckin' hot," Alan said as Skip's tongue played in my mouth and his hands gripped my ass. My hands were kneading his mounds, and our cocks nearly tore through our shorts.

"Where's Lane?" Tye asked for a second time.

"He's late," Alan finally answered needlessly. "We can't wait here. I hear the drums and flutes. Pan calls."

We ran across the wide meadow and up the side of the butte. Our magical circle stood in a high place, under soaring, glaciated peaks and surrounded by a circle of junipers.

Never with words could anyone describe the moods our rituals evoked. Of course, we loved the hot sex, the masculine bodies locked in spasm, the mouths contorted in the rictus of orgasm, but our homoerotic orgies transcended the physically profane. I have heard people describe sex as degraded, sick, nasty, dirty, filthy, and sick. But our games were not dirty. Our orgasms were sacred, dedicated to the eternal powers, and our magical rituals refreshed our souls.

Lane did not arrive by the time Apollo closed the circle, and his absence provoked considerable speculation. Barring sickness, no initiate ever missed our monthly revels. He had called no one, and nobody could imagine why he wasn't there. We worried over him, fearing some tragedy, but our rite had to proceed.

Hyacinthos decreed that we would sweep the circle that night, so he directed Orpheus, Moloch, Ibreez, and I to don female attire and pick up our brooms. Though the sweeping ritual was serious, we giggled as we pulled up girls' thong underwear, which we covered (barely) with exceedingly short skirts. We put on blouses with padded boobs and placed colorful long wigs on our heads.

The other fellows acted out hilarious scenarios of sexual harassment as we minced and pranced with our brooms. Acting our own parts, we played prissy and sissy as we swept all baneful spirits out of our magical circle. In jocular play, we swept out fear, disease, hunger, violence, homophobia, racism, authoritarianism, and conventionality.

❖

Tipper's Tale

Though I was wishing that Thad would quit trying to describe everything and get to the sex, I could not help but interpret the cross-dressing/sweeping ritual. In a vast number of pagan cultures, ministers, shamans, conjurors, and select men who fulfilled discernible religious functions dressed and lived as women. The Manangs of the Pelew

Islands, the Bassirs of Borneo, the Sea Dyaks of Borneo, the Bugis of South Celebes, not to mention the American tribes such as the Illinois, the Sauks, the Dakotas, the Pitt River Indians of California, the Koniags of Alaska and others had their effeminate sorcerers.

I had a book of paintings, one nineteenth century *Dance to the Berdache*, drawn by George Catlin among the Sac and Fox Indians of the Great Plains. Catlin depicts a taunting dance to attain the identification with the two-spirit man. Despite the mockery, the dancers achieve honor through the berdache recognizing them.

Sometimes they cross-dressed for specific purposes, as Thad had apparently done in the ritual he was describing. For instance, Frazer describes the female men of the island of Rambree, who upon some calamity, evoked the assistance of the Idol by dancing around a tall pole. Frazer suggests that the assumption of woman's dress may disguise a man to deceive demons. In other words, men lived as women, enduring either their community's reverence or contempt, out of a desire to please some gods and deceive others.

❖

Thad's Journal: The First of July, continued

After we swept the circle, Priapus, Sandes, Skip as Osiris, and Narcissus took our brooms and held them erect. Orpheus, Moloch, Ibreez, and I formed a square, falling to our knees and deep-throating the cocks of the broom holders. I had perfected the art of taking a cock deep into my throat, having practiced since the night of my initiation with carrots and bananas. By the night of our final full moon, I could throat fuck a thick dick without gagging.

I had hoped to get my mouth on Skip's cock, but Chip (Ibreez) claimed him. Not that there was anything lacking in the magnificent phallus Priapus brandished. I licked Crane's bobbing dick head, relishing its thick succulence. Opening my eyes briefly, I saw Tye standing in the row of the unchosen, fingering the head of his cock and wishing me in hell. If he was still enthralled to that cruel myth, I would have to enlighten him. Hells are of our own making. We are absolutely free. Of course, Dr. Bromius would have taught him that in the first day's lecture—providing the lesson had not been corrupted by the community college's abject submission to insidious neighborhood gossip and restrictive local mores.

Those thoughts flitted through my consciousness in the briefest of moments before I turned my full attention to the cock touching my lips. I puffed over Crane's dick head, kissing it, licking it, and wetting it with my mouth. My head going down on Crane, his cock glided deeper and deeper into my mouth. The salivary glands under my tongue were spurting as his cock slid deeper. My throat was wet for him by the time he reached my uvula.

Proud I was that I did not gag. His cock hit my uvula, but it was no different from a choice bite of steak or some other savory that I was swallowing. I swallowed the head of his cock until the shaft itself filled my mouth and its broad head stuffed my throat. I went down once, twice, and thrice, bobbing my head so that his cock head slid into my slick throat. Only then did I come up for air, so to speak.

I drew a breath; then I deep throated him again. "Ah, you brilliant cocksucker," Crane howled. "Oh, Thad, I mean Adonis, man, you give awesome throat."

Crane's cocksucking talents would have made a satyr blush, so his words were high praise indeed. Nevertheless, I did not have time to bask in glory. Crane was so close to shooting into my throat that I decided to make him come right then. I throated him harder, and he howled with bliss. I felt his cock thicken, so I grabbed his ass with one hand, stroking it, and seized his balls with the other. I milked his balls, squeezing the cum out of them as I tormented his dick head with my lips, my tongue, and my throat.

"Oh, I, ah," Crane said, barely managing the words. "I'm going off, Thad. I'm going to shoot it into your mouth." He could not help bringing up my classroom name. Often in the throes of orgasm, we forgot our ritual names and called each other by the names we knew in daily life. The lapse was a constant reminder that all our hopes and desires were mere flights of our imagination. Dr. Bromius had everlastingly cautioned us not to turn befuddled by the power of the circle. We had to consider the routine precautions, no matter what heights of ecstasy our revels ascended.

With the feeling of Crane's cock still swelling my throat and the taste of his hot cum on my tongue, I rejoined the group. Standing in my skirt beside my naked brother, I glanced down at Tye's erect cock. "Yes, I can still feel his cock in my throat," I replied to his unasked question.

Tye grinned, though his lips conveyed something less than benevolent. Not sardonic. Not cruel. Simply envy, with touches of resentment, naked voracity, spite, and cupidity, in those green emotions' purest figure of brotherly rivalry.

"I'll let you try on the skirt when we get home," I promised, and Tye's jealousy slipped away. I was tempted to add the caution that I might not be allowed to keep it, but I decided not to tempt Tye too far.

Ganymede kindled the Midsummer Fire, a gigantic bonfire that some of the boys had constructed earlier in the day in preparation for the night's revels. Those of us in girl's clothing tossed our garments aside. Our fire walk did not involve our walking through the bonfire, but dancing around it with each boy's right hand holding the next boy's cock. As we danced, Dr. Bromius and our priests decorated us with the nine sacred flowers of summer.

The drums pounded and cymbals clashed. With our left hands, we dancers shook bells and tambourines. The warm air kissed our naked skin, and the eye of the full moon looked upon our taut bare asses, our hardened bare cocks, and our gay bare souls.

Following the dance, the priests held branches of mistletoe above our heads. Every one of us kissed, moving around in two circles. I even kissed Tye, and my brother's lips were soft and warm, and at the same time, hard and desirable. I had to tear my mouth away from the forbidden fruit.

Then we stood holding hands around the bonfire while Attis and Hermes performed a rite celebrating the life and death of Balder the Beautiful. Jim/Attis had donned a costume of forest green, consisting of a hempen shirt, tights, and pointed shoes. Carrying a basket of midsummer flowers, he rounded the circle, kissing each boy and promising good things to come.

In contrast, Hermes/Ralph, playing the mischievous Loki, fashioned a spear of mistletoe, the only plant that Balder's mother Frigg had failed to charm. She vowed that no plant should harm her son, but she forgot the mistletoe. As we pelted Balder with summer blossoms, Loki slipped the mistletoe spear between Balder's legs, and Jim held the plant as if someone had stabbed his groin.

Mourning the death of Balder the Good, we lifted Jim and pretended to fling him into the flames. Following the sacred ritual, we sat for our customary celebration of cakes and ale, that night symbolized by seeded pound cake and pungent punch.

The moon illuminated our naked skin as we ate the cakes and sipped the punch. The holy flowers floated on the surface of the punch. The punch made my head swim. There was no alcohol in it, so the flowers themselves must have contained a narcotic quality.

We sat upon the flowery heath, drinking punch, eating seedcakes, throbbing to the drums, and swaying in the moonlight. The moon grew brighter, and the stars threw down their spears.

Without warning, other lights strobed across the meadow. We sat frozen, unable to credit the evidence of our senses. Not until the lights formed a semi-circle that joined with the circle of the dark wood and a harsh masculine voice barked orders through a megaphone, did we fully understand that Sheriff Douglas's deputies had surrounded us.

Young Joe Kern was howling through the megaphone. Kern was a sheriff's deputy who longed to become a pastor were there any church insane enough to have him. He barked orders to us as if we were escaped felons.

"Bromius, give yourself up," he shouted, as if Dr. Bromius were public enemy number one and a prime candidate for the hot seat.

"I'm right here, you deluded fools," Dr. Bromius shouted, striding forward toward the assembled group. He walked naked as if he were walking toward the classroom podium, and I had never felt so proud of him. Sheriff's deputies grabbed our professor as though he were a common thug, forced him face-first into the meadow flowers, and handcuffed him behind his back.

I jumped to my feet when they handcuffed Bromius. Tye stood beside me, and Skip on my other side. I thought that my heart could not sink any lower. Then I saw my father standing beside Bobby Beacon, Deke Talbert, and a few other diehards from the family's church. Skip's parents were there as well. I felt some minor relief that my mother wasn't there. Somehow, having my mother see Tye and me naked would have been more than I could stomach. My heart went out to Skip. His mother was standing right beside the sheriff and pointing at Skip as though he was the much-anticipated and long-delayed Antichrist.

Only then did we see the turncoat. When Deputy Kern stepped aside, Tye shrieked, the cry emergent from his anguished soul. Lane, Baal the betrayer, had led the posse to our sacred circle. So we stood, betrayed, and the moon's deep circle illuminated our nakedness, our defiance of the god of these country folk, and our wayward homosexuality.

After we dressed, we were released into the custody of our families, except for Dr. Bromius who was placed naked in the back of a squad car. Dad's pickup truck was parked down the slope. He forced Tye and me to walk ahead of him, but he made us ride home in the bed of the truck while he occupied the cab alone.

Arriving home, Dad sentenced us to our room. Little Tipper slept through our arrival, which was the only good thing that happened that night.

"What about the bathroom?" I asked.

Whirling, Dad balled his fist as if he meant to punch me. I had never seen him so angry. He drew a deep rasping breath. "You two can have parole down the hallway. But no contact with Terry. You're not to touch my last remaining son."

"He's our brother. We love little Tipper."

"My last son is not going to take the pansy route," Dad shouted. The shrieks rose behind him. Little Tipper had awakened and wandered to see what was going on. He would not have known the words pansy route, but he was still traumatized. I grabbed him up to comfort him, but Dad snatched him from my hands, which made Tipper scream all the louder.

Tye threw himself on his face on his bed and began sobbing. "Come on, Tye. Mom and Dad are our family. What are they going to do to us—really? They'll come around."

"That's not why I'm crying, Thad. Lane is a frigging Judas. He told the sheriff where to find our circle."

"Yeah, it looks like it, Tye. Maybe he didn't have a choice. Wait until you hear his side of the story."

"What side? There's no side that I could understand. I don't care about the pressures the church put on him. Or his parents. Or fuckin' Deputy Kern, that asshole. I sucked Lane's dick, Thad. I've digested his cum."

"Shit, Tye, why don't you say that a little louder? I'm sure Dad heard you, but just in case he didn't…"

As I write, I don't know what is going to happen. This evening, the night after our exposure, Tye and I are still confined to our room with brief trips to the bathroom permitted. Mom has carried in plates of food, but she refuses to speak. She won't even look at us, while little Tipper has been pitching tantrums at not being allowed to play with us.

Late in the afternoon, we saw the preacher's car pull into our drive, and the church elders and deacons followed after. Then came the sheriff and his deputies. For the past five hours, our parents have kept in close conference with those beacons of authority. Tye and I sit on the sides of our beds, waiting glumly. We both recognize the writing on the wall: the expulsion from Eden, the banishment of the light-bearer from the divine radiance, the shunning of the transgressor. We know that our future bodes ill.

❖

Tipper's Tale

Thad wrote nothing further. After scanning the empty pages, I closed the notebook. My heart was pounding and my brain whirling. I got up and walked around my room, but I couldn't shake my confusion. I was wearing only my black briefs and a T-shirt, so I dug out a pair of shorts, slipped them on, and checked out the window. No sign of car lights.

I had one volume of Thad's collection of esoteric writings hidden under my mattress. I grabbed it and Thad's final notebook, replaced them quickly, and inspected my brothers' room. I remembered Tye's satyr design silver neck pendant that I had borrowed. I put it where I originally found it. When I was certain that every item was exactly the way it had been on the day I first entered, I inspected the carpet. Then I softly closed and locked the door with my key for the last time.

Part Two

The Revelations

CHAPTER TWELVE

The next morning, I toyed moodily with my breakfast. Pop was reading the business section of the paper, so I grabbed the sports pages and set them in front of me. I didn't want Mom asking whether I was sick. I downed enough of my eggs to make a dent, and dumped the remainder in the garbage while Mom was pouring more coffee.

Rick and Mart picked me up before we got Jeep and Lyle. The two breeder boys did not have a clue, but Lyle knew instantly that something was wrong. Jeep gave me a quizzical look, but I shook my head. With Rick and Mart radiating heterosexuality, I could not explain why I wasn't myself.

The day was the longest I'd ever lived. The only consolation was that we didn't have swim practice—I don't know how I would have kept my mind on the team that day. However, we had planned a grueling lower body workout at Beaver Dam Fitness Club after classes were over. Every boy on the team had to work his legs and butt until every muscle was failing. After that would follow a twenty-four hour period during which we would consume lots of peanut butter and do a lot of stretching.

Jeep called me from Lyle's house mere seconds after Rick dropped me off at home. "Can you meet us?"

"Yeah. After supper."

I was not looking forward to supper with my parents. My parents were acting as they always did, but the way I thought about them had changed. I could hardly stand to be around them. During that meal, no mention was made of the momentous family decision still hanging over our heads.

I was hungry after the heavy exercise. Mom had fixed an underdone rib roast, and I ate my salad, but I avoided the potatoes. Then Mom enticed me with strawberry shortcake, and I succumbed to temptation. The meal lightened my mood, so that I was positively beaming at my mother by the end of it. My father was still on my shit list, though he didn't have an inkling.

Claiming a homework assignment, I drove to Lyle's house right after dessert. Lyle and Jeep were upstairs, and both rushed me with questions before I could sit down.

"What happened?"

"What's wrong?" Jeep asked.

"We both saw it this morning. We know you too well."

"Yeah, your face is an open book."

"To us. Rick and Mart didn't guess a thing."

"They were oblivious. So what's happening?"

Jeep and Lyle were wearing nothing but T-shirts and abbreviated sports briefs, leading me to wonder what they'd been doing while I was eating. I still had my jeans on and my socks. I'd removed my shoes at the door out of courtesy to Lyle's mother.

Their questions brought me down from my shortcake intoxication. I picked up the notebook and read aloud my brother's final entry.

❖

"Holy shit! What do you think happened? You think maybe your pop blasted them with his shotgun and buried them in the cornfield?"

I favored Jeep with a particularly disgusted scowl, even though the same thought had crossed my mind. "Jeep," Lyle said. "Show a little human feeling. That's Tip's family you're talking about."

Jeep didn't appear to be embarrassed in the slightest. "It was years ago." As if the passage of time made the pain less.

I looked at Lyle's bedroom clock. "Tomorrow evening, I'm gonna talk to Skip again."

"Uh, Tip," Lyle said hesitantly. "Tomorrow, we get out of school at noon so we can board the fuckin' school bus. By evening, we'll just be finishing up the four-hour ride to Astoria."

I'd forgotten. I'd totally forgotten. "The Fur Traders. The goddamn Fur Traders. How could I forget about them?"

Lyle patted my thigh suggestively. "You've had a lot on your mind, Tip. You need to relax."

"Yeah, you're kinda tense," Jeep said, his thumbs massaging my nipples through my cotton T-shirt.

"Come on, guys. I don't have the gumption for sex tonight."

"Gumption?" Lyle said. "What's good sense got to do with it?"

"Look at the moon." Jeep pointed at the moon, not having much better diction than I.

"It's not full," I said.

"No. It's all tipped over. Like it's ready to pour." Jeep had been working at my chest during that conversation, while Lyle's roving hand had reached my cock. He unfastened my jeans.

"Knock it off, guys." I felt weak. I wasn't sure I wanted them to knock it off. When both boys stripped off my jeans, my briefs along with them, I was too far gone in lust to protest further. My cock was standing tall.

Then Jeep's mouth was on my dick, sucking my dick head, licking my shaft, taking me all the way so my dick fucked his throat. I half-expected him to retch, but he came up for air, tipped me a grin, and went back down again. If that wasn't enough, Lyle's hot breath tickled my ass crack. He kissed my butt cheeks, kissing both and licking them. I had never felt anything so erotic. He licked along the crack of my ass, but he did not go deep into the crack. Jeep was taking my cock into his mouth with quick strokes. Jeep pulled his head back until his firm lips massaged my cock head. Then he swooped down, letting my cock ride along his tongue. My cock head passed into a wet tunnel while Jeep's tongue stroked the underside of my cock shaft.

As Jeep sucked my dick, I pictured the way his curvy ass looked in his team swim briefs. He was such a sexy boy, as was Lyle. I saw him too, standing bent for his plunge, his tight buttocks stretching his seamed crack. The beginning tingles of approaching orgasm signaled in my cock head.

"You have a super ass, Tip," Lyle said into my ass crack.

"I'm going to come." No sooner were the words out than both of my friends pulled away. For a second I thought that my dick would spurt anyway, but my orgasm stilled and died a quiet little death, leaving me rather uncomfortable.

"Shit!" I shot Jeep an accusing look. "My balls are aching."

"All part of the grand design," Lyle said. He pushed me forward, bending me at the hips. His hand crept into my ass crack. He had already lubricated his hand so it slid easily between my cheeks. I felt his fingers pushing into my asshole.

As Lyle lubricated me, he handed me the bottle. Jeep tipped me a wink, moved close, turned his ass toward my dick, and bent forward. "Do unto others."

Lyle raised his head and flashed a wicked grin. "Whatever anyone may say, thou shouldst not do unto others as thou wouldst have them do unto thee before having made certain that your tastes are the same."

"What's that quote from?" Jeep gasped as I slid two slick fingers up his ass and twisted them to and fro.

"A great book," Lyle said, giving my ass the same treatment. "One whose author should have won the Nobel Prize."

"The only fuckin' prize I want—"

Jeep finished my sentence, "—is your dick."

I pulled out my fingers and pushed my dick into Jeep's ass. "Ah, fuck, yeah!" Jeep howled.

"Are you boys all right?" Lyle's father shouted from the foot of the stairs.

"Okay, Dad," Lyle said, pressing the head of his cock against my asshole. "We're rehearsing for the class play." I felt the pressure against my ass again, that still new yet familiar pressure, so I drew a deep breath and pushed as if I was trying to fart. The sense of fullness increased. Lyle's dick was pushing into my ass. I thrust to take him all the way. Jeep's asshole rimmed my dick head as I impaled my ass fully upon Lyle's cock.

"Don't pull it out." Jeep reared his butt back to skewer his hole all the way.

Rhythm was hard to maintain. Lyle would pull out of my ass as I rammed deep into Jeep's, and I would lose Jeep altogether as I pounded my buttocks against Lyle's lap. Yet, after a brief practice session, we developed a stroke that worked for all three.

I had been close to coming in Jeep's mouth, and the short wait had not chilled my fervor. I was soon close to shooting my load. "I'm not gonna hold out, guys. I'm going to unload in Jeep's ass."

"Ah, let it fly, Tip. I'm about to give you my cum too."

"Fill me with it, Lyle. Oh, Jeep, here I go. Oh, man, I'm gonna come right now."

"I'm not ready to orgasm with you guys," Jeep said. "Shoot it into me anyway."

I wished that my dick had made him come, but I was over the edge of orgasm then. I was committed. Lyle was humping my ass harder, moaning absurdities as he shot his juices into me. My dick was in raptures. The cum ejaculating into my ass enhanced my orgasm due to the power of sympathetic magic. Orgasmic raptures seized me. The mind-blasting pleasure knocked me three feet behind my body as my muscles at the base of my penis contracted. From the dizzying heights of rapture, I looked down upon Lyle fucking my ass and me shooting cum into Jeep's ass. And for every burst I shot, I received one from Lyle. Lyle was coming in my ass, coming hard, filling me with his wet spunk. Even as I unloaded, swooping back into my body, I realized that in our sexual frenzy, in the throes of our mindless lust, we had done the deed that Bromius had always warned against: we had gone bareback.

Five minutes later, the three of us were in the shower, washing naked rectum from our dicks and considering the path our lust had taken us. But as we stood under the spray, we saw that Jeep's cock was standing hard.

"Are you a clean boy, Jeep?" Lyle asked.

"Hell, yes." Jeep said. "I've been careful. If you wanna know the truth, I've never done *anything* with *anybody* but you two."

"Yeah, that's what I thought," Lyle said, presenting our Bolivian friend with his bare Japanese ass. "Then you should fuck my ass.

Bareback. Just like I shot my cum into Tip. Just like he shot his own load into your own unprotected rectum."

Jeep was agreeable. "*Sí*, Lyle. *El gusto es mío.*" And right in front of me, using soap, spit, and a little oil as lubricant, my best chums fucked, and the moon tipped to spill its delirious stuffing onto our willing world.

❖

The Astorian High School Fur Traders were looking dazed, dismayed, and dazzled. Never had I swum so powerfully. Something had sparked in me that evening, whether a zip gained from the previous evening's sexual frenzy or a hope that the mystery packaging my life was about to be unwrapped. I left the competition circling the pool drain. Inspired, Mart, Rick, Jeep, and Lyle surpassed their previous performances. The Muskrats pulled it off.

"We're on our way to the state championships," I said buoyantly as we boarded the bus for the grueling trip home. "Only one more team to beat."

Jeep did not share my confidence in our victory. "The Professionals. Ah, shit!"

The Professionals was the team from Portland Technical High School. Like the Muskrats, they had won every meet this year. Unlike the Muskrats, they had won every meet for the past seven years. They were considered unbeatable.

The guys were enthused, but beneath their enthusiasm lay an undercurrent of something unspoken. "We whipped the Traders' asses," Mart said as we took our seats in the rear of the bus. "But they looked cooler."

Rick promptly agreed with Mart. "Yeah. We gotta talk to Coach Reece about ditching these faggy bikinis." He said it loud enough so that the sophomores and freshmen, who had to sit near the bus driver, could hear every word.

"Those full bodyskins are what we need. These red swim briefs are just too fucking gay."

When Mart uttered the word *gay*, Jeep looked uncomfortable, and Lyle positively blushed. The driver put the bus into drive and we pulled away from Astoria High School.

The Astorian Traders had worn black high-tech suits that covered every square inch of skin from the neck to the ankle.

"Rick." Jeep's throat was so tight that he had to drag down a couple of deep breaths before he could voice his protest. "The team wearing those bodyskins just exposed their asses to the whole world." Jeep's criticism was partially true. One of the Fur Traders' suits had split up the back, showing his butt crack to all present, not to mention those in reach by camera phone. Naturally, the local news stations relished an opportunity to show a high school boy's wardrobe malfunction to an eager world bent on embarrassing any human they could. The boy had kept swimming, to his everlasting credit, even after his coach had screamed at him to climb out of the pool and throw the match, and his principal had shouted his expulsion through the microphone.

I added my own objections to the proposed change. "The National Federation of State High School Associations has ruled that high-tech suits are no longer permitted in high school competition. The Traders were wearing banned suits, and we still beat them."

"Besides, swim briefs are traditional, and they don't rip up the ass," Lyle said. "You gotta admit that we look damned good in them."

I hated the thought of losing our red swim briefs. "Like Jeep said, we beat the team wearing the *superior* swimsuits. Just how far should technology go in aiding the athlete?"

Lyle was also fighting for his right to keep his swim briefs. "We beat the high-tech boys with our lower tech skills. Think about that. Not to mention, our swimwear is cheaper. Those fancy suits cost a fortune and have to be custom fitted."

"It's the best swimmer that wins the races, not the best swimsuit."

Rick positively sneered at that idea. "Tell that to Michael Phelps."

"NFHS guidelines say that we can wear suits that extend from the waist to the top of the kneecap," Mart said. "We could wear jammers."

"We could wear stainless steel, but it wouldn't help us. Besides, jammers look ridiculous."

"Tracy hates these red bikinis," Rick said. "She says we look like fairies. She says that red is especially bad because big faggots used to wear red bikinis to advertise to other faggots."

"Let's cut out this homophobic bullshit." My voice was loud enough to draw the bus driver's attention as he pointed the nose of the bus toward the terrible hill leading down to the highway. "*Gay* isn't a dirty word anymore, and saying *faggot* is as bad as other words that put down groups."

"You should know, Tipper," Rick said, bringing the underlying tension into the open air of the bus. The bus nosed downward. The hill was so steep that we could see ships navigating the Columbia River. "What's that supposed to mean?" I prayed silently that the bus's brakes would not fail. Lyle gasped, Jeep turned pale, but Mart stuck out his jaw aggressively.

"We need to know if the captain of our team is gay." As he issued the challenge, Mart stuck out his chin even farther. I wanted to tap his chin with my fist to teach him to keep it pulled in.

Rick backed Mart up with a hard state. "Are you? Are you queer, Tip?"

"Yeah," I said. If *yeah* wasn't clear enough, I threw caution out the bus window. "I am gay. Like that makes any difference."

"Fuck," Lyle said. I'd spoken loudly enough for the entire swim team to hear.

"Makes a lot of fuckin' difference to me," Mart said, insolently tipping back his cowboy hat.

Rick jumped in again. "You're challenged—which is politically correct sissy speech for *you have a fuckin' problem, cocksucker*."

"I'm heterosexually challenged. You're homosexually challenged. That's your problem, Rickety Pussylicker."

Lyle had been sucking down a restorative slug of root beer when I made that remark, and the root beer came foaming out his nose. Even Mart snickered, in spite of himself, while Rick was still trying to work out whether he should feel insulted.

"At least you faggots are funny," Mart said, including Jeep and Lyle with a sweep of his arm.

❖

After we got off the bus at the Muskrat Creek High parking lot, Jeep drove Lyle and me home. We rode in silence until Lyle shattered our private moods with a shriek that nearly deafened Jeep and me. "Do you know what this means, Tip? Do you realize what you've done?"

"I came out to Mart and Rick."

"You came out to the whole goddamn bus," Jeep said helpfully.

Lyle's mortification was manifest as he enlarged my claim. "Which means *we* came out to the whole fuckin' community. If you are out of the closet, you dragged Jeep and me out with you."

"Oh shit fire," Jeep said. "We're in a world of shit. *Mi papá* will shoot me *muerto*."

My heart was thundering as I anticipated my own parents' reaction, but I tried to calm my friends. "It's not so bad," I said, trying to soothe. "Are you guys ashamed of what we've been doing?"

"Not for one second," Lyle said. "But you know what this community is like."

"Tizzy," Jeep said. "You'd better warn Tizzy."

"Tizzy won't be touched by this. We didn't out him."

"You outed all of us. You outed every friend you've got."

"Jeep's right," Lyle said. "As far as the churches are concerned, we're toxic waste. Anybody who touches us is toxic waste. People have seen Tizzy with us."

That called for a protest on my part. I didn't feel toxic, and nothing we had done had been a waste. "They've seen Mart and Rick and whole team with us too. Rick can't tell on us without becoming toxic waste himself."

"You just wait, Tip Trencher." Lyle shook his head. "Wait until Monday. The whole school will know by noon. You'll see."

Lyle was worse than right. I didn't have to wait until Monday. The next morning, Saturday, I drove to the Muskrat Creek Shopping Plaza and parked in front of the K-Mart. I walked down the sidewalk past Albertsons supermarket, turned a corner, and tried to brush off an army recruiter who offered me a free college scholarship and a lifelong *Hustler* magazine subscription if I would join up.

The recruiter's spiel, not-to-mention the *Hustler* centerfold he kept waving in my face, shredded my patience. I whirled, gripped him tightly, and breathed suggestively, "I love making out with a pushy man in uniform."

The recruiter whipped away his sample magazine as if I would sully its pages. Standing well back, he watched as I entered Skip's Security Service.

"Holy shit, little Tipper," Skip said when he saw me cross his threshold. "What did you say to that army guy?"

"Forget about him. I read Thad's last journal—the one about the night of the full moon in July."

"What?" Skip said, looking bewildered. Had I struck him with a memory he had long repressed? Or one that drove him every night to drink enough beer or wine to fall asleep?

"The night the cops showed up," I said. "You were there. What happened?"

Refusing the evidence of his ears, Skip turned the conversation to current events. "It's all over town. You got caught taking it up the ass during the Astorian swim meet."

I had to bite on that monster. "That's a complete fabrication. You know what it's like when the whole community is making up shit about you, Skip. People must've told all kinds of lies about you. Fifteen years ago. After the cops busted Dr. Bromius. After my pop took Thad and Tye home." I gripped his arm. "I have to know, Skip. I have to know everything."

My cell phone warbled, and I saw that Lyle was texting me. "OMG," it read. "R pstd pix. Emld u lnk."

Rick had posted pictures on the Web? So what, I thought. What did we have to lose? Lyle was making much out of nothing. So what if an e-mail was awaiting me with a link to the photos? I couldn't check the link then; I had to press Skip for answers.

Maintaining his silence, Skip edged toward the curtain that covered the rear of his shop. I had been wondering where he lived. Perhaps he lived in the back of his shop, which would be a violation of the stringent rules of the corporation that owned Muskrat Creek Shopping Plaza. "Don't run from me. You've been feeding me a banquet of lies, but you're gonna disgorge it all now. Right now, Skip. What happened that night?"

Sweating then and speaking brokenly, Skip gave up the story. "The fuckin' cops showed. Lane betrayed the group. Not his fault entirely. Bromius should have prepared him better. How does a nineteen-year-old boy resist a preacher who keeps telling him he's going to get roasted in a lake of fire if he doesn't tell all? The evangelists have been lying, stealing, killing, and vandalizing everything that challenges their lies for the past two thousand years. Why would Bromius think that a community college student would hold out against that kind of threat? The man liberated us, but he led us astray. He took us off to the edge of the cliff, but he didn't care to—or know how to—give us a way off the precipice."

"Are my brothers still alive?"

"Yeah, Tip. Thad writes to me a couple of times a year. He writes to you too, but your father intercepts the cards and destroys them."

That made sense, in a horrible way. "Where is Thad? Where is Tye?"

"Only your father knows. Thad never gave me his address, but he once told me that he keeps your mother and father informed about where he and Tye are. That's all I know. Oh, fuck, the sheriff told me he was gonna put me in prison for corrupting youth. They made up all kinds of shit. The reverend was ready to lie under oath that they found child pornography in my room."

I slipped out of Skip's Security Service feeling like a microbe under the microscope. I dropped into Albertsons and bought five quarts of Chunky Monkey ice cream, Pop's favorite. My car sat under the spring rain, cooling except for the gay rainbow triangle stuck on my bumper. The sticker hadn't been there before I parked.

Sitting in my car and leaving the sticker intact, I checked the website Lyle had sent to me. The headline read, These Boys Are Queer!!!

Under that caption was a picture of Lyle, Jeep, and me. The picture had been taken the previous evening just following the defeat of the Fur Traders, but I didn't remember behaving any different from usual. However, the three of us looked like we were ready to drop our swim briefs and go after one another on the spot.

Under the picture was the next caption: How to Identify a Faggot.

I gazed at the photo of me in my red swim briefs staring at Tizzy's ass. Perhaps I had glanced that day in Silverton, but I had not stared at his ass. The photo implied otherwise.

For the final straw, the perpetrator of the website had included an innocuous picture of Lyle and Jeep hugging at the edge of the pool. Coupled with the innuendo, it spoke volumes.

❖

On the way home, I pulled into the parking area of a neighboring farmer's vegetable stand and called Lyle. The growing season was too early for any profitable sales, so the vegetable stand was locked up and I had the gravel lot to myself. On the other side of the road was a field of hops with immigrant farmhands diligently preparing the young plants.

"Tip, have you seen it?"

"If you mean Rick's Facebook page, yeah. That fuckhead."

"Are you all right?"

"Yeah. I just left Skip's business. Can you believe that somebody stuck a gay pride sticker on my car while I was inside?"

"Same thing happened to Jeep. He peeled it off and stuck it on some random SUV."

When I stopped laughing, I told Lyle, "I haven't removed mine. I thought that an army recruiter looking for payback stuck it on there. If Jeep got one, then Mart or Rick or both are targeting us."

"Maybe it's somebody else. Could be a church group. Or any other collection of homophobes."

I paused and looked at the field of hops. The trellises and poles were bare, awaiting the young vines, which farmhands were training to climb the twine supports. "The rumor mill is open for business, Lyle."

"What have you heard?"

"Outlandish stories are flying all over town. Skip heard some wild fairy tale about what we did in Astoria. Total bullshit, but you know how the gossip flies around here."

"Some asshole busybody will be calling my parents."

"Guaranteed. I know it sucks."

"Maybe less for me, Tip. Jeep's cultural heritage is more homophobic than mine. Maybe even more than yours."

A cold chill ran up my spine. Could any bastard be more homophobic than Pop, the man who'd thrown away two of his sons? "I'll call again when I get home."

Another half mile down the road, a blue light strobed behind me. I pulled over and grinned at the cop. It was Officer Martin, who'd pulled me over several times before.

"License and registration," he demanded.

"Hey, Officer Martin, it's me."

"Just hand over your license and registration." As I gave him the documents, he asked if I knew how fast I was going.

"I guess I was hitting seventy. I still have a lot of energy in my legs after we whipped the Fur Traders last night."

Still pretending that he'd never let me off every other time, Officer Martin handed me a citation. The citation gave me the option of appearing in court or paying a two hundred and sixty dollar fine.

In no good humor, I pulled into my parents' drive and parked beside a strange car. With a start, I realized that it was Pastor Kern's buggy. The urge to strip that mysteriously planted rainbow sticker off my car was acute, but I squared my shoulders and approached the front door. However, harsh voices issued from the side of the house. Pop had not invited his pastor inside. Peeking around the corner, I saw my father facing down Pastor Kern and Deacon Beacon. The buckaroos, staring in awe at my father's rage, were gazing out of the bunkhouse.

Our alpacas were also watching nervously. Anxious twitches passed through the herd as Pop raised his voice. "I lost two sons by listening to you and your predecessor."

"The Bible says—" Pastor Kern began.

"Then there's something wrong with the Bible," Pop interrupted. "You're telling me that my third son is also queer. You want to know something, pastor? I don't give a rat's ass if he is. I think my son is suffering. I know that my wife has been suffering for years and years. Is that what your religion brings? Suffering? Pain?"

"Consider the state of your soul, Frank," Deacon Beacon interjected.

"Maybe you should consider the state of yours, Bobby Beacon. Where is your daughter Mary right now? And you, Joe—maybe you should pull out that shriveled up tail dragging monkey you call a soul and replace it with a generous spirit. I remember when you were a sheriff's deputy, before you got fired for shooting a Modoc Indian woman with too much wine in her skin."

"She was a lowlife. A throwaway," Pastor Joe Kern shouted. "I ought to haul your ass in right now."

Even Deacon Beacon backed away from the pastor as he forgot himself so thoroughly. The former deputy's racism, his homophobia, his judgmental cruelty, his abuse of power, his complete disregard for humanity shone through like a sulfurous glow to the lowest levels of hell. I thought it high time to show Pop some support. Carrying my load of Chunky Monkey, I sauntered around the barn as if I owned the world and tipped my father an encouraging grin.

Pastor Kern backed away from me as if I were Beelzebub himself, picked up two sticks coated with alpaca shit, and formed the sign of the cross. Deacon Beacon emitted a sigh and asked rather softly, "Are you a practicing homosexual, Terry?"

"Deacon, I'm not eager to embrace the vocabulary, simply because some churches and some supposed Christians have abused the words so horrifically. Let's just say that I have reason to suspect that I might be gay."

"Abomination unto God. Unclean. Unclean," Pastor Kern howled.

"Reverend, I'll thank you to leave my property," Pop said, his voice almost strangled.

"Abomination. Sodomite. Unclean."

"I'll take him home, Frank," Deacon Beacon said.

"Thanks, Bob," Pop replied. "I need to spend some time with my son. Without any distractions."

The deacon ushered the raving pastor into his car and drove down our long drive. Pop watched them go, sighed mournfully, and asked me to come inside. He was shaking and unhealthily pale. He said nothing else, so I followed him through the door. Pop sat at the kitchen table and called for my mother.

"Barbara," he shouted a second time. His face was white. I went for the liquor hidden under the sink. I poured him a glass of whiskey and handed him a bottle of aspirin. Pop took a sip of the whiskey, but he held the aspirin in his hand as if he was tempting the gods to slay him.

Mom appeared shortly. "Barbara," Pop said. "Hand me that key."

Mom gasped, unable to believe what he was asking. "What key?"

"The key to our children's room. Give it to me." He clutched his chest suddenly. He turned blue. "No, hand it to Tip."

Mom looked stricken. "Frank, please. Don't cast out my last child." She broke down sobbing as she pulled the black ribbon from around her neck.

"Thad. Tye. My sons. My begotten sons. I threw them away." Pop slumped over the table. I took his pulse in his neck.

"Mom, we need the paramedics. He's having a heart attack."

CHAPTER THIRTEEN

On Sunday evening, I heard automobile tires crunching in the driveway. I looked out the door, expecting to see Mom returning from the hospital for something she had forgotten. Yet, I knew it couldn't be her. She had hardly left Pop's side, and if she needed anything, she would have called me to bring it to her.

"Tizzy," I yelled as I saw him hop from his Mazda pickup.

Tizzy ran to the door. He was dressed in deliciously tight shorts and an even tighter Lycra shirt. His sneakers were sea green. "How's your father doing?" he asked once I released him from a breathtaking embrace.

I shut the door against our buckaroos' prying eyes—not that I still cared what the buckaroos thought. I got Tizzy an icy cola, and learning that he had skipped his dinner, I seated him at the kitchen table while I fixed sandwiches.

"Pop's gonna be okay," I said, slicing tomatoes. "The doctors say it was a fairly mild attack. He should be out of the hospital in a few days."

"Your mother's with him?"

I grinned. "Yeah. She'll be there all night. We have the house to ourselves."

His face flushing, Tizzy yawned and adjusted his hardening cock. I laughed as I smeared mustard on the sliced turkey. "A yawn is one sign of approaching sexual arousal."

"Don't you feel funny? I mean, talking about gay sex while your father is in the hospital. Lyle said that he had a heart attack when he found out about you." He emphasized his words by squeezing my left buttock.

"Lyle has it wrong. Everybody is jumping to conclusions. Pop had a heart attack after he told off his pastor."

Tizzy took a bite of his sandwich and popped potato chips into his mouth. "What about his pastor?" he mumbled around his food.

"Yesterday, Pop had a nasty epiphany. He finally admitted that the teachings of our family church had robbed him of his family. He found out what kind of a louse our pastor really is. It wasn't the fact that I like cock."

Tizzy grinned at that one. I brought him up to date about my brothers, about the notebooks I had read, and about Dr. Bromius. "Pop caught Tye and Thad at that gay pagan celebration and disowned them. Probably ordered them to go away. He was about to tell me the truth when the attack hit." I picked up my mother's key. "He told her to hand this to me."

Tizzy instantly understood the significance of the key. "I'd like to see your brothers' room."

"Finish your sandwich first."

The door to Thad and Tye's bedroom was standing open. I had opened it after I left the hospital that Sunday morning, and I intended that it should remain open. That door symbolized years of lies, hiding, deception, and denial. When Mom and Pop returned home, I wanted the yawning entrance into my brothers' room to confront them.

I showed Tizzy my brothers' books and journals, and we went through their things more thoroughly than I had ever before dared.

"Tye had a girlish taste in underwear," Tizzy commented, holding the pink briefs in front of his crotch.

"They might look good on you," I suggested, growing more randy.

"Would you mind if I tried them on?"

"Of course not. Tye wouldn't object if he were here. From what I know of him, he'd urge you on. And I'd dearly love to see you looking like a sissy."

"Bet you say that to all the boys, Tipper." Tizzy pulled a golden thong out of Tye's underwear drawer. "How about you wear this?"

I had always been so careful in my brothers' room. I had tiptoed, fluffed the carpet, and left no traces. Not that night. Tizzy and I dropped our clothes on the floor. Standing naked near to him, I wanted to go directly for the sexual action. Tizzy was more subtle than I. "Not yet, Tip," he said when I reached for his dick. "Let's play."

"What are we playing?"

"It's called sissy boy."

"Who called it that?" I asked as he pulled Tye's pink panties over his ass. Tye's underwear fit Tizzy to a tittle. They tantalized, tempted, and teased as they hugged his buttocks and defined his cock.

"Get into the game, Tip. Try to tempt me. Make me want your gay ass."

"I can't help it. I'm a jock. I'm a country boy." What was I saying? Tizzy was a jock too. Were both competition swimmers, whether or not the beer-guzzling football louts thought of us as fellow jocks.

"You're a horny homo boy. Start acting like one."

I pulled up Tye's thong underwear and wiggled my ass into them. Adjusting my cock, balls, and butt cheeks, I felt my face flush. I could not tell whether I was embarrassed or aroused. Tizzy didn't help when he howled at the sight of me, "Oh, Miss Thing."

"Nobody ever called me that before," I said, catching a glimpse in the mirror. From the front, I looked only slightly more lascivious than I looked in my team swimsuit. Then I turned.

"Oh, yeah. Love that booty."

Tizzy's flattery did embarrass me, but my butt was sweet. The thong cut into my cleft, disappearing in my deep crack until it reemerged between my legs to hold the cup of my balls. "Let's trade,Tizzy. I want to see you in the thong."

Tizzy handed me the pink underwear that looked so much like panties, but my cock had hardened and I had a difficult time with them. Tizzy looked great in the thong, but his cock was also stiff.

"Maybe we should try on something else, Tip."

I ran my hands over his ass. His bare skin felt even silkier than the thong. "Maybe we should go into my bedroom."

Tizzy rubbed his erection against mine. The flimsy cloth held our hard dicks close. Moving gently we nuzzled our dicks together, producing a friction that was unbearably erotic. Gripping Tizzy's buttocks, I rubbed our cocks together harder. Tizzy's face pressed closer to mine, his eyes drifted shut, and his breath came soft on my face. I met his lips with mine. He rubbed his hands over my pink nylon briefs and pushed his fingers into my cleft. I kissed him harder, slipping my tongue over his lips. We pressed tighter together as we kissed, pulled each other tighter by gripping ass, and sucked tongue with ferocious intensity.

"Ah," Tizzy gasped, breaking away. "Quit or I'm gonna come right now."

Without thinking what I was doing, I swooped him off his feet. He weighed as much as I did, but his lithe, sexy swimmer's body felt light in my arms. I kept kissing him, sucking his tongue in my mouth, feeling his heat. I carried him to my bed, where I lowered my body atop his.

While we kissed, our fierce erections pushed against each other. We caressed one another's ass, and we lost ourselves in lust. The desire was overwhelming, but I fought against it and leaped to my feet.

"Wait a second, Tizzy."

"What for?"

I rummaged in my drawer and found my box of condoms and lubricant. I was going to need them. Tizzy was an ass man, through and through. But first, I was going to taste his dick, and I hoped that he would like the taste of mine. I leaped into bed beside him and planted my lips on his. We kissed, osculating with our lips, probing with our tongues.

Still kissing him, I pushed my hand into the thong imprisoning his dick. I had to push hard to free the thong from his butt cleft; it had been wedged deeply. I smelled the fresh, slightly salty scent of his crotch as I pushed down the thong. The Copperheads swam in a salt water pool, which contributed to Tizzy's tasty crustiness.

"You practiced tonight?" I asked. The Copperheads would swim against the Fur Traders next Saturday afternoon, but their meet was only for show. They were no longer in the running for the state championship. The Copperheads and the Fur Traders had both lost to the Portland Professionals, and we Muskrats had beaten them too. For Tizzy, serious high school competition was over.

"I practiced. All the Copperheads practiced. We're gonna beat those damned Fur Traders next weekend. Then we'll root for you Muskrats to spank the Professionals until they cry like a bunch of babies."

While we were talking, we had kept stroking each other's dick. The pink panties were off of me by then (to my relief), and Tizzy was thumbing my dick head. "Shift your position." I didn't wait for his agreement. I turned until my mouth was brushing the head of his cock.

"Uh, I'm not much into cocksucking, Tip," Tizzy said. "I take it up the ass."

"I know. Just take it a little bit. Give it a taste."

"I have a high gag reflex," Tizzy warned. "You gotta remember that."

"Trust me," I said. "I'm not going to ram my dick down your throat."

"I bet you say that to all the boys." To shut him up, I licked his cock. Meeting no resistance, I mouthed the head of his cock. I probed down the side of his cock shaft until I reached his balls. He had trimmed away most of his pubic hair, so I met no tongue troublers. I licked back up the underside of his dick, going slowly. Reaching his dick head again, I twisted my lips around it.

He held out until that point. When I started lip fucking his dick head, he broke down and touched his tongue to my cock. He licked around my dick head, around and around. The tip of his tongue flicked against my piss hole. I knew that I had him then. Despite his protests that he did not suck, he was getting the feel of a cock in his mouth. Nobody, of any gender, could resist the taste, the texture, the feel, the penetration, or anything else associated with that wonderful suck tool. Think of all those cock shaped treats that people love to stick into their mouths: Popsicles, lollypops, hot dogs, Twinkies, sausages, eggrolls, pickles, and big bananas. Those gay goat gods hardwired every human to suck dicks—though some people don't know it yet. Tizzy was finding out the great secret.

Tizzy worked my cock with his lips, just as I worried his. I let my mouth pop over his cock head and let his shaft slide along my tongue. Tizzy was licking down my shaft as I took his dick deeper into my mouth. I heard funny little noises emitting from him, noises of pleasure. What had disgusted him when he anticipated the sensation now delighted him. He moaned around my dick as he popped his lips over my dick head. He moaned again as he lowered his head, lowered irresistibly as he let my dick slide along his tongue. *Now you're a cocksucker, Tizzy, I gloated. Just now, you're beginning to realize that you love having a cock in your mouth. Soon I will come in your mouth, Tizzy. I'll shoot hot cum onto your tongue and into the back of your throat. And to your shock and surprise, you will swallow.* And Tizzy continued to go down on me as I went down on him.

According to the great poets and singers, man born of woman loves to suck. Tizzy sucked, and where the flamboyantly homosexual bee sucked, there sucked I. Echoes of twelfth grade English class flickered in the hallways of my brain as I took Tizzy's cock into my throat. I took him as deep as his length would reach, fucking his dick head with my lips, my tongue, my whole mouth, and my throat.

As I sucked, my cock grew heavy. My ball sack tightened and loaded my cock with cum. It softened slightly as my cum rose, a sure harbinger of orgasm. The softening lasted for only a few seconds before it hardened even harder than before. My cock was preparing to squirt.

Tizzy was close to coming, so close that he would swallow my spunk without hesitation. He had passed the threshold of denial. I had made him a cocksucker.

Swallow, I thought. Swallow, I demanded. Swallow, and then shoot.

A throbbing catlike purr rose from deep in Tizzy's abdomen. The tingles grew in my dick head, and those tingles exploded into wild raptures. Over the edge of orgasm, I was committed to come. I wanted to tell Tizzy, warn him, mayhap, that I was going to shoot semen into his mouth, but his dick filled my mouth. I am your cocksucker, I dreamed, explosions of pleasure erupting throughout my body and lightning of pure pleasure disrupting my brain.

Then I was coming. My cum shot into Tizzy's mouth. I painted his tongue with my cum. I shot deep into his throat, so he was left with two choices. Would he swallow or barf? *Take it down, Tizzy. Take it down. Drink my semen into your body. Take me into your stomach. Digest my love.*

I tasted his cum as his dick bucked hard in my mouth. I took his cum into the back of my throat without gagging. I swallowed it like a rich dessert. Devouring his cum, I accepted his beingness into my body. His essence became my essence, and mine became his.

Without thinking about what we were doing, we swallowed until our orgasms passed. Then we sprawled, gasping with amazement as our hearts returned to normal rhythm and our breathing slowed.

"Holy fuck, I sucked your cock, Tip. Ohmigod, I swallowed your cum. I didn't puke. Your cum is in my stomach."

"Isn't that fun? Think about it, Tizzy. Your stomach is digesting meat, bread, sweets, carbs, fruits, lettuce, and semen."

"Fucking gross!" Tizzy pretended to gag himself, and then grinned at me.

"You mean fucking tasty."

"Oh, yeah. Let's rest for a couple of minutes. Then I want your cock up my ass."

That was inevitable—not that I was averse to buttfucking him, nor having him get off in my own posterior. I was an ass man too. "I'm going to fuck you, Tizzy. I promise. Every time I see you in your little yellow swim briefs, I just about come in mine. The way your briefs draw up your ass crack drives me crazy. I could fuck you all night. And Jeep and Lyle think the same."

"Oh, fuck, yeah."

"But you gotta return the favor."

"You mean you want my dick up your ass?"

"Yeah. But I'm patient. I'll come in your ass first. Then you can come in mine."

"Oh, Tip, I love your hot butt. Your ass is so hot. You can't believe how good you look in your bikini briefs. That seam up your crack, man. Oh, man, I look at your ass and I wanna die. Even one straight boy on my team said that your butt looks good enough to fuck."

"Maybe you should check him out."

"I tried. Mike is like your Rick Jecks—an asshole, stuck on himself—with a girlfriend whom he treats like shit and she loves him for it. It disgusts me. Mike should treat her right, but he keeps saying that the worse you treat them, the better they love you. Are women really like that? Does your Rick treat his girlfriend like garbage, and does she dote on him and excuse every insult as if it's her own fault?"

"I don't want to talk about Rick right now, Tizzy. Rick is the asshole who posted all that shit about me on Facebook."

"You're sure he did it?"

"Who else? I want to be fair about this, but who else? Fuck! Now I'm completely out of the mood." Tizzy looked stricken by my declaration, but I could tell that he was feeling down too. "Did my getting outed affect you?"

"Yeah. A little. Not your fault."

"Maybe not. I shot off my mouth."

"So what? Are we supposed to walk around hiding what we are forever? We're all gonna have to come out, Tip. I don't care if they plaster a picture of my face on the front page of *The Portland Bugle* or *The Silver Falls Times*. I'm here, I'm queer, and I take cocks in my rear."

I laughed so hard that my tensions fell away. I rolled against Tizzy and kissed him hard. I kissed him, licked his throat, sucked his nipples, and tongued his ear. Despite my erotic moves, a depression still hung over us, the result of rank conservatism and oppressive religion. "How about I read from my brother Thad's journal? I'll read about the night of his initiation in Dr. Bromius's gay pagan cult. That will put us back in the mood."

"Yeah, I'd like to hear about that." Tizzy's eyes were glistening. I made a mad, naked dash for my brothers' room, searched through Thad's journals to find the correct entry, and hurried back to Tizzy. He was stretched upon his back, naked, flaccid, staring at the ceiling, and lost in uffish thought.

As I began reading, he rolled onto his side and rubbed his dick against my thigh. I read on, describing Thad's initiation. The night deepened into eternity.

"Let's do it now. I want you to come into me. I want your cum inside me. Take me bareback tonight, Tip."

If it had been Jeep or Lyle, I would not have hesitated. But Tizzy was a Copperhead, not a Muskrat. He was swimming for the other team, and I could not be certain where his ass had been.

"I have to play it safe, Tizzy. We have a responsibility to gayboys everywhere." I sounded like a mealy-mouthed Pollyanna or a Mrs. Grundy, but Tizzy bought it. I was caressing his ass at the time, which helped convince him. I glided my hands over his curves and slid my finger along his cleft.

"Sure, Tip," he gasped. "You're right. We gotta set an example." He reached for my cock as I fingered deeper into his anal crack. I dolloped lubricant onto my fingers and handed Tizzy the bottle. He slicked his palm. I brought my fingers to the small of his back and slid slowly down the deepening crevice. I parted his butt cheeks with my fingers and approached his asshole.

"Oh, that's nice. I love the way you handle me," Tizzy breathed. I also was loving the way he was handling me. He kept playing with my cock as I fingered his ass. When I reached his asshole, he started flipping my dick head with his finger. As I drove my wet finger into him, opening him up in preparation for my cock, he worked my cock head with his palm. Holding his hand flat, he made a circular motion around my pee hole. I probed him deeper, dribbling lubricant along my forefinger as I finger-fucked his ass.

Howling like a wolf with ear mites, he gripped my dick with a death squeeze when I hit his prostate. I gave it to him in a way he wouldn't soon forget. I massaged his prostate until he was excreting prostatic fluids and a little urine. Fortunately, I'd possessed the foresight to place a folded towel under his dick, so he didn't stain my bed. "Ah, fuck, you're killing me," Tizzy yelped.

"You want me to stop?" I had been careful not to massage him too vigorously. I kept it safe, but stimulating.

"Fuck, no. I just want your dick." I flipped him a condom.

"Then stop playing with my cock and wrap it."

Tizzy squirted a couple of drops of lubricant onto my dick and unrolled the condom over it. When he had me ready, I pulled my finger out of his ass, rolled him onto his back, and lifted his legs.

I kissed his lips hard as I pushed my cock against his relaxed and lubricated asshole. "I'm going to give it to you now, Tizzy."

"Slide it in, Tip. I want it."

So went the night, taking and giving, riding and driving. In the wee hours, Tizzy slipped out of bed, kissed me, and headed back to Silver Falls. It was Monday morning, the beginning of another week of high school classes.

❖

The Portland Professionals had won every meet for the past seven years. I would love to state that we stole their title, but we did not. By the night of our meet, the Muskrats were a broken team. Rick had seen to that. I swam my heart out, as did Jeep and Lyle. Mart swam with a loser's limp and Rick came in dead last, such was their plan to humiliate me.

Most of the sophomore and freshman boys swam hard, but the churched followed Rick's example. The Muskrats lost the meet and the championship, and the Portland Professionals retained their title. However, some of the guys on the Professionals team acknowledged that the Muskrats had deserved to win.

"I saw what happened," one boy said. "Those homophobes fucked you over. They didn't care whether they lost, just so long as you lost. That guy"—he gestured toward Rick—"threw the match."

The humiliations did not end there. Coach Reece screamed at me, as if the failure were mine alone, and Rick, with Mart as a reluctant cheering section, urged him on. Lyle and Jeep tried to speak in my behalf, but the coach shushed them. Of course that final lecture happened about two minutes before Principal Relish grabbed a microphone and oh-so-publically fired Coach Reece.

In the Calvin Coolidge Technical High School locker room, Rick and Mart stripped off their swim briefs. With a disgusted gesture, Rick tossed his red briefs, his Muskrat team uniform, into the trash. A second later, Mart followed suit.

"What's going on?" one of the Professionals asked.

"We don't support faggots," Rick said, pointing at me.

"You're way out of line."

"Flaming Portland liberals," Rick sneered. "When you get done hugging trees, I'll bet you hug all the faggots."

Tizzy came into the locker room then. He had watched the match, cheering the loudest as I swam.

"There's another one, a queer Copperhead," Rick yelled.

Tizzy stood by while Lyle, Jeep, and I showered and changed. The Professionals were lining up against Rick and Mart, so those two dressed without showering and headed for the school bus.

Tizzy had driven to the match. Lyle, Jeep, and I piled in with him so we did not have to ride the bus home with the saboteurs. I felt a little guilty about leaving the freshmen and sophomores, but considering the growing anger and resentments, I decided that they would be better off without our disrupting presence.

❖

"I could use a drink," Jeep said, gasping somewhat because all four of us were scrunched into the cab of Tizzy's Mazda truck.

"Nobody's going to sell it to us."

"Screw alcohol," I said. "I'd rather have some cum. Right now, I want to take it up the ass—bareback. Fuck the risk."

Tizzy sucked in his breath audibly. The hiss had no sooner died a joyous death than Jeep pointed toward a budget motel. "Let's rent a room."

Lyle pointed toward a sex shop across the street. "Let's go there first."

We spent several minutes examining the various butt plugs, miming with the most enormous and obscene looking. "We don't need these," Lyle said, shuddering over the diameter of one wicked looking toy. "Didn't we come to buy lubricant?"

"Can you recommend a really great anal lube?" Tizzy shouted to the guy behind the counter.

"Jeez, Tizzy." I tried to make myself invisible.

"This is Portland, Tip. Nobody knows us here."

The guy had come from behind the counter by then, and was pointing out the various lubricants. "If you're going to use the butt plugs or the prostate massagers, you'll want a thick lube," he said.

"If you're just going to use your cocks on each other, then you can go with something lighter and less sticky."

Jeep pulled a gigantic anal vibrator off the shelf and aimed it at my butt. "Can Tip test-drive this one?"

The clerk turned to me. "I thought I recognized you. You're the captain of the Muskrats. I watched you swim tonight. My boy's one of the Professionals."

Even Tizzy looked somewhat abashed, but the clerk went on talking. "You didn't swim against him. He's only a freshman, but definitely an up-and-comer," he mused while he selected the best anal lubricant for us. "You Muskrats should have won. You were better than the Professionals this year. It was those two boys that threw the match for you."

We bought the lubricant and headed for the hotel. All of us chipping in on the room, we enclosed ourselves inside.

"I feel like crying. All we worked for was tossed aside."

"Let it go, Tipper," Lyle said. "Nobody cares about a high school swimming competition. Whatever glory we found is already passed. Right now is what we've been working for—to be free. Absolutely free."

"Free from doubt. Free from fear."

"Do you boys really want to get stuffed bareback?" Jeep asked. "You and I and Lyle have done it with each other. We don't have any diseases. We don't know where Tizzy has been, no offense, Tizzy."

Tizzy shook his head. "It's a fair question, Jeep. If you hadn't spoken first, I would have had the same doubts about you. I've fucked around with five guys on my team, but we always kept it safe. Condoms all the way."

"Then we'll do anything you want, Tip," Lyle said.

"How about Tizzy gives it to me in the ass bareback while I suck your cock, Lyle?"

"What am I supposed to be doing?" Jeep's complaint was justified.

"You can wait and take care of Tip after we've come."

"You could make Tip come when we do."

"You could jack off on Tip. Give him a cum bath."

"I'll sit back and watch," Jeep said. "Then when you get done with Tipper, two of you can make me the middle of the sandwich, the same as you're doing with him."

By the time the rest had finished deciding, I was on the bed on my hands and knees. Tizzy lubricated his fingers and worked them into my ass. Sparkles of rapture rushed through me. "Why does anal penetration feel so good?"

"It feels good to us because we were created to be gay," Tizzy said as he twisted his fingers. "The gods designed our asses to feel pleasure during penetration." I wiggled my ass. "You wiggle when you're fucked. A straight boy would resist until he was screaming in agony." My cock was harder than steel, and his fingers sent throbbing rushes up my ass and down to my cock head.

Lyle's cock was hard. He was on his knees in front of me, so I lowered my lips to his jutting cock head. Tizzy pulled his fingers out and positioned his cock against my asshole. While I licked around the head of Lyle's cock, I pushed my ass back. As Tizzy's slick, naked cock entered me, my head swam with the growing pleasure, and my asshole dilated in paroxysms of ecstasy.

Tizzy bounced his lap against my buttocks. Gripping my sides, he reared back. Sucking furiously on the head of Lyle's cock, I demonstrated my coordination by tightening my asshole as Tizzy pulled back. His cock slid out, creating tingles that traveled up my anal chute and down my cock. My hands were gripping Lyle's buttocks. I squeezed as I pulled his cock deeper into my mouth and rocked my ass back to meet Tizzy's forward thrust.

My fingers crept into Lyle's butt crack. Jeep slopped lubricant onto my fingers and down Lyle's crack, so I drove into his asshole with two fingers. Tizzy was pounding me harder by then, slamming my ass with great urgency. I met his thrusts while I sucked Lyle's cock and twisted my fingers in his ass. Lyle emitted a low moan.

"Oh, I'm coming, Tip," Tizzy groaned. "Oh, lover, I'm coming in your ass."

As Lyle's cock grew taut and bulky, I tasted cum. Lyle wailed as he convulsed orgasmically. I swallowed as more cum spurted onto my tongue and into the back of my throat. I kept swallowing as I received cum into my body from both ends at once. My cock was trembling near orgasm as gusts of sexual excitement tore through me.

When both boys had emptied their balls, we collapsed in a heap. Left out, Jeep stared with doleful eyes. "Don't look so sad, Jeep," Tizzy said. "We'll give it to you any way you want. You can do my ass bareback, if you'd like."

"Tipper hasn't got off yet either, Tizzy," Jeep said. "I want to take it the way Tip did, but not right now. Right now, I would like Tip to fuck me. I want to be his bottom."

Jeep stretched out on his stomach and pulled his left leg up. "Take me this way, Tip. Lyle and Tizzy can watch you fuck my ass."

The curves of Jeep's ass were enticing, and my cock was soaring. I reached for the lubricant, but Lyle seized it and stroked it onto my cock. I almost came right then. "Not too hard, Lyle. Don't grip it like you mean it."

Giggling at my lust, Tizzy anointed Jeep's asshole. He opened Jeep and fingered a generous amount of lubricant into his rectum. "He's ready for you, Tip. Climb aboard."

Jeep giggled at that. I pressed the head of my cock against his asshole. "Here it comes, Jeep."

"I'm ready," Jeep said, drawing a deep breath. "Push it into me."

I drove my hard swimmer's ass down, which pushed my cock through Jeep's anal sphincter and into his chute. He emitted a joyous shriek as I drove into him. "Oh, God, I'm coming." I rose and plunged, driving the cum out of his cock. I had not stroked five strokes in his ass before the ripples of pleasure surged through my dick head. Waves of sexual rapture followed. Caught in the storms, I shot my cum into Jeep's ass while he was still unloading onto the besmirched bedclothes of that budget motel.

We showered together, all four. After we washed and toweled each other, we stood naked around the bed and regarded each other questioningly. "Do we sleep here?" Lyle asked, wrinkling his nose at the sheets.

"I'm hungry," Jeep said. "I want eggs, ham, bacon, pancakes."

His rash words made my mouth water. "Let's find an all-night restaurant. Then I want to head home. It's after midnight. My pop comes home from the hospital this afternoon."

❖

We had no more swim meets and no coach; swim practice was over for the school year. Lyle, Jeep, and I continued working out at the gym, and we practiced in the gym's pool. Often, Tizzy drove down from Silverton to join us, even though Beaver Dam Fitness Club did not appreciate the three of us using our guest privileges to sign him in.

High school seemed strange without Coach Reece's presence. I heard that the principal was interviewing prospective swim coaches, and I hoped that the younger swimmers coming along would get a better deal than we had received that year. Coach Reece hired a lawyer to sue the school, but his own statements to the press turned the community's opinion against him.

Surprisingly, I did well in all my classes. I concentrated upon my studies, and reading Thad's journals had awakened my interest in more scholarly pursuits. I found that I was reading a great deal of the time.

Lyle, Jeep, and I avoided Rick and Mart as much as possible, but those two had created a faction against us. One late morning, a group of our fellow students, mainly members of my former church, formed a human wall in the corridor with the intent of not letting me into the cafeteria. Lyle and Jeep joined with me, as did a surprising number of non-gay students, and we formed a human wedge that sliced through the wall. Once inside the cafeteria, we jeered and taunted the other group. Their forlorn expressions almost made me feel sorry for them. One confessed later that Pastor Kern had assured them that the power of God would link them into an unbreakable wall to befuddle the deviants. When God failed to show up on demand, like a cosmic bellhop on an unauthorized cigarette break, the homophobes were the befuddled. Like a bride jilted by her bridegroom on that day of all days, they turned tail rather than confront us. Nothing much came of the incident; Principal Relish did not admonish either side, but during the next day's English literature class, Ms. Malcolm delivered a scathing lecture against bullying.

The day of our high school graduation dawned with balmy June weather. I breakfasted with Mom and Pop, both of whom had changed since Pop's heart attack. That morning, they were sharing secret smiles and kept asking about my plans for the day. Their sudden interest was dreadfully weird and nauseatingly parental.

A few hours later, I was standing against the fence watching our alpacas and talking with two of our buckaroos who had become strangely chummier since I came out as the friskiest gayboy in Cougar County, when Jeep and Lyle pulled into our drive, bringing Tizzy along with them. The trio helped inspect the alpacas, though we exchanged wordless glances that were not lost upon the buckaroos.

"It's unusually warm for an Oregon June. How about we hike down to Muskrat Creek and check out the old swimming hole?"

"Good idea," said Tizzy who had never seen our favorite outdoor swimming hole.

"Mind if Rojo and I tag along?" Ricardo the Buckaroo asked. "I think we should keep an eye on you boys."

Pop saved us. Not knowing what was transpiring, he emerged from the house and ordered Rojo and Ricardo to deliver a John Deere Windrower to Hungry Hill Farm in Crabtree. Only then, his sense of duty fulfilled, did Pop return to the couch where he was continuing his convalescence in front of the television.

"I'm kind of disappointed," Jeep said as we trudged across the flowery meadow. Rojo was cute, and did you see the size of the bulge in Ricardo's pants?"

"I'm not going to put out for the help, guys. I've heard that the bunkhouse is a hotbed of gay sex, but those men are my family's employees. Fraternizing with the servants only leads to trouble."

❖

Muskrat Creek was running high after the spring rains and the snowmelt off the peaks of the Cascades. The water was chilly, but the sand was surprisingly warm. First to toss all clothing aside, I dove into the deep hole. Being wet and naked felt good. When I emerged, the sun kissed my skin.

My dearly departed grandmother, Pop's mother, saw me in my red swim briefs just once before she died. That night she whispered a great secret to me. "Nice display, Tipper," she said. "Always remember this prescription: the less clothing you wear around the water, the happier you will be."

I grinned. "Grandma Trencher, were you a skinny dipper?"

"*Were*, Tip?" she snorted. "Still am. I catch the bus from the old folks' home and sun my ancient ass at Collins Beach on Sauvie Island. I'm not alone either. We all know that the senior center is a holding tank for the funeral home, but some of us are going to keep on gathering our rosebuds right up to the bitter end." She got even more confidential. "Tell you a secret. Your holier-than-thou father used to love the nude beach when he was young, before the church warped him."

Picturing my grandma, I was naked as I grabbed the old rope dangling from a high limb and swung over the deep pool. I let go at the strategic moment, soared and fell, splashed, and went to the bottom. I kicked hard, broke the surface, and swam to shore.

By then the rest were naked, and all three took their turns on the rope swing. After a dozen plunges each, we sprawled nude upon the sand and talked of our hopes and fears. "Tonight we graduate," Tizzy said.

"Yeah, but you're graduating from Copper Valley High School and we're graduating from Muskrat Creek," Jeep added.

"So what?"

"Are you going to the university?"

"They offered me a scholarship," Tizzy said. "But I'm going to get an associate's from Cougar Ridge Community College first. Those universities flunk forty percent of their freshmen and a lot of sophomores. Once you're a junior, you've got it made. Community college is cheaper and less stressful. The professors are there to help you get through, not to weed you out."

"And Cougar Ridge has a swim team," Jeep said.

"They wear *green* Speedo swim briefs," Lyle said as if that were an objection.

"You don't like green?" I asked. "Your ass would look damned good in green."

Lyle turned bottoms up to reflect upon the subject. "If I'm going to be wearing green swim briefs, then I'll have to get my truck repainted."

"Who wants to go for some afternoon sexual raptures?"

"It's hardly eleven in the morning, Tip," Tizzy said.

"Is that a *no*?"

"That's a *yes*. But let's not make it complicated. Let me jack you off. You jerk Lyle's dick. Lyle will beat Jeep's meat. And Jeep will give me his best hand job."

Within a few seconds, our cocks were hard and our hands were busy. Jeep came first, followed by Tizzy. My orgasm was deep and vigorous. My cum flew as my body fell into the spasm that follows the potency. Lyle shot his at last, and our cum decorated the sands. We washed our bodies and our weapons of penetration in the old swimming hole, and finally meandered back to my parents' house.

"Will they feed us?" Lyle asked, echoing the thoughts of my two other companions.

"The family's finances feed a whole bunkhouse full of buckaroos three or four times a day, Lyle. I think that my parents, who are the highest taxed parents in Cougar County, can afford to spread themselves for lunch."

Lunch was somewhat delayed. A strange vehicle stood in our drive, a green Element with California license plates. In the living room, two men in their early thirties sat conversing with Mom and Pop.

All four stood as we had entered, me in front and my three friends behind. "So this is our little brother Tipper," one of the men said, his voice cracking with the emotional strain, and I knew at once that he was my brother Thad.

The other, the more effeminate one, suddenly squealed at me. "Tipper? Little Tipper."

My breath caught in my throat. My heart was pounding hard. "Tye?"

"That's me."

I turned to the other. "Thad. I read your journals. Every last word."

He looked abashed, so I added, "I feel what you feel. You set me free."

Thad's eyes widened, and Tye grinned wickedly. Meanwhile, Jeep, Lyle, and Tizzy were plastered against the wall beside the door, looking for all the world as if they were patterns on the wallpaper. I knew how they felt: foreign, out of place, strangers in a strange land, bastards at a family reunion, like they just didn't belong. Turning back from my friends and lovers, the dam of my emotions cracked and burst asunder. Without meaning to do it, I launched my body toward my brothers just as I had done as a child. My arms were wrapping them and I propelled them backward, virtually bowling Mom and Pop aside.

Tye threw his arms around me and dropped to his knees. Thad was a little more sedate in his manner of hugging me, but his eyes were brimming with tears. In the end, Jeep, Lyle, and Tizzy did stay for lunch. Rather than fixing it ourselves, Pop told Ole' Cookie to send over a spread from the chuck wagon and serve it on the big picnic tables on the edge of the cornfield. Rojo's eyes took in Lyle, Jeep, Thad, me, Tye, and Tizzy sitting in a row. "Are all of you fellows gay?" he asked with wondering approval.

Mom turned pale, but Pop spoke up promptly. "Yes, they are," he said clearly. "And I'm damned proud over each one of them."

"Not only are we gay," Tye spoke up, "but we're pagans to boot."

Pop blanched at that statement, but he recovered quickly. To my shock, he started asking Thad and Tye about paganism as a faith and a ritual, and soon we were merrily discussing the advantages of circle casting.

❖

That evening, we were together again, with the exception of Tizzy who had to attend his graduation from Copper Valley High School. Of course there were others present. Skip for one. Also Lyle's and Jeep's families. No mention was made of homosexuality then, for not all family relationships are wrapped in warm, soft fuzzy-wuzzies. Jeep's parents, his father particularly, were completely in denial even though Jeep had tried to explain his sexuality to them. His father had raged, and his mother talked of a cousin who had once expressed a similar "malfunction," but had "gotten over it" in time to marry a girl from a good Chilean family. Tió Augusto merely shrugged and looked vaguely amused.

Fortunately, we had ignored Tye's suggestion that we wear gay pride stickers on our graduation gowns. In Muskrat Creek, such a flagrant display would have raised a stink, not to mention gunshots.

Then later, much later, after we ditched our families and Tizzy drove down freshly graduated from Silver Falls, we conspired together, Tizzy, Jeep, Lyle, and I, along with Thad, Tye, and Skip. I learned then that Thad and Tye were college professors and writers, but they had changed their last name from Trencher to Tempter, which explains why my searches had failed. Thad taught religious history and wrote books about neo-paganism, ritual magic, and Wicca. Tye taught English literature and mythology. It turned out that, under a pseudonym, Tye was a famous author of gay erotica.

Of course, we talked about how I had discovered Thad's notebooks and how Jeep, Lyle, and I discovered the joys of gay sex.

"They discovered me too," Tizzy said.

We talked until the early morning hours, and before Tye and Thad drove back to their college in California, we made our secret preparations.

Part Three

The Initiation

CHAPTER FOURTEEN

Three weeks after our high school graduation, Skip drove Lyle, Jeep, Tizzy, and me across the Oregon border. We spent a night in a remote cabin in northern California, owned by a member of Dr. Bromius's coven. The next day, we came to a picturesque, three-story lodge high in the mountains where the coven met for its monthly rituals. Tye and Thad were there, and they introduced us to a gorgeous man of forty-three. He embraced me and said, "Merry Meet, Tipper. I'm Buck Bromius."

Some of the members of his original coven were there, now all in their thirties. Of course Thad was thirty-three and Tye thirty-two. But there were younger members, many our age, and Lyle, Jeep, and Tizzy found much eye candy around the swimming pool.

"I've never seen so many scrumptious looking guys," Tizzy said.

On the same night, we four were initiated into the coven under the warm beams of the July full moon. The coven did not break the incest taboo, so Tye and Thad did no more than conduct us to our initiation. Of course, unlike most initiates, we knew what to expect, having read Thad's notebooks. I was the first to be conducted to the sacred space.

"We're going to blindfold you," Tye said.

I nodded in agreement.

My brothers secured a sash around my eyes. After scrutinizing my blindfold, they spun me and led me around in circles until direction was meaningless.

"Don't touch your blindfold. Ganymede and I are going to undress. Then we'll strip you naked."

I heard unzipping, rustling, and caught cloth. A few more seconds passed before Tye said, "Let us undress you."

When I was naked, they led me along a smooth path.

"Don't even think of playing with your cock," Thad said.

"I wasn't." Then I remembered that the initiate was ritually mocked before entering the circle.

"I saw you fingering it."

My brothers led me through a gauntlet of hecklers, who accused me of every perversion under the sun and others that they invented. Mere anal and oral submission was reduced to the commonplace compared to their mawkish taunts.

"I'm sure he fucks goats."

"Sheep, too."

"Only goats and sheep? How droll. I saw him do a chicken once."

"They say that a whole herd of satyrs gang-banged his ass."

Unseen hands gripped my cock, patted my ass, tweaked my nipples, kissed my lips, and stroked my thighs. My cock was hardening; I could not touch it, but I sensed the blood rush that swelled and elongated my dick. Fairy fellows slapped my growing erection lightly as it rose. Above me, the full moon shone so brightly that I perceived shapes through my blindfold.

My brothers released me and stepped aside. Someone placed a hand on my chest.

"Seeker, you come to us trusting, though blind and humiliated, mocked and defiled. You have passed the test of will. Do you still seek to join the Uranian brotherhood?"

"I do."

"Will you sacrifice your consciousness to the homoerotic frenzies?"

"With pleasure."

"Will you sacrifice your flesh to give pleasure to men?"

"Without reservation."

"Will you sacrifice all possibility of wife and children?"

"Gladly."

"Will you sacrifice approval from any society save ours?"

My heart was pounding hard. "I already have."

"Will you accept social ostracism, familial rejection, religious persecution, and sexual discrimination, so that you may serve the Uranian gods?"

"With all my heart."

"Do you promise to commit your soul and body to unrestrained homosexual delights exclusively, for all of your days?"

I chose the path of my brothers. "Yes," I said. "Of course. It is what I want."

"Do you promise to keep our rites secret, to tell no one what we do during our holy rituals?"

"Certainly."

The cheers and clapping warmed me. Pipes shrilled, drums boomed, and tambourines rattled while my questioner anointed me with the holy oil and gave me the ritual kisses I had read about in Thad's journal.

"Enter the sacred circle." I stepped forward.

"Seeker, I, stag-horned Hyacinthos, open the path of boys who live to give pleasure. Now you shall fulfill the three great rites of our Uranian god. Seeker, if your vows have meaning, drop to your knees that you may kiss the holy phallus. Free your soul from doubt as the Uranian god courses through you. He is the throbbing excitement you feel. Now do as thou wilt."

The familiar shape of a cock head touched my lips. Pushing my head forward, I opened my mouth to receive the cock. The cock head slid over my lips and along my tongue. I took the cock farther into my mouth. I tightened my lips around it and started sucking harder.

"*Evoe*, Pan; *Evoe*, Pan; *Evoe*, Pan; *Evoe*, Pan; *Evoe*, Pan."

As I sucked harder and faster, the tempo of the drumbeats increased. The cock grew heavy in my mouth, so I sucked harder to draw the cum from the balls.

The drumbeats reached a fevered pitch. Tambourines and bells rang wildly, and the chants came wilder still. I felt a tremor as the man's muscles shot the first blast of semen into my throat, and the cosmos whirled around me. I was part of a cosmic event as I swallowed the cum until I had downed it all.

As the spent cock passed over my lips, the head of another cock touched my anal cleft.

"Do you know how to receive anal penetration?" Hyacinthos asked.

"Yes," I said. "I love taking a cock in my ass."

Some unseen man pulled my butt cheeks apart and pressed his cock head against my asshole. I felt a fabulous pressure. His hands gripping the top rounds of my buttocks, the pressure against my asshole did not decrease. It grew more intense, and my rectum was full and heavy. The pressure increased, but I drew deep breaths and pushed. I felt the deep pleasure of anal penetration, which I love so much. The man gripped my waist and pulled me back. Deeper and deeper, his cock impaled my ass until his loins pressed hard against my butt.

"You've got Marduk's dick inside you now." Hyacinthos's announcement was followed by the exultant concord of bells and tambourines echoed off the mountain crags. Robust male voices bayed homoeroticism, hedonism, and submission to the moon. I fucked my ass on Marduk's cock until my asshole throbbed with extreme bliss. Marduk met my backstrokes with his thrusts, and soon we were fucking in rhythm.

I joined my wails to the cries of the worshippers as the pleasure exploded. My asshole sang like a galloping Valkyrie as the strokes rippled my vital nerves. My contracting asshole squeezed Marduk to orgasm. His cock thickened; every stroke massaged my prostate, firing raging gusts in my dick head. My balls constricted, and my cock sizzled for eruption. Marduk howled in explosive orgasm. His cock twitched as he launched salvos of spunk. He thrust savagely as he moaned and, between moans, begged me to take it all, as if I would refuse his surging cum.

Before I could attain orgasm, Marduk's contractions stilled, and he pulled his cock from my ass. Helping hands assisted me to my feet.

"Initiate, you have opened the way of the catamite. Are you prepared to see the circle?"

"Yes," I said. Hands untied my blindfold, and I stood blinking at the full moonlight.

The circle was much as Thad had described, though located in a different wild realm. We were standing in a mossy clearing in a lofty gorge under the summit. A two-hundred-foot waterfall filled a deep basin at the far end of the dell, and the mountain stream swept away toward another waterfall at the other end of the gorge. The group consisted of a more than a hundred males from eighteen to forty, all naked in the yellow moonlight. They stood in a circle around me. Tye and Thad waited side by side, smiling upon me. Many held tambourines, hand bells, or musical pipes. A group of drummers sat within the circle. I saw Marduk, a gorgeous hunk about my brothers' age, removing a used condom from his cock. Marduk smiled at me as he indicated the bubble of cum in the condom.

Dr. Bromius sat on a flower and vine bedecked wicker chair near the center altar, which held ritual objects, flickering candles in glass bowls, and smoking incense. Flanking Dr. Bromius were two boys, one masked as a bull, the other as a stag.

The man wearing the bull mask said, "You have met my lover, the Priest of Hyacinthos. He has initiated you, mouth and anus, into the way of catamite. I am the Priest of Apollo, and to me you must prove your worth in the manner of Zeus. Behold the offerings."

Apollo waved his hand around the circle. With the exception of my brothers and the drummers, each man turned, bent, and wiggled his bare ass. "Make your selection."

As he intoned the words of the command, the Priest of Apollo lubricated my hard cock and slipped an extra-strength condom over it. He lubricated the condom again. I turned, surveying the proffered butts. Every man did his utmost to entice me.

I made my selection based upon shapeliness, protrusiveness, and eagerness. The man I selected had an ass to die for, and he knew how to offer it. I placed my hands on his hips to indicate that he was my selection. "I am Priapus," he said. I did not mention that I knew that Priapus was my brother's old classmate Crane. Priapus and I walked hand in hand toward the altar. He bent and gripped the altar, and stuck out his ass for my pleasure. The rest of the fellows turned again and each gripped the cock of the man next to him.

I slid my cock between Priapus's buttocks, and his rosebud burned my dick head right through the condom. Priapus pushed back, impaling his asshole while I drove forward. His butt chute was tight, hot, and coarse. His ass sucked my cock in until I slammed his round buttocks. I pounded his ass again and again. His asshole was unbelievable. He milked me off without mercy.

"*Evoe*, you're making me come," I wailed. Sparklers crinkled the head of my cock. My cock throbbed. The sparklers matured into exploding firecrackers. My balls twisted like fire snakes, and my nipples felt like pinwheels. Cherry bombs of pleasure vibrated through the head of my cock. Skyrockets of pleasure traveled up my cockshaft. My lips grimaced and my eyelids fluttered as my cum surged in great explosive gouts.

When we pulled apart, Priapus kissed me gently before returning to his place in the circle. Then I joined the circle of men, standing between my brothers, as one by one, Lyle, Jeep, and Tizzy were initiated into the Brotherhood of Uranus.

Watching my friends experience the same ecstatic mystical participation I had felt, we fell into an eternal moment in which past, temperature, future, matter, light, vacuum, and energy collapsed into a single point where we shared our rapture in a sacred circle which had existed for time out of mind and would exist as long as men prevailed. As the orgasms shook my friends, symbols of time and desire, we were all lost and all found in an event nameless and indescribable, and the moon whirled above us, casting long, deep circles around the point that was the cosmic orgasm.

The End

About the Author

A resident of Portland, Oregon, David Holly often sets his stories in the environs of the Pacific Northwest. He is fascinated by the human penchant for odd mythologies, bizarre rituals, diverse religions, forlorn hopes, and broken dreams.

David is the author of more than ninety published stories of gay erotica and romance. His stories have appeared in four anthologies from Bold Strokes Books: *Nice Butt*, *Erotica Exotica*, *Black Fire*, and *History's Passion*. Find out more about David Holly and his publications at facebook.com/david.holly2 and gaywriter.org.

Books Available from Bold Strokes Books

20th Century Un-limited by Felice Picano. The 20th Century is over and done with and nothing can be changed. Or is it? Felice Picano's two short novels take delicious what-if peeks at outwitting Time's (seemingly) unbending Arrow. (978-1-60282-921-3)

The Moon's Deep Circle by David Holly. Tip Trencher wants to find out what happened to his long lost brothers, but what he finds is a sizzling circle of gay sex and pagan ritual. (978-1-60282-870-4)

The Left Hand of Justice by Jess Faraday. A kidnapped heiress, a heretical cult, a corrupt police chief, and an accused witch. Paris is burning, and the only one who can put out the fire is Detective Inspector Elise Corbeau...whose boss wants her dead. (978-1-60282-863-6)

Raising Hell: Demonic Gay Erotica edited by Todd Gregory. *Raising Hell*: hot stories of gay erotica featuring demons. (978-1-60282-768-4)

Pursued by Joel Gomez-Dossi. Openly gay college student Jamie Bradford becomes romantically involved with two men at the same time, and his hell begins when one of his boyfriends becomes intent on killing him. (978-1-60282-769-1)

Promises in Every Star edited by Todd Gregory. Acclaimed gay male erotica author Todd Gregory's definitive collection of short stories, including both classic and new works. (978-1-60282-787-5)

Tricks of the Trade: Magical Gay Erotica edited by Jerry L. Wheeler. Today's hottest erotica writers take you inside the sultry, seductive world of magicians and their tricks—professional and otherwise. (978-1-60282-781-3)

Straight Boy Roommate by Kev Troughton. Tom isn't expecting much from his first term at University, but a chance encounter with straight boy Dan catapults him into an extraordinary, wild weekend of sex and self-discovery, which turns his life upside down, and leads him into his first love affair. (978-1-60282-782-0)

The Jesus Injection by Eric Andrews-Katz. Murderous statues, demented drag queens, political bombings, ex-gay ministries, espionage, and romance are all in a day's work for a top-secret agent. But the gloves are off when Agent Buck 98 comes up against The Jesus Injection. (978-1-60282-762-2)

Combustion by Daniel W. Kelly. Bearish detective Deck Waxer comes to the city of Kremfort Cove to investigate why the hottest men in town are bursting into flames in broad daylight. (978-1-60282-763-9)

Young Bucks: Novellas of Twenty-Something Lust & Love edited by Richard Labonte. Four writers still in their twenties—or with their twenties a nearby memory—write about what it's like to be young, on the prowl for sex, or looking to fall in love. (978-1-60282-770-7)

Night Shadows: Queer Horror edited by Greg Herren and J.M. Redmann. *Night Shadows* features delightfully wicked stories by some of the biggest names in queer publishing. (978-1-60282-751-6)

Secret Societies by William Holden. An outcast hustler, his unlikely "mother," his faithless lovers, and his religious persecutors—all in 1726. (978-1-60282-752-3)

Wyatt: Doc Holliday's Account of an Intimate Friendship by Dale Chase. Erotica writer Dale Chase takes the remarkable friendship between Wyatt Earp, upright lawman, and Doc Holliday, Southern gentlemen turned gambler and killer, to an entirely new level: hot! (978-1-60282-755-4)

The Jetsetters by David-Matthew Barnes. As rock band The Jetsetters skyrockets from obscurity to superstardom, Justin Holt, a lonely barista, and Diego Delgado, the band's guitarist, fight with everything they have to stay together, despite the chaos and fame. (978-1-60282-745-5)

Strange Bedfellows by Rob Byrnes. Partners in life and crime, Grant Lambert and Chase LaMarca are hired to make a politician's compromising photo disappear, but what should be an easy job quickly spins out of control. (978-1-60282-746-2)

Sweat: Gay Jock Erotica edited by Todd Gregory. Sizzling tales of smoking-hot sex with the athletic studs everyone fantasizes about. (978-1-60282-669-4)

The Marrying Kind by Ken O'Neill. Just when successful wedding planner Adam More decides to protest inequality by quitting the business and boycotting marriage entirely, his only sibling announces her engagement. (978-1-60282-670-0)

Boys of Summer edited by Steve Berman. Stories of young love and adventure, when the sky's ceiling is a bright blue marvel, when another boy's laughter at the beach can distract from dull summer jobs. (978-1-60282-663-2)

Calendar Boys by Zachary Logan. A man a month will keep you excited year round. (978-1-60282-665-6)

Buccaneer Island by J.P. Beausejour. In the rough world of Caribbean piracy, a man is what he makes of himself—or what a stronger man makes of him. (978-1-60282-658-8)

Twelve O'Clock Tales by Felice Picano. The fourth collection of short fiction by legendary novelist and memoirist Felice Picano. Thirteen dark tales that will thrill and disturb, discomfort and titillate, enthrall and leave you wondering. (978-1-60282-659-5)

Words to Die By by William Holden. Sixteen answers to the question: What causes a mind to curdle? (978-1-60282-653-3)